THE WIND CANNOT READ

RICHARD MASON

"Though on the sign it is written:
'Don't pluck these blossoms'—
it is useless against the wind,
    which cannot read."

—JAPANESE POEM

PAN BOOKS LTD : LONDON

First published 1947 by Hodder and Stoughton Ltd.
Published 1952 by Pan Books Ltd.,
8 Headfort Place, London, S.W.1
New Edition 1958
3rd Printing 1958
4th Printing 1958
5th Printing 1959
6th Printing 1960

TO
THE MEMORY OF
MY MOTHER

All characters and incidents in this
book are fictitious

PRINTED AND BOUND IN ENGLAND BY
HAZELL WATSON AND VINEY LTD
AYLESBURY AND SLOUGH

BOOK ONE

CHAPTER I

I

It took all of April and May to get out of the jungle. My birthday was at the end of April, and I had laid my gold watch against Peter's signet-ring that I should never live to celebrate it. He would have had the gold watch by April 27th had it not been smashed beyond repair. I told him to take it and sell the gold; but he said we hadn't been able to celebrate the birthday anyway, unless another jungle sore and a sock full of rice could be called a celebration; and, in any case, if the other thing had happened, he wouldn't have left his signet-ring for the Japs to loot from my corpse. "And what do you mean, *sell* the gold?" he added. We did not think even then we would come through to civilisation.

Behind us they were fighting their way out. Our only concern was retreat, but no one knew exactly where the line was, and once the Japs had crept ahead of us and blocked the road. We had to abandon our transport and get through the jungle as best we could. All our equipment had gone, except for a water-bottle and a haversack and a sock for rice.

Many people were dropping out altogether from fever and exhaustion. They were left—whilst we had these things still— with a rifle and five rounds. They were supposed to have only one round because of the ammunition shortage, but we left them five to use as they liked on the Japs or themselves.

There were bad dysentery cases, too, who discarded their pants and went on in their shirt tails. I had dysentery mildly; but my worst complaint was the sores that had started—four of them the size of half-crown pieces that ate into the flesh like acid, down to the bone.

At night we slept on the side of the track, when there was a track to sleep on the side of, and to hell with mosquitoes and malaria. And to hell with tigers, for that matter—though fortunately we never saw a tiger to say to hell with.

The nights were harder to bear than the days, especially when you slept. In the day there was some defence: a cynical humour,

5

companionship, the preoccupation of sipping water, or longing for water, or dragging yourself up a hillside; and distances and sizes were what you expected. But in the dark your fears reared up grotesquely. You were terribly small and alone. No British Army, no Indian Army, no General Alexander; only yourself in the clutches of a nightmare. I think a nightmare can be more real than the real thing; for you do not know it is a nightmare when you are sleeping, but when you are awake you can pretend life is all a dream.

Once when we awoke in the morning Peter had gone. Two miles up the track we found him coming back to meet us. He had gone off in his sleep, thinking we had left him behind. Another time a sergeant woke me. "I can see them!" he cried. "Look!" He pointed into the moonlit jungle. The perspiration was streaming down his face. Then he asked the time, and rolled over and was quiet. Afterwards he did not remember.

Sometimes deserters joined us from the fighting battalions. Later, in India, most of them were awarded long sentences of imprisonment by a General Court Martial. We could not desert because there was nothing to desert to, and I was often glad there was not that alternative.

So we crawled back, ill and shattered and depleted. I never saw a Jap outside of my dreams, not until later when one was shot down out of his aircraft 15,000 feet over Assam. You could see a dent the shape of his body in the paddy-field, arms out like a cross.

It was the jungle and the sun that had broken us; and God knows how through all that one nurses the life spirit. I did not know I could suffer this much and live, nor that I could remain sane through such torments of mind. Yet I was nothing like the worst.

We thought that we would die and that the Japs would stick our rotting corpses with bayonets for fun. We did not die. We reached a camp near the Indian frontier, and the newly dead were carried from their beds to make room for us. Then there was a lorry and at last a train. On the train there were five hundred sick and wounded, with no doctors, no medical orderlies and no destination. We seemed to go all over India looking for a hospital that was not already too full to take us. At stations we made the natives unravel the muslim *dhotis* from their waists, and we washed them to use as bandages. We also put down the dead at stations.

We were three nights on the train, and it was nearly midsummer and the fans were not working. I thought the heat and the smell of sweat and wounds were as bad as anything in Burma.

On the afternoon of the fourth day we reached Kachatola, and there were ambulances at the station. By five o'clock we were in bed. The hospital had hardly been completed but there were white sheets and fans, and cool rooms with clean white walls. There were white nurses, too. And there was tea, and hot water, and medicine, and the attention of doctors.

I knew that I was not going to die; at least, not yet.

II

I lay between the cool, white sheets, and there was the smell of hospital. I thought, heaven will smell like this, and angels will wear starched things like nurses and God will operate with rubber gloves. It will be just like this; you will come dirty and worn from the jungle of life, and you will be sponged and shaved and given fresh, beautiful clothes, and your pain will be assuaged and your sores healed, and there will be anodyne for the griefs and the bitterness and the hatreds of the soul. Then, purified and shining, you will step out amongst the lawns and the flowers and the fountains. . . .

There were no flowers or fountains in the hospital compound, only the brown earth and burnt grass; but it was near enough to heaven for me, especially when I woke suddenly in the night to find myself searching for my revolver in frenzied terror. Then I would discover that the dark shape I had seen was not a Jap but one of the posts of the verandah, and I would sink back on to the pillows with indescribable relief. It is curious how persistent were those retrospective nightmares. When I asked the doctor about them, he said:

"Perhaps they're to intensify your joy when you find out where you really are."

"And when I dreamt of home in the jungle?" I asked. "Was that to intensify my horror when I woke up to reality?"

I was only three weeks in bed. After that I used to sit in an arm-chair on the balcony, smoking and thinking. It was not at once that I found I could think clearly again. All through Burma my thoughts had been feverish and sick; I had said to myself a thousand times, 'Was it I that had sat on the lawn by the river at Tewkesbury, reading fine, leather-bound, good-smelling volumes?' And reason, what remained of it, had said, 'It was you, the same body-you. But not the same mind-you.' That was it, the body was the common denominator; and except for the body I was someone else, someone alien, doing things that had no connection with the self that I had been long ago.

Now, very gradually, serenity descended upon me once more and my old self drifted back. I felt a continuity with the person that I had been; yet when I sent my thoughts back to England it was not, so to speak, as the crow flies, but through Burma; through the jungle, through that period of time when my real self had been almost extinguished. So, like a convict whose completed sentence always has a place in his consciousness, I was in that respect changed.

I savoured this peace in delicious content, and I wanted it to continue. I wanted to go on for ever smoking cigarettes and thinking, and sitting on the balcony just out of the sun. I did not want a woman, or whisky, or to play poker or listen to the wireless. In the ward they kept the wireless on all day long, anything at all so long as it was noise, and mostly it was the awful metallic cacophony of a jazz band. Instead I watched the tree rats in the compound; because, of course, they were not rats at all, but had tails like squirrels, and jumped like monkeys, and moved jerkily like lizards; and they were very pretty with their striped fur. I watched these and listened to the birds, and at night to the haunting cries of the jackals. I was happy, not wanting to come to grips with life again. Often I thought I would have done well to get something worse than jungle sores and dysentery, something painless but incapacitating.

I was in no hurry to leave the hospital, though when the time came I was given a month's leave, and went up to Simla. They all said, you won't remember a minute of it, with all your accumulated pay you will be drunk for twenty-four hours a day. But I remember it all, not the effects of whisky and gin, but the long line of the snow-covered Himalayas behind the town, and the cool walks amongst the deodars, and looking down 6000 feet to the hot, dusty plains, and feeling like a god. I found a servant, a bearer, who suited me well. He was a gentle person called Bahadur, who spoke English and understood my moods, though I think he was offended when I refused to let him dress me. He had soft brown eyes, and I liked him because he spoke fondly of his family and did not offer me his daughter for three rupees a night.

In the evenings I sat in the garden of the hotel, sipping long drinks of gin and lemon, wishing that this month could be for ever. All the same, I knew that if it were for ever I should want to step down into life again, to my friends, and to change, and disorder, and new, interesting things. It was six weeks since I had seen Peter. He had been out of hospital before me and gone down to Madras, believing in a livelier recuperation. I didn't want to see him again at once. But in time I should need the stimulation of his friendship and his conversation. My serenity would at length desert me, and I should lose that supreme detachment with which I gazed on the plains. I was never made to live in a cloud; I needed earthier sustenance.

Besides, there was no choice. Beggars can't be choosers—nor airmen, either.

It was early September. Bahadur said, yes, Sahib, he would always be my bearer, he would come with me to Delhi; indeed, he must come with me to Delhi to see I drink no bad water on the train. He must see I do not wear one shirt two days.

Thus, together, we descended to the plains.

CHAPTER II

I

I KNEW I was through with flying, and I wasn't sorry. When I was in Burma and the dizziness had started, I had pretended nothing was the matter. After two or three bad scares I nearly crashed the aircraft and that was the end. For the last three days before we got out I stood on the airfield and watched the others take off, feeling like a worm.

There was good reason for feeling like that. I think the dizziness had come because part of me was afraid and did not want to fly any more, just as once appendicitis pains had started when I was scared to go back to school. There must have been some cause, and though the doctors would not say so, I still believe that was it. If I had not been dizzy, I would have gone on flying, because the fear of being thought a coward is the biggest fear of all; but the mechanism of the subconscious is so damnably clever.

I felt like a worm, then, when the others were still flying; but later on the jungle made short work of my lingering heroics, and I did not care if I never saw an aircraft again in my life. If anyone asked me why I was off flying, I told them without any bad conscience of the dizziness. It was one of the little dishonesties that I allowed myself.

I had a Medical Board in Delhi, and was officially 'grounded'. They might have added 'with honour', for the Wing-Commander patted me on the shoulder, and shook my hand, and said:

"It's not so exciting at ground level. But life is good fun."

He fluttered the certificate which he had signed; he knew what his signature meant.

"We'll find you something interesting," he said.

"Quick promotion and staff pay?"

"You never know," he said.

I did not care a great deal. The war in Europe would last a long time, and in the East it would last longer still. I would be in it to the end. I saw time stretching away, and I saw it in terms of the hot, sandy plains of India, insufferably dreary. Perhaps the dreariness would drive me at length to flying again. . . .

"Is there a good bar in Delhi?" I said.

"There's Davico's," he said. "Or the Imperial."

"Life is good fun," I said with a weary jest, and he smiled.

I began to stroll down the long avenue. After a while I found myself perspiring, and called a tonga.

"Davico's," I said.

The horse moved off at a trot. I said: "Slowly!" to the driver, but he did not understand. He flicked the back of the horse with his whip, and we went faster. I was banged about uncomfortably in the narrow open carriage, and was glad when we reached the bar.

"Two rupees," said the driver. He could see that I was a newcomer. I don't know what it is, but they can always tell.

I held out to him a single rupee note. He took it between his fingers, looking at it as though I had insulted him by giving him an old cigarette end. Then he followed me with reproachful eyes, and as I went through the door of the bar I could hear a plaintive cry of "Sahib!" I went on, feeling uncomfortable, and angry with him for trying to cheat me, and sorry for him because even if I had cheated him the police would have taken no action. I remember once I saw two drunken soldiers get out of a carriage and refuse to pay. When the driver demanded his money, one of the soldiers struck his hand. There was a policeman close by, and he came over reluctantly; but it was only to tell the driver not to cause trouble.

As I went to the bar I saw Peter was there with Mervyn Bentley. It was an exciting reunion. We didn't know where to begin.

"I should have known you were here at the best bar," I said.

"Only because it's the best whisky."

"You find that fast enough."

"I've been here weeks," Peter said. "Doing my Lutyens."

"I've done it this morning. It's utterly soulless."

"I'm so glad you agree with me."

"It costs a rupee to get from one building to another, and then you can't get in because it's the Viceregal Lodge or the Commander-in-Chief's house."

"You must be an Air-Marshal," said Mervyn, "and have a supercharged Chrysler. Then New Delhi's a paradise."

"The avenues were built for supercharged Chryslers."

"And the marble palaces for stuffed shirts."

"It was the right idea," Peter said. "I'm going to be a stuffed shirt—very soon."

"It was bound to happen sooner or later," I said.

"Yes, I'm going to be a stuffed shirt. I'm going to join the Gymkhana Club now. Hurry up with that whisky."

I drained my glass. It was Scotch whisky, and it made me feel very happy. I forgot all about my serenity in Simla, and was glad to be with Peter again, and even with Mervyn, though I did not like Mervyn as much as I liked Peter. I had been with Peter on the boat from England, and again in Burma and in the jungle. He was only twenty. He had been so young when the 'phoney' war was on that he had been allowed to go to the University of Grenoble to study French. Then the break-through had come, and he had been trapped in Unoccupied France. He had had a good time ski-ing in the Pyrenees, until he thought it was time to come home and join the Air Force. He walked over the Pyrenees, but they picked him up with a forged visa in Spain and put him in prison for six months. By that time there was something wrong with his ear, so that he was disqualified from flying. Now he was an Intelligence Officer in the Air Force.

His name was Peter, but everyone said that it ought to be Algernon, because of the moustache that he had carefully cultivated, pushing it up at the ends. In London he used to take it to Maurice's for its upkeep, and that is proof of how keen he was about his moustache. He was thinking particularly about its future, when it would be quite grey and exquisitely groomed. He liked to think of himself in the rôle of English Gentleman, which in fact he was by birth. He also wanted to be a good conversationalist, a connoisseur of wine and food, and a writer. He was doing excellently for his age in all these respects.

"For God's sake!" exclaimed Mervyn. "Isn't this a lousy, rotten hole!"

The fury and hatred in him had suddenly blown up like a gale, and his voice shook with vehemence. It was no particular surprise. We had seen too many of Mervyn's neurotic outbursts to be either alarmed or impressed.

"I was such a damned fool to come!" he went on.

"Come where?"

"To India, of course."

"Of course," I said. "What a pity you didn't ask the Air Ministry to cancel your posting overseas."

"I could have got out of it."

"Could you?"

"I was a coward," he said. "There were a dozen ways. I always let myself get into a mess through indecision."

"You should have been in Burma." I couldn't resist that, though it sounded dreadfully priggish.

"Oh, I know what you went through. I should have shot myself."

"You'd never shoot yourself."

"I'm afraid you're right."

"Nonsense!" Peter said. "Mervyn's going to shoot himself, and you're not to discourage him. He promised last week that he'd do so, and he's sending us invitations. 'You are invited to be present on the steps of Government Buildings at 21.30 hours on the evening of 23rd September, 1942, to witness the outstanding social event of the season.' I'm going to keep the bullet as a memento. 'It was with this bullet that Mervyn Bentley took his own life as a protest against the imprisonment of Mahatma Gandhi.' "

"To hell with Gandhi," said Mervyn. "As a protest against the enforced detention of myself in the unspeakably horrid country of India."

"India's all right. You love it really."

"As a matter of fact, it wouldn't be intolerable in the right circumstances. It's the circumstances that are so appalling. I'm going home. It's quite possible."

"You're going to Bombay," Peter said. "You don't know about that yet, do you, Michael? We're all going to Bombay. I've been waiting to tell you."

"How do you know what I'm going to do?" I said.

"I've arranged it. I've been arranging it for weeks. You're going to have a Medical Board."

"I've had a Medical Board."

"And you're grounded? That's fine. Now you're going to Bombay."

"Why Bombay?"

"It's a nice place. There's the Taj Mahal Hotel, and Juhu beach, and the most beautiful women you ever saw. But that's not why we're going there. We're going to learn Japanese."

"I've never been able to master even Hindustani," I said.

"I've often heard you say *dhobi* and *baksheesh*. Anyway, you mustn't let me down. I've told the Squadron-Leader that you're a polyglot. I said you learnt Serbian in three weeks without a master."

"I didn't know there was a language called Serbian."

"Nor did the Squadron-Leader—that's what impressed him. You've only to say I was exaggerating, and he'll like you all the more for being modest. We're all going to have a wonderful time learning Japanese. Even Mervyn, though he doesn't know it."

"It'll have to be very wonderful," Mervyn said.

"Aren't you looking forward to it?" I said.

"I don't mind. It's all the same to me. It's all the same waste of time."

"There's a war," I said. "There are a lot of people wasting time."

"Don't preach."

"Don't be selfish."

"I've never pretended to be anything but selfish. I'm not interested in war."

"What would you do at home that isn't wasting time?"

"I should live. This isn't living, here. Everyone's dead."

"You're wrong. Some people are more alive here than they are at home."

"Well, one man's meat. . . ." Mervyn said.

"It will be a good thing, this Japanese," said Peter. "It's going to take a year. I always had the instinct to return to the womb. Returning to school is a step in the right direction. We shall have long holidays, too, because it's a great strain. Besides, it's quite a compliment. Only the best brains can learn Japanese. It requires a reorientation of the mind. You think backwards and write upside down."

"That'll be fun. And what happens then?"

"You wait until a Jap is shot down out of the sky. Then you ask him his name and Where the Big Attack is Coming."

"It's already come," I said. "Didn't you know that's why we got out of Burma?"

"Well, then you ask him about his Weak Points. It's all quite safe, because you do this at Headquarters, and there are two Gurkha guards pinning down his arms."

"The Japs don't use parachutes," I said. "So there won't be any air prisoners."

"That's why they're only going to teach a few of us."

"Well," I said, "it sounds all right."

"I tell you, it's the best job of the war."

"Then it's just what I've been looking for," I said.

II

When we had finished a round of whiskies, we left the bar to find somewhere for lunch. Mervyn came along moodily, his hands plunged into his trouser pockets and his shoulders rounded. He looked as though he had spent the night in his khaki bush-shirt, which was probably the case. When we had been in the same cabin on the boat as far as Ceylon, he would often pace the deck until five or six in the morning, chain-smoking, and then collapse on his bunk without removing his clothes. He had the temperament of an artist and a strong artistic sense; but he could not harness himself to creation. He was better suited to attract by his conversation, which cost him no effort, than through the medium of paint or the written word; and his personality had brought success to his Chelsea bookshop.

We had lunch at a Chinese restaurant, and ordered wine. The waiter said: "I will give wine, but in the hot middle day it is killing. I do not advise." We thought this was very nice of him. Afterwards Peter swore he had said: "in the hot day's middle."

But at any rate he did not advise, and we drank water with our fried rice and noodles.

In the afternoon I went to Headquarters, and was interviewed by the Squadron-Leader in the Intelligence Branch. I confessed that I did not speak Serbian, but had not found French and Spanish too difficult. He spoke to me fluently in both. I said I knew a few words of Polish, and he said: "I bet they're *na zdrovie*!" It was a good thing I had not said I could speak Russian.

"You're keen to learn Japanese?" he asked.

"There's nothing I should prefer."

"I'm told it's a short-cut to the madhouse."

"There are a lot of short-cuts," I said.

He added my name to a list he had in front of him.

"The course begins on Monday," he said. "You can get a ticket voucher and catch a train tomorrow."

CHAPTER III

I

It is not the most beautiful or varied part of India that lies between Delhi and Bombay. There is no grandeur in the parched land that stretches grudgingly away to flat horizon. Rivers flow with a muddy sloth, and shrubs have to struggle to push out dry, dusty leaves. And at the stations nothing tempts you to leave the train and explore.

At one of the stations at which we stopped I noticed the name *Dhanapore,* and I remembered that I had been at school in England with the Nawab of this state, who for some reason was not sent to Eton. I had always imagined his lands to be lush and jungly, because he had once spoken to me of tiger shooting. Now we were passing through it, I discovered that he ruled over a desert, with little villages as cramped as beehives, but dirtier and not so well organized. Nevertheless, the palace of which I caught a glimpse had a gigantic splendour. The train inspector told me that the Nawab was exceedingly rich and that he entertained all the bigwigs in India. He said that the Nawab's wife had to keep to strict Purdah, but once on the train she had asked the inspector if she could be seen from outside the carriage. When he said it

15

was impossible, she removed her cloak with its tiny lattice window and lit a cigarette.

"You must write and ask him to invite you to stay," Mervyn said. "You'll be well away. One should make a point of visiting a Maharajah."

"I haven't got the clothes. It's altogether too big a proposition. I don't know anything about manners in Oriental palaces."

"Oh, that's easy," he said. "They emulate us in things like that."

I did not think, all the same, that I would write to the Nawab. Not unless I was very bored with Bombay. And if ever we were given a long leave I should want to get away to the hills.

There were four of us in the compartment, and in the next compartment there were three other officers who were also going to Bombay to learn Japanese. One of them was a Flight-Lieutenant, who had come up to us on the station at Delhi with a conscientious hail-fellow-well-met manner, showing off his Hindustani by unnecessarily ordering about the porters. My dislike was instantaneous; but I wondered if I was being unjust until Peter said:

"I shall have difficulty in preventing myself being vile to that man."

"He is trying awfully hard to be popular with us," I said.

The fourth person in our own carriage was called Mario Vargas. He was good-looking in a fine, swarthy, aristocratic, Latin way, with eyelids that fluttered like those of a coquettish woman. He was Portuguese, though his English was almost perfect; he had affected a little stammer that gave him time to think before a difficult word.

Mervyn had met him before in Delhi.

"He's a grand fellow," he assured me. "He's the best person I've met in this God-forsaken country."

"How's that?" I said.

"He's one of those people who always send for the manager. He's frightfully good. He was in billets, and they wouldn't give him any hot water in his room. He had a first-rate row with the woman. When he said he would leave, she refused to give him back his money. He took out the electric-light bulbs all over the house, packed them in his suitcase, and went off to an hotel in the middle of the night."

"Has he any other good qualities?"

"Oh, he's a person," Mervyn said. "He's not one of those narrow emasculated puppets."

Mervyn was not always reliable on character. But this time I agreed with him. Mario was the nicest person I had known with eyelids that flutter beautifully when they stammer. There was all kinds of goodness in him. He must have been a wild success with women, but he was reticent over his conquests.

There was no corridor on the train. The first-class compartments were the width of a carriage, with four bunks. My bearer, Bahadur, was in the servants' carriage, and at each station he came running along the platform to make sure that I was all right and had not been drinking any dirty water. He also put things in order in the compartment, and sat there like a watchdog when we changed to the restaurant car for dinner. When we came back he was as pleased to see us as if we had been away for months. He was exactly like a spaniel, only he had no tail to wag.

After dinner we played poker. We put two suitcases in the middle of the floor, and sat on the two bottom bunks. As we had not sufficient change, we made matches into counters, four annas, eight annas, and one rupee. Peter played boldly, raising high; Mervyn was very cautious. We often had to wait whilst he tried to make up his mind whether to spend four annas, which is fourpence, to see someone's hand.

Whilst we were playing, the train stopped in a station and a young boy came into the compartment with a tray of oranges and bananas. I thought he had a fine white smile and lovely eyes. I would like to have bought his fruit, but already we had too many oranges.

"No, thank you," I said.

"Very nice, Sahib. Good, Sahib."

"I don't want any," I said.

"Good oranges, Sahib."

"No," I said.

"Very cheap, Sahib."

Mervyn leapt suddenly to his feet and waved his arms in the air.

"Get out, you little devil, or I'll break your blasted black neck!"

The boy turned and disappeared like a frightened animal.

"That's the way to treat them!" Mervyn said. He was vastly amused. "That gets rid of them all right."

"Another way's to shoot them," Mario said.

"Did you see him move! 'Get out, you little black devil!'" He chuckled reminiscently. "That's the way to move them."

"You're a nigger beater," I said.

"It fixed him all right."

"It scared him, certainly."

"'I'll break your blasted neck!'" he repeated.

"It wouldn't surprise me if you did, either."

"Nonsense," he said. "I was only pretending."

"Nonsense," I said. "You're a damned hypocrite."

"I don't do anything I don't profess."

"You're always talking about the poor Indian people being exploited by the British, and you behave like a third-rate imperialist."

"You say silly things," he said. "If you don't pretend to be angry with these people, they make your life a misery."

"What about the poker?" Peter said.

"I can't afford to lose any more," said Mervyn.

"You only lose because you're mean."

"I never have the cards."

"I've had no cards at all," said Mario. "You're so easy to bluff."

"Ah, *c'est Mario qui blague*."

"Say that in Japanese," I said.

"The first thing I shall ask Japanese prisoners is can they speak English."

"You won't ask," Peter said. "You'll say to them, 'If you don't speak English I'll break your blasted neck.'"

"You little yellow devils!" Mervyn said, rolling the words over his tongue with delight.

"I thought you were their champion."

"Please will you desist from misinterpreting my words. I am not their champion."

"You're their apologist," I said. "You're always justifying them."

"On the contrary, I don't try to justify anybody, certainly not the Japs. I wouldn't justify ourselves, either. I can't use a word like justification. I don't think I'm qualified to say this is right and that is wrong, and I don't think you are. In my own life I don't admit other people's standards with their arbitrary right and wrong. I base my own behaviour on what is expedient, so long as I have sufficient control over myself to base it on anything at all.

In the same way, so far as I support the war it's because it's expedient to defeat the Germans and the Japanese. If they defeat us, life would be even more inconvenient than it is in normal times. But to say that our cause is just and the cause of the enemy unjust, stinks to me of prejudice and cant."

"Why did you join the Air Force?" I asked Mario. "Did you join to fight for cant?"

"I told everybody I would join if there was a war. I had to save my face."

"You told all the girls at Estoril," Peter said.

"He's a liar," Mervyn said. "He's a hundred per cent idealist."

"It's only a question of my face."

"I don't believe you," said Mervyn. "You can go back to Portugal tomorrow if you want."

"You can't say you're going to join the Air Force, and then walk out in the middle of a war because you don't like it."

"You could if you were me," said Mervyn. "I should go without a blush. I should tell them what they could do with their Air Force. That's what I'm going to do, anyway. I'm going to get out."

"You've been saying that for months."

"I know people who got out of the Army. They were mentally unfit. One was put in an asylum, and someone kept jumping out of bushes at him to condition him to something or other. In the end he was allowed to go back to his firm. He wrote a book about his treatment, but no publisher would touch it. It was too hot."

"Nobody can deny that you're mentally unfitted."

"We shall all be mad by the end of this war," Peter said. "You can't live under unnatural conditions like this and not go mad."

"It's the sun," Mario said.

"And bad whisky. It's all very unnatural."

"It's just how one had imagined India," I said. "I always said my India would be different. But it's curious how helpless you are against circumstances."

"Let's drink some rum," said Mervyn.

He passed round his bottle, and we gulped down the liquid in turn. It was raw and burnt a channel down to my stomach. Peter found some cigars, and we sat there until after midnight, rattling along to Bombay. Then we climbed into our bunks. I remember lying in the dark with the fan purring on the ceiling to the right of my head and wondering why I was there. There were thousands of millions of people in the world, and I was the one lying on the top right-hand bunk on the train going from Delhi to Bombay. And I was going to Bombay to learn Japanese.

How very odd, I thought; I wonder why I wasn't born to be the Nawab of Dhanapore. And I turned over and went to sleep.

CHAPTER IV

I

WE arrived on Friday afternoon, and were sent out to a unit on the outskirts of Bombay.

The Adjutant said: "Oh, you're the Jap-wallahs—good show," and sent us in the back of a lorry to a hotel in Harrison Street. It was run by a woman called Miss Jackson. She was an Anglo-Indian, thirty-five perhaps, with Jewishly handsome features that showed signs of softening and running to seed; but there was a ripe attraction about her still.

The hotel was clean and not badly furnished, and there were fans in all the rooms. As we went into the hall, Fenwick, the Flight-Lieutenant, said in my ear:

"As I'm the senior officer, I should really have a single room, but I'm willing to share it with someone. You could come in with me."

I said: "Thank you, but Peter and I arranged to share."

"Perhaps Vargas would like to share my room," he said.

"Perhaps," I said.

We went upstairs and there were no single rooms, at least all the rooms had had two single beds put in to accommodate us. Peter and I took one, and Mario went in with Mervyn.

"You're coming in here," Miss Jackson said to Fenwick. Her tone was commanding. She swept forward and led him into a room in which there was already an officer who had arrived on another train from Karachi. "Now are you all right, boys?"

"Where is the bath?" Mario asked.

"At the end of the corridor."

"What time do we eat?"

"You eat at eight o'clock. On other days you may eat earlier by request."

"I hope your food is well cooked."

20

"We are used to catering for officers."

"That means nothing," Mario said. "We're very particular."

"I am particular, too," Miss Jackson said. "I am very particular about whom I have in my hotel. I hope you are all nice boys."

"We pay for what we have," Mario said. "We're as nice as that."

"I think we shall understand each other."

Fenwick stood in the passage. He was still annoyed by the way he had been ordered into the room; he had also heard Mario talking to the proprietress and was jealous of this independence. He thought it was time to display his seniority.

"How do you think I can wash my hands in the basin when the tap doesn't run?" he said.

"There is a tap on the pipe."

"Oh," he said with forced jocularity. "That's different. Why didn't you say so before?"

Bahadur began to unpack my clothes. He laid them neatly according to his invariable pattern, with my blue shirts and my khaki shirts in different piles, and pants and vests laid alternately ready to take out in pairs. In one of my socks he found a hole, over which he shook his head sadly. Then he went into the bathroom to place my towel and soap by the bath. He would not go down to the bazaar to find himself a place to sleep until I was dressed for dinner. This was because he was afraid that when his back was turned I should put on the same bush-shirt that I had been wearing all day. He made it clear that in this respect he did not trust me farther than he could see.

II

On the following day we went to the school for an interview. Two flats had been taken over for our purpose in a large modern block; and the big, cool rooms overlooked the harbour, with its liners and naval vessels and graceful fishing-boats. When a new troopship came in from England, we could see it from the windows. Often, later on, we looked out of the windows at these things instead of thinking about Japanese.

The chief instructor was a retired Brigadier, a fine, cultured man, small of stature and well-preserved. He had spent many of his sixty-five years in Japan, and we were to find a refreshing lack of prejudice in the way he spoke of the qualities and the short-comings of the Japanese people.

We sat down at the desks in the classroom.

"Tell me how much Japanese you know," he said.

"*Sayonara*," said Mario.

"*Hara-kiri.*"

"*Kimono.*"

"Good," he said. "You don't know much Japanese. We can start from the beginning. First I'm going to give you a test."

He turned the blackboard round. On the back there were a dozen ideographs. We studied them intently for two or three minutes. After that he rubbed them out and drew twelve more. He numbered them. On a piece of paper we wrote down the numbers of those that we thought had appeared before.

"That is to test your visual memory," he said.

Then he wrote on the blackboard some word-by-word translations of Japanese sentences. *Man as-for comes time at me to informing condescend*. We tried to make sense of them.

"There is not time enough in one year to learn both the spoken and the written languages," the Brigadier said. "I shall divide you into two sets."

He came and sat down by each of us in turn and examined our papers. I was the first in the front row.

"You haven't got all the characters right," he said.

"I haven't got a good visual memory."

"You can pick up words well by ear?"

"I learn best that way."

"Very well," he said. "You can do the colloquial."

He went on to Fenwick.

"You would also be better at the spoken language?"

"I got hold of French and German without difficulty."

"That is settled, then."

I thought that was a pity. I should have to work with Fenwick. But there would be Peter, too, and the other officer called Lamb who had been at the hotel, and a number of Army officers also. Mervyn and Mario elected to learn the ideographs.

"I will introduce you to your instructors now," said the Brigadier, and led the way from the room. We followed him across the passage into the Common Room. Four Japanese sat there reading newspapers. They stood up and bowed as we entered, and when they had finished bowing they inclined their heads several times

22

more and sucked in their breath noisily. They were all small of stature, and two of them wore thick-lensed glasses. They had all been in India when the war broke out; now in pedagogy they had been offered an alternative to internment.

We shook hands.

"How do you do?" one said meticulously. "How do you do?"

"There is another instructor on the way out from England," the Brigadier said. "Meanwhile we're lucky to have these gentlemen."

"Yes, indeed," we murmured, and the Japanese inclined again.

"Very well," said the Brigadier. "Will you please be here on Monday morning. I hope half-past nine is not too early?"

III

Although I did not expect to find Mr. Headley in his office on Sunday, I called on the offchance at No. 211 Cornwallis Road. I had been given his name and address before leaving England, and for some reason it had remained in my mind long after my address-book had been lost in Burma.

Mr. Headley was a social worker; a man who—so I had heard —had the attributes of a saint. I thought he would give me the best introduction to Bombay.

His office was like a musty bookshop; I had seen nothing like it before amongst the well-ordered homes and places of business of other Englishmen in the Orient. There were dusty books everywhere, in the chairs and on the floor and stack along the corridor. On the walls there were old calendars, curling at the corners and out of date; and on the desk, a chaos of papers and junk.

But Mr. Headley himself was not there. In his place was an Indian youth who beamed at me in a fashion that was recognisably Christian.

"Mr. Headley is out?" I asked.

"He very soon return."

"What time?"

"At twelve he must return. He has not taken with him his instrument, and therefore he must return. At twelve he must be with his instrument."

"I will come at twelve," I said, though I did not understand what he meant about the instrument, and I went off to do some shopping.

23

I went past the big European stores, which were closed because it was Sunday, and into the bazaars of the side streets. I felt like the stranger I was—with no comprehension of the life seething round me, not even of the simple processes, the mixing of potions, the side-stepping from the holy cow that sniffed at a cart of vegetables, the smoking of hookahs or the eating of chapattis—I didn't understand the language or the feelings, how these brown-skinned people made love or worshipped, what they enjoyed and what they hated. The streets were full of filth and noise; children played naked in the gutter, and deformed beggars in stinking rags called out for alms in husky whispers. I thought how easy it was to lose your pity and grow contemptuous, how easy to despise what you didn't understand. The syphilitic mendicant was too low for sympathy, too remote from your own experience, too animal. You needed a genius for sympathy if you were to comprehend. I turned away and went back to Mr. Headley's office, and all the dusty chaos had a friendly and familiar English look.

Mr. Headley, from behind his desk, called me in as though I was a regular visitor.

"Come in, come in," he said. "Don't you look hot!"

"It's very hot outside," I said.

"Excuse me," he said. "I'm one of those stupid people who must jab themselves to the clock."

I saw that his hand held a syringe. He was pushing the needle through the rubber cap of a small bottle.

"Marvellous stuff, insulin," he said. "Kept me alive for twenty-two years. How old would you say I am?"

"That's difficult to guess," I said. "Fifty, or fifty-five perhaps."

"Sixty. No illness—nothing. That's insulin."

"Splendid," I said.

"Look at this."

He unbuttoned his shirt and squeezed a roll of flesh between his fingers. He was a small, wiry man with thick hair.

"Look," he said, and pulled up one of the legs of his short khaki trousers. I looked at his thigh.

"Not a mark!" he said. "I've punctured myself twice a day for twenty-two years and not a mark. A different place every day—that's the trick. Do you know how long it takes me to get round my body?"

"I've no idea."

"Eight months. Take a look."

24

He inserted the needle into the flesh of his leg and began to squeeze in the liquid.

"You won't see this puncture. Haven't used this spot since last February. Now I shan't use it again until next June. Now," he said, still squeezing, "sit down. Tell me who you are."

"My name's Michael Quinn," I said.

"Quinn?" he repeated. "Never met anyone called that before. What are you? I don't understand uniforms."

"Air Force, as a matter of fact," I said.

"Good," he said. "Stay to lunch, if you don't mind taking pot-luck. It'll be along in ten minutes. Have to eat to the clock, you know, because I'm a diabetic. How did you get here?"

"Mrs. Bostock gave me your address—she used to know you in Birmingham."

"Mrs. Bostock? Can't recall the name at all. . . ."

"Her maiden name was Beresford."

"Ah, I've got it, Lucie Beresford. A perfectly charming lady with no morals whatsoever—used to be an old flame of mine. Does she still eat cold sausages off sticks? Never met a woman with such a passion for 'em."

"I don't know," I said. "She's a friend of my father's."

"Of course. I still think of her as twenty-five, but she must be fifty now—no chicken. Is your father an old flame, too?"

"I don't know."

"Expect so. Who's Bostock, anyway—the circus fellow?"

"I think he manufactures bicycles."

"Fool!" Mr. Headley said. "What's your father?"

"He was in advertising."

"Doing all right out of it, I expect."

"He makes both ends meet," I said.

"Of course. Gives you plenty, I suppose?"

"If I need it, he gives me some."

"See that he does—you need it when you're young. When you're my age, no need. Live quietly. Did you meet my boy?"

"The chap who was here when I came first?"

"That's him—Jack. An untouchable—but you don't call them Untouchables. Depressed Class—Scheduled Class. They're on the upgrade now. Jack'll show you round, he's doing social work with me. Now here's our lunch. Don't mind eating in the office, do you? It's easier. Must eat special food when you're a diabetic."

After lunch I walked with him down the Mahatma Gandhi Road towards the Taj Mahal Hotel.

"Tell me something about India," I said.

"India? Certainly. Size, one and half million square miles. Population, approximately four hundred million. About five hundred thousand villages and eighty-three important towns."

"No," I said. "I don't mean statistics."

"The Hindus wear turbans, Muslims fezes, and the Parsees wear hats like a cow's hoof. They also put their dead on the Towers of Silence. You can see them on Malabar Hill over there. Devoured by vultures in half an hour. That's hygienic, you know."

"Anything else?" I asked.

"Do you want to know about India?"

"I have to live here," I said.

"You must live here for thirty years, and you'll find out something about India. Now I've got a meeting—please excuse me. Go away and be young. It's a good thing to be young, you know."

IV

I lay on my bed with a towel over my middle and looked at the fan, and did not think it was always so good to be young. Why, I was not even that, I was forgetting. Five years ago I was young like Peter. I was always forgetting how those five years had slipped away. It was necessary to get used to this—to accept the truth that I was no longer someone who had just left school and had all his life before him. When the war was over I should be practically middle-aged; and it was no use hoping to take up life again where I had dropped it in nineteen thirty-nine. This wasn't a slice out of life; it was part of life itself that must be lived to the full.

I lay looking at the fan. In my chest was a hollowness—the sort of hollowness that usually came in the afternoon or early evening —a sense of utter futility. Sitting before a blazing log fire with a good book in my hand, I never experienced that hollowness. I never experienced it when I thought I was in love, nor when I was passionately interested in a thing. Nor at any time in England, for life was too full. But in India it came often; and it was necessary to study its treatment. Not a difficult study—it was merely a question of learning to drink; or if you already knew, of

26

finding out where and with whom it was nicest to become intoxicated. It was an infallible way of filling in the hollow. It was also an admission of defeat.

It was gravely wrong, I told myself, looking at the fan, to be on the way to middle-age and still have a hollow. When you were young, when you were Peter's age, you could legitimately have a hollow, for it was something that you expected to be filled in as age brought you experience, philosophy, love or religion. But I had none of these things—except perhaps for experience; and what had experience done for me except to bring home to me the futility of all things? What I needed was a religion, that greatest Filler-in-of-Hollows. If you had a religion you need not bother any more about blazing log fires and women and stamp-collecting. It was a great pity not to have a religion. But I was not anywhere near having one—not unless there was a miracle and God appeared to me suddenly in the midst of my hollowness.

The air from the fan was cool on my body. I removed the towel and lay naked, and all of me was pleasantly cool. I bunched the pillow under my head, and looking down I could see how white and clean was my body from the shower. Then I thought of four hundred million other bodies in a million and a half square miles. If only it were possible to think, "But they are brown, they are black, they are inferior. I am white. I am great!" But I could not adopt even that conviction.

I thought, there is a war, and God knows when it will all be over.

I am no longer young; no longer free to shape my life as I choose.

This body is me; and this mind is me; and I can no more change these things than I can change water into fire—and I can no more escape from them than a prisoner can escape from a cage of iron.

v

When Peter came in he said:

"Why are you depressed? You're not often like that—you're so interested in things. When you walk through the bazaars you're perfectly happy. All I think of is what vile, ugly people. I'm glad I can't understand the vulgar things they say to one another."

"You always talk like that," I said, "until suddenly you give a

27

brilliant discourse on the mental processes of a scavenger—full of intuitive understanding."

"Probably one of my ancestors was a scavenger. I shall really have to hush it up. I don't approve of that kind of thing at all."

"I've never really found out what you do approve of."

"I approve of the Taj Hotel," he said, smiling. "Inside it's so clean and beautiful, and you don't have to think about scavengers. Let's go there for dinner. We'll have a nice brandy, and you can tell me all about the women in your life, and that'll make you feel fine."

CHAPTER V

I

I BEGAN to like learning Japanese. Half the reason was that I liked the Brigadier. He made his classes amusing and coloured them with anecdotes of Japan.

He knew a great deal about the culture and the social life of the country. Sometimes he would break off a class to give a demonstration; clearing the top of his desk, he would climb on to it to show the sitting posture of the Japanese, or he would go the length of the room, bowing and sucking in his breath, in imitation of a Japanese meeting an acquaintance in the street. Then he would mimic the high-pitched songs of the geisha; or with curious grunts from his belly show how Japanese generals gave their military orders.

"But Miss Wei will tell you about Japanese women," he said. "She's the new instructor who ought to be here next week."

Our second instructor was Mr. Itsumi, or Itsumi San as we called him, for San was the Japanese equivalent to Mr. He was only twenty-nine or thirty, with an owlish student's face. He had been studying British business methods in England, and on the way back to Japan when the war started, his ship had docked in India. He had been released from internment to teach us.

He was strikingly yellow. I had not met many Japanese, and I did not know that they were really this colour, a deep brown-yellow. When he was angry it turned to a grey-yellow, and that happened often, for he easily took offence. I suppose it was an inferiority complex. He would misunderstand a word, and believing himself to be insulted would fall suddenly silent and nurse a grudge for days.

When he came to teach us the first time he delivered a prepared speech.

"I am speaking frankly. I am a civilian, you are officers. To me that is nothing, for I am an instructor. Therefore let us discount distinction. Without such a discount, I cannot teach. If you are wrong, I will tell you without standing upon ceremony. I shall also reprimand."

He meant that he had no intention of calling us 'Sir'. I did not like him, though it was not for this reason, but because I knew a great deal of scheming went on behind his expressionless eyes. Everything he said was carefully worked out in advance, and when he scored off someone it was a premeditated revenge.

In the same way, he planned his lessons with remarkable industry. Each day he would give us a list of new words, round which he had written sentences. These were inscribed in meticulous handwriting in his black file, the Japanese characters by the side of the English translation. Some of them showed a curious knowledge.

"The sun is ninety-three million miles from the earth, but the moon is only two hundred and forty thousand miles away."

"In England there are sixty-six varieties of butterflies."

His information was always correct.

He was also fond of giving us tests. He would go round the class putting a series of questions to each of us in turn. Then without passing any verbal comment, he would write something in Japanese characters opposite our names. We were never told what he had written down.

His favourite was Fenwick, because Fenwick was the hardest worker. When the rest of us were happy to let the class deteriorate into an informal discussion, Fenwick would look irritated and eventually blurt out, "I'd like to remind you fellows that you've come here to learn Japanese". In the evenings he would study at the hotel, and then he began to get up at six in the mornings and put in an hour before breakfast.

"The application of an Asiatic clerk!" Mervyn said about Fenwick, and we all felt scornful, as though it was a base ambition. But it was very soon clear that he was getting a good start on us. If he had not been there, perhaps we too should have worked in the evenings, and during the long middle-day siesta, but Itsumi

San held him up to us as an example, and demanded that we should emulate him. The thought that it was emulation was sufficient to deter us. We left our Japanese mainly to school hours.

Itsumi San would scold us. If he asked me a question that I was unable to answer, he would look for a long time at his file in silence, as though pondering upon the best line of correction. He would then lecture me on the error of my ways. It was my duty, he told me, to pay more attention. In the same way it was his duty to teach me. He did not want to teach me any more than I wanted to learn, but he was doing his best. Then a sentimental note would creep in. Did I not think he was a good teacher? Was there any improvement in his method that I could suggest? Did I realise that when he was angry it was for my own good? Was it not clear to me that his only concern was to see that we passed the examination, that he wished, not to bully us but to help us? The lesson was resumed. Mollified now, he would give me some easier sentences to translate, and for the time being all would be well.

I did not let any contretemps upset me, and I settled down to the routine of learning. I became interested.

One night I met the Brigadier in the bar of the Cricket Club.

"You're all making good progress," he said.

"Itsumi San is less complimentary."

"You mustn't take him too seriously. He's in an awkward position."

"But he can teach," I said. "He takes a lot of trouble."

"You find Japanese difficult?"

"It's worse than Greek or Latin."

"It's really very difficult," he said. "But it's fascinating, isn't it? It's a pity you can't learn to read and write, too—but you'd have to know at least five thousand characters to make it worth while."

"If I can talk the language that'll be enough," I said.

"There are few who can do that. It'll be a valuable knowledge for after the war."

"After the war I shan't have any use for it."

"You won't go to Japan?"

"Perhaps for a holiday. I shan't live there."

"But there's no knowing," he said. "Life is full of surprises."

"I shall live in England or France—where there are people that I like."

"There are also good people in Japan, you know."

"I'm prejudiced," I said. "I've fought them in Burma. I've run away from them. I've had nightmares about them. They killed my brother."

"In the war?"

"He was in Hong Kong. They did some pretty cruel things there."

"Yes," said the Brigadier. "They can be cruel. Soldiers can be cruel. When they're drunk they do wicked things."

"It isn't only when they're drunk."

"No," he said with a sigh. "It isn't only when they're soldiers, either. There are a lot of wicked things in the world. Sometimes it's very hard to see round them at all."

"I'm not trying to see round them," I said.

"You don't hate all Japanese?"

"I haven't any reason to love them."

"You don't hate the instructors?"

"I don't love them, either."

"Miss Wei, too, is Japanese. I don't think you'll hate her."

"At any rate," I said, "I promise not to show it."

II

I saw the ship arrive. It was a great three-funnel liner. It came in the evening and anchored in the harbour, and three launches went out to it. Their wakes, darker blue than the blue of the undisturbed surface, spread out into huge arrowheads that converged at their tips.

It looked very proud and magnificent and stately lying there, ignoring the fishing boats that drifted in and clustered in front of it.

It looked huge and old and nature-made, like a mountain.

I took a pair of binoculars to examine it more closely. Along the decks were a thousand white pinpoints that were British soldiers.

Night came down. In the morning it lay there still, immensely strong and solid in the glistening harbour.

I watched it from the classroom, saw it move with gigantic sloth until it was hidden by the great stone archway that is called the Gateway of India.

III

She came in with the Brigadier.

Of course the Brigadier had told us before: "Wei is a Chinese name. She is using it because it is not advisable to have a Japanese name now. But Miss Wei is Japanese—you will find she speaks the best Tokyo language." That was all he had told us. We had waited expectantly; most of us had never seen a Japanese woman before.

We were all silent, watching her. She stood nervously by the Brigadier, looking at the corner of the desk, very slim and tiny in a light summer frock.

"I will introduce you," the Brigadier said. "This is Miss Wei."

We murmured, "Good morning."

"Good morning," she said with her lips, and gave a quick little stoop, a suggestion of a curtsy.

"Miss Wei has come all the way from England to help us out." He smiled at her gallantly and gratefully. She smiled too, dropping her eyelids in self-depreciation. Then she sat down next to him behind the desk.

There were general signs of approval: Miss Wei had passed the first test—she was pretty. She was a spot of fresh colour in the schoolroom, with its blackboard and its piles of books and its tables and its inkpots. For a time nobody looked out of the window, and there was a certain amount of winking.

"She is exquisite!" Peter whispered.

"Yes," I said.

"We are going to have delightful classes."

"We probably will."

"Once she has got over her shyness," he added.

It was not surprising that she was shy when there were ten of us there, ten strange faces ranged in front of her. Ten of us judging her critically as a woman.

The Brigadier took out an exercise book.

"I want you particularly to imitate Miss Wei's pronunciation," he said. "I will ask her to read a paragraph, and afterwards we'll all repeat it."

She started very softly. Then she cleared her throat and began again.

"I think it would be better," the Brigadier said, "if you wouldn't mind reading a little bit slower."

She looked up and blinked and her eyes were almond-shaped and enormous.

"I am so sorry."

32

After a while the Brigadier left us, and she said to us in Japanese:

"If you will ask questions one by one, I will do my best to answer them."

She used the most formal and polite words; it was as if she had said:

"If you will kindly deign to ask questions, I will answer humbly."

"Did you have a good journey?" an Army officer asked in halting Japanese.

"It is kind of you to ask," she said. "It took a long time, but there was somehow always something to do. I tried to read a lot of English books."

She had in front of her a register containing our names.

"The next one? Quinn, is it?"

I had been preparing a question on a piece of paper, looking up the words in a dictionary.

"Is it true that when Japanese husbands return home drunk, their wives sit at their feet and untie the laces of their boots?"

Miss Wei shook gently with laughter. She hid her face behind her register so that we should not see her laughing. All we could see was her black hair over the top of her book. She remained there for a minute.

"Is it true?" I insisted when she looked up.

"I cannot say. It is a funny question."

"You don't know?" I said.

"I expect they do sometimes. Now, who is next?" She looked at her register. "Is it—Fenwick?"

I suddenly noticed that Fenwick was flushed with anger, and the veins were standing out in his neck.

"Yes," he said.

"You have a question?"

"I've not got a question," he said in English, "but there's one thing I should like to point out." He pressed his hands down on the table; his hands were red too. He had worked himself up into a kind of frenzy, in order to force himself into raising this blunt objection. "We're all officers in this class. It's usual for our rank to be used when we're being addressed. If you don't know our ranks, as a matter of courtesy you might use Mister."

There was a long silence. The rest of the class was horrified.

"Of course as a foreigner," Fenwick went on, trying to make a clumsy conciliation, "it's rather difficult for you to know our customs."

"Shut up!" Peter said in a loud whisper. "My God!" he said, "isn't it quite unbelievable?"

Miss Wei was lost in confusion. She buried her face in her register. At last she said:

"I am sorry, I did not realise. . . . I had heard the Brigadier speak in that way."

"That is hardly the same thing," Fenwick said.

"It was very rude of me," she said. I was afraid that tears were on the point of welling in her eyes. But they did not come.

"Has anyone any more questions?" she said, the scarlet fading a little from her cheeks. She was afraid to use a name now.

"I hope," said Peter in Japanese, "that you're going to stay here a long time. We are glad to have a new instructor."

He said this kindly, to show that we were not all of us sympathetic with Fenwick's crude complaint.

"Thank you," she said, bowing her head. "I do not deserve that compliment. Thank you very much."

After the class we did not speak to Fenwick. He gathered his books together with studied nonchalance, whistling through his teeth, expecting us to comment on the way in which he had stood up for our rights; but we said nothing.

"Coming home, you fellows?" he said.

"Shortly."

"Make it snappy if you want a free ride in a ghari."

"We aren't as poor as all that," Peter said.

"It's up to you."

We let him go by himself. When he had gone the rest of us went outside to look for a carriage. The road was empty.

"I'm going to the bazaar," I said. "I've got some shopping to do."

I turned off along the front, and then because I was still angry and rather hot, I decided that I would first go to the Cricket Club and drink a John Collins. I turned round and started to walk back along the front of the flats. I was close to the school when Miss Wei came quickly out of the entrance. There was still no carriage. She turned in my direction.

"You're in a hurry," I said.

"I beg your pardon?" she said, stopping. She looked at me in a frightened, surprised way.

I repeated the same thing in Japanese.

"Oh, I was running!" she said in English. "I don't know why."

"I hope it isn't because you're already so pleased to escape from the school."

"No, please don't think that."

"You must think very badly of us."

"For a month," she said, "I don't know how you speak Japanese so well."

"I didn't mean Japanese, but our manners."

"What is the matter with manners?"

"That outburst," I said, "about handles to our names."

"I can't think how I was so stupid."

"The rest of us hadn't noticed."

"But it was so silly of me. I didn't know what I was saying. It is first time I have tried to teach, and there seemed to be so many people."

"Only ten."

"At first it seemed like a hundred."

"You'll get used to our faces. We aren't very frightening, really."

"Oh no," she said.

At that moment an empty ghari came by on the road. The horse clopped to a standstill. The driver wore a red Muslim fez and had a black moustache that hung in a half moon over his mouth.

"Ghari, Sahib?"

He smiled down at us from his high seat. His teeth were red as though from pyorrhœa.

"May I drop you?" I said to Miss Wei.

"I am going to hotel."

"It's on my way."

"You know where it is?" she said.

"No, but that doesn't matter."

"But I don't want to take you out of your way, please," she said. "You take this and I shall find other ghari."

"What is your hotel called?"

"The Mayfair."

"Then it's on my way. To the Mayfair," I said to the ghari-wallah.

I climbed in after Miss Wei. The black hood was pulled down

against the sun, far down at the sides, so that we were almost shut in. Only the flanks of the horse were visible in front of the driver's seat.

It was months since I had sat close to a woman. It was probably as long as two years. In Rangoon I had not known any women at all. On the boat out from England there had been some nurses; I sometimes thought it would have been nice to have an *affaire* with one of the pretty nurses, but long before I had decided that they were all deeply involved with people who had more initiative than myself. When you are in the Services you have to take a lot of initiative to have a woman, because there are so few to go round.

Then at home . . . the last woman I had sat close to was my mother. I had sat next to her in the back of the taxi on the last journey to the station. I had tried not to look at her closely, because she was screwing up her face in an effort to keep herself from crying. I was keeping my own face set for the same reason. Before that, since the beginning of the war, I had only sat next to women I did not care about, and that is not like sitting next to a woman at all.

Now I was all of a sudden aware with all my senses that I was sitting close to a woman. This sharp awareness was quite unexpected and surprised me, and I remembered what a pleasant thing it was. I remembered that when I had thought of women in places where there were none, I had forgotten about the subtle pleasure and remembered only the crude ones. At this moment I was deriving an intense pleasure from the faint, dry odour of perfume, and the fainter aura of cosmetics, and seeing the movement of beautiful fingers. Then I looked up at her face and saw that it was like ivory, a round little face full of gaiety and gentleness, with these brown, tremendous almond eyes.

Japanese, I thought—don't I hate the Japanese?

("You silly idiot," I heard Peter saying. "You don't know what you do hate. You're so impossibly muddle-headed."

"I think I could hate this woman for being Japanese."

"You *could*?"

"If once I thought of her as being Japanese instead of a woman."

"She is both," Peter said. "Stop talking tripe.")

"This is better than the Delhi tonga," I said to Miss Wei. "You face the right way, and there is no fear of falling out."

"But the driver has hurt mouth," she said sadly.

"You haven't been in India before?"

"No," she said. "Are they all hurt?"

"They all chew betel-nut. You can see them selling it in the bazaar. They make it into a sticky paste and spread it on a leaf."

"What is bazaar?"

"Where the Indians go shopping."

"Can you go and see?"

"I'm going there now."

I tried to divine from her expression whether she would like to come too. I waited, half hoping she would ask, but she was silent.

"Have you time to look round with me?" I said, and found myself full of apprehension, not that she would not come, but that I was making a proposal she would find it embarrassing to refuse.

"Oh, please!" she exclaimed, with sudden brightness, like a child offered an orange. And then as though she thought she should not have shown such excitement, she said doubtfully, "But perhaps you would not care to take me?"

"Why not?"

"You are perhaps already meeting someone?"

"No," I said.

"But you are sure it is all right?"

"What could be the matter?"

"Well . . ." she said.

"Well?"

"I am Japanese. You are sure you won't get into trouble?"

"Certainly. You're my teacher. We're talking Japanese."

"Then let's go to bazaar," she said. "I think that is such a nice word, bazaar. It must be very exciting."

I called to the driver to go to Chandragupta Road. He pulled on the reins of the horse, and we came to an abrupt standstill. Then we turned round in the middle of the road and fitted into the traffic going in the opposite direction.

"It was really out of your way," she said.

"A few yards."

"I am sorry to be trouble."

"I'm enjoying it—the first time I've ridden with a lady in a ghari. It's a great event."

"*O-seiji . . .*" she said.

"I don't understand Japanese."

37

"It means you were speaking compliment."

"It is true," I said.

We stopped the ghari at the corner of Chandragupta Road. Facing us as we alighted there was a smooth plaster wall, and on the wall was a poster. It was a poster I had seen all over India.

It was the face of a Japanese—a smiling and not unpleasant face. But this face was only a mask. Beneath it, teeth bared but not smiling, eyes narrowed and cruel, was the real face of yellow flesh; and beside it the caption: 'Beware the mask of friendship —it may hide Japanese treachery.'

I looked at Miss Wei; she had seen it. Her eyes took it in, and then the lashes hid them and she looked at the ground and turned away towards the bazaar.

"It is difficult for you," I said.

She was suddenly bright:

"It is also difficult for you."

"That is different," I said.

"You don't mind?"

"Mind?"

"Showing me the bazaar?"

"Yes," I said, "I am very particular whom I show bazaars to."

"Oh dear! . . ."

The brightness went, and a pathetic, crestfallen look came into her face; her eyes were large and round, watching me to try to make me out. I brought the joke to an end quickly.

"That was just my idiotic sense of humour."

"Really," she said. "Honestry, you don't mind?" She pronounced the 'l' of honestly like an 'r', and there was something charming in this little serious appeal of hers that brought a rush of sentiment into my breast. It amused me, as though it were some quaint thing said by a child.

"Why you laugh?" she said.

"I'm sorry, it was rude."

We began to walk along through the bazaar. The street was thronged with people, and there were wooden carts drawn by bullocks rumbling over the stones, and a great deal of noise. And as many smells as noises, but chiefly the dry, sharp smell of burning charcoal. It was very dirty. People pushed by us, hardly noticing us. Only the shop-keepers called out in arresting tones, as though we had dropped something.

"Sahib!"

"Look, Sahib!"

"A minute please!"

"Sahib, very cheap shoes!"

Miss Wei was wide-eyed like a child. She skipped from one side of the street to the other, pointing at things, touching them, like a perfectly unselfconscious child in a toyshop. I was looking at her, fascinated. I began to think she was the prettiest thing I had ever seen; and then I purposely thought of the poster, and after that of 'the Japanese', of what 'Japanese' had always signified to me, and of Itsumi San. But I knew it was being an effort for me to think of Miss Wei as 'Japanese', and not simply as a woman.

A dirty grey cow wandered aimlessly and in holy immunity past her.

"Look!" she cried. "Look!" She laid a daring finger on its horn. It swung its head round, brushing her dress with a dry, lazily inquiring nose, and she jumped a foot backwards, withdrawing her hand as if it had been bitten.

She looked at me in surprise.

"Did you see it had whiskers?" she said. "I didn't know cows had whiskers."

"Don't you have cows in Japan?"

"Yes, but I have never touched. I have never been close before. Why do they have cows in bazaar?"

"Nobody dare turn them out."

"Oh," she said, thinking it over. And then: "I think bazaar is awfully exciting. I am going to buy."

"A cow?"

"I will buy anything. It looks fun to buy. Could I have fountain-pen?"

We found a store where there were some for sale. The storekeeper was fat and sat cross-legged on the threshold. He reached for some pens and began to hand them to us one by one. His hands were thick and brown, with big, dry nails.

"Is this good?" Miss Wei said.

"I will show you our best. It is this. It is a genuine Blackbird."

"It is honestry good?"

"You see written—super-fine."

"How much this?"

"Fifty rupees only."

"I will take."

She began searching in her handbag.

"No!" I said.

"Please, I would like to buy."

"It's too expensive."

"But I want good pen."

"It's not that good."

"How much worth?" she said.

"Offer him twenty-five."

"It is worth more than fifty," the shop-keeper said. "It is a super-fine pen. I sell specially cheap for Memsahib. For anyone else it is sixty rupees."

"Twenty-five," I said.

"I cannot sell for less than fifty."

"Twenty-five."

Miss Wei looked at me beseechingly. I took her arm and started to lead her away.

"Come on," I said. "We'll buy the same thing cheaper somewhere else."

"Forty rupees, Sahib. Special price."

"Make it thirty," I said.

"This is genuine super-fine Blackbird."

"Thirty rupees."

"Thirty-five, special for Memsahib."

"Very well," I said. "Thirty-five. You're very fortunate that Memsahib is so generous."

Miss Wei's face brightened. She pulled the notes quickly out of her bag before anybody changed his mind. She took the pen and tucked it away inside.

"You must never pay all they ask," I said as we turned away. "They expect you to bargain."

"But he looked so poor."

"He was pleased to get thirty-five. Did you see his face?"

"He didn't think I cheated?"

"No, he thought he could cheat you."

"Then you have saved for me fifteen rupees. Please let's spend on something for you."

"I don't want anything."

"Yes," she said. "It is your fifteen rupees because you saved for me. I shall buy that."

"I'm afraid I don't wear braces."

"Oh dear," she said plaintively. "It is naughty of you not to tell what you would like. Oh, look!" she said. "There is orchestra!"

She pointed down the street to a crowd of Indians, from the midst of which came the monotonous squeaks of some musical instrument.

"Don't look," I said.

"But it is perhaps charming snakes."

"No, it is something horrible."

"Please, I would like to see."

"It'll upset you," I said.

"What is it, please?"

"Some kind of begging."

"Then why mayn't I see begging?"

"You can see it if you want to—but you won't like it."

"You are—squeamish!" she said, delighted with herself for having found such a nice word.

"All right," I said. "We'll go and look."

We pushed our way through the brown, thin-legged pedestrians until we could see the musicians. The leader was an old man with long, black, matted hair hanging about his shoulders. His face was only a little less black than his hair, and his cheeks were swollen as he blew into his gourd-like flute. Behind him were two young boys, almost naked, whose cheeks too were swollen like little brown footballs, and their eyes projecting grotesquely. The stream of sound from their instruments was penetrating and incessant.

"There is nothing bad," Miss Wei said. "Look, they are blowing so hard. . . . Oh!" She stopped suddenly. Her mouth fell open in horror. She stood staring, transfixed with a dreadful fascination.

Between the spider legs of the onlookers something had emerged into view that resembled a fœtus, with enormous head and useless match-stick limbs drawn up into a shrunken belly. Its ash-smeared body was the size of a child's; yet there was nothing in the paralysed face to indicate whether it was for five or fifty or five hundred years that this hideously misshapen creature had harboured its tiny spark of life. Only one arm was mobile and with this, inch by suffering inch, it dragged itself along the gutter.

The pain was deeply engraved on Miss Wei's face; but she did not move.

"Come," I said.

"Please wait."

She fumbled in her purse and found some notes. There were

41

twenty or thirty rupees. She handed them to me. I noticed that her eyes were quite dry; but the misery stood out in them like tears.

"Please give," she said.

"But . . ."

"Please," she said, and moved away out of the crowd.

I pushed through the row of spectators. The old man with the long hair saw me, and held out one hand without stopping his music, peering over the wooden instrument to see how much I gave. I stuffed the three or four notes into the hand. The monotonous sound seemed to rise for a moment in an unexpected squeak, and then fell back to the old tuneless rhythm. The old man inclined his head slightly, and the eyes of the two boys goggled more than ever. I turned and fought my way out.

"You're very generous," I said to Miss Wei. She did not say anything. "Normally he wouldn't get so much in a month."

After a while she said, "It is the most terrible thing I have seen."

"It is terrible," I said. "It's difficult to believe, but sometimes they mutilate young children on purpose, so that they can make a livelihood begging."

"Oh," she said with a tiny whisper. "That is so wicked."

"Yes," I said, and echoing the words of the Brigadier: "There are a lot of wicked things in the world."

We walked for a time in silence, pretending to look at the things in the bazaar, but we were no longer spontaneously enjoying ourselves. I felt shattered, partly because of the monstrous thing we had seen in the gutter, partly because all the charming gaiety had gone out of Miss Wei, and now she was looking ineffably sad. I made some frivolous remark, but she only looked at me and forced herself to make a sad smile.

When we reached Hornby Road she said goodbye, thanking me as though I had done something very wonderful for her. Then she made two or three little curtsies before getting into her ghari.

"It has been such experience," she said.

"Yes," I said. "It has been an experience."

I called for a ghari myself and gave the name of my hotel.

CHAPTER VI

I HAD a cold shower, and then wrapped a towel round my waist and lit a cigarette. It is a fine thing, a cold shower in India—better than alcohol, or a cup of tea, or a sleep. You can go under it tired and footsore, perspiring, oppressed by worry, and emerge like a new being. Of course, the cigarette is also an important adjunct. Except for the after-breakfast cigarette, it is the best you can have.

I pottered about in bare feet, feeling immensely fit and aware of my body. In England that was a thing that I had been seldom aware of, except in so far as satisfying its needs were concerned. Those needs only served to underline its nuisance value. Even exercising for exercising's sake was an intolerable waste of time.

On the boat out from England it had first been brought home to me how much more conscious people became of their bodies as they neared the equator. There was a Burmese girl on board who was pretty and vivacious and quite intelligent; and clearly the fires of passion could burn hotly within her. An Army doctor, a Captain, became quickly infatuated with her—before we had even got down the Clyde. And by the time we had begun our zig-zag course in the Atlantic, an *affaire* was in progress that could not be entirely clandestine. I began to wonder what would happen, for both of them were married. They even spoke of a double divorce. That idea, however, was hatched in the cold northern climes, when she was still shivering within the folds of a huge fur coat and he within an Army great-coat. When we got down to the equator, nature straightened out the difficulty into which it had pitch-forked them. Basking in the sun, her nut-brown body came to life again; something that had long been dormant was reawakened. As for the Captain—he reluctantly changed into tropical kit, revealing a pair of knobbly knees and a white skin that the sun soon turned to a painful pink. They lay, one in the sun and one in the shade, he beginning to envy and she to despise. North of Ireland they could be lovers—in the tropics their differences were irreconcilable.

So it is that the sun brings out this body-awareness; though for me Burma, and being in hospital, had done the same thing. Rebuilding my body had served to remind me that it belonged to me, that I could neither exchange it for another nor do without it, and that it was something more than a complexity of inconveniences.

I smoked a second cigarette and read a few pages from a book. Then I dressed in khaki slacks and a loose bush-shirt, and took a ghari to the Yacht Club. Peter had left a note to say that I should find him there.

He was drinking with Mervyn and Mario. I had a whisky, and then we went upstairs to dine. It was a tall, cool room with many big fans. The waiters were smart and dressed in white, and they walked bare-footed on the polished floor. We ordered a bottle of wine to go with the delicious food.

"I am getting to like Bombay," Peter said.

"That's the trouble," said Mervyn. "I'm afraid of liking it too much."

"What do you mean?"

"Life's simple when everything revolves round the King's Road in Chelsea. There's always a hub to your wheel."

"It's nice to find it bearable to live on the rim."

"I don't want my wheel to get out of shape."

"The Quinn wheel is going cock-eyed," said Mario good-naturedly. "Very soon the hub will be stuck on the end of a spoke."

I looked at him questioningly.

"Aren't you making plans here?" he said.

"I don't understand."

"Of course he is," said Peter. "Michael always gets his life organised. The moment he lands in a town he buys a map. He marks places of interest in blue, and local dignitaries in green, and the residences of beautiful women in red."

"What is all this about?" I said.

"Our spies have told us everything, and we're very hurt. You get rid of us cleverly and pretend to go away. Then you come slinking back to your tryst."

"Miss Wei?" I said.

"That's what we're told."

"I can assure you it was an accident."

"Getting into the ghari, too?"

"That was instinctive gallantry," I said.

"There's great scope for gallantry when you find yourself with a beautiful woman beneath one of those hoods."

"You think she's beautiful?"

"Of course she's beautiful," Peter said. "She's altogether exquisite. I've never seen eyes like those in my life before. It's like looking into one of those bottomless pools you find amongst the rocks on the Cornish coast."

"It sounds a bit as though you're jealous," I said.

"Certainly I'm jealous. I can't imagine why I didn't think of doing this myself."

"I didn't think of it—it just happened."

"You watch your step," Mervyn said. "Don't forget she has a yellow skin. These things can get you."

"Her skin isn't yellow. It isn't like Itsumi San's at all. It's as pink as yours."

"The principle is the same. It's a question of warping your taste. I'm told if you once chew betel-nut you lose all interest in cigarettes."

"Good heavens," I said. "I don't see what all that's got to do with me. The only reason that I spoke to her was to apologise for Fenwick." My protestation sounded rather over-vehement and humourless, for something in Mervyn's words had given me an unpleasant jolt. I was not absolutely sure why I had been affected in this way, and I made a mental note to work it out afterwards. Meanwhile it was better to guide the conversation to a safer topic. "Fenwick quite surpassed himself today, don't you think?" I said.

"He's unspeakable!" said Mervyn. "In peacetime you simply wouldn't have a man like that in your house. You wouldn't even let him use the service stairs."

"Some people get taken in by his back-slapping," Peter said. "They can't see it's all part of a plan to better himself."

"It isn't even back-slapping. Have you seen him with the Brigadier? It's sycophancy. It's crawling up the honourable backside."

"But it's that kind of person who gets on," said Mario. "You wait and see. When we're still Flying Officers he'll be a Group-Captain, and there'll be nothing we can do about it. He'll be a Group-Captain because he's good at his job. And there'll be no weapons with which we can fight him, because we shan't be a quarter so good."

"There's a lot to be said for the old days," Peter said, "when you couldn't be an officer without five hundred a year and a father

45

in the Guards. I suggest a motion deploring the passing of the Old Days and recommending the foundation of a club for survivors. The President will be the Colonel whom I met in the Cricket Club."

"Tell us about the Colonel."

"He said, 'I want you to ask yourself three things. Firstly, do the right-thinking Indians want the British to leave India? Secondly, is it to their advantage that the British should leave? And thirdly, do the British want to go, and if not, why the hell should they?' He had a real God-given conviction that we were a superior nation carrying out a divine mission in India. He was absolutely sincere and kind, and at least seventy-two. He also had a twinkle in his eye and talked about the stage-door at the Gaiety. He hadn't lost his eye for a shapely ankle, either. He said to me, 'I know I am an old diehard, or Blimp or whatever you call old fogies like myself nowadays. . . .' There should be a monument to the diehard and the Blimp. I should like to preserve him for ever and ever—put him in Madame Tussaud's or somewhere, so that all the nasty little children of the future, all the precocious little Fenwick children, can be taken there to see him."

"I don't believe Fenwick will have any children," Mervyn said. "He's a slug."

"But I must tell you about my uncle," Peter went on. "You'd never believe about my uncle—he's altogether too good to be true. He's a squire. We never call him Uncle. He is always 'The Squire'. We're all very fond of the Squire. The only thing he can really do well is ride a horse—you've never seen anything so wonderful as the Squire on horseback, doing the rounds of his estate. Of course the estate is losing a very steady six hundred a year; but that is one of the burdens it's his duty to bear—it would be a break with tradition if he were to make it pay. He was at Cambridge about fifty years ago, when only tradesmen's sons took degrees. Naturally he did not take a degree, but that didn't prevent him from becoming a JP of Worcestershire—he was cut out absolutely for the job. Now he is not a JP, but there is still a morning ceremony called 'attending to business'. 'Attending to business' takes place at half past ten, when the Squire retires to his study. He sits down at his desk, and clears his throat very fruitily, and strokes his moustache, which is a symptom of the profoundest thought. Then he turns over the pages of *The Times* one by one. When he reaches the end, he turns the whole paper over and starts at the beginning again in case he has missed any item of importance. If you interrupt him in the middle of this he scowls over the top of his reading glasses and says, 'Couldn't the matter wait, dear boy? I'm attending to business.' At half past eleven, with business attended to, he can get into the saddle with a clear conscience and inspect the clumps of elm trees that he's been trying to decide whether or not to cut down for eleven years.

"After dinner there's always port and cigars. Once I was brazen enough to ask him to give me a bottle of champagne. I waited until he was in a good humour, but it came as a terrible shock to him. I had to repeat the request several times before he could believe his ears. Then he said, 'Hum, hum, hum', and made the ferocious noise in his throat and twirled the ends of his moustache. 'I'm afraid we've drunk the last bottle, dear boy,' he said at last. But I'd already inspected the wine cellar. I told him so. It was clear he was very disappointed in me, and there was a long interval while he put on his reading glasses so that he could scowl at me over the top, and took them off again, and made some more fruity noises—long noises in his throat, working up to a crescendo and then starting lower down again like a car changing gear. War or peace for a nation might have been in the balance. Finally he said with enormous solemnity, 'I shall think it over, dear boy. I shall consider it', and that afternoon he had an unexpected session of 'attending to business'. But I'm afraid that before I return to England the Squire will have been gathered, and the country won't be the same. Meanwhile I shall appoint him Hon. Secretary to the Survivors of the Old Days' Club. He will fill the rôle to perfection."

"You should be happy in India," Mervyn said. "This is the last stronghold. Look at all the stuffed shirts in this room."

"Oh, but it isn't a stronghold at all. The bastions are crumbling. There's too much sedition and go-getting, and the war has caused an influx of young whipper-snappers—just like ourselves. No principles. Look at Michael here, with his queer ideas that Indians are people you can ask to dinner. And now he's in love with a Japanese."

"You're drunk," I said.

"No, I can see it in your face. You've gone crazy about the new teacher."

"I've done nothing of the kind. I think she's very beautiful, but

47

she probably has a lover already. Whenever I meet a beautiful woman she's always passionately attached to somebody else."

"Yes," Mario said. "I should say you're right about that."

"What do you know about it?" I asked, because it sounded a strange thing for Mario to say.

"She's sitting behind you," he said. "So is the third corner of the triangle."

I turned round. Two or three tables away I could see Miss Wei. Her back was half turned towards me. Sitting opposite her was a man with horn-rimmmed spectacles. He had a broad forehead, an aquiline nose, and thin, pale lips.

"There," I said. "I hope that convinces you. I'm not chasing after the Japanese lady."

CHAPTER VII

I

On the following Saturday afternoon I went to the races with Peter and Mario. We left Mervyn lying on his bed in one of his purplest depressions. When he was like that it was useless trying to humour him; you might as well have tried to coax someone out of a drunken stupor. We had begun to suspect that he was cultivating his moods, seizing hold of any little irregularity in his state of mind and magnifying it, driving himself mad. When you are mad, you get sent back to England.

It was Mario who was enthusiastic about the races; he said his soul was going dead in him and he wanted movement and colour, and he wanted to see beautiful women in smart clothes, women who would remind him of European capitals. Peter was going because he wanted to make some money. He had a system. One ought to have a system, he said; in fact, from now on he was going to start systems for everything. He had only just discovered the value of them—he was using a system of mnemonics for learning Japanese words. He was going to organise his whole life on a number of systems, and then eventually he would be bound to get somewhere.

I was going to the races because I had no system for anything and could think of nothing better to do. At least, I could think of better things: I would really have preferred to read a book at the Cricket Club or work on some Japanese, but I knew that on

Saturday afternoon I should find it impossible to sit still and concentrate. It wasn't only that way with me on Saturday afternoon, either. The peace I had known in Simla was gone, and a kind of restlessness was besetting me. I didn't know what I wanted to do, nor why I was restless. I went to the races because it meant moving about, and it would pass the afternoon.

Although the temperature was over ninety degrees, the racecourse was crowded. There were dozens of limousines lining the road and the grandstand was full of Maharajahs. The Brigadier had lent us badges that admitted us to the paddock.

"Isn't it simply marvellous," Mario said. "I love to be amongst the best people."

"It's excellent," Peter said. "You see, the Indians have best people too. I'd got it all wrong. I thought all Indians were *babus* and sweepers."

There was plenty of colour for Mario. All the Indian women were wearing their silk saris, very soft and colourful, and wholly feminine; the English women moved amongst them like a different sex, half-way to masculinity. These Indians seemed to glide as they moved, and the diaphanous material, exquisitely bordered in silver or gold, floated behind them; they stood in twos and threes like bunches of soft-petalled flowers. Mario was smiling his white Latin smile with æsthetic delight.

"I am losing money every minute you stand there entranced," Peter said. "I must go and study the field at once."

We left Mario in the crowd, and went off and looked at the horses. Then we went over to the bookmakers and placed bets on the first race. The minimum bet was thirty rupees. Thirty rupees for us was two days' pay.

"That'll make your system very expensive," I said.

"I shall use it all the same. The whole point about a system is that it must be rigid. Then if I lose my money I can lay all the blame on it. If you have any sense, you'll start one too."

"I just back the agreeable names and colours."

"You're not nearly cynical enough," Peter said. "You don't understand life. The nasty names and the loud, clashing colours always come in first."

We took our cards, and went back across the paddock to the grandstand. It was no use trying to find Mario again in the crowd, so we found seats and smoked a cigarette waiting for the first race to begin. People began to flow through on to the grass in front of

49

the stand, thronging the fence that lined the track. All the voices merged into a roar that rose and fell like the sound of the sea. It was cooler in the grandstand, but I was still perspiring. I was beginning to enjoy myself, catching the expectant mood in the air. I had only got ninety rupees, enough for three races, and I thought if I won some money I could find plenty of things to spend it on. If I won, I thought, I should ask Miss Wei out to dinner. I told Peter.

"You're crazy," he said. "You could take her out anyway. It isn't a question of money."

"It will make the race more exciting."

"That's like the stupid game of avoiding the joins on a pavement—'If I step on the line, I shall fail my exam'. You're hopeless. You're not my type. I don't know why I have you as a friend."

"I'm part of one of your systems."

"At any rate, it proves we were right about you in the Yacht Club. About you and Miss Wei."

"You weren't," I said.

"If you put your women on a horse..." he said.

"It was just a whim."

"Let's see if your horse wins."

We didn't have to wait long. And it didn't win. Except for one horse a furlong behind, it was last in the field from the start. I saw the salmon pink and the sky blue, the jockey colours that I had chosen, hanging there at the back of the bunch, and the jockey never seemed to be trying. Peter's horse came in fifth.

"That's fine," he said. "In my system it's no use winning on the first bet—you don't get enough, and you have to start at the beginning again."

"I've lost Miss Wei," I said. "But I'll probably have to take you out to dinner instead if you lose all afternoon."

"I'll manage. You'd better put your woman on the next race again."

"No," I said. "That's all over."

We went down to the bookies again and made some new bets. I stuck to salmon pink and sky blue, and Peter had a horse called 'Tintinnabulation'. We watched the race from the rails. I saw mine as they came by, well back, but Peter never saw his at all. We couldn't see who had won, and Peter was on tenterhooks until the numbers went up, and neither of ours was among them. I put my last thirty chips on something called 'The Colonel's

Daughter', and Peter put ninety on the same horse. It came in third, but we had both backed it to win. After that I fell out, because I had no more money left in my wallet. Peter offered to lend me some, but I had purposely only come with ninety chips, and I told him to use it up on his system. On the fifth race he laid a hundred and fifty rupees, and his horse galloped home at ten to one. He almost went mad queueing up at the bookmaker's to collect his hundred-odd pounds, afraid that the money would run out. After that he put thirty on the last race, and I took thirty from him, and we both lost.

We waited at the paddock gate until we saw Mario coming out with the crowd. He looked so pleased with himself that we thought he must have had as great a success as Peter. But he asked about us before he told us anything.

"My system was wonderful," Peter said.

"Next time it will let you down," said Mario.

"It'll do nothing of the kind. The genius of my system is that you never use the same system twice running at the races. Nobody has ever thought of that before. Now what have you won?"

"More than you."

"I don't believe it. You didn't have enough capital."

"You've lost your soul," Mario said. "And I've gained the world."

"I hate people who talk in riddles."

"I've gained heaven, too."

He was trying to suppress his smiles, but all his face was smiling, and his eyes were very bright and happy. He looked extraordinarily handsome—handsome in a dark, suave way, without being wooden.

We let him keep his secret until we had got into the taxi, and then we pressed him, and he said with diffidence and as though he was a little surprised:

"Well, as a matter of fact, I've met the most wonderful girl."

"Oh, hell," Peter said, "I should never have let you out of my sight."

"I never quite expected to find anything like that out here."

"I suppose you've fallen for one of those tantalising saris. What a shock you'll get—those garments can turn mountains into molehills."

"It's an English girl," Mario said.

"One of the best people?"

"Certainly—she was with her parents."

"One of the very best, obviously."

"I just looked at her and thought she was wonderful. I went on looking at her, and she looked at me, quite frankly, and I knew all about her at once. I went straight up to her, and began to talk to her as though I'd known her all my life. I've never experienced anything quite like it before. It makes one believe in all kinds of new things. Divinities that shape your ends, and all that. And she has an exceptional name, too. It's Dorcas."

"Yes," Peter said. "That's a good name. I can imagine those frank looks."

"I spent all the afternoon making bets for her. We lost every one."

"Not that it mattered in the least!"

"Once we forgot to watch the race, because we were so busy talking."

"And the parents?"

"They thought from the way we were talking that we must be old friends. The father is a Major-General. A little gouty."

"You're going to be so happy," Peter said.

"Of course, I don't know what will come of it. It may just be one of those beautiful isolated moments, a happy combination of chemicals in the right atmospheric conditions. Anyway, I'm meeting her for dinner next week."

"Not tonight?" Peter said. "Then we'll have a celebration. We shall celebrate your beautiful moment and the vindication of my system. Only I'm not going to have Mervyn because his blues are infectious."

When we got back to the hotel Mervyn had disappeared, anyway. He had left his bed rumpled and his clothes scattered everywhere. We bathed and changed, and then we went out and ate a Chinese meal; we ate shark-fin soup because that was the most expensive thing on the menu and Peter's wallet was bulging with the notes he had won. Afterwards we went to the cinema; but we were not in the right mood for two hours of sentimentality, and we made frivolous comments that annoyed the audience round about us. When we got up to go they expressed their relief with purposely audible mutterings.

Mervyn was not in when we got back. We went to bed, and I lay awake thinking of the races and the film and the shark-fin soup, and occasionally of Miss Wei. It was dark outside, but the fan was shorting and I watched the sparks dancing round the motor above my head. Then I heard Mervyn coming up the stairs, breathing heavily like an animal.

"What's the time?" I said, as he passed my door.

"I don't know," he said.

"You've got a watch."

He shone his torch on to his wrist. He looked at it for a long time, leaning against the door, snorting all the time. He might have been drunk; but Mervyn did not have to be drunk to get himself into that sort of state.

"Three o'clock," he said at last.

"Good night," I said.

He did not say 'Good night', but went off clumsily to his own room. I could hear him kicking off his shoes, and then the springs of his bed squeaked as he threw himself heavily on to it without taking off his clothes.

II

Miss Wei taught us in the afternoons. Once her first shyness had gone her classes became the brightest hour of the day.

Everybody teased her, and she began to think it was great fun, and all through her hour she was putting up the red-backed register in front of her face to hide her giggles. But we learnt a great deal of Japanese from her. We used to look up odd phrases and words in a traveller's dictionary and bring them out in conversation, and she would have to hide her face and laugh again at the strange sound of them on our lips. She wanted to know who had taught us these things. Then one afternoon she was absent from the school. The Brigadier came in to announce that she was sick; she would be back soon. We searched the phrase-books for all kinds of condolences. But she was not there the next day or the next.

Once I thought I saw her in the street. I stopped my ghari and jumped out, and chased after the person along the pavement. It wasn't her. After that in the street I seemed to recognise her over and over again in distant figures. When I found out my mistake, I experienced that same sense of frustration and disappointment as when she did not arrive for her class. The days were long and dreary; there was a gap in them that had not been there before she came to the school. It came as a little shock to find out how much I was missing her.

I felt a sudden urge to send her flowers. In the lunch-time siesta I went to Matier's and ordered a bunch to be sent to her hotel.

"You have a card to enclose?" they said.

"No," I said. "It doesn't matter about a card."

I thought just sending her the flowers was enough, and would relieve the feelings that were pressing inside me. I found that I was thinking of her all the time; it was like a disease, and I wanted to rid myself of it, because it distracted me from things that I really wanted to do. I felt better when I had sent the flowers, and in the evening I went to the Cricket Club and bathed and thought I had been behaving like an idiot. I ordered an iced coffee, and drank it in a deck-chair by the side of the swimming-pool, reading a book and taking in most of what I read. I felt perfectly at ease and happy, and was glad I had sent the flowers without a card. I was all right until I was in bed; and then it all came back with a sudden surge and I desperately wanted to see Miss Wei, and I promised myself that the next day I would go to her hotel. The next day was Saturday, and I went in the afternoon.

I stood about in the hall whilst a bearer went up to inquire. The hotel was called the Mayfair, but it was more like one of the older hotels of Belgravia, rather gloomy and hang-dog and full of Victorian fittings. It had seen better days, but kept up its prices despite everything. I began to wish I hadn't come: not because of the hall's gloominess, but because I now felt some trepidation. One moment I thought that coming here was an obvious gesture of politeness, beyond criticism, and that if she was in bed and did not wish to see me she could easily send down a message. And the next, I wondered if it would be clear to a child that I had been pitchforked into this by a ridiculous infatuation, and that I was making a fool of myself. On the whole, I wanted to drop the business and go; go and forget it all in a fan-cooled cinema. But I knew if I did that, when the surge came again I should despise myself for my cowardice. I knew I had to live up to my feelings even when they were absent.

The bearer reappeared.

"It is number forty-three room, please," he said.

"I'm to go up?"

"The lady says please to go."

I was carried to the second floor by an old clanking lift, and ejected into a corridor. I found the door of No. 43, and knocked. Miss Wei's voice called me in.

It was a big room with a high ceiling, lighter than the rest of the hotel, but dingily furnished. Only the bed looked new, with its perfectly white sheets and white pillows; and there Miss Wei was sitting, propped up against the pillows, very small and a little forlorn all alone in the room. But I had never seen her looking so lovely as this, her black hair framing her little, pale face, and her slender hands lying on the sheet beside her. All the reluctance left me at once and I was filled with delight, and I wanted to say all kinds of things to her that I knew were impossible. Instead, I went through the rigmarole of genteel compliments and sympathy, and sat down in the chair several yards from the bed.

"Really," she said, "I am just swinging lead. It is only a little headache."

"You've seen the doctor?"

"He comes and gives nasty pills."

"I expect it's the sun," I said. "You ought to have taken things easily at first."

"I am lazy woman, that is the trouble. I think at school everyone will be angry with me. Please, did the Brigadier send you to scold?"

"Yes, he's furious with you."

"You're pulling leg now. That is very naughty."

"We were all very worried about you," I said.

"Somebody has sent me beautiful flowers. Please can you tell me if it was school people?"

"It might be."

"You are teasing," she said. "I think you know who sent flowers."

"Is there nobody else but school people who might have sent them?"

"There is one friend, but he has already sent nice grapes."

"Have you only got one friend in Bombay?"

"Yes," she said. "That is all. Except for the nice school people."

"You are *sabishii* . . .?" I thought that was one of the best of all Japanese words, the most expressive, *sabishii*—said lingeringly, like the wind sighing sadly. But it was not sadness, not loneliness; but something between, a sad-loneliness, a sentimental yearning. Miss Wei was *sabishii*—I could tell by her eyes, although at first they had seemed quite gay.

"I am very happy," she said. "I have got lots of reason to be happy, except for sick headache. And now I really have two

55

friends—I have person who sent grapes and person who sent flowers. It is nice of people to be friendly with Japanese."

"It doesn't matter what you are," I said, "so long as you have a good heart."

"I have got selfish heart."

"I don't think so."

"Yes, I have. All I think of is me."

"Is that why you've come all the way out from England to help us?"

"That is because I like English people; and they have been good to me. In Japan there is a lot of badness."

"It isn't easy being with people who are fighting your own country."

"I try not to think much about fighting own country," she said. "Please, would you like to drink tea?"

She pulled an enormous Victorian bell-rope that hung by the bed, and the bearer came. He brought the tea, and we did not talk any more about fighting Japan, though we talked about living in Japan, and tea ceremonies, and wearing Japanese clothes, and sometimes we talked a little bit of Japanese. I found that I could make her laugh, and when she laughed in front of me alone she did not put anything in front of her face as though she was crying instead. Her laugh was very pretty and gentle, and for a time her eyes were not in the least *sabishii*. I also laughed a great deal, though it was not because there was anything funny, but because my blood was joyous and singing through my veins. I thought that in all the world there could be no greater pleasure than gradually getting to know a beautiful woman, and being with her alone.

When I left, I did not call a ghari, but walked all the way home. I was still smiling, and all the uncomfortable pressure inside me had burst out of the safety valve.

III

Then my dysentery started again. I had suspected it for a day or two, and that morning it became a certainty. The germs were tearing out my inside, and I knew it was useless to try to stop them with a chemist's potion. Instead of going to the school, I went to see the Service doctor.

56

"Pack your bag, old son," he said. "You're going off to hospital."

I returned to the hotel in an ambulance van to get my things, and leave notes for Peter and my bearer, Bahadur. After that I told the driver to go round by the school. I went up to see the Brigadier and collect a Japanese grammar from my locker. Whilst I was talking to the Brigadier, he told me that Miss Wei was coming back to teach in the afternoon.

That made me more than ever regretful that I had to go into hospital. It seemed absurd that one's body should suddenly let one down in this way, and I was angry with my bowels as I might have been with a person who had treated me inconsiderately.

The hospital was six miles out, not far from the racecourse at Mahalkshmi—a dozen long, low buildings in a compound. I was taken to the dysentery ward. The officers sitting on the verandah in their pyjamas looked at me with mild curiosity. I followed the Sister into a room where there was one empty bed and two already occupied. I felt like the last person to get into a railway carriage.

"Amœbic or bacillary?" one of the two officers asked. He was an Army officer called Gregory.

"Bacillary, I hope."

"If it's amœbic you're in for the hell of a time."

"It was bacillary last time," I said. "I never quite got rid of it."

"I've got amœbic. I've been here a month. The fifth time this year. Now I'm for the boat."

"That's some compensation."

"I don't want to go," he said. "I like India."

I took off my tropical clothes and put on pyjamas.

"Where's the holy of holies?" I asked.

"Through that door."

I went out, and afterwards I wrote my name on a piece of paper and left it there. I got into bed, and before long an orderly brought lunch on a tray. There was soup and chicken mince and jelly. I was quite hungry, and, except for the inconvenience of the disease, I felt in good health. I hated being a patient and having to eat thin, unappetising food, and I thought Gregory looked like the kind of Army officer who was dumb from the neck up, not the type to be shut up with. The other officer was asleep. He woke up for his lunch, and nodded a dim hallo, and after he had eaten he went to sleep again. The wireless didn't disturb him. It was

57

Gregory's wireless, and he kept it on full blast. The room was palpitating with jazz.

I began to think how wretched it would be if my dysentery turned out to be amœbic. No more Japanese probably. No more Bombay. No more fun. I should go home. But not straight away; there would be a year, perhaps, spent in and out of hospital, like Gregory, until its incurability under Indian conditions was proved. No more drinking. Amœbic or bacillary, it was probably drinking that had started it up again now. Drinking bad whisky and gin.

And now I didn't want to go home. After Burma, I would have been glad of amœbic dysentery, malaria, a wound, anything that would have given me also a passport back to Tewkesbury. All I wanted was to see the green meadows full of buttercups, a glimpse of the abbey's tower or the Malvern Hills, and the warm stone lintels of the house, welcoming me as I came up the drive . . . how I'd longed for those! A refugee from the jungle then, I had seen heaven in the cool, clean sheets and in the mute efficiency of English nurses. But now, in a better hospital, these things meant nothing. I didn't want them. I wanted to go on living as I had been. All of a sudden life had seemed exciting.

I was restless and irritated as I lay in bed. The wireless was insufferable, but I thought I had not been in the ward long enough to start complaining of such things. Captain Gregory began to tell me about his job. I don't remember what it was, but it was a staff job of sorts. Only four months before he had been a Second-Lieutenant. Now he was Captain on staff pay, and smug in a way that only staff can be smug when they retrospectively mistake a lucky chance for their own astuteness. Listening to him I understood the feeling that I had noticed in Burma—a feeling which ran backwards from the front positions, each man more contemptuous than envious of those behind him. The forward man in a platoon, perhaps only the width of a road in advance, would think, 'Those damned non-combatants in the ditch behind! No bullets flying there!' And the platoon commander in the ditch would be thinking of the soft jobs at Brigade HQ, and the Brigade officers would think of the *babus,* the office-wallahs, at Division. And so on, right back to GHQ in New Delhi, where the red-tabs sat in the air-conditioned Secretariat. And in summer, even the red-tabs were thinking of their colleagues in the hills.

Well, you can't put GHQ where snipers can pot at it. Nor can you blame a man for being pleased to be on the staff; but there was no need to speak of the men in front of you as though it was only through ignorance and stupidity that they had found for themselves no safer or more remunerative positions.

I knew I should quarrel with this Gregory. It was after a news bulletin that he said:

"The little bastards. The slit-eyed monkeys."

"Who?" I said, though I knew quite well whom he meant.

"The Japs."

"Perhaps they're not all bastards," I said.

"Perhaps they are."

"Do you know many Japanese?"

"I don't know any, and I don't want to, thank you."

"Then how can you condemn them so sweepingly?"

"I know sufficient about them to hate the lot. Don't you hate them?"

"I thought I did once, but I don't really. Not all of them."

"You'd hate them if anyone you liked had got into their hands."

"Do you know someone?"

"I know people whose sons were at Singapore. I can appreciate their feelings."

"My brother was at Hong Kong," I said.

"He was captured?"

"Yes. I don't suppose he died very nicely."

"Well, all I can say is you've no depth of feeling."

"That is illogical," I said.

"It's perfectly logical. If you have any feelings it's only natural to hate the people who killed your brother 'not nicely'."

"If my brother was killed by a car whose driver was drunk, I should hate the driver but not all the passengers."

"O God!" the Captain said. "You're one of those people, are you? There are good Germans and bad Germans, good Japs and bad Japs. I hope there aren't people like you in power after the war."

"What do you think should happen to the Japs after the war?"

"I think they should all be exterminated."

"You don't mean that," I said.

"Certainly I do. It would be easy. You could wipe them out with gas. You could kill them in their millions. It's easy to gas them."

"I hope you're not in power after the war," I said.

"If I am, I shan't have people thinking sloppily like you. It's damn treachery."

"It's stupid to say that."

"Well, do you want to win the war against the Japs or not?"

"We've got to win it."

"We won't win the war by saying they are nice people. 'Awfully sorry, old man, and all that, but I shall have to shoot you.' You've got to be fanatical."

I would like to have said, 'It must be frustrating to feel fanatical with a pencil in your hand all the time, wishing it were a bayonet.' But that sarcasm was too cheap, and anyway who was I to talk, with a safe sedentary job and wings on my tunic that referred to the past?

"I'm afraid I'm not fanatical," I said. "I think this war is a damned unpleasant duty, like shooting mad dogs." And I added, "I hate war."

"That is obvious," he said.

"But I hate most of all what it does to people, and that is not so obvious."

"Well, anyway," he said, "let's have some music."

He twiddled the knob of the radio and a torrent of sound deluged the room. I lay trying to think and trying to stem the waves that assailed my ear-drums. When the Sister came round with a thermometer my blood was still angry, and it sent the mercury up to 99 and my pulse beat to 96.

"You're not feeling well?" she said.

"I'm all right."

"You look feverish," she said, entering up my chart.

"It's nothing at all."

And yet like a fever the thoughts of Miss Wei came back to me. It was on her account that I had so bitterly resented the words of the Captain; I had changed all my ideas to include her. I had said, "I don't hate them all . . ."; but I was only thinking that Miss Wei was beautiful and had beautiful hands, and that she had deep-brown eyes with a look that was *sabishii*. I began to remember all the expressions of hers, in the classroom and in the bazaar, and whilst we drank tea in her room, and everything about her seemed more pretty and gentle than anything else I had ever known. I told myself, 'But it is too quick. You know nothing of her, nothing! Your imagination is creating someone for you.'

But my imagination was on fire, and in its flames these protests of my reason were burnt like brittle dried leaves, and their ashes lifted away and lost in the air.

IV

Next morning my temperature was normal and my pulse ticking over at a steady 65. The doctor came on his rounds and delivered his sentence:

"Bacillary dysentery. Don't worry—we'll clear you up in ten days."

The Sister proffered four white tablets on a spoon. I crunched them in my mouth and swallowed them with a gulp of water. They were as tasteless as chalk.

I felt fine. I got up and examined the hospital books on the shelf; but the covers were torn and dreary and the contents looked drearier still. I wandered out on to the balcony and sat down in an arm-chair just out of the sun, watching the lethargic construction of a bungalow across the road. Women moved at snail-pace, carrying baskets of bricks or pieces of roofing on their heads—women heavily draped in red with carriages proudly erect. After a while a motor-car drew up and the Sikh contractor, magnificently bearded, white-turbaned, egg-paunched, got out and swaggered across. But no one paid any attention to him; in the morning heat the Indians went on working in slow-motion. A bullock-cart passed. The animal looked dreamily unconscious of the yoke hooked over its hump, regarding one side of the road and then the other, the loose folds of skin flopping beneath it. Behind it the cart rose and fell creakily with each turn of the roughly hewn wheel. Then a taxi rushed by, blowing its horn, and through the windows I caught a glimpse of two pink faces and the glittering buttons of a uniform. It was gone, leaving a thin cloud of dust; and whilst this still hung in the air two figures emerged from it—a tall, lean man with a muddy *dhoti* and bare, dusty feet, and a few yards behind him his wife, bearing on her head all their household chattels. They moved past me, mutely. Another car sped by, swirling up the light-brown film that had hardly had time to settle on the surface of the road. After that, unhurried and supercilious like an old duchess, a camel moved noiselessly on its soft flesh-padded feet.

I sat on, enjoying the Indian scene with its hurried Occidental interludes. The sun came round the corner and I could not be bothered to move. I closed my eyes and the heat lay heavily on my lids. I began to doze.

I was woken by Bahadur. I was glad that he had come out to see me. He had discovered all kinds of things that he thought I ought to need in hospital. He placed his suitcase on the floor and produced them one by one, explaining why he had brought each of them. There was a pair of nail scissors, because even though I was lying in bed my nails would grow just the same; three more pairs of pyjamas, and would I please give him the ones I was wearing for the *dhobi*; and a writing-pad, since it was my filial duty to write home every week; and here was a little book that he had seen in a shop, and which he would like me to accept from him as a present, because once in his presence I had expressed a desire to know more about Indian birds, and he was ashamed that he didn't know the names of any except something with white on its wings called a *shama*. Now, with this book I could sit on the verandah and compare the birds I saw with the illustrated plates.

Then he stood over my chair and gazed down at me sorrowfully over his drooping moustache.

"I should not have let you eat bad food," he said.

"It was not your fault, Bahadur. It was a germ."

But Bahadur did not believe in germs. He shook his head and smiled tolerantly, as though it was I who was superstitious and was speaking of evil spirits that inhabited my belly.

"When Bahadur is not there, you go to bad places to eat and have hot, bad Indian foods that disagree. You are an Englishman, perhaps one day you become a great Englishman, but there is no use trying to be an Indian man with an Indian stomach."

"I will try to behave," I said.

"At four o'clock in the mornings you must not eat old eggs in bad Indian places."

"Who told you that?"

"Peter Sahib tells me all that you do."

"You tell Peter Sahib from me that he's not to give away any more of my secrets."

"Peter Sahib and I talk for a long time about Michael Sahib. There are many things which I hear."

"And you're not going to leave me?"

"I remain with Michael Sahib if Michael Sahib still wishes Bahadur."

It was not until he was on the point of leaving that he took two or three letters from his pocket. "I keep purposely these nice things to the last," he said, but I suspected that he had not given them to me before lest I should be too interested in reading them to listen to his admonishment.

There was an airgraph and an airmail letter from home, and the other note was from Peter:

> *Cher ami.* So there's disease in them there bowels! Hard lines. But this will enable me to slack off for a day or two without feeling I am dropping too far behind you. So it's an ill wind, etc. Had a scare myself at lunchtime when Mervyn told me I looked yellow. Visualised an attack of jaundice being used by the Air Force as an excuse to drop me over Tokyo, a Lawrence in natural disguise. However, it was only the peculiar light, not bile, and I am saved from the Nipponese firing-squad and the other little inconveniences that would have transformed me overnight into the Great British hero of World War II.
>
> Mention of your tropical malady started Itsumi San off on a half-hour diatribe on dirty water—excrement—methods of disposing of same in all countries of the world (this man is a guide-book, with an absolutely ubiquitous curiosity)—hygiene—great cleanliness of Nips as compared with Chinese. I really think he is under the orders of the Emperor's Ministry of Propaganda. The lovely Wei, of course, quite *desolated* by your absence. I am wildly jealous.
>
> *Sayonara,*
> PETER.

I read the letter over twice, and the final sentence several times more. Of course it wasn't true. It couldn't be true. But was it perhaps a half-truth? Had she noticed my absence, had she commented on it? Or was it all Pete's joke, a leg-pull, a long-vowed retaliation for the time when I had slipped the cellophane from a box of his scented soap, and inserted oranges, and let him go back angrily complaining to the shop. But no—he would never expect me to take this seriously at all. Quite *desolated*, indeed!

And then I suddenly found myself thinking; I shall write a letter to Miss Wei. It is absolutely necessary for myself that I do so. It is impetuous and mad and letters are dangerous, but I shall write her a letter because I cannot exist in hospital for another week and do nothing. I shall write saying that I am glad to hear she is better, and that I am sorry I am missing her classes, but perhaps when I am better she will come and have dinner with me— and please don't bother to reply, and I am hers—hers what? I am

63

hers sincerely. No, I am hers affectionately—nothing very outrageous in that. And she would have to reply. It would take one day for my letter to reach the Mayfair Hotel. She might not answer immediately. Allow two days—and one more day for the letter to arrive. Four days in all. An eternity! And even then, what could I expect except a formal note? That would be something, anyway.

I took the pad Bahadur had brought me, and ten minutes later the letter was written, in an envelope and sealed.

Then, because it was written and the impetuosity had expended itself, I was not sure that I would send it. I put it on the bedside table, and lying back on my pillow tried to make the decision. But the wireless was blaring hideously. I was quite unable to think.

I was still in a dilemma when the Sister came into the ward to tidy the beds. She saw the letter.

"Do you want this posted?" she said.

"Oh—yes, please."

I was glad it had gone; for the time being a little bit more steam had been let out of the safety valve. I felt better, but still evil-tempered with the Captain called Gregory. I asked him to turn down the wireless. I suppose I might have asked him more politely. We began bickering like fishwives, and he said:

"Ever since you came into this ward you've been damned impertinent and unsociable. What's the matter with you?"

"For heaven's sake let's stop tearing at each other's throats," I said.

"Of course you want to stop now."

"We've got to live in this room together," I said.

"Well, you might learn some manners."

"Great Scot!" I said. "If you had any manners you wouldn't inflict that excruciating noise . . ."

The Sister came back into the room, and I was ashamed to be caught engaged in this childish squabble. "Oh, hell," I said. "Don't let's go over this again."

"You're Flying-Officer Quinn, aren't you?" the Sister said. "There's a visitor to see you."

She held open the door, and in that instant I thought, 'Good, this is Peter—he will cheer me up, and I can ask him to explain his letter, and I shall hear about Miss Wei.'

But it was not Peter.

It was Miss Wei herself who came into the ward.

"I hope you don't mind," she said.

For a fraction of a second I thought she had come because of the letter; and then I remembered that I had only completed it half an hour ago and that she must have come of her own accord. I was trembling with excitement like a schoolboy.

"I don't know whether it would matter coming," she said. "Is it honestry all right?"

"Of course it is," I said. "It's wonderful."

I got out of bed and put on my dressing-gown, and we went out together on to the verandah. We sat down in two arm-chairs in the shade, and for a moment I could think of nothing to say.

"Tell me," I said at last. "How's the school?"

"I am so bad at teaching. But everyone is good to me."

"Even Fenwick?"

"He hasn't been nasty again. We have had lots of fun playing games. There is no need for me to teach when we play games."

"What sort of games?"

"Someone thinks of something, and then everyone asks questions in Japanese to find out what it is. It is always something funny. Mr. Lamb thought of the Brigadier's grandmother."

"Did you think of anything?"

"Yes, they made me."

"What was it?"

"I don't want to say."

"I shall ask Peter," I said.

"It was somebody's little finger-nail."

"Whose?"

"It was yours. We had been talking about you because you were ill—that is how I knew you were here. But I got into awful trouble. I didn't know whether finger-nail was animal, vegetable or mineral. I said mineral, and nobody could guess. They were all very angry with me." She sniffed her diminutive nose sadly, and her big eyes were warm and brown and humorously solemn.

I looked at her in silence. It was the first silence we had had without any embarrassment, and you can tell a lot by silences.

"You shouldn't have sent those flowers," she said.

"Shouldn't I?"

"It was naughty of you to spend money."

65

"How did you know they were from me?"

"Afterwards I went to the shop, and they described person like you. But I guessed already, because I had found out you were kind."

"I wrote you a letter today," I said. The Sister to whom I had given it was standing farther along the verandah. I called to her and asked her if she had still got the letter. She took it from her uniform pocket and handed it to me.

"There's no need to post it," I said.

"Please show me," Miss Wei said.

"There's no need. I can tell you everything that's written in it."

"Please." She held out her hand.

"Really," I said. "There's nothing in it."

"I would like to see."

"No, it's a silly letter."

"But it is addressed to me, and has stamp. It is not your letter any more."

"I've got it," I said.

"Give it to me," she said, with mock sternness. "I am your school-teacher. You have got to do as you are told."

"All right," I said, and handed it to her. She tore open the envelope and read it through, taking a long time, and then she folded it up carefully and put it in her handbag.

"It's rather embarrassing to have one's own letters read in one's presence," I said.

"It was kind of you to write. It is a nice letter."

"It isn't a true letter. It's formal and silly, and not in the least what I meant to say."

"What did you mean?"

"That if you didn't reply I should be angry and sad, and sit sulkily through your classes, and that even more than a reply I should like you to come and see me in hospital. But if I had said that you wouldn't have come."

"I might."

"I shouldn't have deserved it. I would also have asked you in my letter why you sometimes looked *sabishii*."

"But I try to look happy."

"That isn't the point," I said. "It isn't how you try to look. It's how you are."

"I am really happy."

"Perhaps that's true," I said. "Part of you is happy, and full of

66

sunshine. When you laugh you're very happy. But there is also part of you that's *sabishii*."

"I don't see how you know."

"It's because you have expressive eyes."

"I shall wear spectacles, and then I shall become real schoolmistress. I shall use stick."

"You'll still feel the same," I said.

"But you will not know how I feel behind the spectacles."

"Do you mind my knowing?"

"Not if you don't care about *sabishii*."

"I think it's very beautiful and soulful," I said. "I'm going to call you *sabishii*. Only it had better be *Sabby* for short. Sabby! That's rather a good name—perhaps better than your real name."

"My real name is Hanako."

"The Flower Child! That's a good name, too. But I'm going to call you Sabby."

"I already know what you are called," she said.

"Quinn is such an easy name to remember."

"But I also know other name, because your friend always uses it at school. It is Michael."

"What is it?"

"Michael. Isn't that the way I should pronounce?"

"Yes, that's the way."

"Michael," she said.

"Sabby."

"Well?" she said.

"Well?"

When she went I walked to the gate with her in my dressing-gown and slippers, and saw her into the taxi. The driver had gone to sleep with his mouth open, and I had to wake him by shouting into his ear. Then I went back to the ward. As I entered the Captain looked at me disagreeably.

"You can put on your wireless," I said. "I don't care if you blow off the roof."

"Thank you very much," Gregory said with forced sarcasm.

"Not at all," I said, and I began to laugh. And then suddenly I realised that I couldn't stop laughing.

BOOK TWO

CHAPTER I

I

I WOULD like to write a book about being in hospital. For many people it is an experience unique in their lives, when the mind, no longer bound to the routine of wage-earning and domestic habit, has the opportunity to take wing like a bird released from a cage—and so often, flopping about in new freedom, learns that its wings are clipped; and learns, too, on what an intricate mechanism it is dependent, infinitely more intricate than an aeroplane engine, and more difficult to control, more difficult to repair. I think that as many philosophies have been formed in hospitals as in any study or garret; and as many resolutions made there as in any parlour on New Year's Eve.

Then I would also like to write the story of the people who passed through a ward in which I was bedridden, and how each one, by the things he brought with him, by a gesture, a word, a look, dropped clues to his personality. Like a wild animal advancing over soft ground, each man leaves his spoor. He may tiptoe or sidetrack; but the clever hunter will follow through a labyrinth to the secret lair.

I thought I would like to try my hand at hunting in the hospital at Mahalakshmi. The Captain and the Lieutenant were discharged some days before me. Their beds were occupied by others; and because these new cases turned out not to be dysentery, after all, the beds were emptied again and filled again. I saw six new patients in all; and it was amusing to guess from their faces how they would call the sweeper, or from the way they called the sweeper how they would react to an anecdote. It was like playing jigsaws, fitting together the pieces of each personality. To each picture there were a thousand pieces, and sometimes the wrong ones linked comfortably and for a time were deceptive. And I soon found that when you play jigsaws it is dangerous to guess too soon at the nature of the picture. If there is a ship it is not necessarily on the sea; a child may be floating it in the bathtub. The bird may be stuffed and on somebody's hat.

I watched and began to make up my mind about people. And then I thought: but they too must be making up their minds about me, unconsciously perhaps, by the way I call 'Sweeper!' and the books I read, and my face and my accent and the ordinary things I say to them. They will be thinking I am a good fellow or a snake in the grass, or that I am pleased with myself or have an inferiority complex. They will have a picture of me.

But how curious to be pictured in this way—what a different thing to picturing somebody else! For how can it be said of yourself that you are this or that, you are good or bad; for you are this and that and good and bad, you are a good fellow and a snake in the grass, and there are a hundred different people inside you. You have a hundred facets—and how, when the centre to which they turn is darkly incomprehensible to yourself, may others understand it and pass judgment on the actions and feelings that originate there?

It is because we do not really understand that we pass judgment. 'What a fool,' we exclaim, 'to marry a little bit of stuff like that!' —as though the man had been able to make a rational choice of whom he married. We rarely look deep enough; yet we often expect others to look more deeply into ourselves, so that they might see through our eyes the person whom we love, the 'exquisite mirage'.

So I thought it might be said of me by people who did not understand, 'What a fool to get himself mixed up with a Japanese woman! What an idiot!' And I did not believe that anyone else could see in her all that I saw—poetry in a tiny movement of her hand, and in a look from beneath her dark lashes, a warm, flowing, generous passion.

When I was a boy at school I had written a story about a man and a woman. The English master was a poet with a great understanding of human nature, and in red ink at the end he had written, 'Yes, my dear, but people do not fall in love as quickly as all that, you know.' I think my characters had declared their mutual love at the second meeting. The poet may have been right about love; but I afterwards found out that a lot can happen very quickly. If you put a flaring match-head to another, that too will flare up, because it is already a potential fire. In the conflagration they will stick to one another. But the flame will die. . . .

I did not see why this fire that had flared up in Bombay should not die, as fires have died in a million hearts elsewhere, and in my heart too. I expected it to die; but you may warm your hands before hot red coals this afternoon that by midnight will be cold grey ashes.

When I went out of the hospital at Mahalakshmi it was in the afternoon.

II

As I went up the stairs of the hotel, I met Miss Jackson, the proprietress.

"Ah, it's Michael Quinn," she said. "How is the funny tummy?"

She spoke with the mincing articulation of the Anglo-Indian. She was neither very young nor beautiful, with her full, rather Semitic face and her podgy, ringed fingers; but she had a bright, teasing manner, and I am sure that if she cared to set about it she could have aroused a great deal of ardour in a man. There was something about her which seemed to indicate that she had often cared to set about it, and with success; and that now she did not care so much as she did, but that she had forgotten how not to be provocative.

"Thank you," I said. "It's much better."

"It isn't a romantic disease, is it?" she said, smiling over her shoulder as she turned the corner at the bottom of the stairs.

"It isn't."

"But it was nice having Sisters to look after you. They are nice girls, Sisters, aren't they?"

"I called our Sister 'nurse'," I said. "And she never quite forgave me."

"Oh, that is bad. You should not be rude to Sisters."

I had tea sent up to my room; then I lay reading for an hour. A delicious calm pervaded me. I remembered when I had lain on this same bed weeks before and felt only a hollowness, and I was glad that this had gone. It was natural that it should have done so.

At five o'clock I bathed and shaved. When I was dressing, Peter came in with his fat dictionary and exercise books under his arm.

"Ah, the prodigal son!" he said. "I'm glad to see you're doing your toilet preparatory to taking me out to dinner. We've all been saying you'll have saved enough money to treat us for weeks."

"I'm convalescent," I said. "It's your duty to pamper *me*."

"We've no money. I've borrowed from Mervyn, and Mervyn

70

from Mario, and Mario from the Brigadier. The Brigadier has turned out to be an absolute treasure. We all adore him."

"What else has been happening?" I asked.

"There are no really succulent morsels of scandal. But this will please you. You must get a pencil and write it down before you forget, in case you ever write a book and want to use it. It's about Fenwick."

"I don't think I shall ever write a book about Fenwick."

"Well, anyway, he came into the bar at Green's the other day full of his nauseating brand of bonhomie and said, 'Let's have a discussion. I maintain that rugger is a better game than baseball and brings out better qualities in a man.' Of course he's never played either in his life. Whilst he was enlarging on his theme all the half-wits in his audience were nodding their heads solemnly, and afterwards one of them said to me, 'Isn't Fenwick a grand chap! He must be most interesting to work with.' I reserved this specially for you. No copyright. And that reminds me of some more news. . . ."

I hoped that he was going to speak of Sabby, because it was only of her that I really wanted to hear. But he was talking of Miss Jackson now. He had spent a whole evening 'looking into her', and had found her an uncommonly interesting study, besides being a woman of great sympathy with a heart of gold. And when Peter said that of someone, you could be sure it was true. I never knew anyone like him for ferreting out what was worth-while in a character, nor for that matter did I know anyone like him for so ruthlessly discarding the trivial and dull, not caring whom he offended or angered.

"Her name's Rosie," he said. "And you'll do well to be on the right side of her, my young fellow, because she knows a lot of gairls. She always talks about 'gairls', exactly like the wife of a vicar at home. 'She is such a nice gairl, with such nice cairls.' All Rosie's gairls are nice gairls, too. And she thinks we're all such nice boys. She told us that before the war she used to live in Rangoon. She came out on the last ship, with all her gairls on a string. It was sheer patriotism that made her leave; she didn't say so in so many words, but there's no doubt about it. She wasn't going to leave her protégées to the mercy of the Japanese warriors. And so here she is, running a respectable establishment. Only she can't bear to see young men like us, thousands of miles from home and family comforts, deprived of the solace due to our sex and noble vocation. Oh, Rosie is a jewel—and her anecdotes about *pukka sahibs* déshabillé are uproarious."

"It's all most interesting," I said. "And I suppose you've also been making great strides with your Japanese?"

"No. I've been writing a book. I go back to the school in the evenings and write it in the classroom. It's going to be the great book of the war. An epic. What *All Quiet on the Western Front* was to the last war, and *For Whom the Bell Tolls* to the Spanish war, my book will be to World War Two. Unfortunately I can't make up my mind whether it shall be *The War Office Murder*, or *One of Our Bodies is Missing*. But my detective wears an eyeglass and went to Eton, and will stand alongside Mr. Micawber and the Scarlet Pimpernel as one of the great original characters of literature. He will also make me thousands of pounds so that I may entertain one of Rosie's gairls in all the best places. Don't you think it's a good idea?"

"I think it's wonderful."

"Then I shall have gold-backed hairbrushes, and a thirty-horse-power automobile with a horn which is worked by an expensive device that detects earnest and impoverished souls that are pursuing art for art's sake. Whenever it passes one of these in the street it will automatically scream 'Sucker!' My lips will then twist into a smile of cynical derision, and I shall turn back to my immodestly perfumed mistress. Now what about this dinner?"

"I can't go with you," I said.

"But you can't discard me in this way, like an old sucked orange. I shall go with you."

"You may if you like."

"No, I was only joking. I know everything."

"I doubt if you do."

"You're meeting the delectable Hanako at six-thirty in the entrance hall of the Taj."

"How did you know that?" I said

"She told us in class."

"I don't believe it," I said.

"Oh, she's a little minx. She tells us everything."

"She didn't tell the whole class?"

"Very nearly. She was so excited this afternoon that anyone sufficiently perspicacious would have known she was going to a tryst. But fortunately for you I'm the only one writing a detective story. You see, I'm becoming very clever. I can tell from that ash-tray that you've been here at least an hour."

"But the place and the time?"

"That's clever, too. You're all ready to go out, which means you'll be at the Taj at six-thirty. Of course it's the Taj, because in Bombay nobody meets anywhere else."

"You gave me a fright," I said.

"I meant to. You're going to have such a happy time, it's only just you should have a fright first. But you can rely on me to swear to all the world that you've taken Rosie to the pictures. Rosie will swear too."

"You're a great friend," I said.

"Oh, that's nothing. I'd do it for anyone. I like to see young hearts beating together in romantic ecstasy."

"Go and drown yourself," I said.

Outside I took a ghari, because I was cool and wanted to remain so. If you get hot and then cool again, it is never quite the same as if you had not got hot at all after your shower. It was also cool in the Taj. I was ten minutes early, so I looked through the books on the kiosk. There were a great many about Japan—*Japan's Feet of Clay, The Yellow Peril, Bushido and Terrorism*. Several of them had hideous caricatures on the front, like the caricature we had seen on the poster, of the Japanese face with its prognathous jaw. Then I saw one called *Two Faces of Japan,* on which the cruel male face stood out in front of a faint drawing of a kneeling woman. The woman was pretty. I looked inside the book, and there were a great many more pictures of pretty, laughing Japan-ese girls. Facing each there was a picture of steel-helmeted Japanese youths, or a threatening display of bayonets, or a Japan-ese atrocity in China. Most of these were horrible to look at; they were all of them photographs. They turned my stomach, so that I replaced the book and drew another one from the shelf. It was called *The Three Bamboos*. I thought it looked interesting, and I began to turn the pages. Then I turned back to the beginning to see who was the author, and as I did so I noticed the dedication. It was 'to the gentle, self-effacing, and long-suffering mothers of the cruellest, most arrogant and treacherous sons who walk this earth—to the women of Japan—who will, as always, reap the richest harvest of suffering as their reward'. I read the sentence over several times, because I thought I would like to know it by heart. I was still reading it when I felt someone at my side.

73

"How are you?" Sabby said in Japanese.

"*O-kage-sama de* . . ." In Japan it is always 'by your honourable shadow', by your influence, that one is in good health. After three weeks in hospital, it was about all the Japanese I could remember.

"You are honestry better?" she said in English.

"Honestry," I said.

"Oh, you are teasing me."

"I'm not teasing," I said. "Please always say honestry. It is beautiful."

"You must teach me to speak proper English. Honest-ly. Honest-ly. Oh dear, it is so very difficult!"

"After a drink it won't be so hard."

We mounted the palatial staircase and sat down by a table by an open widow overlooking the bay. The waiter hovered over us.

"What will you have?" I said.

Sabby shook her head.

"You don't want anything?" I said.

"No, thank you."

"There must be something you'd drink?"

"No, really."

"You ought to have told me before we came here."

"I would like to see you have drink. It is nice here."

"I'll get you a soft drink."

"Please, I don't even want even soft one."

"It makes one happy to drink," I said.

"I shall be happy without drink. With drink I shall perhaps be very sick and ashame you."

"All right," I said, and I turned to the waiter to order something for myself.

"It doesn't shock you if I smoke cigarette?" Sabby said.

"I'm sorry, I'm very rude—you ought to have one of mine."

"Please," she said. "These are open."

I took one from her case. It was a fine silver case with an intagliated design, and her initials engraved in the centre, H. T. I knew what the H meant—Hanako, the Flower Child—but she had never told me about the T, her real Japanese surname before she called herself Wei. It made me wonder all of a sudden about her past, whereas up to that moment I had only thought of Sabby in the present. But I was not in a hurry to know about the past. I watched her snap the case closed and put it in her handbag; then I

74

lit a match for her and held it whilst she sucked in the flame with the tip of her cigarette.

I looked at her face very closely, objectively; I wanted to see it as I knew on some future occasion I might not be able to help seeing it. I began to search it for any little imperfection that could irritate me, a twisted mouth, a bad chin, a nervous habit, any ugliness that might later cause me to wonder how I had loved despite *that*. But there was nothing with which I thought I could ever find fault. Like her hands, her face was fashioned with the exquisite delicacy of an Oriental figure in ivory; and yet it was impossible for me to regard her as an ornament only, for I seemed to see strange depths of experience in her, as though all the suffering and happiness of womanhood had been hers. I looked at her eyes, just aslant and almond-shaped when she smiled, trying to brush aside my feelings and see them as Oriental eyes were supposed to be, cruel or sly or inscrutable. But there was nothing like that to be found there, and I allowed all my feelings to come back again with a rush, and was certain that they were the most expressive and tender and beautiful eyes in the world, East or West. I felt guilty at having been so calculating and mistrustful, and letting Sabby detect it.

"Why you look so curious?" she said.

"Curious?"

"Perhaps it is not curious I mean. I wish I could speak clever English. I mean you look at me through window."

"Detached?" I said.

"Yes, that's it."

"It was only for a moment. I wanted to find out if I could ever dislike you."

"Can you dislike?"

"No."

"Can you always like me?"

"Why not?" I said.

"That is not answer. No, please don't say anything. I wish I had not asked such silly question."

"It wasn't silly."

"There is no reason why you should like me at all. Look, there is very beautiful woman behind you who is intelligent and sophisticated. I am awfully stupid and childish."

"That is modesty," I said in Japanese, because I happened to remember the word and because it was really modesty.

75

"No, it is true, I am sometimes awfully childish. I have often been told."

"It's attractive," I said. "You've probably been told that, too."

I drank my whisky slowly, and Sabby smoked three or four cigarettes. Afterwards we went in to have dinner. There was a band and dancing, and the room was full of uniforms and *saris* and evening dresses, and movement and kaleidoscopic colour. I was not in the least drunk with whisky, but I might have been drunk the way my senses recorded this swirl of people around us, out-of-focus and dim, and all that was in-focus and real was Sabby and the table between us and our little cave of stillness stolen out of the festivity of the room.

"This is first meal together," Sabby said.

"We had tea in your room."

"That was the second time of meeting. Private meeting, I mean."

"This is the fourth."

"Ought I still to say Mr. Quinn?"

"It doesn't matter what you say. You can say Mr. Quinn if you like. It doesn't make any difference."

"But I would like to say Michael."

"Say Michael, then. Whatever you say, I feel as though I've known you for years and years."

"That is funny thing."

"That's how it feels. Sometimes you meet people hundreds of times and you never know them. They might be a gatepost for all they do to you. And sometimes you only have to meet people once or twice, and you feel more natural with them than with people you were brought up with."

"They fit like old pair of shoes?"

"Yes, just like that. If you put on new shoes you don't expect them to feel quite right. It's rather a surprise when they do."

"Am I old shoe?"

"Well," I said, "you feel like an old one."

"But you said it is first time you meet Japanese woman."

"It doesn't matter. I seem to have known you before. I've seen your hands before. Only perhaps they weren't hands then."

"What were hands?"

"They might have been flowers, or clouds, or doves."

"You talk like Japanese poet."

They were very small, pretty, fluttering hands, and afterwards

76

in the ghari, when I enclosed one in my own, I was half afraid that I should crush it because it was so fragile. I thought it was like having the tiny body of a bird in my palm, its soft feathers covering a quivering little skeleton.

In the ghari it was cool and the hood was down, and the driver perched up aloofly, ignoring us, and busy manipulating his horse.

"Do you like Bombay at night?" Sabby said.

"Sometimes."

"Better than in day-time?"

"It is more lovely at night with the lights."

"It is nicer than London?"

"The last I saw of London was in the black-out, bumping into lamp-posts and tripping over kerbs."

"I did that, too."

"I can't imagine you in London," I said.

"I liked London so much. I was very happy there, you see. You ought to die when you are happy, otherwise you must become sad again."

"You're not sad now?"

"No, not now. Now I am happy."

"And you'll always be happy," I said.

"No," she said. "Life is not like that. I must become terribly sad, because now I am so terribly happy."

"That doesn't mean you'd like to die now?"

"No please not—not just now."

We were at her hotel. I gave the driver some money, and we went in. The hall was badly lit and gloomy. The clerk at the reception-desk grinned good evening and the liftman took us up in the clanking lift. But Sabby's room looked lived-in, and the dressing-table was alive—alive and feminine, with its bright pots and bottles, and profusion of things that were in use.

"I am so ashamed," Sabby said. "I have left everything untidy. I am a scatter-brain, an *awatemono*. Please forgive."

I went out on to the balcony whilst she pottered about barefooted in the room. On the balcony you could look up at the stars or down at the street, and it did not matter which you did, for one was serene and had the beauty of eternity, and the other was a little colourful glimpse of the huge mosaic that was life—and both in their way were exciting; and on the balcony one was in between. I leant on the balustrade and looked down at the movement below—each brightly lit shop a miniature scene on its own,

77

framed by the gloom. The dry smell of charcoal fires drifted up to my nostrils. Mysteriously draped figures glided along the pavements; others were seated in a circle round a fire on which something was frying, and the flames gave to their faces a strange unreality. A beggar looked up and caught sight of me; and because he could see my face was pale, he lifted a skinny hand like a claw as though to drag an apple from a tree. I made no movement and he kept his hand raised, and a feeble trembling voice, inarticulate, floated up to me. He stood there like a Moses gazing up to heaven, his face desiccated, and yet with a dull light of hope burning in his eyes. Hope for an anna, a penny. I threw him down a coin and it tinkled about the street. He went after it like a monkey, on all fours, pushing between a forest of brown legs. When he found it he examined it curiously, turning it over in his fingers. He did not look up again. He continued down the street, unevenly like a drunk.

"Michael."

I looked back into the room. At the door of the balcony Sabby stood motionless. She had put on a Japanese kimono, richly coloured and embroidered, with a deep blue sash and folds of drapery beneath the sleeve. She had combed her hair, and it was very black and soft about her face.

"You would like to see funny Japanese writing-brush and ink?" she said.

I did not say anything. I wanted to fix that moment in my memory, because I knew it was one of the beautiful moments of my life; and yet it did not seem to have any more reality than the faces dancing in the flames in the street below, and I had to tell myself: this is real, this is true, neither time nor misery can ever take this moment from you.

"Well?" Sabby said, so softly that I hardly heard it.

"Don't move," I said, and her eyelids gave a little questioning flutter. She did not say any more. For perhaps a few seconds we stood there; then all of a sudden she was in my arms, her head on my breast, her tiny bird-hands clinging to my shoulders and my own hands supporting her trembling body.

"Sabby, Sabby, darling."

"Oh, Michael! Michael!"

I stooped and lifted her up; and she was as light as air, and I could not see her face because it was buried in my shoulder. I laid her on the bed, and she lay still, with her eyes closed, as though she were sleeping; until I covered her eyelids with kisses and felt the lashes brush my lips, and her long, slender fingers run through my hair.

III

"Oh, darling," she said. "Do you think I am so bad and selfish? Do you think you will hate me because I have been bad? Was it wicked to love you? I wanted you so much, so terribly much."

"Perhaps not so much as I wanted you," I said.

"You did not only come because I wanted you? You are kind and sweet, and perhaps it was because I was sad and *sabishii* that you are good to me. Oh, darling, can you like me, can you like me a tiny bit?"

"Sweet darling Sabby," I said.

"Please say honestry, can you like me?"

"Honestry."

"You are a tease. I don't like you to tease." She pretended to whimper.

"Of course you are bad and selfish," I said.

"Really?"

"No, not really."

"You really think it is so?" she said.

"I don't, Sabby."

"Yes, you think it."

"I shall bite you."

"I don't mind."

I took her nose between my teeth. It was a funny little nose, broad at the bottom and soft. I worried it gently. She cried out, and I released it and bit her ear that was like a pretty white shell.

"Bully."

I ran my lips over her face and into her hair. There was a soft womanly odour. I took a curl in my teeth and pulled.

"Michael!"

I let her go; my mouth returned, exploring over her forehead, down the brief ridge of her nose, across the mouth, round the chin. I buried it in her neck.

"Why don't you say something, Michael?"

"I'm too happy."

"Oh, Michael," she said, and squeezed her fragile body against mine.

"I've never been so happy before."

"There is no need to say comforting things," she said. "I just want to know that you don't really hate me."

"I've never been so happy," I said.

"I won't be a nuisance to you, I promise that."

"Listen," I said. "Don't you believe me, darling? I swear I've never been so happy. Nothing has ever meant so much to me as this."

"It would be nice if that were true."

"It is true."

"Then will you please promise me something?" she said.

"What is it?"

"Promise me."

"When I know what it is."

"You are horrid. I want you to promise. It is necessary to promise in advance."

"All right," I said.

"When you are tired of me, you will not pretend?"

"Pretend what?"

"Anything that is not truly what you feel."

"I will promise that," I said. "On my honour. So long as you promise too."

"There's no need for me."

"What if I pester you until you're sick to death?" I said.

"Please pester, darling."

"You'll get so tired of me."

"I'm afraid I shan't be able."

"Why afraid?"

"Because you will get tired of me first, and I shall still want you terribly like I want you now. I shall get hurt."

"I shall never hurt you, darling," I said. "Never. Please don't think I shall hurt you. You're too beautiful to be hurt."

CHAPTER II

I

THERE was a letter waiting for me at my hotel. It was from Mr. Headley, the missionary. Come to supper, he said.

I rang him up, forgetting that it was only eight o'clock in the morning. But it didn't matter. He was already up and full of insulin, and he would not accept my excuses. If I was meeting someone else, bring along the someone else by all means. Take pot-luck.

"It's my instructor," I explained. "She is Japanese."

"She is a human being, isn't she?" the instrument vibrated.

"Yes, indeed."

"Well, that's that. Eight o'clock. 'Bye."

I went upstairs. Peter was still asleep, and there was a cup of cold undrunk tea by his bed. His moustache hung dolefully like Bahadur's. I woke him, and he turned over and automatically pushed it up at the ends. It made all the difference to his face which way the ends pointed.

"Well," he said. "Did you enjoy the pictures with Rosie?"

"It was a fine film."

"It must have been," he said. "You look as though the spell's still on you."

I pulled back the covering from my bed and ruffled the sheets. Then I realised it was no use doing that because early-morning tea had been brought when I was absent. Oh well, who was Rosie to care!

"Are pavements hard to sleep on?" Peter asked. "I've always wondered."

"You get used to them."

I washed and shaved, and when I returned to the bedroom Bahadur had arrived and laid out a clean set of clothes. He pretended not to watch me dressing, but he kept glancing from the corner of his eye to make sure that I didn't sneak into yesterday's pants; he looked upon it as a kind of game in which I was bent upon cheating him. He also never quite rid himself of the hurt expression that arose from my not allowing him to dress me; though as a concession I permitted him to tie my shoelaces. If it had not been for this, he might long since have left me for a sahib who was unequivocally *pukka*.

"You have shopping today?" he inquired.

"I'm going to do it myself, Bahadur," I said. "I'm excused duty for a week."

"But in the shops it is tiring."

"It will do me good."

"Bahadur can assist?"

"Not today," I said. "You can go away and enjoy yourself."

I went down to breakfast in good spirits. The time I had got up seemed hours ago, and I kept looking at my watch. It was a quarter to nine. Then it was nine o'clock. Then after another age it was a quarter past. I was surprised at my own excitement. I went into the lounge and tried to read the newspaper, but I found myself skimming over the lines without taking anything in. At a quarter to ten I went out and walked slowly through the bazaars, and at half past I was outside the Army and Navy Stores.

So was Sabby. She was exactly on time. She jumped out of the ghari and came skipping across the pavement; and then she remembered about paying the driver and rushed back to push a couple of notes into his hand.

"You are too skittish," I said. "It's not decent."

"Why?" she said. Her eyes were enormously round and innocent.

"You'll give the show away to everyone."

"You regret about last night? Do you regret?"

"Of course I don't."

"Then I don't mind if everyone knows. Everyone." She skipped gaily up and down.

"It's more than your job's worth."

"I shall tell the Brigadier this afternoon."

"All right," I said.

"Would you mind if I did?"

"I should mind if you got the sack."

"Then I won't tell the Brigadier."

"You can't help telling him unless you look a little more *sabishii.*"

"Very well, I am *sabishii* to please you." She put on a sad expression and puckered her nose with a sniff; but her eyes did not look sad.

"Come," I said. "What do you want to buy?"

"Everything."

"You must stop being frivolous."

"I feel frivorous."

"Frivorous?"

"Oh, you are unkind," she said with a quaint little whimper. "Fri-vol-ous. Fri-vol-ous."

"You can do it if you try."

"You can speak Japanese if you try. You must speak it always and then you will be cleverer than all the others and I shall be very proud of you."

"Well, what are you going to buy?" I said in simple Japanese.
"That."

We were in the pharmaceutical department. She pointed to a big jar of green liquid.

"It is a beautiful colour. Please, how much that?"

"Fifteen rupees," the girl assistant said.

"I will take." She put her hand in her bag and brought out the notes. They were the equivalent of more than a guinea. "Isn't it beautiful!" she said. "Please, what is it?"

"Pine extract. It is for baths. Very soothing."

"You are crazy," I said. "Buying stuff when you don't know what it's for."

"It is certain to be useful. It is such nice colour, like English lawn."

I carried the bottle for her; it was the size of a large pickle jar, and as heavy. We wandered into the food department.

"It is like Fortnum & Mason's," Sabby said. "Don't you wish it was Fortnum & Mason's? Then I could buy you a delicious chocolate trifle and we could eat it at home. We could have little private meal."

"That reminds me. I've got an invitation for tonight."

"Yes?" she said, trying not to appear crestfallen. "Of course you must go."

"It's for us both."

"For me, too? Oh, please may we go? It would be fun, wouldn't it?"

"You don't know who it's from."

"That doesn't matter if we may both go together. But I don't want to be a burden; please tell me when I am nuisance, and I shall go and jump into deep water."

"I've already promised. Look, here's the café—what about some iced coffee?"

"Oh yes, let us have some iced coffee."

We sat for a time drinking the liquid through straws. At other tables people stole glances at Sabby, and when they caught my eye, looked away quickly as though I had surprised them in some shameful act. I wondered whether they were looking at her because she was pretty or because she was Japanese; though of course it was Chinese that they thought her to be, and sometimes I could hear the word 'Chinese' on somebody's whispering lips.

Sabby did not mind; she did not notice; and I was delighted by her lack of selfconsciousness and her gay nonchalance, and I could have swept her into my arms and covered her eyes with kisses. I felt younger myself, gayer, and proud as a youth who steps down Piccadilly with the first girl he has kissed.

After we had drunk our coffee, I bought a new pair of shoes, and a pair of flannels and a sports shirt. I did not need them, and since it was close to the end of the month I had only a little money left. But I had caught the carefree spirit. I bought Sabby a silk handkerchief for her head, and ordered some flowers to be sent to her room. Sabby bought me a new watch strap that was made of silver. I protested. It was no use, I said, it wouldn't fit. I would take it back. But I couldn't make her listen. Finally I told her it was a lovely gift that I should always, always treasure; and that was the truth.

We left the store. Inconspicuously in the street we squeezed hands. It was perfectly true: I had never been happier. I was laughing nearly all the time—and when I was not laughing I was smiling. I felt silly to be so happy, because I knew that Sabby had been right and happiness like that does not last. What was going to happen? I wondered. And then as though Sabby's thoughts had been following mine she asked suddenly:

"Michael, what is fool's paradise?"

"Why?"

"I have heard the expression, that's all."

I tried to explain.

I said: "If you sit in a room with a bottle of gin in one hand and a lovely girl on your knee, and think yourself happy—and all the time there is a time-bomb in the cupboard—that is a fool's paradise."

"Do you think there is a time-bomb in our cupboard?"

"I can't hear it ticking," I said. "Can you?"

"I don't know, Michael. I don't know if I am deaf. Don't you think sometimes one is deaf purposely?"

We had reached the Eastern Empire Bank.

"I am going to cash a cheque," Sabby said. "Please come with me. Perhaps if you stand at my side the manager will not see."

"Won't see what?"

"I don't want him to see me."

"Have you got an overdraft or something?"

"Oh no," she said. "I have got plenty of money."

"Then what's the matter?"

"Afterwards I will explain. It is nothing."

We entered the vast building where hundreds of bespectacled *babus* pored over ledgers. Sabby went to a counter and wrote a cheque, and a flabby-jowled Indian beamed at her between the bars of the grille.

"You would like to see Mr. Scaife?"

"Not just now—I must hurry."

"He is just in his office."

"No, thank you, really . . ."

Outside I said: "Tell me about Mr. Scaife."

"I am really in his care."

"How do you mean?"

"You see, he is a great friend of my guardian. I haven't told you about my guardian. There is so much to tell, I can't think where to begin."

"At the beginning," I said. "Tell me why you were in England."

"You see, my father went to Europe on business, and my mother and I went too. They were angry with me because I would not marry the man they had chosen for me. At least, my father was angry, and my mother was very sorry. They thought after I had been away I would change my mind. Then I was obstinate and didn't want to go back. English people were so kind to me that I was happier in England than I had ever been in Japan. My father said, you have got to come—you are a scatterbrain and cannot look after yourself, and I am not going to give you any money. So to show him that it was not true I got job."

"How did you manage that?"

"Oh, darling," she said, "do you really want to hear all about it?"

"Yes, please," I said.

"Well, it was because I was too cheeky. I did not mean to cheek, but afterwards my mother told me it was naughty of me, and I had to apologise. You see, in Japan it is a very great art to arrange flowers, and it is taught to girls so that they may make their homes beautiful and have successful tea ceremonies. We are taught to try to understand flowers and be sympathetic about their natures. I was taught every week from when I was ten to when I was nineteen by a very clever master. Well, in Regent Street there is a flower shop, and when I saw the flowers in the window I remembered all that I had been told, and it made my heart cry. I remembered a beautiful poem I had once heard in English:

> *'Poor foolish blossom,*
> *How thou shinest for him who*
> *Dishevels thee, and withers thee.'*

"So I went in and said: 'Please let me arrange.' The manager did not understand, so I took the flowers from a bowl and broke the stalks in the way that made them most lovely, and took some away because there were too many. He said, that is certainly very nice, and he called one of his assistants to see. But then afterwards I told my mother, and she said you must return and say you are sorry, because otherwise they will say rude things of the Japanese for interfering. When I went back the manager was not at all angry; he said he had been thinking it over and would like to have a special window display of Japanese flower arrangement. He said, would I please stay and work for him. Of course I wasn't going to do it—not until my father said that I could not look after myself, and then I did it just to prove. That is why I stayed in England."

"With your guardian?"

"Yes, because he is a very good, kind man, and he and his wife promised my mother they would look after me."

"Who is he?" I asked.

"He is called Wilbraham Durweston."

"That is Lord Durweston, isn't it?" I said.

"Yes, that is who it is. Before there was a war he was a friend of my father in business, and that is why we stayed with him. Then when it looked as though there must be a war, he tried to make me go home. That made me unhappy. As last he said he would look after me, and when the war came he made promises for me, and I was allowed to stay in his house."

"Are you sorry you didn't go back to Japan?"

"No, darling. I don't want to marry anyone that I am told to."

"But now there is a war, and you're a long way from home. You're on the wrong side of the line."

"No," Sabby said. "I'm lucky. I'm terribly lucky. It is my mother who is on the wrong side of line."

II

I returned to school in the afternoon. It was not necessary, because I had a certificate in my pocket to say that I was excused duty for a week. But I wanted to be at Sabby's class; or perhaps it was that I did not want the others to have her when I was not there too. I did not want to fall far behind in Japanese, either. Already, in three weeks, the rest of the class had made a great deal of progress. They used words and expressions that I had never heard. Itsumi San laid stress upon this.

"I am going to see how much you have forgotten," he said. And then in Japanese, "Since when have you been in hospital?"

"Since three weeks."

"In the hospital bed did you with might and main study the Japanese language?"

"That is not so," I said.

"Your illness was too severe?"

"That is not so."

"Then for what reason did you not with might and main study the Japanese language?"

"Because when someone else in the hospital is playing a fearfully loud wireless it is not possible to study anything with might and main." Only I said this with difficulty and ungrammatically.

"Once more the same sentence, please," Itsumi San said.

"There was a fearfully loud wireless," I said.

"What else?"

"For that reason I did not study in the least bit."

"How old are you?"

"That is a rude question," I said, because I could never think of numbers quickly.

"Did you read today's newspaper?"

"It is so."

"What was the most important item?"

"It concerned Russia."

"What about Russia?"

"Oh hell," I said in English. "I'm excused duty. Please go on to somebody else."

"You don't want to learn Japanese?"

"Yes," I said. "With might and main I wish to study the Japanese language. Only my brain has not yet recovered."

87

"I think your illness was an illness of the belly."

"That is correct."

"Therefore you must now endeavour——"

"With might and main," everyone said in chorus.

"This is a very serious, important thing," Itsumi San said. "It is not a joke. It is serious. It is serious and important. Moreover, it is for your own good. To me it does not matter in the least whether or not you learn to speak cleverly. I am thinking of you. Upon your proficiency will depend your promotion. I would like to see you all high officers. I am a civilian. But notwithstanding this, it is my desire to see you successful. Some people in my position would not care. But I work at nights with might and main to prepare lessons for you. I would prefer to go out and entertain myself. I do not do this. I think of your promotion. Therefore it is also your duty to study."

"I understand," I said.

"Please then pay attention. It is for your own benefit. I will ask you one more question. Where were you born?"

"I was born at a place called Tewkesbury in England."

"Very good. Very good indeed. If you try you can succeed. Now we will continue. . . ."

When Sabby came in, she was less severe. She did not look at me at first, and then she looked quickly and away again, and she blushed a little. Later on she grew cold. She began asking questions round the class, and when it came to my turn she asked, "Are you a person who keeps promises?"

"It depends on the promise," I said.

The next time round she said, "Do you keep promises that you make to women?"

I said: "It depends on the woman."

Her eyes twinkled mischievously. She thought it was great fun, this personal allusion in the middle of the class: she did not think that anyone could possibly suspect that there was anything behind it. And everyone thought that Sabby was great fun, and I could see that during my absence the formality with which she had been received at first had given way to an easy intimacy. Her hour went quickly. She tried to teach some grammar, writing words up on the board, and rubbing them out before anyone had time to see. After she had rubbed something out she put the duster up on the side of the board as though there was a hook there, and when she let it go it fell to the ground. When she needed it again at first she could not find it; but always she tried to put it where there was no hook and was surprised when she saw it on the floor. And somehow in this little careless action there was a naïveté that started a responsive wave of tenderness within me, and I found that I was whispering to myself, 'Sweet darling, Sabby, my child Sabby.'

Yet she was not a child, she was a woman, and there was as much woman as there was child in her, a deep age-old womanliness. I wondered how she could be so womanly, so warmly responsive, so passionate, and yet retain that wide-eyed innocence. Perhaps the others had wondered, too, because someone asked:

"How old were you at the time of the great earthquake?"

"I was seven." She knew it was a device to find out her age, and she did not care. We all counted on our fingers. She was twenty-six. But what did the years matter? It takes more than the passing of time to make an age. Sabby was seventeen and seven and seventy all at once.

After the class Lamb spoke to me.

"You know," he said, "Hanako's the goods. I didn't know I could fancy anything East of Suez. But this is talking, what do you think?"

What I thought was that his words sounded crude; and there was a nasty taste in my mouth, and I felt for perhaps the first time a spark of the pristine gallantry, 'How dare you, sir, speak thus of a woman's name. Choose your own weapons!' But also I thought, how comic to feel this! And I wondered whether my uprush of indignation was a form of hypocrisy. As a kind of counteraction to hypocrisy I said:

"She's the goods all right." (How easy to be misjudged by one's words! I thought.)

"I've a good mind to ask her out to dinner."

Jealousy plucked lightly at a chord within me. I had liked Lamb, as a kind of gay ruffian. His moustache was bushy, almost intentionally villainous, and he did not care for pretences. Now suddenly I disliked him.

"Go ahead," I said.

"I think I shall see what's doing."

"Good luck," I said.

He went off. I went to the window, and I saw him appear through the doorway below and stand waiting on the steps, with his books under his arm. He looked up, and screwed his face into a grimace that meant 'This is something good', and he stuck up his thumb above a clenched fist and waved it. I was ashamed. It may have been that I was ashamed of him; or else that he was making me feel ashamed of myself. Then I remembered that I was happy, and that I thought Sabby was happy too, and I could not see any reason why I should feel badly like that. And yet wasn't this grimacing and thumbing exactly the same thing as I had done—only differently expressed? And wasn't my way more insidious, more dishonest? There are various ways of picking pockets—you can do it promiscuously in a tramcar and risk the consequences; or else you can do it under the cover of friendship, by creating a trust and then abusing it, knowing you will not be arrested as a common thief. Of course the second way is more cowardly.

"I have never been so happy in my life," I had said. I had said it three times. Yes, and I had meant it, I had really meant it and believed it, I had never, never been so happy. But supposing Lamb also were to have said that, and to have meant it, and to-morrow to have said it again and meant it again in the arms of one of Rosie's girls? It is so easy to say things and mean them when you say them.

O God, I thought, what is the matter with you? Why this guilty conscience all of a sudden?—you have never felt like this before. Is it because Sabby is half child, because of the way she naïvely hangs the duster? Do you think you've bitten off more than you can chew? Are you afraid of responsibilities, and after one night's bliss would like to call it a day? Would you like to do that?

And here was Sabby on the steps below. I could see her come out, gaily swinging her bag. She went quickly down to the pavement and looked about for a ghari. Lamb followed. I could see he was saying something to her, but I could not hear what it was. She smiled questioningly. Lamb touched his moustache and beamed like a gay buck approaching a pretty woman to whom he has not been introduced. He spoke. Sabby looked shy; I could tell somehow from the position of her head that her eyelids had drooped. Lamb brought a hand into action; he spread it flat and moved it through a semicircle, making specious offers. Sabby's head inclined; it said: 'I'm frightfully sorry, please forgive me.' Lamb was sheepish; he made a final desperate appeal. He touched his dictionary—of course, he wished to dine with her to improve his knowledge of Japanese. Why not? Sabby's head, her black hair, were eloquent, 'Please understand, please.' Lamb shrugged. A ghari had drawn up. Sabby made her series of half curtsies. 'I am so sorry.' She turned and climbed in, and sat down with a scarcely perceptible but extra haste, and was gone. Lamb looked up at me. He made a wry face and his thumb pointed downwards. Then a second later his expression was devil-may-care.

"*Shikata ga arimasen,*" he called—the fond phrase of the Japanese ('It can't be helped; there is nothing to be done'). "After all," he said, "what is thirty rupees between friends?" He was whistling as he went away.

And I was singing. For a moment I did not notice it, but then I found a sudden joy was bursting out of me. Good for Sabby! And good for me; for perhaps, after all, I was not like Lamb. (But don't be too sure, I warned myself, don't be too sure.) I did not want to call it a day, not with any part of me; or else I should have rejoiced, not in Lamb's rejection, but in his acceptance. Good for Sabby, darling sweet Sabby. . . . I do not want to be treacherous, I want to make you happy. But what will come of this? What is going to happen to us . . .?

"You are coming?" said Peter.

"Oh yes. . . ."

"You've a lot to tell me."

"I don't think so."

"Perhaps not. You've told it already. You were flirting outrageously in class."

"Nonsense," I said.

"But you were. And Hanako! I've never seen anything like it. You'll both hang for this. It's *lèse-majesté.*"

"Nobody but you would notice."

"But you must be careful. You must tell her to be good. She's such a light-hearted little thing she'd gaily embrace you in public. You must keep billing and cooing out of the schoolroom. Be wise. Be expedient."

"I'll try," I said. "But I don't feel very wise."

"Of course you don't. You're in love."

"Oh!" I said. "It's so easy to say these things about other people."

"You talk as though I was saying you were a fool."

"Weren't you?"

"No, I wasn't saying that."

91

"Let's talk about the weather," I said. "It's very hot."

"Yes, it's pretty hot. In summer it'll be hotter still."

We took a ghari back to the hotel. We had calculated that we could only afford to take a ghari on special occasions; but it was wonderful what an aptitude we had developed for investing occasions with a special nature. It was a special occasion when we were happy, and the happiness obliterated all thoughts of the expense; and it was a special occasion when we were sad, for it was worth the extra money to make life that much easier. This was a happy special occasion. At least I was happy, and Peter was maintaining satisfactorily the *status quo* of his equanimity.

Bahadur was waiting quietly in our room, sitting cross-legged on the floor; he insisted that this was the position he preferred, and it was probably the case, though even had he preferred to use one of our chairs or the bed, I think he would have refused our invitation to do so. He knew 'his place' and all his instincts compelled him to this as the force of gravity brings a pendulum to its position of rest. And as reluctantly as the pendulum yields to the power that swings it, he yielded to pressure that tried to elevate him; and with the pressure removed, back he would swing to 'his place'. Instead, on the chair were my garments for the evening, laid out like the display window of a tailor's shop— a clean handkerchief folded with no overlapping edges, and placed with geometrical precision on the centre of the seat, and a sock either side of it folded in the way proved to be the easiest for the insertion of a foot. And in the bathroom, all my paraphernalia parading regimentally for my use, in the order Bahadur had observed I used it—first my toothbrush and tube of paste, and then the shaving-brush, the soap, the razor, an antiseptic tube in case I cut myself, and then my face flannel, a snow-white towel and a tin of powder. I dared not think with what horror Bahadur would have gazed into the chaos of any servantless apartment I had occupied; and yet in England I could have returned gladly to chaos. Here in India, however, I thought Bahadur was worth his weight in gold. But it took him a long time to earn even the weight of his little finger in gold; his wage was only fifty rupees a month, and that is not two rupees a day, not two rides in a ghari. And these fifty rupees, in arrears, he received not avariciously, but with such gratitude that I might have been opening up to him the coffers of a Maharajah. He salaamed worshipfully, not only on his own behalf, but on behalf of his wife and his daughter, for whose roof and garments and daily rice I was through him responsible. He did not think that he lived in poverty. He lived respectably, and in comfort, and happily. I said to him:

"Bahadur, wouldn't you like someone to lay out your socks and your jacket and your turban?"

He was vastly amused; and he chuckled as though I had told him some funny story about Eskimos, for the subject was no less remote to him than that. It was an entirely new idea. I might have asked, 'Bahadur, wouldn't you like to be an elephant?'

"I am very pleased to do these things for master," he said, afraid that I was suspecting him of discontent. And he added as an afterthought, as though to show after all that there were some things of which he disapproved, "But I think it is time the Sahib bought a new pair of shoes. . . ."

When I had changed my clothes it was only half past six. I wished it had been half past seven, because I had told Sabby that I would call for her at a quarter to eight, and I was impatient for the time to pass. And then I could not wait for it to pass, and I went downstairs to the telephone and rang her.

"You still want to come tonight?" I said.

"Don't you want me to?"

"I thought you might prefer to have dinner with Lamb San."

"Oh, Michael darling," she said unhappily, "was it terribly rude of me to refuse him? Was it, darling?"

"You could have gone with him another night," I said.

"I want to be with you another night. You know I am selfish. I am hard-hearted bitch."

"Say that again. I love to hear you say it."

"Bitch," she said. "It is all right when I say it, but when you begin to say it to me I shall jump in river. Perhaps already Mr. Lamb is saying it."

"He was disappointed to find that you weren't one."

"What do you mean?"

"Never mind," I said. "I'll explain later. But why didn't you go with him?"

"Darling, he has such awful moustache. It is really not nice at all."

"If I had a moustache like that, would you still go out with me?"

"Yes, darling."

"Then I'm not really like Lamb. I mean apart from the moustache?"

"That is a silly question to ask."

"You really mean I'm not like him?"

"You are nothing, nothing like him at all."

"You are biased," I said. "But that's all right. I just wanted to make sure that you were biased. I was fishing."

"What is fishing?"

"I'll explain that afterwards, too. I'd like to come straight away and explain it."

"Oh, please," she said. "Please come straight away."

"All right. I think that's what I'll do."

I took a ghari; it was a special occasion, very special, and I said *"Juldel!"* to the driver so that he whipped the horse anything but gently and we galloped away with the air quite cool on my face. Then when we arrived I gave him twice as much fare as was necessary, and thought, so this is true what one reads in books—in happy towns the happiest people of all must be the cab drivers.

Sabby was in her kimono, in the middle of changing.

"Please look the other way," she said, wrapping it tightly round herself. On the carpet I could see her feet, and feet are usually anything but beautiful, but I thought that these were lovely; little ivory feet, delicate like her hands. When I went out on to the balcony I could hear them pattering about the room. I liked even this sound. Could I ever listen with such joy to the pattering of English feet? Something Mervyn had said in the Yacht Club butted its way into my memory; something about the taste of tobacco after betel-nut. But I did not care for this intrusion, and I pushed it back where it came from and said:

"Why aren't I allowed to watch you dressing?"

"It is a convention."

"It's like being given a dinner by someone, with champagne; and then borrowing a tuppenny ha'penny stamp and insisting on handing over the coppers."

"You must not say things like that."

"It's true," I said. "We've had champagne."

"Tell me about fishing, please."

"You fish for compliments. You dangle a well-baited hook like, Do you think so-and-so is prettier than me?'; and up comes a salmon, 'My dear, you make her look like an old bicycle saddle.' Or else you get your desert in the form of an old boot, 'There's normally no comparison—only she's not looking her best to-night.'"

"I am going fishing," Sabby said. "Please look round at me. Do you think I am prettier than old bicycle saddle?"

I turned round. She stood with her towel held up to her chin. Her bare arms protruded at the sides, and her knees below.

"Do I?" she said wistfully.

"You look quite unlike anything I've ever seen before," I said. "Is that salmon or old boot?"

I went close to her. She did not move, but she kept the towel held to her chin. I kissed her lightly, and her lips were cool; she had just come from the shower. I could feel her body touching mine through the towel. I wanted to clasp her; but there was an intimacy in this faint contact that we had not experienced before. We looked at each other for one of those moments that are time-less, because afterwards they live more vividly than whole mean-ingless weeks. And then because feelings on this level wear them-selves out—it was perhaps only a few seconds that it lasted—she reached up on her tiptoes and brushed her lips over mine and then scurried into the bathroom with the towel trailing behind. A second later her head appeared round the door.

"Please, Michael," she said sadly, "did you say salmon or old boot?"

"Salmon," I said. "Very pink."

She disappeared again, and from the bathroom I heard her singing, "Sabby is a salmon, a salmon, a salmon. . . ."

At a quarter to eight we went off to Mr. Headley's. We went to his flat that was close to the office which I had already visited. The Indian 'scheduled class' boy opened the door to us, and a moment later Mr. Headley appeared, a little whirlwind in bed-room slippers, extending both his hands, one for each of us.

"Hullo, hullo, hullo. No need to have dressed up, you know. Pot-luck—not a dinner party. All the same——" He looked at Sabby's dress, still holding her hand. "Charming. Quite charm-ing." His thinning hair was tousled. He wore an open khaki shirt and short khaki trousers. Indicating the latter he said, "You don't mind, do you? I'm on the right leg this month. Saves undressing. Pump it right in. What did you say your name was?"

"This is Miss Wei," I said.

"Really?" He extended his neck to look at Sabby closely, as though he were short-sighted. His eyes were screwed up quizzically. "Nonsense," he said. "Count on your fingers. Count up to five."

Sabby looked bewildered; she did not know whether this curious man was being funny or savage. She held up a doubtful hand.

"That's right. Count. One, two, three, four, five."

"One, two, three, four, five," Sabby said uncertainly.

Mr. Headley burst out in delight.

"There you are. Did you see? Did you see the way she did it? Started with an open palm and closed the fingers one by one. Ever seen a Chinese do that? Of course not. They count like the English, starting with a closed fist. Japanese!" he diagnosed triumphantly.

Sabby's expression was shamefaced; she thought for a second that she was going to be thrown out of the house. She began to apologise for the deception in the name, until Mr. Headley held up a silencing hand.

"Not a bit of it! Very fond of Japan; been there myself and made a lot of friends. Don't need to hide your name, though. We're glad to have you. Not a war of nations, is it? War of ideas. You've got our ideas. That's fine. Not always perfect by any means; but not so bad, eh?"

"I told you I was bringing a Japanese," I said.

"That's right, you said schoolmistress though."

"I am schoolmistress," Sabby said.

"Nonsense. You a schoolmistress? Wouldn't mind being at your school."

During dinner Mr. Headley talked about Japan. He let off explosive questions at Sabby.

"What are your politics?"

"I really haven't got any," Sabby said. "I suppose it seems silly. I don't think I understand politics."

"Why should you. Don't understand them myself. But you have *feelings*?"

"I think if only everybody could be nice to one another—if only they weren't selfish . . ."

"That's it. Doesn't matter if you can't read or write so long as you know that. Bad people, bad world. Good people—and everything solves itself. Think of India. I've no idea what the political solution is. Nor have you. Damn tricky. The trouble is the attitude—my mind, your attitude. A week after I arrived here

96

I bought a bicycle. Pedalled off down the road and almost bowled over an Indian; don't know whether it was his fault or mine, probably both. Do you know what I nearly said?"

We shook our heads.

"You'd never guess. I'm a missionary. Rum kind of missionary you may think, but that's what I am. And what I darn nearly said was, 'Get out of the way, you black so-and-so!'; words were on my lips. No idea where I picked them up; probably overheard someone once. 'You black so-and-so!' I nearly said. Well, it was a good thing I didn't say it. Because once you say that kind of thing, you're done for. You find it's the easiest thing in the world. Fellow doesn't hit back. Makes you feel a little bit bigger, and for that matter it makes him a little bit more of a so-and-so. And it solves the whole problem—it was his fault. It would have served him right if he'd been run over. Just saying something like that begins to create an attitude. Words. You've no idea what words can do to you. Don't be too eloquent. You may fool other people; but you'll certainly fool yourself. This young woman's got the idea; I can see it all right in her eyes. Wonderful eyes. They tell everything. Don't try and express things in words. Be yourself."

"That's not always easy," I said. "You can get wrong ideas about yourself just as you can about other people."

"Naturally—you're a youngster. Just go on living. You'll find out about yourself in time. Get some surprises. And disappointments. Wonderful what there is in life. I tried to write a book about it once—about life. Words, words. What's the use of it? Life is smells and pain and hopes and regrets, and winding up your watch and pumping insulin into your thigh. Don't worry. Just go and live."

Later, as we were walking back to the hotel beneath the deep blue canopy of the night sky, Sabby said:

"I like Mr. Headley, he is so gruff, and then you discover it is not gruffness at all. It is a pity that she died."

"That who died?"

"Oh, he did not say, did he? I think it must have been his wife, or else the girl that he loved very much indeed."

"I didn't hear him mention it."

"He didn't say anything, but you can tell. You can tell that she meant everything to him. But please, what does he mean when he says that you must live it? I don't see how you can help living unless you are dead."

"You can be dead and alive at the same time; it's even an expression in English. You can be dead to everything that goes on—dead to beauty, and to ugliness, too; you can be dead to all the little subtleties of experience, just as you can be numbed by cocaine in the dentist's chair."

"Perhaps it is sometimes a good thing to be dead. It would be good to be dead to suffering."

"It works both ways. You can't be dead to suffering without being dead to happiness, too."

"Oh dear."

"But why do you always have to think of suffering?" I said. "What are you going to suffer, darling?"

She did not say anything. She clung more tightly, more dependently, on to my arm, as she might have done if there had been a cobra in our path.

"That is the child in you," I said. "You have never got rid of the fear that there is a dreadful supernatural *thing* in the corner of the nursery."

"Yes, that is it. I shall not be child any more. I shall be grown-up."

We walked on silently. The air was warm, a soft night air. The deepening blue of the sky overhead was faintly dusty with stars.

And suddenly I began to wonder: Is it Sabby who is grown-up already, and I who am the child? The child who plays at being big and important and protective . . . until something frightening happens and then it runs away in tears?

CHAPTER III

I

ABOUT a week later I ran into Mr. Headley in Marine Drive.

"I meant to ask you about yogis," I said. "I'd like to know about them. I'd like to know something about spiritual India."

He laughed. He only had a few teeth, but he looked very merry when he laughed.

"When you go to heaven," he said, "you'll buttonhole St. Peter at the gate and say, 'Look here, St. Peter, tell me all about angels.'"

As though he could put you *au fait* with the subject with a few brief sentences."

"But one must know something about these things. When we go home, everyone will ask about them. I'd like to see a yogi. Just one."

"I expect that could be arranged."

"I know you have all these things at your finger-tips," I said.

"No, I've never met a yogi. But I can put you in touch with a connoisseur. Go and see Scaife. Eastern Empire Bank man. An expert. Say I sent you."

I remembered that it was Scaife who was supposed to be looking after Sabby's interests in India, and when I saw Sabby again I asked her to take me to see him. I explained about the yogis.

"Oh, darling," she said. "I don't want to take you. Please don't let's go."

"But aren't I presentable?"

"It isn't that."

"You needn't tell him all about us. You can just say I'm a student. An exceptional student bent upon discovering the secrets of the East."

"Please, I don't want to go."

"But why not?"

"I don't like him," she said sadly and with shame, as though confessing to a sin. "He is very queer. I don't want to meet him."

"In that case it doesn't matter."

"You see, it is true, I am selfish. Poor darling, you would like to know about yogi, and I am not trying to help you."

"You don't mind if I go and see him alone?"

"Of course I don't. It is so stupid of me. Please go and enjoy yourself, darling, if you can find out about yogi."

I went on the following day. I went to the bank, and sent in a slip to Mr. Scaife to say that I should like to see him on personal business. I was kept waiting for ten minutes, and then a Major came out of his office and the *chaprassi* waved me in. Scaife sat behind a massive, highly polished desk. Everything in the room was polished, and it was a big, airy room with two fans swirling from the ceiling. A secretary sat typing on a noiseless machine, facing the wall.

I remembered Scaife's face, for I had seen him with Sabby that night in the Yacht Club. I remembered that he did not look like a bank manager; though in the East it is less easy to judge an occupation by an appearance, because the social life has a greater moulding influence than the office files, or the chemicals, or the mining machinery, or whatever is one's stock-in-trade. He wore horn-rimmed spectacles, which lessened the effect of his broad forehead, but because they were so large his mouth looked tight and small. He might have been a scholar; and, in fact, I found out that he was something of the kind—an intellectual who had taken the wrong road at the beginning, being directed by his parents to a place behind the grille of an English bank. And then when he had woken up to find that he had been already five years counting notes and checking ledgers, he had only had sufficient courage to compromise with circumstances—to take half a new life out East, with the other half still given to drudgery he hated. Nevertheless, I believe he was a good manager. He despised the work and, despising, conquered it. He did not care for spit and polish, but his room was like an operating theatre. He was like someone who dislikes football but, dragged into a game, plays with an energy and ferocity unequalled by the devotees.

I told him Mr. Headley had sent me. I was interested to learn something about yogis and fakirs and maharishees—a rather casual interest, but I should be glad of his help.

He would gladly assist me, he said. He leaned back in his chair and opened his mouth and looked at the ceiling. The tips of his fingers were together. I wondered if this was a yoga attitude of meditation; but it was only that he was pleased for a moment to forget the business of the Empire and turn his thoughts to something else. Yes, he said, looking down again, he could arrange something for me. He would ask Mr. Munshi to meet me, and Mr. Munshi would be a willing guide. What about supper? An early supper—say seven. I could manage it? Good.

I went to the Mayfair to tell Sabby. It was the first time since I had come out of the hospital that we had not had dinner together, and now, having accepted Scaife's invitation, I felt reluctant to go. Imagining an evening with Sabby, I visualised a happy instant that would no sooner have come than gone; but this evening seemed to stretch before me like a sweep of desert, without oases, that I wondered how I could bring myself to cross. Nevertheless, I was glad I had accepted. I told myself it was good to break the habit of being with Sabby, to go without the drug once in a while to prove that it could be done.

But I did not like telling her. I knew what she would say and how she would look.

"That is lovely for you!" she said brightly. "You are going to see just what you want, lots and lots of yogi." Even her eyes were bright, but it was not a real brightness. I did not want it to be. If she had not been at all sorry that I was going away, I should have been more unhappy than I was because I had made her a little sad. And then she said quickly, to cover up anything that I might detect as reproach, "Darling, what is yogi?"

"I will tell you tonight. Or else you could come, too, and find out."

"But it is Scaife."

"I don't know why you dislike him so much."

She shrugged.

"Oh," she said. "I don't understand him. He is funny. Perhaps it is because he likes yogi. Please, don't go and care for yogi so much that you are like Mr. Scaife."

"Are you afraid that I shall?"

"Perhaps that is it," she said, and she sniffed in the pathetic, humorous way that made me feel so big and protective and loving, and that made the evening seem blanker still. But I kissed her and went, and if leaving her left a hole in me, it also made me think I was being strong-willed and sensible. I might have been resolving to renounce her forever.

Mr. Scaife's house was a fine porticoed building on Malabar Hill—the arm of land that forms one side of the bay and is the exclusive suburb of the town. As my ghari went up the drive I saw Mr. Scaife through a window. He also saw me. But he did not come out; a servant came out, and I stood on the doorstep while my presence was announced. After a minute he appeared.

"Ah!" he said. "You have arrived." He led the way into the lounge. "Mr. Munshi—Mr. Quinn."

I shook a soft, good-humoured hand.

"Dis is a pleasure," Mr. Munshi said. His round, fat face was full of well-fed smiles. "I am so pleased we are meeting."

We sat down. Mr. Scaife waved a hand. The servant brought whisky and began to pour it out. He did not make a sound. We indicated our needs mutely. Mr. Munshi took only lemonade, holding up a flabby finger to indicate the amount. He sat on the edge of a chair, and I could see his brown legs beneath his *dhoti*, and his sandalled feet turned outwards. He looked as though he was very used to feeling out of place in a drawing-room on Malabar Hill. Mr. Scaife held a cigar in his teeth passively. The lenses of his horn-rimmed spectacles were thick, and behind them his eyes floated like something seen through the glass of an aquarium. In the office I had noticed his eyes; perhaps they were his business eyes for studying balances. These were curious, off-duty, detached eyes, for reading the books on the shelf at his elbow—a handsome collection of books whose vellum and leather bindings spoke of first editions and recondite subjects.

The servant moved silently into a shadowy part of the room and hovered there.

Mr. Scaife gazed at nothing.

"To de host I drink good health," said Mr. Munshi.

"Ah!" When he said "Ah!" Mr. Scaife opened his mouth like a fish and looked at the ceiling. He lowered his gaze to me. "Mr. Munshi has kindly consented to show us something interesting tonight."

The Indian grinned self-deprecatingly. He lowered his head and looked at his hands.

"I hope you will find dat it is so. I hope so very much."

"It is very good of you," I said.

"Please do not make mention of it. It is so rare dat de visitors to dis country are interested in de spiritual India. But I have not de same knowledge as Mr. Scaife. He has a fine knowledge of dese things. He has taken much time to study."

"Alas," Mr. Scaife said, "only study by halves. A dangerous thing, very dangerous. Now, if you don't mind, we shall start supper. Best to get off early, don't you think, Munshi?"

We took a taxi. It was a huge car with a tattered hood and no side-screens, and the three of us sat in the back. Mr. Scaife on one side of me was thin and bony; and on the other side I could feel the ample flesh of Mr. Munshi bouncing comfortably with the motion of the car. He kept his hands folded in his lap. There was still the smile on his face which broadened for a moment whenever we went over a pot-hole or swerved to avoid a pedestrian, and then resumed its normal dimensions.

"Where are you taking us, Munshi?"

"I dink we might pay a visit to Lala Vikrana."

"Ah! Might as well drop off at Grant Road and show him the devil before God."

"Very good. Very good."

The roads became narrower and more crowded. We advanced like a juggernaut, the horn bleating continuously. In front of us the milling figures parted and closed again the moment we had passed. Eyes, caught in the glare of the headlamps, stared from brown faces.

"Here, Munshi."

"Very good."

We tumbled out, and I followed after the other two down the sidestreets, selfconsciously. Here everyone was Indian. They stared at Mr. Scaife and me, the two white-skins, so that I was glad Mr. Munshi was escorting us; it made me feel a little less alien, less of an intruder. Nevertheless, I had the feeling that we were trespassing, that at any moment we would be told to get out —or that the crowd would turn on us suddenly and tear us to pieces. Yet they seemed perfectly docile. Even the beggars, if you showed anger, removed their suppliant hands. But the children were plucking at my trousers. I said: "*Jaow! Jaow!*" but still they went on chattering round me. They grabbed at my hand. I withdrew it quickly, wiped it on my shirt. I thought rather sneakingly that afterwards I had better have a disinfectant bath. They said you couldn't catch diseases in this way, but all the same . . . there was something repulsive in the bare contact with these depraved-looking children.

"*Jaow!*" I said.

"*Baksheesh! Baksheesh!*" If it would have sent them away I would have given them their annas. But it wouldn't.

"*Challo, challo,*" Mr. Munshi said. They looked at him to see if he meant it; for a minute they could not make up their minds. Then he added something else in Hindustani, and they fell behind, all the animation suddenly gone out of them because the hope of their penny had gone. A penny would have bought them a meal.

"Not many places in the world you'll see this," Mr. Scaife said, indicating the houses at the sides of the street.

The shops had now given way to buildings in which every door and window was barred like a cage; and through the bars we caught glimpses of brightly painted lips and powdered cheeks, and brass ornaments hung from ears and noses . . . whilst above, in upper windows and balconies, silhouettes of hair and shoulders were framed invitingly by the dim orange light of inner rooms. Somewhere music was being churned out mechanically and there was a babble of voices. It was almost gay. And at night these old, unpainted façades of the houses had a beauty of their own.

Then there were shops again, cafés, sudden explosions of light. And then only the dark fronts of houses with beds out on the pavements and people already asleep there.

"Not far now," Mr. Scaife said. "No question about it being all right at this time of night, is it, Munshi?"

"It is a time when Vikrana has many disciples," Mr. Munshi said. "Mr. Quinn will find here some difference from what he has just seen. It is not often in one evening dat one visits de extremes. We must hope dat de worldly scene will bias our friend to de spiritual."

We had come to an open space where arid grass struggled through parched brown earth. Ownerless dogs scampered about, and here and there figures sprawled like corpses forgotten by a battle. We began to cross this space. A small shack came into view, surrounded by a fence and a locked gate. At this Mr. Munshi stopped. He shook it gently and the chain rattled.

From behind the hut there came an old man, of no more than pigmy stature. He came slowly, and clutched two bars of the fence and peered through; his eyes were old and distant like a madman's, or like the eyes of someone who is blind, and I did not think he could see what he gazed at. But when Mr. Munshi spoke, he inserted his key at once in the lock and the gate creaked open. We went through and on to the verandah of the shack. Through the cracks of the door I could see a light. But there was no sound apart from the clank of the chain behind us as the old man again fixed the padlock.

Mr. Munshi did not look round. He lifted the latch of the door and pushed it open, and the light fell on his plump, beaming face; only now his smile was not what it had been. It was not the broad smile of Malabar Hill when he had held his glass of lemonade in his lap, and it was not the Grant Road smile of toleration; it was a faint and peaceful and holy smile, a candlelight instead of a beacon. It was a smile that fitted the scene within.

There were half a dozen people seated in a semicircle on the floor, lightly garbed in cotton cloth or muslin. At their focus was another figure sitting cross-legged on a dais, naked except for a loin-cloth. From his erect body his neck rose like a pillar, squarely holding his head with a broad Socratic forehead, like a marble bust; and the eyes were more than ever like marble, with the pupils revolved upwards out of sight above the unblinking lids.

Mr. Munshi beckoned us in. He closed the door behind us, and the latch clicked sharply in the silence. His hand waved to a place on the floor, and then he subsided neatly without moving his feet, as though all of a sudden the bones that supported his flesh had melted. Mr. Scaife squatted next to him with only a little less ease, the bones of his knees sticking out through his thin trousers, and his head high. I followed suit clumsily, taking my weight on my hands and lowering myself on the coarse coconut-matting of the floor, I tried to pull my feet well under me, but my joints were stiff and pained me. I relaxed them, and placed my arms round the outside of my legs to keep them in, clasping my hands in front. My back was sloped. When I straightened it there was also a pain in my spine, so I let it remain as it was. My head hung in physically essential humility.

I stared at the Master. I was the only one who was staring, for the disciples were lost in their own contemplation. They had not even glanced in our direction as we entered, though the pupils of their eyes were not, like the Master's, rotated out of sight. Their eyelids blinked and they breathed. At first, I did not think the Master was breathing. Then I watched carefully a point on his breast where the yellow light from the oil-lamp shone on his skin. I watched for a long time and I saw that it rose and fell slowly, perhaps once a minute. But it was difficult to judge time. I tried to guess, after a while, how long we had sat there. It might have been ten minutes, or twenty, or a couple of hours. I had a feeling that the room was timeless. I looked at the white sculptured eyeballs and wondered if they were sending me into some kind of trance. A queer sensation passed over me, and I closed my eyes to try to think more clearly. I was not sure whether or not I was dreaming, and I pulled my foot in sharply so that the heel of my shoe came against the back of my thigh. I felt its hardness; I was not asleep. Nevertheless, there was something dream-like in this. Or as though I was a little drunk. That same dizziness. . . . I opened my eyes again. No one had moved. In the lamplight those white eyeballs were like twin moons. The body was still frozen, statuesque. There was no doubt that something had gone out of it. When you look at a dead body you can see that something has gone, and this body was like that of the dead. And in the room was the stillness of death, the timelessness. When you are dead there is no more time.

Yet I could feel that this was no ordinary death. I could feel something else, something positive, that was flowing into me. As it came into my shoulders I grew more comfortable. And then it seemed to be seeping down from my shoulders like a soothing oil and, like oil in a machine, it eased my body. I began to experience a strange tranquillity. I no longer wondered what length of time we had been in the room, but only how long this pleasing sensation would last.

It was only for a short time. As though I was waking from sleep, part of my mind clarified and became practical and I looked at the figure on the dais and saw an old Indian in a trance, and I realised how uncomfortable, after all, was this uncustomary position. I saw Mr. Munshi's felicitous smile and thought of him bouncing in the taxi-cab, and I remembered Mr. Scaife in the office of the Eastern Empire Bank, with the secretary at the noiseless typewriter, and I thought of myself and how amused Peter would be, and Mervyn and Mario, if they could see me thus cross-legged with a pain growing in my joints. It was ridiculous to suppose that in my moment of tranquillity I had been brushed by the spirit of the fakir, or that I had stood on the verge of another world. In this queer atmosphere my imagination had played tricks. Meanwhile, enough—I was aching. If somebody did not move soon, I should have to let myself out quietly. I could drop a word to Mr. Scaife, and wait outside, stroll amongst the pie-dogs and the littered bodies of the homeless. At any rate, it was life outside. This was death, after all, though these people would call it Life, Life with a capital L. Very well, take Life if you will renounce dinner at the Taj and conversation with Peter, and meeting new people and bed with Sabby. Life with a little 'l'—there was a lot to be said for it. . . .

There was a sudden movement—a simultaneous relaxation by everyone as though they were responding to a common impulse. The Master Vikrana's eyeballs rolled. Dark pupils appeared and coursed rapidly round, and finally settled in the centre. His eyelids blinked and his breathing took up a normal rhythm. He moved his hands. It was as though, preserved in ice for a time, he was beginning to thaw.

Mr. Munshi caught my eye and smiled. Mr. Scaife stared at a higher point in the ceiling and opened his mouth; I expected an

'Ah!' to issue forth, but he kept his exclamation silent. The disciples looked at the Master and the Master surveyed the assembly. I was surprised how human he now appeared, how strikingly benign was his face by contrast with the depersonalised mask of his trance.

He made some sign, and one of his disciples moved closer to the dais, sitting just beneath him. Then he took a board from his side on which the Hindu alphabet was written. His finger moved rapidly from one letter to another as he spelt out a message. I remembered I had been told that the Master Vikrana had taken a vow of silence. The disciple was his mouthpiece. The disciple spoke, and he looked at me, and I knew that he was speaking to me although I understood nothing of his words.

Mr. Munshi began to interpret.

"De Master says dat it is a really unexpected pleasure to have here a new visitor."

I inclined my head in acknowledgment of the courtesy.

"De master now asks if it is as a sight-seer dat you come. or if it is dat you are searching for de great Truth?"

"A bit of both," I said, to do myself more than justice, and I left Mr. Munshi to find a Hindustani equivalent of this. His own interpretation was less laconic; he must have added his own diagnosis of my intentions. His voice sounded sympathetic, and Lala Vikrana nodded his white beard understandingly. For a moment or two he meditated. He stroked his beard and he looked at me with penetration, and he went on nodding, and all the disciples looked at the Master and waited for his words of judgment. He looked so wise and Socratic and infallible that I waited with eagerness—though I was not sure what I was waiting for, unless it was to hear that I was damned or saved; and either I could have believed, and his words might have tilted the scale a little more in one way or the other.

At last the Master's fingers began to dance once more over the letters. The disciples' eyes flicked after them, and the pronouncement was made. Mr. Munshi gave it to me third hand.

"De Master has said dat during his trance for a short while only he was aware of you, and dat also you were aware of him. He does not consider dat you were enough determined to enter into de spiritual circle. He says dat you encourage yourself to be sceptical, and dat he can do nothing for you unless you enter your whole heart into de pursuit of dis ultimate Truth, which is ultimate happiness. He says dat if you have a question he would gladly give answer."

"Doesn't the Master consider it possible to find happiness in a lower sphere?"

The question went back, and this time the reply came quickly.

"De Master says indeed dere is great happiness to be found; and he asks why is it dat you put dat question when you have already de answer for yourself. He wishes it to be said clearly dat unless you are prepared to study first de yoga of de body, and den when you have cleared out of your path dese corporeal obstacles, de yoga of de mind, he would not care for you to deviate from de Christian principles which he so greatly admires."

There was a pause while Vikrana's fingers added a paragraph.

"He says now dat he is pleased you did not request him, in de manner of a British person who once visited, to do tricks; for whilst it is in his power to do 'tricks', such as to project his thoughts over many, many miles, dis is to him only de fruit of his understanding of higher things, as de projection of wireless waves is de fruit of de great knowledge of your scientists. He does not himself understand wireless. He says de scientists are great, clever men, but deir chosen way to heaven is a long, difficult way, and all along dere are beautiful mirages. And now he regrets to be discourteous, but he must devote himself for de rest of his time to his disciples. Is dere one more final thing you would care to request of him?"

"No," I said. "There is nothing. Unless he can give me a parting piece of advice that I may always keep in memory of this visit."

Vikrana was obviously anxious to oblige. He stroked his beard in meditation and looked at me with an iron-steady gaze. I looked back into his eyes, and I wanted to look away again, but his gaze was like a challenge. I held it for what seemed like minutes, fighting off the temptation to let my eyes fall away; and then I knew that it no longer required strength of mind to return his stare, that his eyes compelled mine to his and by no effort of will could I now bring myself to withdraw them. I knew that he possessed some power over me; and at the same time I was aware of its benevolence, and the utter abandon with which I could give myself up to it.

Suddenly my eyes began to swim and there seemed to be a fog between us. And through the middle of the fog like two steel shafts his gaze still came, piercing their way into my brain. Next I knew only that the shafts had gone, and that in the dispersing fog I could hear the voice of the disciple, and then of Mr. Munshi.

"De Master says dat you have great power. Dis power is to give happiness and it is not to be used without de utmost awareness. You will give yourself at de same time much happiness and much sadness; and de sadness will be terrible and in de midst of it you will say, 'It has been worth while.' "

And then the three of us were rising to our feet, and placing the tips of our fingers together in the gesture of respect, and going out through the door of the shack; and outside the air was cooler and we breathed it deeply. The old pigmy man who guarded the Master from the mischievous attacks of youths clanked his key in the lock.

"Well," Mr. Scaife said: "What do you think of him?"

"It was very interesting," I said. "But after all, what he said is true of everybody, isn't it? Haven't we all got the power to give happiness?"

III

We went back by taxi, stopping at Toledo to let Mr. Munshi get out. His face shone through the window, not a candle but a beacon again. I thanked him for his kindness; he was a Brahmin, a pundit, a busy man, and he had devoted his whole evening to my instruction. "Not in de least," he said. "Dis is a little matter. Please do not mention it again."

"Better come back and have a drink," Mr. Scaife said to me when the white *dhoti* had disappeared through a doorway.

"It's very good of you," I said. "But I think not tonight. . . ."

"Why not?"

He rapped it out. It was a question to which he demanded an answer. Why not?

"It's getting rather late," I said.

"Only five-to-eleven."

"Oh well, in that case," I said, "just a quick one perhaps." I had known it was only five-to-eleven, but I could not bring myself to make a stand against his insistence. It was a kind of detached and yet passionate insistence, as though I was a woman for whom he cared nothing but whom instinct urged him to possess. I wondered if for some reason he was afraid of being left alone.

The servant was waiting in the house. Mr. Scaife dismissed

him, and we went into the drawing-room and began to drink the whisky and talk about the yogi. He sat opposite me in an arm-chair, and he talked in a curious, lofty and distant and unap-proachable way, though occasionally he would suddenly shoot me a glance as though to confirm that I was still there, like an actor who breaks off a play for a moment to make sure that there is really someone in the stalls. He talked with very selfconscious in-telligence; he ought to have been to a university, and he had not been, and he had never quite forgotten that. And then I began to see that all this intelligence went in circles round himself. He was almost a cultured version of Fenwick; but where Fenwick plunged crudely at the centre with undisguised boasting ('There's nothing I can't tell you about that—I've read all the best books on the subject. . . .'). He spun a clever web round the circumference and from the circumference left you to guess at the centre. And yet you could see that he was struggling to keep his knowledge detached, and knew his own failure and wanted to hide it.

But he really had the knowledge, and Fenwick hadn't; he had the desire to dig it out of dusty books and unfrequented places, and he despised Fenwick's source of information, which was popular encyclopædias and *An ABC of Philosophy*. And on the subject of yoga he was the expert that Mr. Headley had pro-claimed him.

I wanted to know how much he practised it, and I asked him. He was vague; it embarrassed him to be dragged from the circum-ference to the centre, and he escaped back again as quickly as he could. But he did try to practise it, that much was clear. He went down on the carpet and demonstrated the position of the yogi, almost sitting on one foot and the other dragged over on to the opposite thigh. He could do it well, and for an Occidental it cannot be done without practice. But if he had got this far with the yoga of the body, how far behind was he with the yoga of the mind, when the first fetters to be broken were egotism and desire?

Besides, there was the whisky. He drank a good deal, and for some reason, although I wanted to go, I went on drinking with him. The whisky brought him nearer the centre of his circle, and he became more approachable, more human. He talked person-ally. He said suddenly that he hated the bank, whereas before he would not have confessed it. And then he began to talk of Sabby. He began to talk of her as though he could not help it.

He said, "So you are learning Japanese. What do you think of Hanako?"

I pretended I did not understand.

"Miss Wei," he said.

"Oh, of course! She's a good teacher," I said. "Her Japanese is rather formal if we're learning to speak to the soldiery, but . . ."

"What do the others think of her?"

"They enjoy her classes."

He got up and lit a cigarette and started to pace about the room.

"Do you know her well?" I asked. I didn't want to talk about her, not with Mr. Scaife; but at the same time I was curious and did not try to change the subject.

"Certainly. I know her very well. Of course I know her."

"I understand the climate here didn't suit her at first . . ."

He was not interested in her health.

"She is a beautiful girl," he said, and he shot a glance down to me in the stalls, and it made me think; so this is it, he brought me here because he has suspected something between Sabby and myself; in a moment he is going to say, 'This must stop!'

"Don't you think so?" he said, with that blunt questioning manner that insisted upon an answer.

"Yes, I do. I think she's lovely."

"I'm looking after her, you know."

"There are worse jobs than that."

"Her guardian, Lord Durweston, used to live in India. A great friend of mine. He asked me to keep an eye on her."

"Oh yes," I said.

"She's a strange girl."

"She's Japanese."

"Yes, yes," he said. "There is something rather fascinating about Japanese women. I have known several."

He was still standing. He reached down to the table for his glass, and when he straightened himself up again, I saw that he was not quite steady. I saw also that he had forgotten me again; he was not trying to find out what I thought about Sabby—he was telling me what he thought himself.

"Yes," he said. "Hanako is very charming. One could not wish for a better companion."

I got up.

"I must really go," I said. "It's after midnight."

"No, old chap. Stay and talk a bit. I like to talk with someone who knows Hanako."

"I must get back," I said.

"Plenty of time. Have another whisky. I know, we could ring her up. I'd like to talk to her. Tell her one of her pupils is here. Let's ring her up."

"It's too late."

"She won't mind. It's my job to keep an eye on her."

"I shouldn't ring her if I were you," I said.

"That's all right. You could talk to her, too. In Japanese."

"No," I said. "I must go."

"I think I'll ring her up."

"Why not wait till the morning? You can call her at breakfast."

"Better ring her now."

"Well," I said, trying to make him forget this idea, "thank you very much for this evening. It was most instructive."

"One for the road. Come on, old boy, where's your glass?"

"I'm really going."

"What about Hanako?"

"Not tonight," I said. "She'll be teaching me tomorrow."

I went to the door. He poured some more whisky into his glass and came after me, and I thought he had given up the idea of ringing.

"Well," he said. "It's not late. Drop in again. Any time. Just call in."

"Thank you—it was very good of you."

He patted me on the shoulder. He looked more human than he had ever done when he was sober.

"Goodbye, old boy," he said. "Don't forget, just drop in."

I left him standing in the porch. I had to walk half a mile down the road before I found a ghari stand. The driver was asleep in the back seat under the hood, and I woke him up and asked him to take me quickly to the Mayfair. He looked at me without interest, and said "Five rupees", because he did not want to take me any-where. I said, "All right, five rupees", and he climbed out with plaintive grunts and got into the driving-seat. Before he started he made a long raking noise in his throat and spat on to the ground. Then he flicked his whip, and the horse clopped away quickly as though it was glad to have something to do.

It was a little after one o'clock when we got to the hotel. I gave the driver five rupees exactly, and he knew he was lucky to get it, but he looked at it grudgingly and said nothing. I went through the hall of the hotel quickly, looking away from the desk where the night porter was sitting, and hoping he would not see me. I ran up the stairs and knocked lightly on Sabby's door. There was no reply, so I went in. The table-lamp was lit on the bedside table, but the white mosquito-net was draped round the bed and I was unable to see her. I went softly to the side of the bed, and pulled up the net and put my head underneath.

Sabby was sitting up quite wide awake. She was made up very prettily, and the light from the table-lamp shone through the net, illuminating her soft brown eyes. Now they were big and round and non-committal. They did not tell me whether she was angry with me for coming late or whether she was happy because I had come at last.

"Darling Sabby," I said. "Is it very wicked of me?"

"I thought you had forgotten Sabby," she said.

"You didn't think that."

"Yes I did, honestly."

I kicked off my shoes and climbed on to the bed under the net and kissed her. It was like a little tent inside. Usually mosquito-nets are only a nuisance, and in the hottest weather they are stifling. But now it was not too hot, and it made the bed a more intimate place, shutting out the hotel furniture that was Victorian and gloomy.

"How was yogi?" she said.

"It was very entertaining."

"Are you going to become yogi?"

"Not yet," I said. I knew I was not going to become yogi now. I thought that no spiritual attainment could be more beautiful than this, lying close to Sabby and encasing her tiny hand in mine and inhaling her faint perfume.

I saw she had a little note-book and a pencil by her.

"What are you writing?" I said.

"I am doing lessons for tomorrow."

"Nonsense. It isn't that book you use for lessons."

"Well, then it is something else."

"It's a diary. All Japanese keep diaries."

"Yes, it's nice to keep a diary, and then you can remember happy things."

"Please let me see the happy things you've written."

She pushed the book quickly under the pillow and leant on top.

"No, it is very private and secret."

"You're not allowed to have private things from me."

"It is only you it is private from."

"You must let me see it," I said.

"No, you are going fishing."

"What do you mean?"

"That is the sentence that you taught me. You are going fishing after salmon. You think you are going to find nice compliments written about you."

"That's it. I want to make sure that you're really in love with me."

"I tell you, and that is enough for you to make sure. I love you always, darling, from bottom of heart, and that is enough because it is all I can do. And now I want you please to tell me about Mr. Scaife. Did you think he was nice man?"

"I think he's rather odd," I said.

"Did you talk to him about Sabby?"

"Just a little."

"Please, what did he say?"

"He said he thought you were beautiful."

"No, he didn't say that. Please tell me what he said."

"He said it was his job to keep an eye on you."

"Please, did he say anything else?"

"Nothing of interest," I said.

"Oh yes, he did, and you are not telling me. Please tell what he said, and I will perhaps show you a little of diary."

"Honestly, there was nothing else."

"Darling, you are being mean."

"What else should he have said?"

"Nothing, but I am afraid he did say something."

"Why should you be afraid?"

She did not say anything, but her eyes were a little sad and she sniffed gently, and then turned over so that I could no longer see her face.

"What is it?" I said.

"Oh, darling, are you sure he did not say anything?"

"Really he didn't."

"Well, then, it doesn't matter."

"But now it does matter. If you don't explain I shall think all kinds of things."

"If I tell you, you won't want to love me any more."

"If it was something nasty, perhaps I shouldn't—though I might not be able to help it. But I don't believe it's anything nasty."

"Oh yes, it is. I always warned you, I am nasty."

"I don't believe it," I said.

"Yes, it is true. I am nasty, and you won't want to go on loving me."

We lay for a little while in silence. I didn't want to hear, and at the same time I knew that without hearing I should be miserable. At last I said:

"You will have to tell me."

"I always wanted to tell you," she said pathetically. "And now I don't want to, because it will spoil our lovely happiness. Please can't it wait?"

I would have said no, it cannot wait; but at that moment there was the sound of footsteps in the corridor, and we stopped talking and listened. I knew the footsteps were coming to Sabby's door; nevertheless, my heart leapt suddenly when we heard knocking. I thought: "Something terrible is going to happen, this is going to be the end. Our lovely happiness is over; it is fated. The knocking is all part of the end; it has been perfectly timed like a stage entry to elucidate the conversation. It is a landslide, and we are on it. We can't go back, or hold up time. We can't stop the knocking."

"What shall I do?" Sabby said. She was scared.

"Ask who it is?"

She called out in a small voice, and then again, louder. There was a reply in careful English. It was the porter.

"You are requested on the telephone."

"But it can't be me," Sabby said.

"It is a call for Miss Wei. It is a gentleman called Mr. Scaife. He says it is a matter of urgency."

Sabby was flustered. She did not know what to do, and I had never seen her look so unhappy. She shook her head and whispered:

"I'm not going."

"You had better go," I said. It was the landslide, and you cannot stop landslides once they have started.

"No," she said.

"You'd better go and see what he wants."

She hesitated. Then she climbed out under the mosquito-net

and found her kimono and slippers and went quickly out of the room.

I lay and wondered whether I could bring myself to get up and go back to my hotel. This was the end. If I stayed there would have to be tedious explanations, and fuss, and I should have to play a part in the scene and be angry, or resigned and understanding; and I should have to say some sort of embarrassed goodbye. And I didn't want a scene, I didn't really feel at all angry. I just felt immensely crushed and injured, because a few minutes ago I had been up in the sky and insanely happy, and all of a sudden I had dropped to earth. I didn't know exactly what had happened —I should have to work it out later—but the sense of fatality in me was overwhelming, and my heart told me unanswerably that everything was finished.

It would be easiest in the long-run if I went now. But I knew I hadn't the courage to walk out like that, and instead I took off my bush shirt and got underneath the sheet and lay waiting, pretending to be half-asleep. Leave it for tonight, I thought : pretend it doesn't matter. Go to sleep, and see what happens tomorrow.

In a minute or two Sabby returned. She came and got into bed, and when she was in she said :

"He was awfully drunk."

"Oh yes."

She nestled up to me, and kissed me tentatively.

"Darling," she said, plaintively, "don't you love Sabby any more?"

"Why not?" I said drowsily. "But I think perhaps I'm a little drunk, too."

"Please kiss once," she said.

I turned over and did so. It was not a good kiss, because kissing is very hard to pretend to do, like looking happy.

"Thank you," she said, and she did not look at all happy.

"Good night," I said.

"Good night."

It was a long time before I went to sleep. I had really drunk a lot of whisky, and all the different scenes of the evening were whirling in my brain. Even when I was asleep they were whirling. I cannot remember my dream, but somewhere in it there were Lala Vikrana's eyes, and Mr. Munshi's smile and his *dhoti*, and Mr. Scaife sitting cross-legged on the carpet—and there was also Sabby.

CHAPTER IV

I

I DID not look forward to Sabby's class next day. Even then it was a worse ordeal than I had expected. It was the only one of her classes in which I had ever longed for the end.

She came in, looking miserable. When someone made a joke she tried to laugh, and it was no more like her gay, tinkling laugh than a sob would have been. She did not look at me at all, and when she asked me a question she kept her eyes on the book that she held in her hand. She spoke in a very quiet, solemn way, and I gave sepulchral replies, and we were both meticulously polite.

Afterwards as I left the school I came across Sabby on the steps. She did not say she was waiting for me, but for a ghari. A ghari came up, and she said :

"Here it is."

"Yes," I said.

"Would you like me to drop you anywhere?"

"It doesn't matter. I have to pick up something at the Cricket Club, and it's only a few yards."

"Oh yes," she said softly. She was looking away down the road, and I couldn't see her face.

"Peter's organised a party. I promised to go tonight."

"Oh yes."

There was a silence and somebody brushed past down the steps, but she did not look round at him. She waited a moment, and then said, "You must enjoy yourself." And still without looking round at me she went quickly down to the waiting carriage and got in and was driven away.

I did not go to the Cricket Club, because I had nothing there to collect. I had invented the excuse from some perversity, wanting all the time to go with Sabby and dreading the evening without her. I did not quite understand what all my own feelings were about; the events of the night before were confused, and I did not try to go over them, or to make clear to myself what they meant. But they had left their impression, like a stone that crashes through a window and rolls out of sight, leaving a visible trail of shattered glass; and I did not run after the stone to examine it because I could not bear to do so.

I had not invented the story of the party Peter had organised. He had been planning it for a long time, and it was to include Lamb and his girl, Mervyn and Mario, and Mario's beautiful girl friend. And of course, there was to be Rosie. It was really in honour of Rosie, who had proved herself a social asset and a queen of landladies; and for her sake and the sake of making the party bizarre, Peter was willing to forgo the Taj. We were to dine at an Indian restaurant, and it was going to be awfully bizarre. It was to help make it bizarre that Lamb's girl had been invited; for Lamb's girl was one of the fair creatures whom Rosie had whipped from under the noses of the Japanese in Rangoon.

Mario's friend was the lovely girl whom he had met at the race-course, very blonde and Nordic, and slender as a palm. You could imagine her in jodhpurs mounting a horse before the ivy-covered frontage of an English country house; or at a Hunt Ball, still a little wind-swept but perfumed and dressed exquisitely, behaving independently yet without losing her femininity. And now, with the superbly handsome Mario by her side, it was like a picture out of *The Tatler*. Nobody could help remarking how perfectly charming they looked as a pair.

Her name was Dorcas. Rosie's protégée was called Sandra, because Sandra is a Spanish name, and that was what she almost looked and what she sometimes found was the best thing to pretend to be. She was a Eurasian, at the height of her Eurasian beauty, which is as much as to say that she was young, perhaps eighteen or nineteen. Her hair and eyes were dark and her lips a deep red in vivid and provocative contrast, and her nostrils were wide and inquiring like a colt's.

Half the fun of the party was to see how she and Dorcas would react to one another, and to avoid misunderstanding Dorcas had been told of Sandra's past. She didn't mind; on the contrary, in common with Peter she liked the bizarre. And Mario had reported her to have said, "But for the grace of God . . ." She knew it was only by chance that she had been born of English parents, with a silver spoon in her mouth.

The two of them were the high spirits. Between them there was a kind of good-humoured mutual respect.

"I've got a new frock," Sandra said. "Is it nice, do you think?"

"But it is quite the nicest thing I've seen in India. I wish I knew where to get such gorgeous clothes."

"I'll show you where I got it, if you like."

"Oh please, won't you?"

And then later Sandra said:

"I wonder what it's like to be you? I can't imagine it. What do your people do?"

"My father's in the Army."

"I think mine was. I don't know."

"It's awful to have fathers in the Army. People who haven't got fathers in the Army don't understand, do they? One is somehow quite different."

"You do all right, though, don't you?" Sandra said.

"It depends on what you mean by all right."

"Oh, you get around."

"Don't you?"

"In a different way, I suppose."

"I often think it doesn't matter much which way you get around," Dorcas said. "There are always good things and always bad things, and they usually even out."

"I'm not complaining. Life's all right when you get the hang of it. Got to take what comes to you."

"Sandra's a good gairl," Rosie said. "A very good gairl, aren't you, my dear?"

"Oh, I'm all right," Sandra said.

"I think Mr. Lamb's very lucky to be liked by Sandra. You don't care that much for everyone, do you, my dear?"

"Who said I cared for Johnnie?"

"You're mad about him, anybody can see it."

"I never get mad about people, not any more than I get mad at them. I've got too used to them. Johnnie's got money, that's the only thing."

"Don't take any notice of her, Johnnie. She's crazy about you. She knows you haven't got any money."

"I haven't got any money," Lamb said.

"Maybe you can't get gold," Sandra said. She held up her wrist round which there was a bangle. "But so long as it glitters, who cares. Brass, any old thing, I don't care."

"Not so long as you've got that pretty face," Rosie said.

"Oh hell, that'll all go to pieces before long. Would you mind telling me what you do about your face?" she said to Dorcas. "Girls like you look practically the same at fifty."

"That might be a backhanded compliment!"

"Oh, I meant it the right way. You'll look twenty-five when

you're fifty, from across the room. I'd give up Johnnie and all his brass bangles to be like that."

"That's what you'd have to do, my dear," Rosie said.

"Dorcas doesn't have to give up her Mario, and she's got a bangle too. You see, she won't look like a jade at fifty. I'll be an awful jade, if I'm not dead. But perhaps I shall be dead."

"It's not the bangle," said Rosie. "It's the soul. Dorcas has got a sweet soul."

"Haven't I got one?"

"You've got one all right now—a very sweet soul. But what counts is still having one when you're fifty."

"Have you still got a soul?"

"I'm not quite fifty."

"Rosie's got a soul all right," Peter said. "She's got an angelic soul and she's quite certain to go to heaven."

"I don't think so," Rosie said. "There are too many entries on the debit side. I'm going to be burnt, and the only thing I pray for is that it'll be over quickly. I always think it will be. God won't waste His time taking vengeance, He'll just want to get rid of you."

"I'm not afraid of hell fire," Peter said. "This curry is like hell fire inside me, and I'm going on eating it. It's so delicious that I don't care how hot it is. Please pass me some more."

After dinner we went back to the hotel. We walked through the streets, talking loudly as though we had already had something to drink. I was perhaps talking more loudly than usual in order to make myself forget Sabby's expression on the steps of the school (I said to myself, 'to forget Sabby's expression'—and then I remembered that I had not actually seen the expression on her face, but must have imagined it only from the tone of her voice and the movement of her head as she turned it away from me). At the hotel we found two or three bottles of whisky and a bottle of gin, and took them down to Rosie's sitting-room. Sandra sat on Lamb's knee, and Mario and Dorcas sat together on the sofa, trying to conceal the fact that they were very much in love. Mervyn flopped into an easy chair. There were heavy lines down the sides of his face and blue smudges under his eyes, and he kept a morose silence despite the drinks he had consumed. He had been becoming daily more neurotic, though we never knew how much of this was genuine and how much of it feigned. A month ago he had said, "You see, I shall be out of India in six months—

things are going all right." But now when I asked him flippantly, "How are the neuroses coming along, Mervyn?" he turned on me angrily and said, "That's a pretty tactless thing to say, isn't it?" He was still certain he would spend his next summer in Sloane Square.

"I must really get myself a girl," Peter said to me, when the party had got going well enough for a little private conversation to become possible. "You've all got yourselves fixed up."

"That's a frightful expression," I said. "Getting 'fixed up'—as though it was a question of getting a bicycle or a furnished room."

"Well, isn't it like that? One has got to get fixed up with a roof over one's head, and food, and a woman, and then one is complete. You can't really do without these things and say you're living."

"You've never been in love," I said.

"I don't suppose I have. What's that got to do with it?"

"You don't usually go around talking about 'getting fixed up' then."

"It's very fatherly wisdom. Have you ever been in love?"

"I don't know."

"I thought people always knew about these things."

"Well, I have been in love," I said.

"Who with?"

"Some woman in England."

"You don't sound as though you loved her very much."

"That's all she is now, some woman. I believe she's got rather fat and produced a child, and has to do all the washing-up and cleaning of silver because she can't get any help."

"But did you love her very much?"

"I still love her in a way, but only because I can still think of her as I did when she was younger. The plump woman with the infant and the greasy crockery is someone else altogether—quite a stranger to me. Rather more of a stranger than someone that one meets for the first time, because somehow when this kind of thing happens there's a chasm between you that can never be bridged. I don't want to bridge it in the least, anyway. Only it's curious that she can go on living in your mind as the person that she was."

"Well," Peter said, "who else have you been in love with?"

"A nasty, flashy little typist."

"I don't believe it."

"It's true. I bought a sports car so that I could take her out into the country, and I hate sports cars."

"You were just getting fixed up. There you are, you see, it's exactly the same thing. You get fixed up just the same as anyone else, but you think it's a little shameful to get fixed up without clouding the vulgar carnal act with a nice decorous haze of love. You think you're not romantic, and you bandy about all these names like Freud and Havelock Ellis like a between wars undergraduate, and it's nauseating, because if you were honest you'd read Ouida. You're a romantic, and you'd better admit it; otherwise you've no right to object to my saying 'fixed up'. Personally I think you've fixed yourself up excellently, and I suppose you've been able to do it by means of your smoke haze."

"I'm not fixed up so well as you think," I said. "It's so easy to get lost in a smoke haze."

"I hate talking in riddles. Anyway, the point is I'm not fixed up, and I'm very jealous, because Dorcas is without doubt the loveliest girl in India, and Mario will marry her, or at any rate he'll be an idiot if he doesn't. And also Sandra's a beautiful girl, and Lamb is lucky to have her."

"You accuse me of pretending," I said. "But if anybody's pretending, it's you. You're really bristling with principles."

"I haven't got any principles. Look at this book I'm writing. If I had principles I wouldn't write a book about a dead body and the unspeakably boring attempts to find out who made the bullet hole in the head. I'm writing it because I can't write anything good, and because I haven't got fixed up with a woman, and because I hope it'll bring me at least a thousand pounds, excluding film rights."

"I think we're both getting a little drunk," I said.

"Yes, that's it, we're getting drunk. I've been very rude, haven't I?"

"You only said I ought to read Ouida."

"Oh, then I'm not so very drunk. But you know, I'm only rude because you're a great friend, and great friends are the only people you can be rude to without feeling bad about it."

"I'm very glad that's how you feel."

"As a matter of fact, I would like to be rude a little more. Would you mind very much?"

"Please go ahead," I said.

"It's only that I'm curious. I've wanted to ask you when I'm sober, but I haven't had the courage. I think whisky is wonderful stuff; it can make you so personal. But I would hate you to mind."

"I shan't mind."

"It's about your charming Hanako. Please won't you tell me if you were her first lover?"

"I don't think so," I said.

"Thank you very much. It was rude of me, wasn't it?"

"No," I said. "It wasn't rude at all."

Suddenly there was Rosie's voice:

"I think it was very rude."

She smiled at us kindly. There was a lot of cigarette smoke in the room, and the wireless was playing softly. Lamb and Sandra were making love in their chair, and Mario and Dorcas were whispering and smiling and being happy.

"But then it was also rude of me to overhear you," Rosie said. "I've been listening to all your conversation, because the young people are busy together and Mervyn is drinking too much whisky and won't say sweet things to me. So I have heard about your 'fixing things up'. I am so amused."

"There you are," I said to Peter. "Why don't you get fixed up with Rosie? There is nothing wrong with Rosie."

"I wouldn't dare try," Peter said.

"Oh, am I such a dragon?"

"No, you're not a dragon, though you're very exciting. You're a little too exciting, and I'm a bit afraid of you. I think I'd better just be your lodger."

"You see, he thinks I am too old to fix up. It's a dreadful shame. Perhaps when he has drunk a little more he will no longer see my wrinkles."

We could not drink much more because we had almost exhausted our stock. We were not really drunk. I went out of the room quite steadily, and when I returned Sandra and Lamb had gone. Dorcas was saying goodbye. I don't know whether she had drunk less than us, or whether she had a good head, but she was perfectly composed. Mario went off with her to find a ghari and take her home. Mervyn murmured thanks and good-nights and disappeared out of the front door, because he usually spent most of the night roaming the streets. Peter and I remained. We smoked a cigarette and looked at the empty glasses and bottles

and the ash-trays full of squashed cigarette ends, and talked de-
sultorily, and I wondered if Peter was waiting for me to go, because Rosie's wrinkles were negligible, and her age was not more
than thirty-five, and she reclined on the couch with a feminine
litheness, a passive confidence like a tigress that knows itself all-
powerful and waits for certain prey.

"I'm going to bed," he said. "Are you coming?"

I hesitated. I did not know what I was going to do; until I
heard my own voice say:

"I will stay for a bit."

"Good night," Peter said. "It was a grand party. Good night."
He went.

"Well?" Rosie said. She smiled sleepily.

"Well?" I did not move from my chair. I finished my cigarette
and stubbed out the end, and all the time we did not say anything,
because there was nothing to say that was not said by the silent
tension.

Then she shifted her leg a fraction of an inch, and I got up as
though it was a signal and sat down where her body curved away
from the edge of the sofa. I put the tips of my fingers on the
white-brown flesh of her arm, and the effect of this touch ran like
a flood through my body. I began to kiss her, and she was quite
submissive, quite passive, and all the time the smile was on her
face. She did not respond. I kissed her with more urgent passion,
trying to draw out of her more kisses and more passion to mingle
with mine. But her lips only smiled, and her body held its latent
fire.

I did not understand. Without fuel, and insulted, my sudden
passion diminished. I lay still. She was also still for a moment, as
if to make sure this burst of energy was exhausted; and then perfectly gently she pushed me away from her so that I was once
more sitting up.

"What's the matter?" I said.

"What is the matter with you?"

"You were asking for this," I said.

She began to laugh.

"That is true."

"Well?"

"I don't care to have my throat cut."

"What do you mean?"

"I mean, my dear, that already you have a nice girl friend. I

124

have heard all about your Hanako. Peter has told me. He has not told anyone else, but he has told me."

I got up from the sofa and found a cigarette. I had been smoking all evening and there was a dry fur in my mouth. Rosie extended her hand for a cigarette, too, so I gave her the one I had lighted and took another one for myself. I thought I had been made a fool of, and felt an angry shame.

"Go on," I said.

"Michael, dear, how may I talk to you when you are stamping about like a liverish schoolmaster? Please come and sit down once more."

I went back to the sofa reluctantly. She lifted one of my hands and held it in her own.

"Please let me tell you that it is not often now that I have pleasure, and I would have liked you so much to make love to me. If it had been Peter I should have perhaps made love to him, too, because he is a nice boy and now it would be good for him. But for you it is not so good, and I don't need fun so badly that I must make you unhappy."

"Why did you lead me on like that?"

"I dare say it was a matter of my pride. I would like to think I may still make a nice boy lose his head for a minute over me. But you are also a silly boy. Your Hanako is a sweet and good girl. Peter has said so. Very sweet and beautiful, he said."

"If you don't mind," I said, "I think I'd better go to bed."

"Soon I shall let you."

"I'm going now," I said. "I don't want to talk about Hanako."

"If you don't want to talk, it is because you are afraid."

"You don't know anything about it. Nor does Peter."

"I think I know. You are afraid."

"Afraid of what?"

"You are just afraid to face things."

"There are many things that are not worth while facing."

"Oh yes, it is always so easy to say that. It is easy to go through life and say nothing is worth while to face—but it is not a good life."

I withdrew my hand from hers and got up again. My cigarette was not finished, but the end was greasy from the perspiration of my fingers. I threw it away and took another.

"You know," Rosie said, "you could perhaps make someone very happy."

125

"What did you say?"

"I said if only you were a little less selfish . . ."

"Good God!" I said. "Why does everyone tell me that? It's what the yogi said. I'm not a charitable institution."

"But you have a charitable heart. Only it is not always that you remember it. It is for yourself that it is bad when you forget."

"And it was uncharitable of me to make love to you?"

"Yes, my dear. It was uncharitable to yourself. It would have made you very unhappy."

"It might have done a week ago. Circumstances change."

"But not people. People don't change, not as quickly as that."

"Oh, stop all this," I said irritably.

"You had better first of all tell me what is the matter."

I pulled at my cigarette and began to walk about the room. I wanted to break off the conversation and leave; but to have done so would have been an admission of my own weakness.

"Something happened between me and Hanako."

"What was that?"

"I don't know."

"It is not like you to be so silly."

"Well," I said, "you know how atmospheres change."

"Please do not say 'atmosphere'. That is not being honest. What was it?"

"I was jealous. I hate being jealous, and I'm not going to waste my time on it."

"So you ran away."

"Yes."

"You ran away because you had a nasty little pain."

"Before it got worse," I said.

"And perhaps before you had looked into it carefully?"

"Yes."

"Then it may be that it is all a mistake."

"It may be."

"Now we are beginning to find out interesting things. It may be a mistake, and you are not going to try to make sure. And all the time you are perhaps hurting someone a great deal. Don't you think it sounds very funny?"

"Yes, and where does it get us?"

"I think it gets us to a reason for your all of a sudden wishing to kiss an old Eurasian housekeeper."

"Shut up," I said.

"Yes, but it is true. You are afraid to be in love with a girl who is sweet and kind, and you take the first chance to run away. You pretend it is not yourself from whom you are running away; and you make words about atmospheres and circumstances changing, and you throw yourself at someone you don't really care about so that you can blame yourself. That makes everything easier, because you don't really want to blame the sweet Hanako."

"Very well," I said. "You may be right. I'm afraid to love her. But mightn't that be a good thing? She's Japanese and I'm English, and there's a war. Don't you think I'm right to be afraid?"

"My dear, that is your affair, you know."

"You've uncovered the problem. Couldn't you solve it?"

"Do you think that if I said this or that, it would be a solution? Now off with you and go to bed, or I shall start once again trying to make love to you, and afterwards you would have to leave this house because in the morning you would see I am rather old and worn. You would be embarrassed—that is the kind of person you are. Go to bed quickly, and forget everything; and if you are now being honest with yourself, soon you will know whether you are right to be afraid."

I left Rosie, but I did not go to bed. I went out and began to walk aimlessly about the streets; and somewhere else Mervyn was walking the streets because he hated India and was thinking how he might escape. I did not go out to think but because I knew that in bed I could not help thinking, and my thoughts would be hopelessly confused. Walking, I did not have to think. After the air of Rosie's room, the night seemed fresh. I looked at the lights and the dim, fantastic façades of the buildings, and the heaps of rags on the pavements that were sleeping human beings. I went along Marine Drive past the school. The lights of Malabar Hill hung over the bay like a crown of stars, their reflection a jewelled necklace in the sea below. What beauty there was in this great city— and what squalor! Here the fan-cooled luxury of expensive flats, and somewhere behind them the verminous chawls; here books and typewriters and gin and easy chairs, and there smoking cooking stoves and urinating children. The Taj Hotel, and the smelly streets of cages . . . and everywhere men and women reproducing their species, sometimes crudely, sometimes with infinite complexity. And not only in Bombay. All over the world, kings and dustmen, lawyers and sheep-farmers, all like marionettes on nature's strings. And what an endless laugh nature was having, peeping between covers of books and into theatres, into parks and flats and hovels and palaces, to see how seriously and with what variety its simple theme was being played. And the words, the millions of words spun round it. . . .

Stop thinking, I said to myself; you are always thinking. Stop it and use your eyes. You will find out what is good for you without thinking. Go on walking in the good night air. Look at the stars, if you like, look at the vast universe, and go on looking until you know that it is bigger than yourself, bigger than the Taj, and the Gateway of India, bigger than India itself and the world. Bigger than all your own conventions and prejudices, bigger than life. And go on walking. . . .

I don't know how long it was that I went on walking. But when at last, without thinking, I went to Sabby, I know that I was immensely tired.

II

I thought I had never loved her so much. We clung together until our bodies had melted together and my heart was beating with hers, and when she sobbed I sobbed with her. We cried and dozed; and when it was dawn we were wide awake, and we took cigarettes and talked and knew that we were very much in love.

I told her about Rosie and she kissed me softly; and afterwards she talked about herself.

"I wanted to tell you to begin with. It was wicked not to tell, but I was afraid you wouldn't love me. Please now will you promise not to stop loving, because I don't think I could bear it."

"I promise," I said. "But you needn't tell me if you don't want. I don't mind any more—it couldn't make any difference."

"Perhaps it does make difference, and I am so ashamed."

But of course what she told me made no difference at all, unless it was to make me love her more. And if for nothing else, I could have adored her for the way she told the story with a funny forced brightness and tears in her eyes.

"You see, I was still at school when it was decided I must marry Japanese friend of my father's. I thought he was very horrid, and I simply couldn't bear to be even in the same room. I was such obstinate little donkey! I was not like my mother at all. She was always so kind and patient, and oh so much she had suffered! It was not my mother who wanted me to marry, because she loved me too much. It was my father, who wanted to make a nice business arrangement. And when I refused for the third time, he became very stern and said that I was bringing shame upon the family by selfish behaviour, and that even for the sake of my mother I must do as he told. My mother used to cry a lot, but she also told me I must marry. I used to think then that she was crying because I was bad and didn't want to marry. But afterwards I found it was because she also didn't want me to, and it was only duty that made her support my father."

"But you never married?" I said.

"No, darling, I didn't marry. Perhaps I should have married for the sake of my mother, if the nasty thing hadn't happened. I loved my mother very much. I hadn't loved anyone else but my mother, and when my father said that it was for her happiness that I must marry I gave him a promise to try to make up my mind. Sometimes we went to the theatre with the man I was supposed to marry, and sometimes he would come to the house. Always there was someone else with us, until once on purpose my father left us alone to walk in the garden at night. . . .

"Oh, darling, if that had been with you! In Japanese garden at night it is so beautiful with little funny bridges over rock pools, and the moon so round and handsome! I think in Japanese garden you would love me twice as much as in Indian hotel. Only I should not like you to be in Japanese garden with anyone else, because I don't think I should trust you to remember Sabby."

"Didn't the Japanese garden make you want to marry?"

"No, because you see I couldn't think once of garden, only of how much I wanted to be with my mother and how I hated Japanese man. But now I knew it was a *shikata-ga-nai* thing— there was nothing to be done. I let him take me into the summer-house among the trees, and he began to make love to me. . . . Darling, do you think there is need for me to go on?"

"No," I said. "You needn't go on."

"But I think, after all, I had better! I love you so much I want to tell you exactly. You see, I was only eighteen, and nobody had told me what happened when people made love. I thought because my father had sent us into the garden together that this must be what he expected me to do. It was so horrible that I screamed; and then the man I was supposed to marry put his hand over my mouth, and after that I don't remember anything until I was lying in my bed and my mother was beside me in tears. She was so terribly miserable! She thought it had all been her fault, and it made me sicker than ever to see her, because she was the gentlest and sweetest person in all the world. It was such a shock to everyone that my father sent us away for a holiday to the mountains. I don't think he ever quite forgave me for what had happened, because I had behaved so badly and hurt his business; but he did not try any more to make me marry. Afterwards he took us to England, and all the rest I have told you quite truly. I am sorry I did not tell you truly at first, but now you will understand why I never wanted to go back to Japan. In England everyone was good to me, and Lord Durweston was the kindest man I had ever met. Until I met you, darling—only now I think you will not want to love me any more."

I was so moved by the pathetic expression in her eyes and the funny, cheerful smile that she kept on her lips that I could find no words in which to reassure her—and I tried to do so instead with caresses, and by taking her nose between my teeth, and repeating those other familiar little actions that belonged to us and no one else.

Afterwards I asked her about Mr. Scaife and why she was afraid of him; and she told me what I had already guessed, that he too had tried to make love to her, in a furious access of un-yogi-like passion. She had been able to resist; but he had pestered her with a series of letters and 'phone calls which showed the curious unbalanced state of his mind. I found myself feeling sorry for him; and at the same time I felt, not elation at having succeeded where he had failed, but a deep humility—because I knew I had no qualities to make me deserving of Sabby's love.

"And that is all, darling," she said. "Now there is not anything about me that you don't know."

"No," I said. "Not about the past. But what about the future? Do you want to go back to Japan when the war's over?"

"Darling, I don't know. Please don't let us think about after war."

"Some time we shall have to think about it."

"You can think about what you will do after war."

"I shall have to think of you, too."

"No, please don't worry about me, I don't want you ever to think of that. I only want you to love me now whilst we are together, and then afterwards you may go and love who you like.

You may go and love Rosie, darling, and I won't mind. Only please don't love her now, not just for the time being whilst you are loving me."

"I shall always love you and worry about you," I said.

"No, darling, please don't think that. You will never have to marry me. You will hate me if you think I shall always hold on to you. I only want you to give me a little happiness, and then I will let you go. Please remember, darling, always. Whatever happens, you will never have to marry me."

"All right," I said. "I shall try to remember that."

CHAPTER V

I

FROM the middle of June we had thirty-one days' leave. The monsoon was due to break at any moment over Bombay, but we got away in time. We had booked an air-conditioned coach on the Frontier Mail; and although I have always had a childish excitement before starting on a holiday, I have never climbed into a train with such a wonderful sense of happiness and relief.

For weeks past, like children, we had been counting the minutes—multiplying the days by twenty-four, and again by sixty, and that was exactly how long we had to wait, in the only unit of time that was bearable to count. The days themselves went too slowly. A month in the Himalayas with Sabby still seemed to me to be something too marvellous to come about; yet it was the only thing in the future that mattered, and there was no future beyond it. After I had made the reservations I kept taking the receipts from my pocket and reading over and over again every dull word that was printed on them, because they were the only tangible evidence that our idea was more than a dream. And the minutes went by. We lay together and knocked five, ten, twenty off the total. It was good practice for counting in Japanese, because now I was making myself use the language with Sabby.

And then I was waiting on the station. I was early. I had brought a whole battery of thermoses, full of cold drinks and tea, and more fruit than we could possibly have consumed in a week. I had also bought some flowers, arranging them in a jar in the compartment; and a camera, and a tin of Flit, and volumes of books that I knew I should never read. There was also Bahadur. A week before I had told Bahadur that I was in love, and he had said, "Michael Sahib is loving since Miss Wei is in the school"; and it was clever of him, because I had never spoken of it before. Or perhaps it was not so clever, and perhaps he and Peter and Mervyn and Rosie were not the only ones who knew. But what did it matter . . .? For the next month we should be far away by ourselves, and Bahadur didn't mind, he was willing to come. "It is your honeymoon," he said, and he would not call it anything else but honeymoon, although he knew we had not been married. "Because it is your honeymoon, it is necessary that I am with you. By yourself you will drink bad water, and that will be the end of the honeymoon before it is time."

Until Sabby turned up on the platform, I was still afraid that something would go wrong. I had rung her up twenty minutes before when she was on the point of leaving her hotel; but I thought anything might happen—an accident, a broken leg or a last-minute interruption by Scaife. Fate was jealous; it would surely not allow us this happiness.

But Sabby came. She was punctual to the minute. She came with her excitement restrained, and all she said was, "Hullo" very softly, and I also said "Hullo". And then we got into the carriage, and she too had brought thermoses and fruit and boxes of expensive sweets, and she had brought a present for me, a pipe, because I had always said I would take to smoking one instead of cigarettes. It was touching; but what was more touching still because of the thoughtfulness was the tobacco and the packet of white wire pipe-cleaners, and a little gadget for pressing down the tobacco. This also included a cigar-end slicer, and since Sabby could not give a present that was not entirely complete, she had added a cigar. Whilst I was still discovering these, one after the other, the train began to move; and this was the moment we had longed for, and there were no more minutes to count. It was not disappointing. I looked at Sabby and I looked out of the window where the suburbs of Bombay were slipping away, and I tried to savour the moment, because I did not think that in all my life it could ever be repeated.

We went to bed early that night. We lay on the narrow bunk and could only faintly distinguish the sounds when the train stopped in a station, because the carriage was almost sound-proof. It is great fun to go to sleep in comfort on a train, thinking that you will wake up hundreds of miles away; and the first peep out of the window in the morning is exciting. I have been told that it is childish excitement, and that the time comes—as it does in a similar way with so many things—when you no longer bother to peep out immediately you awake; but without some of these childish things life would become dull. However, it always intensifies fun if it is shared, and this was the first time I had shared this particular experience. It was like a new experience altogether. When I got up that morning I felt wonderfully well, and ate with relish the breakfast that Bahadur brought. Sabby stayed in bed and drank tea, and I learnt two Japanese words meaning to lie in bed late in the morning so that I was able to tease her.

During the morning we stopped at a station where there was an awning stretching across the platform. The train pulled in slowly so that a special carriage stopped opposite the awning, and then we waited a long time. When we started off again I saw the name of the station as we passed, and it was Dhanapore. I thought the awning must have been for the Nawab, with whom I had been at school, so I sent Bahadur off to find out if he was on the train. He had never been sent to inquire about a Nawab before, and in his mind this must have made up for my numberless deficiencies as a *pukka sahib*. He came back and said that the Nawab was indeed there, so I sent him back with a note, though he was almost too overcome with excitement to carry out this mission. It was not until the next stop that a letter came back, on fine crested paper and in an elegant hand, asking if I would do the Nawab the honour of lunching in his coach. I was not going to desert Sabby on this important day, and I replied that I had my wife with me. Another invitation came for both of us.

I was not sure how to address him, whether it should be 'Your Highness' or 'Your Excellency', but at any rate it could not be 'old Dhanapore', which is what he had usually been called at school, in the days before he had succeeded his father. When it came to the point, however, it didn't matter at all, and my practice bows in my own carriage were wasted, because he shook me by the hand. He said, "I'm awfully pleased. Have you heard from Miss McCance, and if she is well?" Miss McCance was the Scotch matron at the school, who had always looked after him, hiding her awed respect for his rank behind a grim disciplinary façade.

His own wife was also present, and she had done us the honour —or perhaps it was the opposite—of discarding her purdah veil.

133

She was a beautiful girl of not more than nineteen, with a sleek river of black hair that flowed from her forehead and fell swiftly down her back. She had a small body and tiny hands, and was built delicately and perfectly, like Sabby. They sat next to each other, and were exactly the same height, and if they had not been of different nationalities, one would have said they were twins. I saw at once that there was an immediate bond of sympathy between them. They looked at each other frankly and smiled, and as soon as we two men had fallen to talking about school and raking up old incidents and names, they also began to whisper, as intimately as if they too had been friends before. I began to think of the times at home when my father had invited a friend from the golf club, or a business friend, asking him to bring his wife to dinner; and whilst the men had sat over their cigars, my mother would establish a quick friendship with the wife, discussing things of mutual feminine interest. I would probably be in bed, or else hanging over the landing banisters trying to catch bits of the conversation. And now, half a generation later, I had an adult rôle in a similar sort of scene, on the other side of the earth, with an Indian potentate, and his wife who did not go shopping in Tewkesbury with a big wicker basket, but who saw the world only through a mesh of finely worked lace—and with a Japanese girl whom I loved.

A servant produced whisky. He brought it from a trunk that opened to become a cocktail cabinet, glittering with fittings like an expensive bar. Lunch came from another trunk, even more opulently equipped. I had heard of Maharajahs' picnics, and this was it, with all the plates show-pieces and the food prepared decoratively in palace kitchens, looking like a display in a Lyons Corner House foyer. I had the instinct to say, 'But you do not expect us, you will not have enough for yourselves.' But one did not observe such politeness to Nawabs when there was manifestly enough food for a whole Indian village.

Whilst we were talking about old times, we were schoolboys again in grey flannel trousers and open-necked shirts. And then we exhausted these reminiscences and were suddenly ourselves once more—he the Nawab who was very pro-British and I an officer on leave from Bombay. He became more distant, though still suave and polite. I listened to him with fascination. He talked about agriculture and the government, and after that about the war, and then about the people of his State. He talked about them with the benevolence of someone who is conscious that he has the power to chop off their heads. I looked at the embossed silver finishings of the cocktail trunk, and wondered whether I should like to possess it; but I thought I did not care about it so long as I possessed Sabby, and if he were to ask us to stay in his palace, I would rather have Sabby alone in the cool, remote mountains. But he did not ask us to stay. He gave me a grey hand to shake, and he said wouldn't I kindly 'look him up' some time; and his pretty wife shook hands warmly with Sabby, her eyes quite steady and beautiful, and Sabby's black lashes fluttering happily. We returned to our carriage and had tea out of railway crockery, and because we were thinking of the same things, Sabby said:

"Darling, when you make journey would you rather have cocktail cabinet than Sabby?"

I said: "Yes," but she knew I meant 'No', and when she pretended to sniff sadly I also knew that I had never seen her look less sad. And I asked her:

"Would you rather have a holiday with an Indian prince who could give you jewels the size of blackbird's eggs—or with a poor British officer who can't even give you a nice ring to put on your finger?"

"I don't like jewels," Sabby said. "Couldn't Indian prince give something else?"

"Oh yes. He could set you riding on a gorgeously caparisoned elephant."

"I don't understand caparisoned, but I should like to have elephant."

"Perhaps I will find you an old elephant that is going cheap."

"Please, darling. That would be lovely."

"But really, it is true, you know. I couldn't even afford to buy you a ring with a decent stone. I've got hardly any money."

"Do you wish you had lots of money?"

"Yes, I'd like to have shares in gold-mines, and chemical industries, and Woolworths. It would make the morning papers much more interesting."

"Then you would only be interested in the dull columns of figures and you would not care about me. I am glad you have hardly got any money."

"Wouldn't you like just one ring? I might save up enough money for that, and then people would think we were really married."

"I don't mind what people think."

"Not really?"

"No, darling. Not except you."

"You know what I think," I said.

"I tell myself that I do, because that is the only way that I can be happy. I do hope that I am right, and that it is not just that you are being kind to me."

"There's no need to worry about that," I said.

That evening we reached Delhi, and when we got out of the train the temperature was about 100 degrees. At Bombay it had never been so hot as that at night, and after the air-conditioned coach it was overpowering. We changed into a train on which there were no special coaches, only small fans that did no more than blow a stream of hot air into our faces. We lay on separate bunks because it was cooler, and thought of the Himalayas three hundred miles in front of us. I don't think we slept at all, although we drank a great deal of water, with which we had replenished our thermoses. Bahadur had given his licence for this operation to be carried out at Delhi, which was one of the few places where the water could be relied upon. The next morning, we had another change, and by lunch-time we were at the foothills. I had not seen any mountains since my convalescence up at Simla, and after the flatness of Bombay, and the plains of the Jumna and the Ganges, the sight was exhilarating. We could not wait for the bus that would have taken us the last fifty miles. We said who cares, anyway, about rings with good stones or about Woolworth shares, we were going to have a car. It was an old car with a desperate driver, who went round corners like all native drivers do wherever there are precipices and horseshoe bends. I was scared because it was the beginning of the holiday, and I kept calling to the driver. But he only smiled and nodded his head and drove a little faster. It did not seem to trouble Sabby in the least. She rested her head against the tall back seat, and a smile played softly on her face. Her eyes were round and bright as she looked at the distant peaks that appeared and disappeared again as we swung round the corners. It became perceptibly cooler as we climbed noisily in gear. This new sun, brightening the mountains, might not have been the same one that was burning up the torrid land below. Here it shone down benevolently, creating instead of destroying, giving pleasure to your eyes instead of blinding. We put down the hood of the car, and the air was good. When you have breathed air that is like brackish water, you know that it is a good description to say that mountain air sparkles and is like champagne. Only this was not expensive and in bottles; it was champagne showered over us, champagne everywhere in lashings. It made us a little drunk.

It also made us ready for our tea when we arrived at Jali Tal.

II

It was Mr. Headley who had told us about Jali Tal. I had told him the kind of place I wanted, somewhere quiet and remote; and though I had not explained the reason, I knew that he guessed, because of the wise, understanding look that he gave me and because of the smile in his eyes that was not repeated by his mouth. He said, "Jali Tal is quite nice, quite nice. It's not like the usual Himalayan resort—no dancing there, you know."

If he had said it was Shangri La we should not have been disappointed. And because he had only said it was quite nice, and really it was a place of unimaginable beauty, we were speechless with delight, like a child who tears the paper from a Christmas parcel and is confronted by a wonderful toy he had never dreamed of possessing.

It was a lake set in the mountains. It might have been Switzerland, only instead of a single back-cloth of glittering peaks the mountains towered up one behind the other in an endless succession, each higher than the next, and a different colour, until somewhere in the distance, somewhere that was no longer the same world, the last visible range hung unbelievably in the sky. I have always wanted to climb mountains when I have seen them—but not these. These were not real, and when you are awake you cannot climb mountains that belong to a dream. They were like a mirage, like something that the atmosphere and the rays of the sun had concocted and from which we dare not take our eyes lest they should disappear. They were something that you could not look upon and think small things without shame, any more than you could be foul-mouthed in the depths of a cathedral.

There were only a dozen houses by the lake, and a mile away a native village. Our hotel was a hundred feet up, and from the windows of our two rooms the whole fantastic vista could be seen. Even there, not a third of the way to the snow-caps, we felt our spirits raised above the world of struggling humanity, as though a train fare and a few gallons of petrol had brought us to the state that Lala Vikrana would have had us attain by breathing exercises and chastity. Bahadur carried up tea to our sitting-room, and we sat at the window watching the colours change as the afternoon drew on, greens and lavenders and purples in a dozen hues, and the white crown glowing like mother-of-pearl. And when, the next morning, too late to see the dawn break, we gazed out again, the entire landscape had been washed by its night-bath and young sunbeams danced about the lake; and the mountains stood out in new attire like freshened giants, and above them, still, was the halo of dazzling snow. There was no end to the excitement of these transformations.

In the hotel there were a dozen other guests, all of them English except for a tall, cultured Indian whose name was Sir Ram Nath. If it had not been for the darkness of his skin and also of his eyes, he too might have been taken for an Englishman. He had been to Oxford and the Sorbonne, and he spoke of Devonshire and the South of France with something like nostalgia. Someone had once said to me, "Suspect any Indian with a title. He is a collaborator." But I liked Sir Ram at once. I liked him because of his very gentle toleration of things that were evil, as one so often likes people with a quality one is conscious of lacking. And I liked him for his sincerity and the good reason behind his convictions. Sometimes in the evenings I would let Sabby go first to bed, and I would have a night-cap with him and one of his cigars. He opened himself up to me only slowly; but as the time went by as I realised that, without using the same terms in which I had thought of it, he was teaching me the philosophy of gentleness of which I had caught a glimpse before. The philosophy that Sabby, using no words at all, was also teaching me. He taught me not to confuse gentleness which was love with gentleness which was only weakness.

Amongst the others in the hotel there was a mother with her two young girls, who had come up from Calcutta for the summer. She had another child, a son, at school at Winchester, and I thought she was like so many of the mothers whom I could remember would come down to my school at half-term to see their sons, and would sit watching the cricket match with a masculine interest. Only now I knew the interest was not really masculine, but a very feminine sympathy with the interests of their boys. This woman was of big build, and she wore a tweed skirt and strong shoes. She loved her son more than her daughters, perhaps because he was farther away; and perhaps due to that, as though to make up for it, she would do anything for the girls that they wanted. She went out of her way to show kindness to Sabby and myself, though with a kind of restraint as though she was afraid that we would think she was trying to interfere. I believe she was interested in me because I was English and, to her, young—two things in common with her son. And possibly she was imagining to herself her own son married to a Japanese, and thus making herself peculiarly sensitive to the difficulties, she wanted to help smooth them away. I don't think she ever suspected that we were not really married. We usually spoke Japanese together now, and this must have suggested that I had lived in Japan, and probably been married there. I could not talk about the real reason for my knowledge of the language.

We did not keep up the pretence that Sabby was Chinese. As Mr. Headley had said, there was no need. Everybody was good to her. I sometimes thought that they made too much fuss of her and I did not have her enough to myself; but also I was sufficiently human to feel a reflected glory in her success. The elevated atmosphere had not cured me of my earthly egotism.

We went riding. There were fine ponies there, sleek and strong and sure-footed as one would expect to find in that bold country. The two girls, ten and twelve, handled them fearlessly. They had been here every year since they could walk, and they had been given freedom here, and they knew the animals as they knew the natives and the trees and the valleys and the mountain-tops, and nothing frightened or deterred them. They might have been stranded somewhere all night, and they would have looked after themselves with the knowledge of the woodsman and the lack of superstition that was their Western inheritance. They taught us to ride. Or rather they left me to my own devices with only an occasional prompt, and circled round Sabby on their ponies, and lectured her with serious mature little faces, using technical words that she didn't understand. When she was bewildered they were patient like their own schoolmistresses, and explained in simple terms, helping each other out, as though they were themselves as old as the hills behind them and speaking to a child. Sabby nodded her head, and she was rather like a child, much more like one than them.

"This time, not pull rein so hard," Sabby said. When she was a little confused her English always deteriorated.

"I *won't* pull *the* rein so hard," the girls said in chorus, looking disapprovingly at me, because Sabby had told them that I did not bother to correct her English, and they had appointed themselves very seriously to this task.

"Oh dear," Sabby said. "I shall never learn. This pony is very angry with me because I am stupid."

"It *loves* you," said one of the girls.

"Do you really think so?"

"Of course it does. It thinks you are sweet, and so do we." I could not really see her face change colour from where I was, but I know that Sabby blushed. It touched her to be told this by the children. "But you must not let it think you are not firm with it, or it will try to show off. You must pretend to it that you know a lot about horses."

"How pretend?"

"You must make noises to it."

Sabby made a tentative clucking noise, and said, "Come on, nice pony." I wanted to laugh with delight, because it was charming the way she said it, and she did not think the pony was nice at all now she was sitting on top of it. But Margaret, who was the eldest, gave me a quick, silencing look, and Jennifer, without twitching a muscle, gave her official approval. Of course their psychology was faultless, and in half an hour Sabby was trotting about looking happy and saying "Nice pony, nice pony", beginning to grow honestly attached to it. Then the girls, whose ideas always coincided, said it was time to stop.

"Please," Sabby said. "Please may I ride a bit more?"

"No," said Margaret. "You've had enough for today."

"This afternoon couldn't I have a short time with pony?"

"*The* pony. No, not until tomorrow."

"The pony will forget all about me."

"Oh no; you will see it'll recognise you at once. You have done very well for the first time."

"Honestry?"

"Honest*ly*," we all said.

When we became used to the ponies the girls suggested all kinds of expeditions into the hills, that were to last anything up to a week. They thought our presence would make Mrs. Mather amenable to the idea, and I believe that she would have consented but for consideration for Sabby and me. She was afraid that the children were making themselves a nuisance to us. They had grown fond of Sabby, and now they called her 'Sabby darling', leading her about by the hand and showing her all their local discoveries —ruined peasant huts, bird's nests, the source of a stream. I was only 'Mr. Quinn', and tolerated as her husband; though often they would take me on one side and tell me how I must treat her, and they would watch me to see that I carried out their instructions. Once they found a beautiful yellow wild flower, the name of which I don't think we ever discovered; and this they put in her hair. They were mad with excitement over the result, and I agreed with them that it did enhance her beauty; only she needed her kimono then to complete the picture. She had to wear this flower until the petals were dropping off, and although we searched the hillsides as if prospecting for gold, we never found another like it. I was told that when we got back to Bombay I must arrange for a regular delivery of flowers, as nearly like this as possible, so that Sabby should never be without this indispensable addition to her charms.

It was all Mrs. Mather could do to prevent Margaret and Jennifer from following us on the occasional day that we had completely to ourselves. We went off with a sense of guilt at our selfishness, leaving them standing on the verandah looking after us, like two dogs that had not been allowed to go for a walk. We took sandwiches and a thermos, but we did not go far. We found a comfortable spot under a deodar tree, overlooking Jali Tal and the serried lines of mountains to the gargantuan range at the end of the world. We did not talk a great deal, because when feelings are sure and the surroundings themselves eloquent, there is not a great deal to be said. I began to understand why a yogi like Lala Vikrana would sometimes take a vow of silence; because words, however beautiful, are bound to fall short of a perfect experience; and words are powerful and can drag you down to their level, as they can also bring you up to their level if they are greater than your best experience.

But then if you are an ordinary person you cannot go for long without any words at all. And in beautiful places, and especially when you are in love, you can say very simple things without being ridiculous. So we said to each other little things without much meaning, and asked old questions and tried to think of new answers; and then we went down again to the hotel and thought that in all our lives a day had never been more perfect. And we also thought that about the night when we went out after the children had gone to bed, and the moon was a vivid white disc in the sky and all the lake shimmering. Then we were even closer than during the day, and when we were in bed the moon still drenched half the room. We talked then, until the moon had gone and it was dark.

Sabby painted a little. I remembered now for the first time that long ago in the Taj she had told me she 'tried to paint', and this I passed on to the children, who I knew would not let her hide her talent under a bushel. They had their own box of water-colours, and they asked their friend the carpenter in the local village to make an easel to their precise design. After that Sabby could not refuse. First of all she painted large Japanese characters for them with the brush. She did them beautifully with a swift, easy stroke, and told them that she had written their names. They were wide-eyed with wonder; and when I told them that in Japan such writing was thought of as a work of art, they said impatiently that anybody could see it was a lovely thing, although they couldn't understand the meaning. Afterwards Sabby painted small landscapes. There was no mistaking them for the work of anyone but a Japanese; and yet it was how we had all seen the mountains in the distance, rising up as though on a mist, mysterious mountains that might themselves have been a vapour—and in the foreground, in our world, a deodar like a sentinel, challenging intruders. Then, because we all insisted, she painted portraits. She painted Jennifer first, and then Margaret, Mrs. Mather and me; and though she insisted it was not so, and she had not meant it, we all looked like Japanese. It was partly her style, which was Japanese; but in addition she had given us all, unconsciously, an Oriental physiognomy. When we teased her, she wanted to tear these up. But the girls were delighted, and they took them away and hid them.

The month slipped away. The days fell over each other and were gone, and nothing could stop them; and yet although they passed so quickly, at the same time the school and Rosie and the Mayfair Hotel seemed infinitely remote, as though at least a year had intervened. I could not imagine myself fitting into the school life again after this, and I did not want to go back to Rosie's. Sabby must have thought the same, for it was she who said:

"Darling, I don't like hotel. I should be unhappy after beautiful hills. Could we please have a house together for a little?"

"We should have to keep it a secret."

"We can keep secret," Sabby said.

"It isn't easy to find a house in Bombay."

"We have been so lucky always. Do you think bad luck will begin?"

"I don't know," I said. "I've got a sort of dread. Bombay in the rain. School desks and Fenwick."

"Darling, there will still be Sabby. Do you still love Sabby?"

"Yes, darling."

"As much as before?"

"Yes, and differently."

"Would you like to go back to old times?"

"Yes," I said. "Sometimes I think I'd like to go back to the time when you were the new schoolmistress coming into the classroom for the first time."

"What did you think of me? Did you think I was horrid woman?"

"I thought you were a beautiful woman. I believe that part of me must have known then that we were going to have a month together in the Himalayas."

"You are inventing. At first you did not like me at all."

"That's not true," I said. "I may even have known before. I may have known when I saw your ship coming into the harbour. I had a feeling about it."

"What sort of feeling?"

"I don't know. That's why I would like to go back to the beginning again to find out. It must have been very exciting, only I was telling myself all the time not to be a fool."

"Were you a fool?"

"That is fishing, darling."

"Yes, it is fishing. I like to go fishing. Please will you tell me what you thought the first time I came into classroom?"

"I wondered what it would be like to kiss you. I'd never seen a Japanese woman before."

"Did you think you would try to kiss Japanese woman?"

"Yes, I did."

"Then why did you not kiss when you were with her in the ghari with the driver who had red teeth?"

"Because she would have snubbed me or slapped me, and that

would have been the end. I'm always very sulky when I'm slapped, and I don't try again."

"She would have perhaps done nothing of the kind, because you see she was not respectable woman. She would have done what she wanted instead of what she ought."

"It might have been any of her pupils."

"Oh no, she knew it was a special pupil."

"You didn't know," I said. "But I was telling the truth. I really wanted to kiss you when I saw you. I also thought you looked *sabishii* and wanted to protect you."

"Darling, I am also telling truth."

"You didn't know who I was in the street."

"Yes, I did. I knew you were Mr. Quinn, and when Mr. Fenwick was unkind to me you gave me a nice look."

"You were too embarrassed to notice."

"No, it is exactly what you notice when you are embarrassed, the nice looks. It was nicest of everybody."

"You didn't see Mario."

"He looked handsome. He is a lot more handsome than you, darling, but yours was the nicest look, and that is why I fell in love with you."

"You're imagining it now."

"But I have diary. In my diary it is all written. I will let you see little bits."

"Will you let me see the bit you were writing when I came back that night from Mr. Scaife's?"

"Yes, you may see that, too."

"Tell me what you'd written."

"I had written that Sabby was so unhappy because her Michael had not come back to her, that if she had got courage she would commit suicide. But that because she did not have courage, all she could do was lie and weep. I was very noisy when I was weeping; and then I had to stop to write diary, and then you came in and I did not know what to do."

"I was afraid you hadn't written anything about me at all, but about Mr. Scaife," I said.

"No, darling, there was nothing about Mr. Scaife, except perhaps that I was afraid if he found out about us he would try to spoil our happiness. You don't think he would still do that, do you?"

"No," I said. "We wouldn't let him now."

"Then that is all right. Anyway, we are not going to let anyone spoil our happiness, are we? Everything is going to be lovely. We are going to have beautiful house in Bombay and not mind the rain. There is nothing else to worry about."

"There is one more thing," I said. "Only it isn't a worry. It's exactly the opposite."

"What is that?"

"Now we've had our honeymoon," I said, "will you marry me?"

There was a long silence, and I did not look at Sabby, because I only wanted to hear her answer. And then I realised that she was crying gently.

"I have told you, darling, you will never have to marry me. Please do not ask me again. I want you to promise. Will you please promise, darling?"

III

A few days before we left Jali Tal, Margaret and Jennifer fell out over Sabby. The arrival of their father—a sun-dried Calcutta business man—had done nothing to distract them from their worshipful attachment. But so far their jealousy had been united against me; now they directed it at one another. Margaret had bought a little carved box of native handiwork from the bazaar and made a present of it to Sabby without telling Jennifer. The younger girl had been hurt. She was angry with herself that a similar idea had not occurred to her first; and she went to the bazaar and bought a present that was bigger and more expensive. It was Margaret's turn to be upset then, and for a day they ceased to speak to one another, and they were no more than polite to Sabby. They were both ashamed of what they had done, and did not want to appear to be making up to her. Then all of a sudden there were tears, and they were talking and they were united again. They had come to the mutual conclusion that neither of them had any claim upon Sabby, and that their own affection must be magnanimously subordinated to mine. They put their last annas together and bought a present for me, and asked humbly if they might be permitted to call me Uncle Michael and to write letters to me. On the last day the four of us were wonderful friends.

There were tears in Sabby's eyes when she had to say goodbye. She kissed the two children and Mrs. Mather kissed Sabby, and

Mr. Mather shook us both vaguely by the hand as though he had never discovered exactly who we were. We got into the car, Bahadur in front with the driver and Sabby and I behind. The girls had decorated the car with strips of coloured paper so that it looked like part of a carnival procession. We waved and kept saying goodbye, and blew kisses and promised to write; and at last there was a grating noise as the gear was engaged and we started off with a jerk. We all waved our hands. Then we heard a clattering noise from behind and we motioned to the driver. But the children were shouting excitedly, "Go on, go on!" so we did not stop. Sabby and I leant over the back, and we saw that on the end of a rope there was a tin can and an old shoe bouncing up and down on the road.

CHAPTER VI

I

WHEN we got to Delhi there was the inevitable misunderstanding over our train reservations, and we found ourselves stranded for two days.

After Jali Tal, eight thousand feet up in the mountains, it was like living by the open doors of a furnace. In the daytime the temperature was a hundred and twenty degrees, and at night no less than a hundred. The inside walls of our room were like radiators, throwing out heat, and even the wind came as a scorching blast. In the grounds of the hotel where we stayed there was a swimming-pool, and we spent most of the time in and out of it. But to get into the air-conditioned railway carriage at last was a splendid relief.

In Bombay the monsoon was in full swing. Some of the streets were rivers, and inside everything was moist; and although it was cooler than Delhi, the humidity made it quite as exhausting.

We decided not to return to the school together. I went the following morning, and Sabby took another day's holiday, because people might have drawn conclusions from our late arrival had it been simultaneous.

The first class I had was with Itsumi San. He had already tested the others on the first day of the new term, and now he turned to me immediately to put me through my paces. He asked me where I had been for my holidays, and what I had done, and why I was late, and because I had talked about all these things endlessly with Sabby I answered without any difficulty. I used a lot of words that we had not learned in class but which Sabby had taught me; but I could not help this, because I could not remember now which was which. Itsumi San was surprised, though his face did not show it. He tried out some unusual words himself. He said:

"Did you see any glaciers?"

"Yes," I said, "in the distance."

He was not convinced that I had understood the word. "What were they made of?"

"Ice, of course," I said. I had talked about glaciers with Sabby.

"Did you go mountain climbing?" he asked, using the special word for this.

"No, but I bathed, and rode ponies, and ate big meals."

"What did you eat?"

"All kinds of things. And sometimes there was garlic." I remembered the word for garlic.

He looked at his register for a long time, and then he said with some gratification:

"You have worked with might and main during the holidays."

"I have worked quite hard," I said.

"You are the best in the class."

I did not realise, until I heard the others speak and remembered that I had been worse than many of them, how much I had improved by listening and talking to Sabby. Just as I remembered things easily that Sabby said to me in English, I remembered them in Japanese. I could remember all her pet phrases and the twist she gave to her sentences. And of course I began to copy her, and in the month we were together my own speech had become more idiomatic besides more fluent. And all the time I had been progressing the others had been slipping slightly back, because they were not using the language or working on their books. Only Fenwick had worked hard. He had stayed in Bombay, and I heard that for a few hours each day he had come back regularly to the school, where the atmosphere of the classroom 'disciplined' his mind to study. He had learnt all the rare forms of verbs, and a great deal of other stuff out of the grammar book, but it did not sound like a Japanese talking his language. Itsumi San said:

"It is very good Japanese. You have studied assiduously. But if you speak in this way people will laugh at you." Itsumi San was sensitive about being laughed at, and so was Fenwick.

"Are you suggesting the book is wrong?" he said.

"It is not colloquial."

"It says it's colloquial," Fenwick said.

"It is not. Have you ever heard me speak in this way?"

"You're not the only person in the world who speaks Japanese."

"What do you mean?" said Itsumi San.

"I mean it's possible there may be people who speak in that way even if you don't."

It amused everybody to see a quarrel brewing between Fenwick and Itsumi San. We sat back and waited. Itsumi San looked at the desk for a long time, considering. He had lost face and was wondering what to do about it. Fenwick leant back, tilting the chair on its two back legs, and trying to look as though he was master of the situation.

"You need not stay in my class if you do not wish," Itsumi San said at last.

"That is not the point."

"Do you wish to remain in my class?"

"Why not?"

"If you do not consider I can teach Japanese, I would prefer you to leave now."

"That's just like a Jap," Fenwick said. "You confuse the whole issue."

Itsumi San's yellow skin turned a sullen grey. His eyes narrowed, but their expression did not change.

"You are an officer," he said, "and I am therefore unable to speak to you as I would like." He got up, closed his register methodically and screwed the cap on his pen. There was still half an hour of the class to go. We all waited in silence. He rubbed the board, hung up the duster and straightened his chair. Then he put his books under his arm and went out without looking at any of us, as though the offence had come from us all.

"That's the trouble with these fellows," Fenwick said, trying to sweep us all into his own fold. "They can't stand criticism."

I went out to lunch with Peter. After the holiday we had a lot to say to each other, and we thought we would say it in the Taj. It was a good thing I had Peter, because I had to tell someone about my wonderful time with Sabby, and I could rely on him to be discreet. He was not discreet about what he knew of other people, however, and now he brought out all the stories that he had been collecting for a month. His best story was about Mervyn.

He said the story about Mervyn justified a bottle of hock, and it was partly on account of the hock that it seemed an immensely funny story.

It seemed Mervyn had devoted his leave to trying to get out of India. On the first day he went to the medical officer and beat his brow and wept and said he was unable to go on. "Come, come now," the MO said, "you're letting circumstances get on top of you; you're an officer, and you must pull yourself together." Mervyn said for months he had been pulling himself together. But this was the end. He was defeated. They could do what they liked with him now. They could shoot him if they liked. But he thought himself the best thing would be if they could put him on the boat. . . . Well, of course, the MO said, that was obviously the thing. Only first there was a little formality, and he would have to bear with them. A few days only in hospital . . . under observation. He would arrange at once for the journey.

They came to collect him on the following day. There were two medical orderlies. They arranged the ghari for him, and they knew all about the trains and they already had the tickets. On the station he bought himself a Penguin book, and he asked the orderlies if they would care for something to read as well. They picked out one or two cheap paper-backed publications, and they stocked up with oranges and were all set for Ahmadabad. It was only a two-hour journey and then they were at the hospital, and there was something in the orderlies' instructions about Mervyn having to report to Section H9. They took him down long corridors to a single room. There was nothing in it except a bed, but since he would soon be on a liner and a little bit later in Sloane Square, what did furnishings matter? Then two more orderlies came and began to unpack his bags. They went over everything carefully. They took out the pamphlets that the first orderlies had chosen, and then they removed everything from the room. After a while he needed his handkerchief. He went to the door and found that it was locked. He knocked for a while, and then kicked, until someone came and opened a small peep-hole in the door, and said in a soothing voice that everything was going to be all right, and there was nothing to worry about, nothing at all. He said he wanted his handkerchief. There was a whispered consultation outside, and then he was told he must wait a little while, and then perhaps it would be arranged for him to have his handkerchief. Afterwards something was brought in for him to eat. He found there was only a wooden spoon, so he kicked on the door again and asked for a knife and fork. They were awfully sorry, they said, but there were no knives and forks, and would he mind just this once putting up with a wooden spoon. When the shutter closed again, he listened for a while at the door, and he heard someone say, "Why doesn't someone tell the poor blighter that he's in H9?" He did not have to wait long after the meal before he was taken back down the corridors, to a room where there were two or three doctors sitting about with cigarettes stuck in their mouths with studied nonchalance, as though they were bent on inspiring confidence. They offered Mervyn a cigarette. On a desk there were two pamphlets. They were the pamphlets that he had bought for the orderlies and that had been left in his luggage. One was called *Spanking Stories* and the other *Curiosa Erotiken*. One of the doctors flicked over the pages, and said, "Excuse me for giving these the once-over. Jolly good yarns, what?" Mervyn said his orderlies ought to know whether they were or not, and would they please give him a knife and fork and handkerchief, and stop this damned nonsense of locking the door, and send him back to England, *pronto*. The doctor said, "Jolly good joke, what! Wooden spoon? All a mistake, dear fellow. Now what was the matter? Just make yourself comfortable on the couch and think back, back, back . . . no, the other two weren't listening, they were just waiting for someone. That's right. Now had he ever been ill-treated by a maid when he was a youngster? What? Only had a butler . . .?"

Of course all this was Peter's story. Somehow Mervyn had got a telegram despatched, and Peter had gone down post-haste, thinking it was a death-rattle setting in. He was let in through the locked door after a preliminary briefing, and Mervyn seized him by both arms and said, "For God's sake, man, you've got to get me out. You've got to get me out! This place is driving me mad!" Peter went in to see the doctors, and they all smoked cigarettes, and according to him they looked at him from all angles like Cecil Beaton taking a photograph, and it was only by the grace of God and the absence of *Curiosa Erotiken* protruding from his pocket that he eventually escaped back to the station without a lock clicking to bar his way. Meanwhile Mervyn's immurement continued. . . .

"But this story is nothing compared with my own news," Peter said. "I've finished my book."

"What are you calling it?"

"I'm giving it a strong title. It's going to be *One Man's Meat,* because when it's won me world-wide renown and opened up the flesh-pots to me, I'm going to write the equally stupendous sequel called *Another Man's Poison.*"

"Same smart-alec detective?" I said.

"Same detective."

When we went back to Rosie's that night, he gave me the manuscript to read. It was a carbon copy. The original copy had been typed on airgraph forms and put in the post score by score as they came off the machine. Altogether there had been three hundred and seventy-three pages, and at three annas a time it had cost him something in the neighbourhood of five pounds. The last airgraph form had 'The End' written on and nothing else.

"It's a very clever idea," he said. "The publishers will never have seen a book of airgraphs before, and they'll accept it because it'll make a good publicity story. It'll help put my detective on the map."

"It doesn't sound like a detective story," I said. It was not called *One Man's Meat* but *The Warring Winds.*

"Oh, you read it," he said.

I read the first page, and I thought at once it was a pity that it was a detective story, because he had a clean, easy style that would have done credit to something better than a conventional corpse. Then I discovered that it was not going to be a detective story, after all. He had been pulling my leg for months.

It was a simple story about an English boy who lived with a French family in the Pyrenees. The war came, and the surrender of France. After some conflict in himself, the boy decided to return home to England by escaping over the mountain range. The book ended as he reached the highest point of his climb and looked down into Spain. Peter had escaped out of France in this way and had been imprisoned in Spain; but he had been strong-minded enough not to spoil this tender book with these latter grim reminiscences. A fine spirit had crept into his pages, almost imperceptibly, as though he had not intended it himself—a kind of deep patriotism that had no jingo about it. I thought it curious that after all the time I had known Peter and all the friendship I had shared with him, I had never really known this side of him.

I was reading the book when Fenwick came in. Peter had gone out and I was alone in the room. I was lying on the bed and I did not take much notice of him because of the book. But even from the corner of my eye I could see that he had something on his mind. He was pretending to be jovial to disguise it. He asked me to join him somewhere for a drink.

"I rather want to stay and read, if you don't mind," I said.

"I'd like you to come out for half an hour."

"Not tonight."

He came farther into the room and looked at the book-shelf and the objects on the mantelpiece, playing for time.

"You're sure you won't come?"

"Sure," I said.

"Oh, well," he said. "That's quite a nice carved box you've got. I've one not unlike it that I ordered specially from Kashmir. I always say that Kashmir work is incomparable."

"Yes," I said.

He wandered round the bed. He was smiling unnaturally. He stood with his back to me, examining a picture.

"If you've got anything you want to say to me," I said, "get it over now."

"Why should I have?"

"Because you look as though you're going to have a baby."

"As a matter of fact, there is something I wanted to discuss with you. I thought it would be preferable to do it over a drink, and then we could keep it on a friendly basis."

"I'm good at throwing whisky in people's faces. Indian whisky burns like acid."

"Oh, I know you'll take it all right," he said. "I know you've got a lot of good sense. And remember, this is entirely informal."

"Well?" I said.

He sat down on the edge of the bed with both hands in his pockets. He had obviously planned this scene to take place with a bar to lean on and a whisky glass to twist in his fingers, but he wasn't going to waste the speeches because these things were lacking.

"They tell me," he said, "that the best way to learn a language is with a sleeping dictionary."

"What does that mean?"

"Surely I needn't explain that?"

"Yes, you need."

"Well, it means you can learn best from a woman."

"Then why don't you get one?"

"As a matter of fact," he said, "I've no doubt that I could have done. I was born lucky in love, you know. I suppose that I've had as many gay moments as anybody else."

I looked at him closely.

"What did you come in here to say?" I said.

"Haven't you got a guilty conscience about something?" he said, taking a half-aggressive offence.

"What do you suggest it might be about?"

"If you don't know . . ."

"Why did you make that crack about a sleeping dictionary?"

I knew that if I had not lost control of my temper I might have kept the whole thing from developing into a nasty situation. When Fenwick was pretending to do things on a friendly basis, his capacity for harm was curbed by the pretence. But when he was openly at war there was nothing to hold him back. He stood up, and we were facing each other, and it became a vulgar little scene. I know that I was the more vulgar because I was the more angry, and I was too angry to be discreet.

"You know perfectly well why," he said.

"Say it if you dare!"

"I'm not a fool. I knew a long time before the holiday that you were having an intrigue with the Japanese teacher."

"Japanese teacher!" I said. "Who the hell do you think you're talking about?"

He went on methodically:

"I also know you went away with her."

"How do you know that?"

"That is beside the point."

"It's very much to the point if you've been spying on us."

"You forget I'm the senior officer at the school."

"Anything about Miss Wei or myself is nothing to do with you," I said.

"I'm directly concerned with your conduct."

"You admitted yourself to being—*gay*."

"I've no objection to you amusing yourself——"

"That's kind of you."

"As you know, I've not even stood in Lamb's way. But it is one thing to have a Eurasian and another——"

"Well?"

"It's quite another matter to let yourself be seduced by a Japanese."

153

I struck him somewhere on the face. My closed fist knocked him hard, but it was not the pain that stunned him. He did not even raise his hand to rub the bruise. He stared at me for a moment, and his eyes were hard and bitter in his limp face. Then he turned and went out of the room.

II

I could not bring myself to think well of him for not making a case out of this. He could have got me into serious trouble, because officially no circumstances extenuate such an impulsive action; but he was not insensible to the pleasure to be had from magnanimity, in which light he presumed I regarded it. On the following morning he said to me pompously:

"So far as last night's incident is concerned, Quinn, I'm prepared to let bygones be bygones."

"Oh yes," I said.

"On the other hand, since it's not a personal matter, I can't, with a clear conscience, forget the point which I raised."

"Did you raise a point?" I said.

"I shall pass the matter on, and then it will be out of my hands. So far as I'm concerned it needn't be any further barrier to our friendship."

"So far as I'm concerned," I said, "regardless of what happens henceforward, it will never be anything else."

He did not waste any time in passing the matter on. He passed it on to the Brigadier, and I suspect that he intended it to result in the dismissal of Sabby, if not in any further penalty for myself. I waited fearfully and in an anguish of remorse, telling myself that my temper might have cost Sabby her job and both of us our happiness. The house that we had planned, still only a dream, could never become a reality. I began to wonder if I could bring myself to go to Fenwick and plead, and flatter him into taking no action. It seemed madness to throw away everything because one was too proud and angry to devote five minutes to hypocrisy.

But it was too late. I was called to the Brigadier's office. He came in during Sabby's class, smiling at Sabby and then at me, and he whispered to me, "May I just have one word with you?" I went out, trying not to look sheepish in front of Fenwick, who himself was trying to look as though the matter was 'out of his hands'.

"Sit down a minute, won't you?" the Brigadier said. "Take a cigarette. How's the Japanese going?"

"I'm just beginning to break the back of it," I said.

"I'm so glad. You still find it interesting?"

"Very interesting."

"That's the thing. It is the most important thing of all, don't you think? It's more important than a natural bent. Once I didn't believe that tortoises beat hares, but of course it's true. I once knew a young fellow at Cambridge . . ."

He told me a long story, and I had another cigarette. Then he asked me about my holiday, and I told him of Jali Tal. I said I went with a friend, but he did not ask me about the friend, only about the ponies and the mountains. We talked about the Himalayas, and then somehow we got on to the subject of Burma, and he said, it was very rude, but would I mind showing him the scars of my jungle sores, because that would interest him greatly? I pushed down my long stocking, and he gently ran his finger over the mottled patch where the flesh was sunk as though acid had eaten into it. I heard the others coming out of the classroom. I pushed down the other stocking, and showed him another sore: only now it was painless, just a trophy.

"Well," the Brigadier said, "I'm afraid I've kept you rather a long time, but I have so little opportunity of getting to know my students well. Oh, and by the way," he said. "No names, but someone has told me there's a rumour about you and Miss Wei. It's very flattering for you—she's so charming, isn't she? I wish I wasn't too old to have a rumour like that started about me. But don't worry, rumours die."

I wanted to say, 'I love Miss Wei', if only to show that I did not wish to keep it a secret from him: but his eyes were saying, 'I know, don't tell me', and they were fine, grey, amused eyes. I thought: 'You are a good man, and when I am with you I can feel you bringing the goodness out of me; just as when I am with Fenwick I feel all the pettiness and rottenness coming out.'

All I said was, "I hope it isn't embarrassing Miss Wei."

"She's not the sort of person to spend sleepless nights over that."

When I saw Fenwick at lunch-time I did not speak to him, but when he asked for the salt I passed it to him, and he said "Thank you".

Later on I passed him the bread, and he said "Thank you very much".

It was Sabby who found the house. She negotiated with the owner who was going away to Karachi, and took it furnished for six months.

Until she got it ready, I was not allowed to see it. Sabby did not always work in the mornings at the school, and when she was free she spent her time in buying things that were needed. But she would not tell me what she was buying.

"Very soon you will see," she said.

"But I would also like to buy things."

"No, you are busy student. I will get house ready, and then you can come in."

I lent her Bahadur. He went shopping with her and went with her to the house, but he was too fond of her to betray her secrets. I asked him if it was a nice house.

"It is not great," he said.

"Do you think I'll like it?"

"I think Sahib would like all houses with Miss Wei."

I told Rosie that I would be leaving her hotel. She said:

"You see, it did not matter what I did, the result is the same. If I had let you make love to me, you would have left. And because I did not let you, you are leaving, nevertheless. You will have to kiss me goodbye."

"As a matter of fact," I said, "I don't want to leave altogether. I'd like to have a bed here, and leave some of my things. Also I still want to use this as an address."

"You don't have to explain any reasons to Rosie."

"I'll pay the rent, of course."

"There will be no rent."

"Make it a retaining fee," I said. "Just so that you'll remember to tell people that I'm living here."

"I will remember that you are still living here. I am not Rangoon Rosie for nothing."

"You're a very dear-hearted thing."

"Because you say sweet things like that, I shall not make you pay a retaining fee."

"That's different," I said. "That's business."

"My business is a matter of the heart."

156

"Then sometimes if I'm allowed I shall come and take you out to supper."

"Very well, then, that is good. I shall let you take me out whenever you like."

Twice Sabby postponed our entry into the house. She said whatever happened we must not move in when it was raining, and I teased her that the only reason could be because there was a leak in the roof. Then on the third day I insisted that we could not wait any more, and, as it turned out, in the afternoon it was fine and the sun shone out of a clear sky, and everything began to steam. The evening was the best we had had for a long while.

At half past seven I got a ghari and called for Sabby at the Mayfair. She was paying her bill for the last time. Her luggage had gone ahead with Bahadur and she only carried her handbag.

"Where shall I tell the driver to go to?" I said.

"Please tell towards Malabar Hill, and I will show way."

We clopped off along the wet roads. We went past the Cricket Club and the school and along the Marine Drive, and I could see the Towers of Silence standing up on Malabar Hill. There were a few vultures circling round, but it didn't look as though it had been a busy day in the Parsee mortuary.

"I'm afraid of you being disappointed," Sabby said. "That is why I wanted fine day. Please will you not pretend to like it if you think it is not nice, and we find another house."

"After all the trouble you've taken?"

"I want you to be happy there, please, darling."

"You needn't worry about that."

"I have to worry about Michael being happy. You see, I am such selfish woman and I want so much of you, and if that makes you miserable I don't know what I shall do."

"If you see me looking miserable, you can scold me for ingratitude."

"Oh no, I don't want it that way. I don't want any gratitude, because there is not anything you owe me. I only want you to love me a little bit."

"I love you," I said. "Only I will tell you more about that tonight in your new house."

"Our new house," Sabby said. "Please always remember it is for both of us."

We started up as though we were going to Malabar Hill, and then we swung off to the right up another hill that was shaded with trees. Half-way up we turned off again, and on either side there were beautiful houses. Sabby leaned forward and directed the driver.

"Look," she said, "it is here."

We turned in between some gateposts, and the horse pulled us slowly up a short, sloping drive. At the top there was a fine bungalow with a pillared balcony and a vivid blue creeper on the wall. At the sound of our arrival Bahadur came out to greet us. For a moment I did not recognise him, because he had a new white uniform and a gleaming white turban, and he had trimmed and combed his moustache to do justice to the occasion. He bowed proudly and said, "Welcome, Sahib"; and I walked through into the sitting-room, and then into the dining-room and bedroom that were on the same floor. Sabby's touch was everywhere. Especially it was in the bowl of flowers, and I knew how long she must have taken choosing and arranging them.

I did not know that she had ever noticed the kind of whisky I liked. But in the sitting-room there was a bottle of my favourite brand, and I cannot think how she had got it, because I had hunted for it for weeks without success. She poured me out a glass, and it was the size of a double *burra peg*. I said:

"You must also sip a little, because this is a special occasion and it is good to be a bit drunk."

"But it also makes sick, and this evening I am going to be well. Please, you drink, and then we shall kiss and in that way I taste whisky."

"Your English, darling," I said.

"What is wrong with English?"

"Nothing. It's charming. I don't want you ever to speak better English."

"You are teasing me."

"No, it's marvellous."

"Yes, you are teasing me, and I shall spank you, because I am schoolmistress."

When Bahadur came in to say that dinner was ready we went through into the dining-room, but the table was bare.

"It is through here," Sabby said.

At the end of the room were french windows. We stepped through these and came out on to a terrace where a standard-lamp cast a soft pool of light on to the table laid with fine silver and glasses and more flowers. The air was deliciously cool after the warmth of the house, and overhead the sky was deep blue and the stars were only faintly appearing. I walked across the terrace to the balustrade.

I had not expected to see anything but darkness or the silhouette of another house. Instead, the whole of Bombay lay at our feet, a shimmering sea of lights, and the sea itself was black, its edges laced with gold reflections. I like to be high up in the daytime and look down upon the roofs of cities; but this was more beautiful and more fairy-like than anything I had ever seen, and it was all the more beautiful for being unexpected. Because she had known how it would thrill me Sabby had never spoken a word of it, and I had not noticed in the ghari how far we had climbed nor how close we were to the edge of the hill. Also, I had not imagined that Bombay could lie in this spangled carpet. The life of the Taj was there and the luxury flats with their radios and servants, and the life of the slums and the brothels—and because we were two hundred feet above it all, they were merged into a myriad twinkling pin-points and there was nothing to distinguish them. I wondered as I stood there and felt like a god whether that was how God always looked upon life, seeing millions of little souls like lights, but too far away to see the misshapen, fly-infested bodies of beggars. From a distance, how marvellous to have created this!

Under the lamp on the terrace it was marvellous too, because now I had seen over the balustrade I felt as though we were on a cloud, a tiny golden cloud, a kind of cave in the darkness, with only the table, and Sabby and myself, and the chairs, and a few paving-stones that were washed by the fringes of the light—and occasionally Bahadur, when he appeared from the shadows like a djinn. Because of the whisky I had drunk there was also the sensation of floating; but Sabby had only tasted the whisky from my lips and she too was floating, and then we were so alone together that the world was not there below us any more, and I smoked a cigar which Sabby had bought me specially, and it was not until midnight that we left our private golden cloud and went back into the house.

When we were in bed, we read for a while. First of all I read aloud, and then Sabby read, but she read over the full stops and commas and stopped in the middle of sentences, and so I did not listen to the meaning, but only to her voice, and sometimes I corrected her pronunciation. She came to the word 'corollary', and I said it several times for her. She said 'cororrary' and 'collorrary' and then 'cororrally', but she could not get it right except by splitting up the syllables. We turned off the light and she went on saying 'cororrary', and then she could not say the l's at all. Her nose was buried in my cheek.

"Cororrary," she said.

I felt my face damp, and I put my finger to it. It was not perspiration, so I ran my finger down Sabby's cheek and found it was quite wet.

"Darling," I said. "You are not crying because you can't say corollary?"

"No, I don't mind about cororrary."

"Then what is it?"

"There is a funny noise," she said.

I listened, and some way away I could hear the regular beating of an Indian drum. It was some kind of festivity because there was singing, and wild shrieks, but these drifted only faintly from the distance.

"They are enjoying themselves," I said.

"Yes, I know; I am silly, darling. Do you think I shall ever say cororrary?"

CHAPTER VII

I

A TELEGRAM came from Lord Durweston. It was about a week after we had moved into the house. It said, 'Expect me shortly. Looking forward to seeing you.'

"It will be all right," Sabby said. "He is a darling man, and he will like you."

"I shall have to go back to Rosie's for a while," I said.

"I don't want you to go to Rosie's. You will perhaps try to love her again."

"We will see," I said.

One night Mr. Scaife came to dinner. It was necessary to ask him to see her new house, and we pretended that I, too, had been invited for the evening. We put everything that belonged to me into drawers, and I was very grateful for the whisky and commented upon the brand as though I had not seen it there before. Sabby and I tried not to look at one another. We asked each other polite questions, and sometimes Sabby gave ambiguous answers, trying to make me smile despite all our resolutions. I could see a delighted little twinkle in her eye, as though it was only a game and it did not matter Scaife knowing we were playing it for his benefit. Scaife sat there distantly, and the light was reflected on his spectacles. He looked at the ceiling, talking to it, though indirectly at me, and he did not seem to notice Sabby a great deal.

"Did you give the happiness Vikrana spoke about?"

"I don't know," I said.

"Ah!"

I thought it was all going off splendidly. After dinner we smoked for a long while, and I began to get impatient because I wanted Sabby to myself again.

"I had better be going," I said.

"Must you really?" said Sabby.

"It is getting late."

I looked at my watch, but Scaife did not look at his, and he made no move, so I pretended to think of a new topic of conversation and forget about going. Some time later I repeated the manœuvre and said there was work tomorrow, and Sabby said pointedly that she, too, had to work. Scaife asked for another glass of whisky. He looked into the glass, gently swilling it round, and went on talking in a high philosophical way while Sabby and I dried up, watching him blackly. When at last he came away he was drifting as if in a world of his own, and he said good night to Sabby automatically, as one might to a servant. We went down the drive together. He went on talking, this time at the stars. The roads on the hill were empty. They were still wet from the last rain, and they reflected the yellow street-lights. The freshened leaves of the trees that lined the road glistened and were still, and there was no sound except for our feet on the road and Scaife's voice. He was talking about mystics.

We came to the corner where the bazaar began, and here there were bright lights in shops, glaring out on to the street.

"This is where I turn off," I said. "Are you going to walk to Malabar Hill?"

"Yes," he said vaguely.

I tried to break away but he held me, not directly, but with his conversation aimed away from me. And yet he was at the same time conscious of me, like someone who is talking to a second person and trying to detain a third.

When we finally parted I went off along the road through the bazaar, and spent a quarter of an hour looking into the cafés and the shops that were still open. All kinds of foodstuffs were being sold along the edges of the pavements, queer, twisted, cracker-like orange things and a dozen different kinds of sweets piled high on tin trays. There were many people in the streets, but nobody took any notice of me, nobody begged. I wore different clothes to them all and I could not speak their language, and I felt as though I was invisible, wandering amongst them. I walked up a side-street towards a dense crowd that was spread right across the width of the road, and over the heads I caught glimpses of dancing figures. There was some singing, and the monotonous, insistent rhythm of the drum—the same sound that we had heard every night for an hour as we lay in bed. I turned away, back through the bazaar, and up the hill towards the house again, going back to the other little world that was Sabby's and mine.

Standing by the gate there was a figure. I knew at once that it was Scaife. I knew first by some kind of instinct, and then because it was a tall figure and the attitude familiar. He was standing motionless, waiting.

I had advanced up the road through the lamplight and it was useless to go back. He was facing me and he would have seen me, and so I came on slowly, my feet padding the silent asphalt. He did not move. The light was full on me, and then I was in the shadows and then in the light again. I thought methodically about what was going to happen. I was not perturbed; I might have expected this. I knew whatever happened I should not lose my temper, nor be afraid.

There was only a dim light at the gate. His form was silhouetted with a dull yellow glow and his face was a dark oval. His hands were at his side, yellow-ringed. He was not standing aggressively but with a heavy patience, and he was not barring my way.

I went up to the side of him and stopped, and he turned round from the waist so that I could see his face. One spectacle caught the light, and the other was still in the shadow, so that he looked as though he was wearing a monocle. The visible eye was expressionless.

"Why are you waiting here?" I said.

He began to smile. It was slow and derisive, and straight at me, not at the sky or the stars. He did not reply until I repeated, "Why?"

"I wanted to see if it was true."

"It is true."

"I was a fool to let this happen," he said.

We went on looking at each other, and I had no idea what he was thinking or what he intended.

"I should go back to Malabar Hill if I were you," I said.

"Would you?"

"You've got a beautiful house."

He said nothing. He went on standing there, half-turned towards me and the one spectacle glinting and the mad, bitter smile on his lips, and I began to feel sorry for him because he was fifteen years older than I and his life had gone wrong.

"Good night," I said.

I waited to see if he replied, but he was silent, and I started up towards the house, and when I was in the darkness of the porch I was out of his sight.

I went in, and there was no light in the sitting-room, but there was a light under Sabby's door. She was sitting up in bed with sleepy eyes, waiting for me. When I kissed her she was smooth and soft, and there was a sweet aura of perfume about her. She was so tender and delicate and pretty like a flower that I only dared to touch her lightly. I took her tiny, soft nose in my teeth and shook it gently, and then she wrinkled it and I tried to do the same, but I could not wrinkle my nose without distorting the rest of my face.

When I was also in bed and the lights were out, I could still hear the banging of the drum going on and on monotonously, and the singing that was like the cries of savage jungle tribes.

II

Lord Durweston's telegram had been delayed, so that it was only a week after it arrived that he himself landed in Bombay. He had already installed himself in the Taj when he rang up Sabby. She went to have lunch with him. Afterwards she said:

"He wants to meet you. He is a very sweet man, and he has asked will we please both have dinner with him tomorrow night."

"How much have you told him about us?"

"Darling, I haven't told him anything, except that you are so nice. But I am not any good at pretending now, and I think I don't mind if he knows anything."

"Then I hope he makes you marry me, so that you become an honest woman."

"Darling, is Sabby not honest woman?"

"Not so long as you don't marry me."

"Oh dear, what shall I do?"

"It's very easy. You've only got to say one word."

"One word perhaps would make you very unhappy."

"It would make me insane with joy, and it would make all this pretence unnecessary."

"No, darling, it would make you unhappy, and your mother and father who live in . . . Oh, I wish I could remember where you live."

"Tewkesbury."

"Yes, in Tewkesbury, they would be so angry because you had married silly Japanese girl with funny little face."

"They would like your funny little face," I said.

"They would never forgive me for being Japanese."

"Is that why you won't marry me?"

"Yes, that is one reason."

"And there are others?"

"There are not really any other reasons. It is just as I told you. I am silly and obstinate, but I want you to go on liking me for a little bit more."

"You don't make things any easier."

"It is the first time you have ever said anything like that."

"I didn't mean it," I said. "It was a kind of blackmail. I shall go on loving you just the same."

I saw Lord Durweston before the following night. I was not sure at first that it was him, but I thought I recognised him from Sabby's description, and he was exactly as I had imagined—tall and greying, with a long, aristocratic face and an aristocratic assurance. He was with Scaife.

I went into the bar of the Taj, and they were sitting at one of the small tables. Scaife was talking and Lord Durweston was nodding gravely, and I thought at once that they were talking about me. As I went by I nodded at Scaife. He did not nod back, but he focused his eyes on me through his thick spectacles and followed me with his gaze. Because he also stopped talking, Lord Durweston looked round casually over his shoulder, and then I went to the far end of the room and sat down at a table out of sight. I drank by myself, trying to think why it was that one could not live one's individual life without the interference of others—the Scaifes and the Fenwicks—and yet not caring greatly. They could not take Sabby from me now, not altogether, because I had known her and loved her long enough for her to become part of me. She was part of my life, had been absorbed into it and had influenced it, she had helped to shape the thing that was me, and whatever happened in the future, that could not be altered. I had possessed her sufficiently to know that in that possession I had gained something I should never lose.

But I was not going to lose Sabby. It may have been in Lord Durweston's power to turn her away from me, but whatever Scaife had said he did not try. When we met him at dinner the next night he presided with a kindly grace. I could see how much he cared for Sabby. He was not too old to love her as a woman, but there was nothing in his manner that was more than paternal affection. Yet although he teased her as a child, he treated her as a woman; and although she liked to be light-hearted, and a little feather-brained, and not serious, I knew he could see through this into that ageless part of her full wisdom and gentleness. I liked him at once, and he treated me with courtesy, elevating my sense of importance with a long-practised skill. He was a diplomat of great charm, and his intelligence was as self-evident as his humanity.

After coffee, we went together to the cloakroom. Here, in this sanctuary, it often happens a new intimacy blossoms between men when they have left the ladies for a moment, and here he turned to me and said, as though it was the most natural thing in the world :

"You're in love with her, of course?"

"Yes," I said.

"Good, you are making her happy."

"Do you think so?"

"There's no question about it. You know that, of course. I would like you to dine with me tomorrow."

When I told Sabby, she was very happy that we had got on well together. But she sniffed and puckered her nose, and pretended to be jealous.

"You men will go away and have fun and leave Sabby," she said.

"We shall be talking about you all the time."

"And you will not say nasty things?"

"We're both your admirers. It's a special session to say nice things."

We said a lot of nice things. We talked about her whilst we had long drinks, sitting on the balcony overlooking the harbour where Sabby and I had had our first tryst; and then we dined at almost the same table. It was appropriate, because this was the first recognition we had had of our love, and I was glad to have it. I felt a warm gratitude towards Lord Durweston. It is sometimes fun to be two against the world, and there is something edifying in defiance; but after a time the pleasure palls and it is good to know you have friends.

It was not until we began to sip liqueurs that we talked about the future.

"I've been waiting to say that I want to marry Hanako," I said.

"Yes, I thought you would tell me that."

"You don't approve?"

He had a cigar and he drew at it for some time, and I waited anxiously for his reply.

"It's not really a question of my approval. She doesn't want to marry you because she is afraid for your happiness. I think you should remember she may be right."

"I'll risk it," I said.

"That is the gallant line to take."

"No, it's not at all gallant, it's what I want."

"If I were you," he said, "I should wait. That is the best thing to do. Wait and see what happens. There may be all kinds of factors that you can't see clearly at present."

"I was hoping that you'd be my ally."

"I am your ally. I want you to remember that. I'm your ally, and I'm banking upon your being mine. I want to be able to rely on you."

"In what way?"

"You knew that I was Hanako's guardian? I often wondered whether I'd done right in allowing her to come to India. Only it was not really a question of allowing. She made up her mind that she wanted to come, and she's a self-willed little thing. I said yes, because she would not let me say anything else. It meant coming right across the world by herself and starting the job by herself, and she was more by herself than anybody else because she was a Japanese amongst people who hated the Japanese. It was I who made her use a Chinese name. She told me she didn't think it was fair on the Chinese, and that she must not pretend to be anything but what she was; but I made that condition on her going. Now she is not by herself any longer, and because my work doesn't allow me to stay here long, I'm grateful to you for this. In a few days I'm going to Delhi. Then I shall fly back to England. I shan't be able to see her again. It'll be a great relief to me to know that she is going to have you during the coming year."

"What about Mr. Scaife?" I asked.

"Mr. Scaife is in many ways an excellent person. He is both clever and capable, and he's a friend of mine. But his mind has been conditioned by a lot of curious circumstances, and it has become a curious mind. I wouldn't like to rely on him to take care of Hanako."

"In two months I shall have finished my special training," I said. "I don't know where I shall be going."

"That's something beyond our control. I only want you to do your best to look after her."

"That's not very difficult," I said.

"You never know. You may have a hard time."

"I love her."

"Yes," he said, "that does make a difference. You love her a great deal, and I'm going to rely on you."

CHAPTER VIII

I

TOWARDS the end of October the Brigadier asked the instructors to make individual reports on all the students.

Sabby said: "Please help, darling. I am no good at report."

We sat on the terrace after supper, beneath the standard-lamp. The rains had gone and this was the perfect season in Bombay. The evenings were delicious. We sat out without being too sticky or hot, and Bahadur brought us coffee and a glass of Madeira for myself, and except for the thought that we should not have this house together for many more weeks, we were marvellously happy.

I took her sheaf of pencilled notes. She had scribbled on odd bits of paper in phrases that I would anywhere have recognised as Sabby's. She had written about me:

"This student is the best. I think he is awfully clever and he speaks very good Japanese. Only his accent is a little funny, but that is not important, because I can understand everything he says. He can say anything in Japanese."

"You are not going to send that in," I said.

"Oh yes, I am. And I am going to put on the end, 'He is also very sweet and I like to bite his ears now and then.'"

"There is no need to add that. Anybody can see from what you've written that you like to bite my ears."

"I don't mind."

"I do. You are not going to say that, because it isn't true. I can only say a few very limited things in Japanese, and most of those are all right for this terrace, but they wouldn't go down with prisoners-of-war."

"I don't care, you are the best."

"I ought to be—I've spoken ten times as much as anybody else. But you're not going to say so."

I looked through the other reports, and most of them were 'fair' and 'quite good', and one was 'rather good'. Fenwick's was the worst of all:

"This person is not half so good as he thinks. He likes to use difficult long words, but he never gets them right. He is not as good as he ought, and if he goes on like this I don't see how he will ever speak nicely."

"All these reports are transparent," I said.

"Like windows?"

"Yes, you can see right through them into what you think about the people."

"Darling, I tried so hard to do nice report."

"I know you did, but, darling, you are such a child sometimes."

"You are awfully unkind."

"I think it's the kindest thing I could have said about you."

"Don't you want Sabby to be grown-up?"

"If you grew up nicely, it would be all right. But most people don't grow up nicely at all, and the nicest parts about them are the parts that aren't grown-up."

"I have only said in report what you have said. I copied because you said Mr. Fenwick is not half so good as he thinks."

"When you're older," I said, "you'll find out that you have to modify that kind of thing when you write it on paper."

"Then please will you write?"

I drafted out new reports, and I said that Fenwick was 'one of the best', which was true, and that I 'seemed to be getting a good grasp of the colloquial'. It didn't matter a great deal, because so long as we passed a reasonable standard nothing particularly hung upon who was best. In any case, there were informal exams, which were carried out by the Brigadier himself and by one or two officers who came down from Delhi. They took place a few days later. We went singly from room to room, and had a short chat with each in turn, and they marked us under five heads—fluency, accuracy, vocabulary, pronunciation, understanding. The results were pinned up on the notice-board, with all the marks totalled. An Army officer was at the top. He must have hidden his light under a bushel until then, because nobody had noticed he was outstanding. But he was Welsh, and his native accent had stood him in good stead, so that under this head he had got ninety per cent. I was told that when I imitated a Welshman speaking Japanese, my own accent improved considerably, but, as a rule, I spoke Japanese as I spoke my smattering of French, in round Anglo-Saxon accents. This got me only thirty-two per cent, and pulled me down to a bad second place. I did not care where I came, so long as I was better than Fenwick, which was happily the case. He was fifth. He went round saying:

"I've no complaint at all to make about my own placing—it was a great surprise to see myself treated so favourably. But I consider the whole method of examination most unfair. For instance, I was given only fifty per cent for my vocabulary, and I can honestly say without boasting that mine is second to none."

Later on his grievance came closer to the surface, and he said to me:

"I suppose you're now patting yourself on the back for getting on to a good thing."

"I don't understand you," I said.

"You got yourself good marks and a bit of —— at the same time." He used a word that is quite common amongst men, and I don't think he can have intended it to have all the effect that it did; but it hit me like a bullet in the groin, and I did not even feel the impulse to strike him, but gasped and stared at him helplessly. My expression discomposed him. He knew he had been obscene and was embarrassed, and he tried to cover his embarrassment with a laugh: "You look as though you're going to burst into tears." That was what I felt like doing, but I only turned away in dreadful disgust.

After the exam, when there was only a fortnight of the course left to go, we had a great celebration. Everybody was there, not excluding Mervyn, who had beaten the Service to an unconditional surrender and was waiting in Bombay for a boat back to England. He looked like a prisoner who had just got his reprieve, which is what he felt himself to be.

Sabby came along, too, because all the other instructors were there, including the Brigadier. An Army officer paid her a great deal of attention. He was rather fat and jolly, and he thought he was making good headway. Later on in the evening I asked him how he was getting on with her, and he said:

"Jove, you know, I don't know why I didn't think of this before. She's frightfully good fun, you know." At any rate, I thought, there were some people who still had no suspicion of anything between myself and Sabby; and I looked at this kind of thing with amusement and without any jealousy now. I let him sit next to her at dinner, and watched him trying to persuade her to drink wine. But she only had lemonade, and in this she drank the toasts.

There was a toast to the King, and then Fenwick got up and toasted the Brigadier. We were all pleased to drink this toast, but you could see that Fenwick also felt glory in our enthusiastic response, because he had suggested it. Then the Brigadier made a little speech about the instructors, mentioning them each by name; and when he came to Sabby he said that his words could do no justice to her courage in coming out to India alone to teach entirely amongst men, and that if ever she had felt her position to be awkward, being a Japanese, he wanted her to remember always that we considered it a tremendous privilege to have someone amongst us who represented the finer qualities of a nation we unfortunately had to fight. He said that because of Sabby we had learnt that the language belonged to a culture and society that no one could but admire; and that once the very evil things were wiped clean out of the way, we should be qualified to play a part in re-establishing what was good.

Sabby blushed deeply and looked down so that we could not see her face, and I knew that it was not only because of her modesty but also because of the shame she felt for her country. Everybody cried "Speech!" but she only shook her head without looking up, and long afterwards she was still looking down into her lap, and I think that she was waiting for her tears to dry.

After that the party became a lot more hilarious. Peter got up and announced that Mario and Dorcas were engaged, and Mario pretended to be angry because he had said he had not wanted it announced. They were sitting there together, the superbly hand-some couple from the society magazine, looking as though they would carry the world at their feet. Dorcas's blonde hair was swept back from her forehead in a grand, careless sweep and her face was marvellously white and English and competent, and in that instant I could imagine the rest of their lives to be spent in restaurants and theatre stalls and country houses, with horses and dogs and fine bottles of wine. We all cheered and drank to them. Then somebody got to his feet and said, "Another engagement. This time it's Lamb and Sandra."

There was a bad moment of silence, because this was quite un-expected and we most of us knew that Sandra was Rosie's friend; and then all of a sudden we remembered that she was also good-hearted and humorous, and there was a lot more noise and thumping of the table, and Lamb, who had obviously inspired the announcement, got up and made a speech, beaming through a pair of horn-rimmed glasses. He talked of Sandra as though she were a vestal virgin, and as though we all thought so, too; and now we were all very happy with drink and we laughed im-moderately.

Finally I got up and said that Peter's book was going to be pub-lished. He had heard by wire two days before. The three hundred and seventy-three airgraphs had arrived at their destination safely and had made an immediate impression. It was another impor-tant thing to celebrate.

We sat round the tables that bore the aftermath of the dinner and talked for hours. There was no shortage of drinks, because we had all subscribed money and the Brigadier had given two hundred rupees. Most of our little animosities were forgotten in a welter of fraternity, but I purposely did not go near Fenwick; I did not trust myself not to shake hands with him and forgive him everything. I knew that if I forgave him I should regret it the next day, and it was ridiculous to forgive someone because you had drunk too much wine and were feeling happy.

I had Mervyn on one side of me. He was gayer than I had ever seen him and drunker than anyone.

"You are suckers," he said. "You're all awful suckers. When you're in the jungle again, just think of me in Chelsea."

"Maybe we don't all want to go to Chelsea."

"Everybody wants to go to Chelsea."

"I don't," I said.

"You're a liar, or else a fool. In any case, you're a sucker."

"Why?"

"Oh, don't argue. It's a beautiful place, Chelsea. In two months I shall be there. I shall have dinner at the Leopard, and drink absinthe and go home and have the hell of a night."

"You can't get absinthe in London now."

"I don't care. Anyway, I shall have the hell of a night. Where will you be in two months?"

"Being dropped behind the lines in Burma, I expect."

"I hope that happens. It will serve you right for being a sucker and not wanting to go back to Chelsea."

"I never lived in Chelsea."

"Well, isn't there somewhere else you want to go back to? You'd like to go back to Bayswater. That's not quite so good as Chelsea, but it's all right if you want to go back there."

"I don't want to go back anywhere. I did once, but now I've got used to it."

"It is only being a mug, getting used to things. It's laziness. If you weren't too lazy to have a place get on your nerves, you'd have been going out with me. It's the easiest thing in the world."

"You nearly landed yourself in the mad-house for good."

"I took a risk. You've got to take risks. I got away with it, and you could if you weren't a sucker. You've been through the jungle once, and now they're going to send you again. This time it'll kill you."

"Nonsense, interrogators don't get killed."

"In the jungle anybody gets killed. You'll get malaria and bullets and those filthy sores again."

"I'll remember to think of you calling a taxi outside the Leopard and having intellectual conversations with artists' models. Then I'll realise it's all worth while, winning the war."

"Don't take that attitude—you little hero!"

"I can promise you there's no heroism in it."

"Yes, that's it, you're like all the rest, you've got to be a little

172

hero. Well, heroes are only suckers. I've done my bit. I've had three years of this being pushed around, and now I'm going home. God, I'm going to make up for those three years."

"That's right," I said, "you've had enough. You go back and have your absinthe, and sometimes send me a postcard and let me know how you're getting along."

"I'll send you a postcard, if I remember. If you're not dead, I'd love to send you one."

At eleven o'clock Sabby and I left. Most of them were still sitting around drinking and talking, but the Brigadier had gone and so had Mario and Dorcas. Fenwick was quite drunk. He seldom took alcohol and he had a weak head for it. He was singing and saying senseless things. I wished I could take a motion picture of him and show it him in the morning. As I passed him he said "Watcha, old cock", with a drunken bravado, still remembering how he had offended me. I said nothing, and he called after me for the benefit of those around him: "Whew, you're on a high horse, talk about stuck up. . . ." I didn't hear any more, because the door closed and I was alone with Sabby after what seemed hours of separation, and we didn't care who had seen us leave together.

We sat back in a ghari and hugged each other to show that we were glad the party was over, only from somewhere deep down there was a sadness welling up, and we had to try to be gay and flippant to prevent it from overflowing.

"Michael is drunk with lots and lots of drink," Sabby said.

"Sabby is drunk with lots and lots of people and party."

"Yes, darling, we're both drunk, only you are drunker, and when we get home I shall have to untie your laces and take off your shoes. Then you will see it is true that Japanese wives do that for drunk husband."

"Did I ever say it wasn't?"

"Don't you remember, it was the first word you ever said to me when you asked is it true."

"Yes," I said. "It was in your first class."

"And I had to laugh behind register, and everybody thought what an awful woman."

"Darling, don't think about the past."

"You want to think about future?"

"No; don't think about anything except that it is a lovely night, and we are very happy and we are going back to our own house."

173

"Yes, of course we are both very happy. Listen at the nice noise of clopping horse."

"Who taught you to say clopping?"

"Nobody, I just copied."

"Did you copy me?"

"Yes. I always copy you."

"Good. I like you to do that, it makes me conceited."

"You are not in the least bit conceited, darling."

"Yes, I am. I'm conceited about you, and especially when you call me darling."

I had not been looking at the driver of our ghari. I suppose he had been whipping the horse because we had been going at a good rate, and suddenly it dropped down in its traces and we were thrown forward against the front of the carriage. Sabby uttered a little cry, and we jumped out and saw the great brown body of the animal heaving in the lamplight. It was lying on its side, pinned down by the shafts, its legs stuck out straight, and it was groaning from its throat as though it was in terrible agony and dying. Sabby rushed round to its head and patted its nose with her hand, uttering little whimpers of sorrow. Then she began to talk to it: "It's all right, horse. Driver's taking away cart—please don't die, horse." She was like a gentle child, and this touched me and all the sadness in me gushed up overwhelmingly. The driver was tussling breathlessly with the shafts. I went over and helped him, and when we had freed the harness we pulled away the ghari, and the horse stopped groaning and lay still. Sabby made the clucking noise that she had learnt in the Himalayas, and held out hopeful fingers to it. After a few seconds it struggled suddenly to its feet and walked a few yards and stood looking straight in front of it as though nothing had happened.

"Poor horse only slipped," Sabby said.

"Thank heavens."

"I thought it was going to die when it made horrible voice."

We climbed back into the carriage and waited for the harness to be fixed again. It took some time because the horse did not like being shunted backwards into the shafts. But afterwards it started willingly, and the driver held his whip without using it.

"Now you are *sabishii*," I said.

"Yes, darling."

"Couldn't you go on being happy?"

"No, darling, it doesn't matter. So long as you love me. I don't mind being *sabishii*."

We held each other closely. I was not really drunk at all. It was a beautiful night, with an almost new moon. As we climbed the hill, up the tree-lined road, there were little scenes that might have been glimpses of Paris, except for the brown faces and the *dhotis*. It was a charming ride, and with the movement of the ghari the air was cool on our faces. Somewhere up to our left were the Towers of Silence, where vultures were perched on the parapets, with fat black bodies and bald heads, sleeping off their meals of human flesh. I asked Sabby if she would like to be a vulture.

"But I am vulture already, eating up Parsee Michael."

"Do I taste nice?"

"Yes, so nice that I don't even eat mustard with you."

When we reached the house Bahadur mixed us two long, cold drinks of lemonade, and we took them on to the terrace. It was still exciting to look down on to Bombay. The lights were like a million little jewels set in the blue, velvety darkness, and those in the distance were tremulous like stars. We sat and watched in silence for a long time, drinking through straws, and then we went inside and had a cool bath. Sabby poured in pine-needle extract so that the water was a brilliant green, and it really seemed to smell a little foresty. After I got out she ran in hot water until I could hardly put my hand in, because that was how she liked her baths, and she came out pink as a lobster and ran round draped in an enormous towel. When I chased her she fled through all the rooms, her tiny feet pattering on the bare floors. I caught her, and she was still warm and soft and flushed from the bath.

We didn't read in bed. But we left the light on because we were afraid of bringing the evening to an end, and we wanted to look at each other and remember every detail. We whispered as though somebody might hear if we spoke louder.

"Darling, I don't want to go back to teach at school when you are gone."

"What do you want to do?"

"I didn't tell you about letter I had this morning. It was from wireless people in Delhi."

"What did they write to you for?"

"They say they want me for job. It is reading over the wireless in Japanese."

"Propaganda?"

"It is only just news."

"Don't you mind reading English news to Japan?"

"Not if it is true. Darling, I want your side to win war."

"Our side," I said. "It's yours too."

"Do you think it would be a good thing to read news?"

"It would be all right if you liked it better than teaching."

"But I couldn't bear to go into classroom with a lot of strange faces when you are not there."

"I won't be in Delhi, either."

"No, but in Bombay I have always been with you, and so it would be worse."

"You would have to give up this lovely house."

"I should give it up, anyhow, when you go, because it would be too sad."

"Darling, I shall come back and see you," I said.

"But almost all the time would be without you. Would you also come and see me in Delhi?"

"Of course I would."

"Really, you would come?"

"Darling, why do you think I wouldn't?"

"I don't know if you can go on loving Sabby when you are seeing all kinds of new things and exciting people. You will remember a little black vulture who tried to eat you, and you will think good riddance."

"Do you really believe that?"

"I don't know. Please, darling, how long more can you love me? Do you think another half year would be too long?"

"Is that all you want?"

"I should always be happy if you could love me that much, because I should have had more than I deserve. Could you promise to love me for half year?"

"Let me see," I said. "That's up to next June. Yes, I think that could be arranged."

"Please say you promise."

"I promise," I said.

"Thank you, darling, you are so sweet and kind to me. But please remember you don't have to, even though you have promised."

"If I promised not to, I should still have to, because I can't help it."

"Is it really true?" -

176

"Yes," I said.

"Then I am so happy, darling. I am so terribly, terribly happy."

She lay perfectly still. She closed her eyes, and her lashes were long and black beneath the petal-smooth skin. The rich light of the bed-lamp fell softly on her face and picked out the faint auburn tints in her black hair. I brushed my lips lightly over her face and kissed her little squat nose. I thought she was asleep. I remembered tonight we had heard no drums, and I was glad, because it was a weird, ominous sound. And then suddenly, as I was still thinking this, they began. There was no other sound in the night, and the strong, insistent, primitive rhythm reverberated in the room as though it came from no farther than the road. I felt a kind of shudder run through me. I knew why Sabby had said she was afraid when she heard this drumming. It was savage, and full of death, and inexorable. It went on with fearful monotony, only occasionally rising to a triumphant flourish, and then falling back to the slow, hollow beat.

I listened, staring at the ceiling. And then when I moved to turn off the light, I saw that Sabby was not asleep. She was crying, quite silently and without grimace, and the huge tears were rolling one by one out of her brown eyes and making tracks across her face. She had not moved her head at all, and there was a wet patch on the pillow where they were being absorbed.

BOOK THREE

CHAPTER I

I

WE left Bombay two or three days after the course had ended, with tickets for Cawnpore in our pockets, and no idea at all what our lives held in store.

It was December, and as we went north it became cooler. After a night in the train, we discarded our tropical clothes and put on our blue uniforms. It was the first time I had worn mine since the holiday at Jali Tal.

We arrived at Cawnpore in the morning. We went into the station restaurant to drink coffee whilst Fenwick telephoned somewhere for a truck. After a time, when the truck arrived, we climbed in on top of our baggage and were whisked away through the bazaars of the town into open country. It was half an hour before we came upon the dark walls of a fort, rising in sombre magnificence above the arid and rocky land. It was one of the old Moghul forts that had once contained a whole town, but all that had stood up to the centuries were the thick outer walls and the huge tunnelled gateway, surmounted by cupolas and minarets.

The dust and loose stones on the road spurted up from under the wheels of our truck as we passed through this gateway. Soon we came to a standstill by a barbed-wire compound where sentries were on duty; and inside I caught sight of a little figure in khaki who was under the escort of a guard. It was a Japanese prisoner—the first Japanese I had seen except for Sabby and the school instructors.

We were interviewed in one of the bungalows in the compound by an affable major. "Well, here you are," he said. "This is a prisoner-of-war camp. We're going to keep you here for a bit and teach you a few things, and then off you'll go forward." We asked many questions, and afterwards we went to the mess and had lunch and fixed ourselves up in bungalows. These were inside the fort, a few hundred yards from the prisoners' compound, and we felt almost like prisoners ourselves surrounded by these massive walls.

178

I shared a bungalow with Peter. We took a new bearer because I had left Bahadur with Sabby, knowing that if I went forward he would not be able to accompany me. The new man was a Pathan, with both fire and humour in his eyes.

In the afternoon I went a tour of the cells. They were lofty rooms built into one wall of the fort, furnished with Indian *charpoy* beds. In front there were exercising compounds shut off by straw matting.

In the first cell that I entered the Japanese got up from his bed and stood at attention, his arms hanging from his shoulders like an ape's. I said, "Good morning", and he echoed the greeting, sucking in his breath and using the politest language. I said:

"What is your name?"

"It is Yamanaka."

"Your rank?"

"First-class private."

"Sit down," I said.

He bowed and sucked in his breath and sat down on the bed. His legs were so short that his feet were off the ground.

"Where were you captured?" I said.

"Arakan."

"What happened?"

"I lost my unit and went to sleep in the jungle. I woke up and saw your troops, and I tried to put a grenade to my stomach, but they caught me first."

"Why did you try to do that?"

"For a Japanese it is a shameful thing to become a prisoner."

"Are you sorry you didn't succeed in killing yourself?"

"*Saaa . . .*" he said. "Now I don't know what to think. I expected to be tortured, and I am grateful for kind treatment."

"And after the war?"

"*Saaa . . .*"

"You will go back to Japan?"

"If I go back I shall be put to death. Prisoners can never return."

"But your family?"

"They will have already received my ashes in a box. Ashes are always sent back to Japan. They will think I am dead."

He was laughing as though this had a funny side which was all he expected me to see and which he was seeing, too.

179

"Don't you dream about your home and long to return?" I said.

"I see dreams sometimes. But there is nothing to be done. . . ."

I went in to see the next man. He had a book and a cigarette. He stood up on his bed and bowed. I asked him the same kind of questions and he answered in exactly the same way, and in all the cells it was the same. Some of them were pleased to have company. They talked very rapidly and it was often difficult to stop them, and when they interspersed their sentences with breath-sucking and strings of little superfluous words I found it difficult to understand them. But I was not doing a real interrogation; only finding out what they sounded like and looked like, and something about their mentality.

I looked at them and wondered whether it was any of these who had bayoneted my brother in Hong Kong. It was difficult to believe so. In their cells or when they were brought into an interrogation room by a guard, they were pathetic, lonely, philosophical little people. Of course they denied all knowledge of atrocities. They might have tried to destroy themselves on capture, but now they were not going out of their way to provoke us into ill-treating them. Japanese atrocities, they protested, existed only in Allied propaganda. British prisoners-of-war in Japan would be excellently treated . . . hadn't the Emperor himself decreed that once the enemy had laid down arms, the Japanese soldiers should show their nobility by being clement?

It was said there were three stages through which a Japanese prisoner passed. For the first twenty-four hours he was stunned by battle and the sudden unexpected fate that had befallen him. He had his own word for it, *muchu*—'in the middle of a dream'. After that he began to sit up and take notice, and remember he was still alive and that there was every prospect of his remaining so. There were no lash-weals on his flesh nor lighted tapers in his finger-nails—but a bowl of rice by his hospital bedside and a doctor patching his wounds. He would be touched by this—for there is no one more sentimental than a Japanese. He would write a poem or two to the nurse saying in thirty-one syllables that he had expected his limbs to be tortured, but the only torture he had received was from her eyes—kind eyes that made him think of his sweetheart in Fukuoka, whom he had unmanfully disgraced. Then when he had sufficiently wallowed in gratitude and sentiment, the third stage would set in—despising his captors for their weakness in thus regaling him. He would become, if not surly, at least stubborn and arrogant.

Of course there were many different types. The officers were the most difficult to handle because they had a greater sense of responsibility, and the peasants were the easiest—the *inakamonos,* who knew more about earth than they did about warfare and politics. Then there were small shopkeepers and lorry-drivers and clerks. I spoke to one of the latter, who blinked in a nervous, owlish way behind thick-lensed spectacles. We had given him the spectacles ourselves because he had broken his others before being taken prisoner. I talked to him for a long time because I could understand him better than most, and he looked sad and lost and an abject victim of someone else's war. The difficulty was not to prevent myself from being cruel to these people who had once been the embodiment of the enemy's ruthlessness, but to be sparing with sympathy. And I had to force myself to recall terrible pictures I had seen and stories I had heard, and to think of my brother's murder and allot to them some of the responsibility. It was not fair to do otherwise. The British guards knew it was not fair; they had come through Burma, closer to the Japs than I, and they knew what they would have done if they had had a free hand. They didn't mince matters. But they kept their boots and their bayonets in their places, and we told them: 'Two blacks don't make a white.'

The place was full of interest. It was a little world of its own there, in the barbed-wire compound and the brown walls of the fort. We talked a great deal about the war in Burma, and knew all about place-names and unit dispositions, but all that was another world. We seldom went out of the fort. In the evenings Peter and I strolled round the battlements, and sat talking in one of the pavilions that surmounted the gigantic gateway. We looked down over the endless plains to the Ganges, and saw the brown, compact villages and the peasants and the oxen who belonged to yet another world—a world I should never know anything about. We talked about our work and the Japs, and a lot about Sabby and the life we had left behind in Bombay—the Taj and Rosie and gin and lemons at the Cricket Club—and how life went on and always on, and how it was useless to try to go backwards or even stay where you were. "*Cuncta fluunt,*" Peter said. 'Everything is in a state of flux. . . .' But this was one of the most difficult truths in life to accept: that unless like Lala Vikrana you were to put yourself outside this world, there was no way of holding up the inexorable flow of time or prolonging happiness beyond its appointed end.

"What do you think is going to happen to us?" Peter said.

"More jungle, that's all."

"Do you think we'll get killed?"

"Why should we? We shall be with Corps. Or at the worst with Division. We're out of the real war."

"Something'll happen. I can't imagine going home."

"You'll go home," I said. "You'll suddenly find yourself sitting at an office desk in Holborn, and this will all be a dream. It'll also be something to talk about for the rest of your life."

"It'll also be something to write about. You forget I'm a great novelist."

"Yes, I forgot that. Then of course you won't be killed. Several bombs will explode under your jeep, but by a thousand to one chance you'll get away with only a scratch."

"What'll happen to you?"

"I don't know. I can't imagine going home, either."

"What about your butler and the silver tea-service and afternoon tea on the lawn?"

"That's two reels ago," I said.

"It's also the next reel but one."

"I doubt it," I said. "Though I sometimes think I'd love to have tea on the lawn again, and listen to the rooks and watch an English sky . . ."

"'If I should die, think only this of me . . .' My God, you've been reading too much Rupert Brooke. Sabby ought to have cured you of all that Grantchester-feeling."

"She's cured me of a lot of things, but not that."

"How do you think she'd look in Grantchester?"

"She'd suit the silver tea-service. And the oak beams, too."

"And shopping in Tewkesbury with the county people?"

"Tewkesbury isn't very county. Anyway, she's been in England before. Can't you think of her amongst the Gloucestershire fruit blossoms!"

"And what about the little Sabby-Michaels?"

"We wouldn't have any children—at least not of our own. Perhaps we'd adopt a little girl."

"You've got it all worked out, haven't you?"

"I have," I said. "But Sabby hasn't."

"Then what are you going to do?"

"I haven't any idea. I'm not thinking about it any more. I'm just thinking about next week-end when I shall see Sabby again, and about going to the jungle and about all the little Nips down there eating rice in their cages. What are you thinking about?"

"I'm thinking about those camels over there," Peter said. "They can go such a wonderfully long time without water. Don't you think it's also wonderful how long human beings can go without things and not go mad?"

II

I saw Sabby three times during January and February. She had gone to Delhi a week after we left Bombay, to begin her new broadcasting work, and Delhi was only three hundred miles from Cawnpore. It took ten hours in the train. I went on Friday night when I could get the week-end off, and travelled back all night Sunday. There were bunks in the carriages, so that night travelling was no hardship; but I wished it had been two nights with Sabby instead of two in the train. Still, I had two days and one night with her, and we told ourselves we were lucky to be able to meet at all.

She was living in an hotel in the residential part of Old Delhi beyond the bazaar. It was a good hotel, much better than her old Mayfair Hotel in Bombay, but full of old dowagers waiting for the signal—the first sign of perspiration—to betake themselves to the stations in the hills. There was a spate of staff-officers, too, who were collected by shooting-brakes and whisked backwards and forwards between the hotel and GHQ.

Sabby worked in New Delhi. For a week or two she had been making voice tests and translating scripts, and now she was taking her turn in broadcasting the news in Japanese. The second week-end I was there I listened on the hotel wireless-set on the Saturday afternoon. It gave me an extraordinarily odd feeling to hear the voice that had whispered so many sweet things into my ear coming impersonally from the radio. I was somehow relieved to see her unchanged when half an hour later she came back gaily into the room, and we had the excitement of kissing as though she had been away for years. I wondered if any Japanese listeners would be trying to imagine the person behind the voice they had heard, and I said to Sabby:

183

"Aren't you afraid of what might happen to you after the war if they find out who you are?"

"I don't care," she said.

She didn't care. She was nonchalant about it all, and when she went out to broadcast she might have been going out to the shops, and she talked about it as little.

When I remarked on this, she said:

"You see, it is because I am selfish woman. I ought to remember I am doing war-work and be serious, but all I can remember is that I want you still to love me, darling. I don't want you to go away again."

"In a few weeks I shall come back."

"Darling, when you come the time is gone in a minute, but when you are not here it is like big centuries."

"I write letters."

"That is best thing after not having you."

"You've got me now," I said.

We didn't go out much during those week-ends. There was nothing to do in New or Old Delhi except go to the pictures or dance, and we wanted to be alone. There were no places to go for picnics—the plain round about for miles was stony, uninviting country, and the banks of the Jumna were dreary mud-flats. So we sat in the garden of the hotel, and in the evenings I had long gin drinks and Sabby had lemonades, and we went to bed early. Sabby put up a white mosquito-net—not because there were mosquitos in Delhi in February, but because she wanted it to be like Bombay. I delivered her a little lecture about not trying to keep things the same, but she pleaded for the mosquito-net, and we slept underneath it and were happy. And on the following night she came to see me off at the station, despite my protestations that I hated station farewells, and she made up my bed neatly on a bunk.

I told her I should not be going forward until about May, and that is what I expected. I thought I should take the place of an officer when he came back for summer leave, landing in the jungle in the middle of the monsoons when the 'shooting season' was over. That had been the plan up to now.

Then suddenly there came a demand for someone at Imphal. It was the beginning of March, and the tour would last until September. I was detailed and told to pack.

"I wish it were me," Fenwick said. "It's much more fun forward."

"You can go," I said eagerly.

"I'd like to. It's a pity I wasn't chosen."

"They'll let you go in my place."

"You've had the orders," he said.

"Yes, but if you *want* to . . ."

"It's useless trying to change."

"If you're so keen," I said, "I'll get it fixed for you."

"I don't approve of asking for orders to be rescinded."

"For heaven's sake," I said, "cut out that pompous language. If you want to go, we'll fix it, and if you don't, I'll go—though I'd rather stay here."

"You'll have to go, as you've been told."

"Then don't tell me again that you 'wish it were you'."

"I'm not shy of excitement, as you seem to be."

"Excitement!" I said. "There'll be plenty of rain and living in bashas, and probably not another Nip to talk to for the rest of the season. You've got all the fun here."

"I'm not going to ask to change."

"I know you're not," I said. "Nor would I, if I were you."

It looked as though I shouldn't see Sabby for six months. There wasn't time to go to Delhi, because I had to leave the next night. The only hope was to meet at Agra, half-way in between. But there wasn't time to send a telegram and wait for a reply.

I tried to telephone. It was hopeless. I wasted half an hour and got nowhere. I was frantic, and couldn't make up my mind what to do. I asked Peter.

"Wire her—and go to Agra—and hope," he said.

"But she has a broadcast."

"She'll be there if she can. It's worth the risk."

I left Peter and my bearer to pack the things I should need to take to Imphal, so that I should only have to pick them up on my return, and I took a truck into Cawnpore and was on the station just in time. It was one o'clock in the afternoon. Peter had sent off the wire which would reach Sabby by three, provided the Indian Post Office was not more than usually apathetic. Her train was at four. Of course she couldn't skip her broadcast. I knew she wouldn't do that, but there were others besides her who could do it. If only she could get hold of one of them—that was the thing to pray for.

I prayed all afternoon. I reached Agra at seven, and took a tonga to the Cecil Hotel. There was a decent room empty, and that was a stroke of good luck, because I had been told rooms in Agra were impossible to get. I wondered if it was too lucky, and I should be mocked all night by that big room, and sleep alone in misery and despair. I went out to the portico to have a drink and wait for the Delhi train at half past eight. By the reception desk I met the manageress.

"You are fortunate," she said. "Tonight the moon will be at its best."

"The moon?" I said.

"Haven't you come to see the Taj?"

"The Taj Mahal?"

"It's at Agra, you know."

"Yes, of course it is—I'd forgotten. I shall certainly go and see it."

I'd never really wanted to see it. I would not have got off the train purposely to do so. I hate seeing the world's wonders because it is difficult to disassociate them from the vulgarity of their fame, and it is better to find one's own little wonders that the world has overlooked. But now I wanted to see the Taj because it happened to be at the place where I might be meeting Sabby, and it had volunteered itself as a background complete with its moon.

By quarter past eight the daylight had gone and the moon was coming over the roof-tops. It was quite full, and still a little yellowish, but it was turning whiter as it rose. I went by tonga to the station and began to pace the platform, chain-smoking cigarettes. Indian pedlars tried to sell me hideous models of the Taj and fans made out of peacock feathers. I said '*Challo, challo*', but they didn't go away, so I said '*Jaow!*' impatiently and turned away myself. I kept looking up the line.

The train was less than five minutes overdue. The red-turbaned coolies swarmed to the doors as it pulled in, and the third-class passengers burst out of their carriages. Then others began to emerge. There was no sign of Sabby. I pushed my way through the crowd, and there was no Sabby anywhere. My whole body sickened.

And then suddenly I caught sight of her in a carriage doorway waving to me brightly, and the joy flooded over me. In a moment or two we were back in the tonga with her baggage and trotting towards the Cecil, and I knew this was our fate and nothing could have happened but this.

"Did you manage it easily?" I said.

"But of course, darling. I simply changed days, that was all. They are all so sweet to me."

"Well, we're going to see the Taj in the moonlight," I said.

"Please what is Taj?"

"I am glad you don't know. It's just a tomb, I think."

"Is it good thing to see tomb?"

"It might be," I said. "We can go and try."

We had dinner first at the Cecil and a dawdling coffee in the portico, and kept the tonga waiting. When we set off again, the moon was high and dazzling in its whiteness, and the air was fresh and warm. We clung together on the narrow, uncomfortable seat, and jogged along the road for a quarter of an hour until we came to a giant archway. We got down, and the tonga-man pointed to the number on his carriage so that we should pick it out amongst the others. He spoke the numbers laboriously, the only English he knew: "Seven—two—nine."

High up inside the archway a lamp of fretted metal-work was burning, dimly speckling the stone. We passed under it; and beyond, framed by the dark masonry of the arch, was the marble face of the Taj, cool and pale in the moonlight.

Sabby gasped and took my arm, and I felt her little body trembling. She was trembling with the beauty of it—the beauty of the minarets and the reflection in the long pool, and the lines of cypress trees standing blackly like centurions against the naked whiteness. In a way, I think it was also the most lovely thing I had ever seen, because the moon on marble cannot help but be lovely, as it is upon snow, and here it gave to this formal scene an incredible stillness and purity.

"Please, is it true I am here with you, or is it dream that I have got to heaven?" Sabby said.

"It is only a dream," I said.

"Please, pinch, then."

"Go on sleeping for a bit longer."

We walked slowly along the edge of the pool until we came to the steps up to the terrace. A *chaprassy* slipped big canvas sandals over our shoes and we went up. The whole surface of the terrace was marble, smooth as the surface of the pool, and extending all round the tomb. We climbed one of the minarets, up and up past two perilous balconies until we were in the topmost pavilion. There were many people crowded there, and there were two young Indian men, very drunk and rowdy; and Sabby clung more closely because if anyone had pushed us we should have fallen over the low balustrade. We only stayed a short while to look at the pale countryside, and then we descended and took off our overshoes and went back along the pool. It was from this distance, from the end of the pool, that it was most beautiful, and we lay on the grass and watched it and knew it was really a dream and almost gone.

"Darling, I would like to die now," Sabby said.

"This is only the beginning of our happiness."

"No, it is the end, and I don't mind dying, darling, I have been so happy with you."

"You must never talk like that," I said.

"It is true, so it doesn't matter talking."

"But our lives are only beginning."

"No, it is the end and you are going away to war."

"I'm not going to fight," I said.

"All the same, you are going away."

"You're not afraid I'm going to get killed?"

"No, I didn't mean that; you will never get killed."

"Well then," I said. "I shall be back in six months and we'll have a month together. We'll go to the Himalayas, to Jali Tal, and meet Margaret and Jennifer again and have wonderful pony rides in the mountains."

"Yes, of course we will, darling."

"You don't say it as though you believe it."

"I believe, honestry."

"Honestly," I said.

"Oh dear, I shall never learn. Honest-ly, honest-ly."

"You are crying, Sabby."

"I know I am. It is only because it is so beautiful. Please look at moon."

"I can see it in your tears."

"All Japanese girls drop big tears when they see something very beautiful. Why is it that beautiful things also make sad?"

"Because there is already sadness inside you."

"Tonight I promised myself I would be strong and not be sad."

"You can't help it, darling, when your name is *Sabishii*."

"Yes I can, I am not going to cry any more."

"And you are going to think about our next holiday in Jali Tal?"

"I promise not to think of anything else," she said.

"You won't wish you'd fallen off the minaret?"

"No; I didn't want to fall off minaret unless you had fallen, and then I would have jumped, too."

"And you're happy again?"

"Yes, because this is the most wonderful night in all my life."

"There's plenty of it left," I said.

"There is fourteen and a half hours until your train, because I have worked out."

"You should only count time until good things."

"Then it is just one hour until mosquito-net, and then I am going to bite nose."

"I shall bite your ears."

"Do you like Sabby's ears better than Taj?"

"Yes, darling," I said. "They are better proportioned and they are just as white."

"Then let us go and bite."

"All right," I said. "We'll go and find the tonga."

CHAPTER II

I

When I came in from the bathroom Sabby was sitting in front of the dressing-table with her hands on her lap and her face miserably puckered. She brightened at once as she saw me, and began brushing out her hair with swift, practised strokes.

"Why were you looking like that?" I said.

"It is only because I have a little ache in head through too much looking at moon."

"Then take an aspirin."

"Yes, darling, please give aspirin. You will find bottle in drawer."

I shook out two, and gave them to her with a glass of water. She swallowed them and smiled and said:

"I am all right now. I didn't mean to look miserable, because it is very happy night."

It had been a long day since I had got up in the morning in the fort at Cawnpore, not knowing that I was going to Imphal or that I was going to see the Taj and meet Sabby, and I had also got a slight headache. When Sabby had gone to the bathroom I looked for the aspirin bottle on the dressing-table to take one myself, but it had gone. I waited for Sabby to come back, and when I asked her for it she took it from her dressing-gown pocket.

"I am so sorry, but now there is only one left."

"There were five a minute ago," I said.

"Yes, darling. I threw others away."

"You've swallowed them, haven't you?"

"It is only to make headache better so that I can sleep well with Michael."

"But, darling, you can't take six—you'll make yourself ill."

"It doesn't matter because I am used to aspirin."

"It's a bad habit."

"But it makes headache well. Please don't scold, darling."

I lay awake for a long time. Sabby's face was close against mine, and I could feel her warm breath on my cheek and her lashes tickling as they brushed my skin. Then I could only feel her breath and thought she was asleep. I drifted into a half-sleep, dreaming of the Taj and the jungle and the Japanese prisoners. I could see their little bowing figures in khaki a size or two too large, and their heads with cropped hair. Then the pedlars trying to sell the icing-sugar models of the Taj, and the jogging of the tonga horse, and everything altogether in a jumble until I must have passed into a deeper sleep with no dreams that I could afterwards remember. I woke up when it was still dark and Sabby was moaning. It was a long, steady moan that began with each breath and tailed away and began again. I listened until I could stand it no more, and then I touched her gently and whispered in her ear.

"Is anything the matter?" I said.

She grunted sleepily, and I asked her again, but she didn't reply. She suddenly put her arms round me and clung to me tightly with her fingers pressed into my back, and she remained like that as though holding me with all her might from escaping, until I had once more dropped off to sleep. In the morning when the bearer came in with the tea she was lying in the same position against me, but she had relaxed the pressure, and her face was so peaceful that I hated to wake her.

My own train was early, before hers. She came to the station, and we kept saying the same commonplace things over and over again for the sake of filling in the awful minutes. She bought me a model of the Taj, but only for something to do, and made me promise to throw it out of the window; and I said I would keep it always and we should have it on our mantelpiece in years to come to remind ourselves of this occasion when we had to leave each other for six months. And I kept telling her how six months were nothing, how husbands who went overseas from England had to leave their wives for years. At last the train started to move, and she grew smaller and smaller, waving her tiny hand, and I could only see a little white spot that was her face. Then we swung round a bend, and there was nothing, no longer any Sabby. I shut the door of the carriage and went into the lavatory, staring into the mirror to see what I looked like with damp eyes. It looked so comic that I laughed or made myself laugh, and then I went back into the carriage and discussed servants with an old dyspeptic Lieutenant-Colonel.

At Cawnpore I got transport to the Fort, but I only had time to eat a quick supper and exchange hurried news with Peter and Mario. Mario was going on leave in a fortnight's time in order to get married, and meanwhile was living in ecstasy. As for Peter, he said he was going to go mad in the Fort without either of us, and why didn't they take over a good hotel as a prisoner-of-war camp just to show there was no ill-feeling? We finished up a bottle of whisky—it was Peter's, because mine was packed—and I began to feel excited about going, though I wished I was not doing so alone. Then I paid the bearer his wages, had my tin trunk loaded on to the lorry, and set off back to the station. The moon hung brilliantly in the sky as it had done the night before; only it was a day older now, and I was a day older, and the night with the Taj was already receding far into the past, like the beautiful dream we had known it to be.

I had a top bunk in the train. I laid out my bed and climbed in straight away, and began to read a book, but my mind was full of other things and I read it without taking in the meaning. I closed it up and put it under my pillow. I began to talk to the man who was on the opposite bunk, a gaunt, middle-aged Army Captain, with the face of a disillusioned artist. He was not an artist, but he was disillusioned; and the story of his life came out bit by bit as we rattled down the valley of the Ganges at midnight. He had been a failure at home in accountancy, tried to sell water-softeners to housewives, and had somehow got to Rangoon and managed a failing cinema there. And then the war, when he had joined the Army in Burma, and retreated through the country and come out with malaria. Now he was going back to the border.

I thought he was charming, because he had no self-importance, no illusions about the causes of his own reverses, and his conversation was full of perspicacity and a gentle irony. I listened for a long time, and then we talked about the war in Burma, and he said:

"I shall get killed this time in some useless little jungle skirmish. It's curious not to mind a great deal one way or the other."

"What's going on up near Imphal?"

"Nothing much. The Japs say they're going to get the place by the monsoons. Perhaps they will. We shall get it back."

He asked where I was going.

"Corps Headquarters," I said.

"You'll be all right there. No snipers."

"Some people in your shoes would have said that resentfully."

"Why should they?"

"I'm going to the rear and you're going to the front."

"That doesn't make life good or bad. I expect your life has its rough passages."

"On the whole, I've been very lucky," I said.

"And happy?"

"I think so."

"I haven't. Even if I'd been lucky I shouldn't have been happy, so I've nothing to complain about."

"There must have been some way you could have turned your life to good account."

"I think not. I'm just a kind of misfit."

"I don't know about that."

It was one o'clock. We turned off the light, and somebody on a lower bunk turned over and began to snore. The moon shone through the window on to the floor of the compartment. I was hot, and removed one blanket and lay under a sheet. I tried to work out whether or not I was happy, and whether the gentle ache under my heart was only the thought of Sabby; but I was not thinking very clearly, and soon I fell asleep with the monotonous clatter of the train.

The Captain's name was Manning. I came to know him well, because we travelled a long way together and there is nothing like a railway journey for making friends.

But our journey was not only by rail. Neither of us had priority passes for the Assam Railway, so that from Dhubri it was necessary to proceed by boat up the Brahmaputra. It was an old, dirty paddle-steamer, and we boarded her at night-time by the yellow light of oil lamps. I could see the black faces of the crew, the sweat glistening and their black hands hauling ropes. There was a great deal of noise and shouting, and some drunkenness. Two of the crew were drunk. They fought on the narrow deck, slogging each other wildly and rolling together to the rails. No one stopped them. The lamps flickered, and everything was yellow and black and unreal.

I dug out my bottle of whisky, and we hung over the rails drinking from mugs, while the paddles churned in the water pushing us out into midstream. It was a wide river, muddy and slow like the Jumna and Ganges, and to me the kind of river that was India, as the Wye and Severn and chuckling rock streams were England. The moon came up late. It was yellow at first like the swinging lanterns, and it rose lethargically from the paddy-fields. Somehow it seemed more like a dying sun.

We began to get drunk. It was good Scotch whisky, and we took it straight. I told Manning about Sabby, and he told me of a girl in England he had loved in 1934, and been engaged to, until he had broken it off because the water-softeners weren't selling and he thought she was too good for him. In Rangoon he had had a jealous little Burmese mistress who had wanted to follow him out of Burma with the Army. Now he thought she would be a Japanese officer's mistress, and as jealous.

We went on talking most of the night. It became cooler, the moon whiter. There was a faint breeze up the river, overtaking the steamer. We had finished the bottle of whisky. Inside me there was a little core that was not intoxicated, a pea-size remnant of sanity, and I tried to grasp hold of it, to keep myself from spinning altogether out of reality. I kept telling myself, 'This is the Brahmaputra. You are going to Imphal. The wooden deck-rail is under your hands.' At the same time I could hear myself talking aloud. My tongue, considering it was working independently, was spinning words with remarkably good sense. It was saying deeply philosophical things about life. I heard it quoting Lala Vikrana. And then all of a sudden I felt a great warmth towards my friends, Mr. Headley and Rosie, Lord Durweston and the Brigadier, and Peter and Mario, and Manning too, and I wished they could all be there on the cramped deck of the paddle-boat with the moon and the reflection in the water and the white, flat paddy-fields. Without them a sadness suffused me; I was becoming sober. I walked up and down the deck, and it was all more real than it had been since we had first come on board. I no longer had to remind myself where I was and why I was there. We went down below, and brought our bedding up on to the deck and unrolled it. It was cool, and the sky was clean and beautiful and immensely far distant.

All next day we went on upriver. We drank coffee and ate bully-beef and sat watching the flat banks with their jungles and tea plantations and paddy-fields. Sampans and paddle-steamers passed downstream, making their way through the slow surface. Our own engines chugged and creaked and pushed us on unhurriedly. It was strange to think that we were going to war.

In the evening we disembarked at Gauhati. There was a waiting train already full of people who had come up by railway. But we found cramped seats, and dozed in them until the morning, when we came to Dimapur.

There was a transit camp there, with bamboo and straw bashas in which we erected our beds, and a perforated petrol-drum hoisted on a tree for a shower. We had to wait for a truck to take us over the mountains to Imphal, to the lush little plain that was sandwiched between India and Burma. We saw two lorry convoys set off, and someone told us 'there was a flap on', the Japanese were on the 109 milestone on the Tiddim Road beyond Imphal, and Kennedy Peak had gone and reinforcements were being 'rushed up'. Because we had arrived individually, nobody seemed to care about rushing us up, and we hung about for two days.

The second day two letters came for me. The mail was flown forward up to this point, and I intercepted them at the Army post-office. One was from Sabby. She said that she was trying to be strong and only crying a little before she went to sleep, and that whatever happened nothing could ever take away the wonderful times we had had together. And she ended: 'Darling, it was such happy times we had, wasn't it? I've never had half that much happiness before, only I do hope you were not just pretending happiness. You have got to be so happy always.' And the quaint Sabby touch to the English, more than anything else, made me think that she was beside me saying these things.

The other letter had followed me through Bombay and Cawnpore, and it was written in a childish hand that I could not recognise. I opened it and looked first at the signature and saw 'Margaret and Jennifer'. It said:

Dear Uncle Michael.—We have been trying to make up our minds to write to you for ever such a long time, and haven't done it because Mummy said we mustn't worry you, but now we simply can't help writing to find out if your darling Sabby is all right. You may have to go away from her, and she won't tell you if she is ill, because she thinks also that you mustn't be worried. But we both think you ought to know everything, otherwise you can't help her, and that would hurt you too when you find out. That is why we are telling you, but on your honour you must not tell Sabby we have written, and we are not telling Mummy either, because in a way we promised not to say anything to you, and the only reason we are breaking the promise is that you are a man and we don't think you can always understand what Sabby is feeling, like us who are women. We think you ought to understand before anything awful happens, so that you will know what to do.

Please don't be angry, we are writing because we think Sabby and you are marvellous, and you have only got to tell us and we will come and do anything for you straight away.

Margaret and Jennifer.

PS.—We are going up to the mountains next week and you can write to us there. Wouldn't it be wonderful if you could come too, we promise not to stop Sabby and you being alone as Mummy said we did last year.

Something seemed to collapse inside me when I read this, and all the sap was gone out of my limbs, and I went in a daze back along the dusty road to our basha, dropping down on to my camp-bed.

"What on earth's up?" Manning said.

I shook my head, feeling too broken to speak.

"Do you want a doctor?" he said. "There's one in the camp."

"It's not that."

He saw my letters.

"Bad news?"

"Yes," I said. "It's very bad."

It was suddenly all so clear. Whatever was the matter with Sabby, I was the only person who didn't know, I who had had the most opportunity of knowing and who had professed to understand her so well. What unbelievable, unforgivable blindness! I had thought only of our happiness, of Sabby's pretty ways and her beauty, of all those things that pleased or flattered me; but my selfishness had prevented me from looking into the depths of her —from seeing what Sabby had been selflessly hiding to spare me. Yet even the children had known! They had discovered in a month what in a whole year had passed by me—and my humiliation at the thought of this was deeper than any humiliation I had ever known. But at the present moment it was not so much this as my fear that was making me wretched. What was this dreadful thing that Sabby had hidden from me? Was it something that was going to take her from me?

One by one there came back to me a series of incidents—or at least I now saw as a series what at the time had seemed by unconnected events—that pointed to something dark and forbidding. I remembered Sabby saying: 'You needn't always love me. Do you think you can love me for a year?' And in the beautiful house at Bombay she had said again: 'Can you really love for another six months?' She had refused to marry me. Wasn't it that she was afraid of giving me a new and terrible responsibility? Then Lord Durweston had said: 'I'm going to rely on you. It may not be easy.' At the Taj Mahal Sabby herself had talked of dying, about not caring if she died after such exquisite happiness; and that night she had taken many aspirins and I had woken to hear her moaning, and she was clinging to me tightly as if she were in pain and afraid. There was her own letter, too: 'Whatever happens, nothing can take away our wonderful time.'

One by one I remembered these things, over a thousand miles away in a basha in Assam, when I was about to move not closer to her where I might comfort her, but yet farther away. I felt a panic grow inside me. I wildly thought of plans to get back to her; to take a train back now and be in Delhi before my absence in Imphal was discovered. But I should not be able to stay with her. It was useless. I was hemmed about by stone walls and trying to batter my head against them, and the bitter sense of frustration sickened me.

Later on I began to see things in a calmer light. Nothing had really happened yet. Margaret and Jennifer were children, and they had no subtlety of expression, and their alarm might be exaggerated. All the other things, too, might have simple explanations. Nevertheless, I went to the Army post-office at Dimapur and wired the girls: 'Please write to Sabby,' I said, 'and look after her if she needs it.' I felt happier because I knew they would look after her with their tender competence.

Then I asked an officer in the post-office if he knew anyone who had a wireless. He said there were one or two in the village; there was one in a *pukka* house a few hundred yards away where someone called Major Crossley was living.

I went off at once and found it; it was only a small bungalow, *pukka* because it was made of stone and plaster instead of bamboo. A servant came out and grinned; he knew no English. The Major himself appeared behind him and dismissed him with a laconic phrase. I called him 'Sir', and began to explain my mission. I wanted to listen to his wireless for a few minutes. He was puzzled but willing, and he led me into his living-room.

I got the wavelength just as the suave voice of an English woman was announcing. It sounded incongruous out here, this voice that made you think of London drawing-rooms and the façades of Piccadilly. 'This is Delhi. For the next quarter of an hour there will be news for Japanese listeners.' There was a pause. The silence petrified me. All my consciousness was concentrated into my ears. It went on and on, the silence. Then it was broken, and the voice was Sabby's.

The relief and joy of hearing her burst inside me. I only heard vaguely what she was saying in the sing-song way she read the news. I began to smile and laugh, and the Major watched me from his arm-chair with a stern, mystified expression. When it was over and I switched off the set, he said:

"For Japanese listeners?"

"It's a friend of mine," I said. "I thought she might be ill."

"You understand Japanese?"

"It's my job here."

He asked me to remain for tea. He was a middle-aged bore, a man on whom experience abroad had made no impression. He was from Yorkshire, as much a piece of Yorkshire as a farmhouse on the Pennine Range. But there was plenty of kindness beneath his grey and stony exterior. When I told him I was expecting to get a place in a convoy up to Imphal the next day, he said that he had to go there himself. He was a transport officer and had a car; if I cared to join him it would be more comfortable than the tedious journey in a truck. I mentioned Manning. There was room for both, he said.

I left him and walked back to the basha. On the way I called in at the post-office and sent a telegram to Sabby. I said that I had heard her voice, and it had made me very happy. I added: 'Less than six months to Himalayas.'

But when I tried to sleep that night I could not bring myself to think of the Himalayas. I was still afraid that the children were not exaggerating.

CHAPTER III

I

THERE were four of us in the car, including a Sikh driver. It was a kind of shooting-brake with high chassis and fat tyres, and not particularly comfortable, but it took the gradient at good speed, overtaking the convoy of trucks that had set off before us. The road had been put into excellent condition. The Major told us that before the war it had been scarcely motorable in wet weather; and now it was metalled and well graded, though the bends followed one another in endless succession. The Sikh tore around these with screeching tyres, the horn blaring ferociously.

He was a Subahdar, a Viceroy's Commissioned Officer—a fine-looking figure, immaculately turbaned and magnificently bearded. I tried to imagine him without his beard, and thought his face would still be noble. Whiter, he might have been typical of the better products of a rugger-playing English public school. And unshaven, in obedience to the tenets of his religion, he was wholly patrician in appearance. He called the Major 'Sir', not obsequiously but with a frank acceptance of rank, his own two silver shoulder pips, set in their thin red and yellow bands, raising him little higher than a British sergeant. He spoke English in a slow, deliberate tone, giving his mistakes an air of correctness. He talked to me now of the time he had fought his way out of Malaya.

"There was too much bombing. All day long we heard the voice of the aircraft. There were aircraft with one fan and aircraft with two fans."

"Now it is different," I said.

"Now we give them too much bombing. It is too much, but it is not enough."

"You don't like the Japanese?"

"Sir, in Malaya I cut off the head of a Japanese with my sharp knife. It is not a nice thing to do, to cut off a man's head. But this I would do again with pleasure."

In the back of the car Manning and the Major were talking about England. The Major was dogmatic and wore a smile of intolerable smugness. Glancing round at him, I caught a glimpse of his face at an angle which revealed all his pig-headedness in his brief, pointed nose and ignorant chin. But as I said, there was a certain kindness in him. So long as you did not try to assail his bastions of ignorance he was amiable. At first he was amiable with Manning, because he was not sufficiently observant to notice the humorous derision with which Manning regarded him. Then he became suspicious; and after that in self-defence he became more aggressive in conversation, the Major deigning to talk to the Captain. He tried to win me: 'Our young airman friend here will bear me out.'

It took only an hour and a half to reach Kohima, perched at five thousand feet on a saddle in the Naga Hills. We arrived there at ten-thirty to find the morning still gloriously fresh and something in the air like an English spring. The exhilarating atmosphere rushed over me from the open windscreen, and I opened my mouth to it and swallowed it like a tonic, and all the cool freshness went through me, but always round the dark, numb core in my heart which had been there since the day before.

I was excited, because in Kohima we seemed suddenly to be in the war. There were troops moving about in a slow, hardy, battle-tried way. There was no nonsense about clothes. They were dressed for the jungle, and had mostly been in the jungle and gained a jungle confidence. Some stood round a tent drawing tea. They looked casual and unhurried; but as though beneath the rather bored exterior there was a fanatical stubbornness. Some of them were joking lazily, and one of these made a rude sign at the car. The sign had another meaning, too, but he meant the rude one; yet not rudely, only as a comical gesture. I expected the

Major to stand on his dignity and show anger or pretend to ignore it. Instead he said unexpectedly:

"It's a good thing we have chaps like those."

I liked him better for saying that. He was not clever enough to have thought of it only to save himself from looking ridiculous, and it was a genuine flash of broadmindedness.

As we came over the saddle the tremendous panorama opened up to us, an incredibly beautiful view. To the right the hills rose high in a range that ran southward, and to the left the jungles of India and Burma merged at an unmarked frontier in fold after fold of deepening blue. I had never forgotten the blue of these jungle hills from the time of my first passage through them—a blue veil whose intensity varied with the sky, that never lifted to reveal the green, tangled valleys and steep, dense slopes. From a distance, and aloft, it was beautiful, and the blueness soft and lavish.

"If I was the kind of person who cared where he was buried," Manning said, "I should like to have a simple grave up here."

"You won't look at it when you've been over once or twice," the Major said. "I do it every week. It's all right once. But you get tired of it. Give me something more compact. The Lake District, for instance."

He was not at all awed by the vastness; nor were the British Army. We passed a column of men, with all their equipment, and later on another convoy of lorries. There were some field-guns pulled into the roadside, and two light tanks travelling along on their own. We overtook them all, and a few miles beyond stopped at an Army rest-camp for a cup of tea. We sat down on benches at a rough table in the open, looking across a valley to a Naga village on a hill-top, and it all seemed like the happiest of summer holidays. In a tree close by a bird was going mad with joy, its song soaring up and up till we thought it could go no higher, but still it went up and up to a little trembling note that sounded in the top of our heads.

A bearer came out with the cups. He had a skin like milk chocolate, and long Mongolian eyes. He put the tray down on the table, and the Major began to pour out, saying: "Shall I be mother? One spoonful or two?"

The tanks had caught us up. Two officers came in, and half a dozen soldiers, and sat down at adjacent tables. One of the soldiers said:

"Another bleedin' doss-house. What wouldn't I give for five minutes in the Odeon Café."

"You wouldn't know what to do with it."

"Do with what?"

"The Odeon."

"Blimey, you wait and see."

"Wait and see what?"

"What I won't do with the Odeon."

"I'll tell you what you can do with the Odeon. Of course, if you're talking about one of them bits of flashlight girls, that's a different blinkin' story."

They were all smoking cigarettes. Their faces were tanned and healthy, and it was hard to think of them in cheap suits in the Edgware Road. Their hands were grimy and looked competent in an unsubtle way. The two officers were quiet middle-class boys with new moustaches. One had sad eyes and a half-intelligent look, and the other was tall with a shock of black hair and a full mouth that the sun had dried and hardened.

"Where are you making for?" the Major said.

"Blimey, that's asking," said one of the soldiers.

"We don't really know ourselves," the tall officer said.

"We're just wandering about lookin' at the blinkin' scenery."

"No Japs around here yet?"

"I'll say there are Japs! Those little beggars get anywhere, they do."

"No, as a matter of fact," the tall officer said, "they seem to be pushing up a bit into the Nagas, but the real trouble's on the other side of Imphal. They're coming up the Tiddim Road. You'll probably find Imphal's got the wind-up."

"As long as they don't get this road . . ."

"Not with our little tin boxes, they won't," the soldier said. "We'll keep 'em off till you get back."

"Keep them off altogether," I said. "We all want to come back."

When we set off again, the tail end of the lorry convoy was just passing the rest-camp. The road clung to the hillside, and there were only short stretches in between the blind corners, so that it took us several miles to pass all the lorries. The Sikh driver nosed up behind one vehicle, and when the opportunity came shot out on to the outside of the road, giving the car full throttle, and then braked suddenly and pulled up behind the next. Occasionally a lorry or a jeep came up from the opposite direction and we had a near collision; but we put the convoy behind us truck by truck and in a quarter of an hour we were free and racing ahead on our own. We passed by one or two little villages of mud houses, and then the road began to snake downwards, still cut out of the hill and sometimes half blocked with small landslides. We saw milestone 85 from Dimapur and 47 from Imphal, and reckoned we should be down on the plain in an hour.

The Major was dozing in the back seat, and Manning looking out of the window with a far-away, reflective gaze. I took out Sabby's letter and read it through, and I read through the last paragraph several times more. I thought it was as characteristic of her as her nose, or her ears, or her tenderly loving eyes, and if there were no tears in my own eyes then it was only because beside this princely Sikh there seemed something quite unmanly in crying. Afterwards I read Margaret and Jennifer's letter again, trying to give it a less bitter interpretation. But I had no bitterness against them for writing to me like this; their instinctive understanding was unerring. If, later still, I had found this thing out, I should have paid even more heavily for my ignorance. It was infinitely better to know now, though my helplessness intensified my anxiety and my remorse. To know. . . . Yes, there was only one meaning to the letter. The children knew and I knew now, not only by the incidents that I had remembered, but by some sense of fatality. I began to feel that subconsciously I had known ever since the night in our house when the drums sounded down the hill; and I had not dared to accept the knowledge into my conscious mind lest a shadow should fall across my happiness. . . .

All of a sudden the car swerved. The Sikh jammed down his foot and the brakes screamed like an animal suddenly wounded. We were thrown forward and fell back, and were abruptly still. The engine stopped. We all stared out through the windscreen.

Across the road there was a barricade—a small tree trunk and a pile of loose branches. Either side the road was empty; behind us was the sharp corner round which we had swung at thirty miles an hour, and in front another blind bend. On the right the ground fell away steeply to a ravine, and on the left a jungle-covered bank rose out of sight.

We all sat staring, and in the short silence the possible explanations for this road blockage came to us one by one, and we at once dismissed the worst.

"Can it have fallen?" I said.

"Perhaps."

"It is very simply removed, sir," the Sikh said. "I will remove it quickly."

"Wait!" said the Major. He made it quite clear he had taken command. We waited, and we looked more carefully at the tree across the road, and saw no root from which it had broken. There was a long silence this time, and without moving our shoulders we turned our heads to look sideways into the jungle. We could see nothing but the creepers hanging from the trees and the intermingling mass of undergrowth. We listened and there was only the raucous screech of a mating bird. We looked back at the tree, and the silence seemed unbearable, so that I longed for the Major to speak again.

"There is obviously a reason for this," he said at last. "There has perhaps been an accident farther on."

We considered this. We were all thinking the same thing. The Major was also thinking it, but it was Manning who had the courage to say it, and he did so with an extraordinarily unaffected simplicity.

"I think it is very probably the Japs. They are waiting for us to get out of the car."

I was petrified by a cold horror that went into all my limbs. I thought this was the end, and in a moment or two I was going to die, to leave Sabby alone to die too, and in that instant I saw not all my life unfolding before my eyes, but a number of imaginary scenes, of which the clearest was in the hall of the house at Tewkesbury, where my mother was about to tear open a telegram that she held in her hands. Then I gripped myself a little and told myself that there were four of us in this, and as yet nothing had happened. I looked at the Sikh. His face was set and wooden and he was staring directly in front of him. The Major had become jittery. His hands were quivering, and when he tried to speak his mouth moved and no sound came. Then he pulled himself together, too, and his voice came out gruffly.

"Better sit tight. The convoy will be along in twenty minutes."

The mating bird clamoured peevishly. It was somewhere in the branches of the trees that overhung the road. I looked out, and ran my eye slowly over the spaces between the leaves. I couldn't see the bird, and I couldn't see any Japanese either. But I knew the bird was there.

Manning took out a cigarette-case and opening it slowly passed it to each of us. My hand was quivering slightly, and I pulled out the cigarette quickly and stuck it in my mouth at a purposely careless angle. The Sikh said graciously:

"Thank you, we Sikhs do not smoke."

The Major lit a match and the flame was unsteady too. Manning leant forward and drew it into the end of his cigarette, and then he leant back in his corner and let out a long, pensive puff of smoke. After that he said to the Major quietly:

"I would like to suggest, sir, that if this is a trap we might be able to save the convoy from falling into it."

"Turn round and go back, you mean?"

"That would make us look foolish if we were mistaken."

The Major barked with nervous impatience.

"Then what the hell do you mean?"

"We could remove the tree, and if nothing happens, go on slowly."

"Remove it?"

"It's only light. A one-man job."

"And what happens if there's trouble?"

"There's only one thing to do. Reverse the car as fast as possible and shoot back up the road until you think you're clear, and then turn round and go to meet the convoy."

"We may be getting ourselves worked up over nothing," the Major said.

"Yes, we may be."

"The Lieutenant at the rest-camp said there were no Japs around here. They'd certainly keep 'em off the road."

"The jungle is very large to hide in."

"Very well. We'll move the tree."

"I would like to do that, sir," the Sikh said. "Will you kindly instruct me to get out of the car."

"It doesn't matter who does it. We're all pretty much in the same boat."

"I think it had better be left to me," Manning said. "The driver may be required."

"Yes, better let Manning go."

"Start the engine," Manning said, "and put her in reverse. Keep your foot ready on the clutch."

"What about you?" said the Major.

"If anything breaks out, don't hesitate for a moment. There

won't be a hope if you do. Get out of it for all you're worth. You understand?" he said to the driver.

"Yes, sir."

"Very well. Here goes. In a couple of minutes we shall probably think ourselves damned idiots for all this melodrama."

"I hope so," I said.

He had a revolver, like the rest of us. He drew it out of its holster, and opened the door of the car, slamming it behind him when he was out. He began to walk at a steady pace past the front of the car. He was very tall and walked erectly. He had left his hat behind and his hair was curly and unbrushed. His cigarette was still drooping from his mouth.

There was only the sound of the engine ticking over, and still the maddening love-call of the jungle bird. We all sat gazing at Manning in a paralysis of apprehension. We saw him cover a dozen yards to the tree without looking either side of him. He surveyed it for a moment, and then stepped over it, and turning to face us he made a French gesture, shrugging his shoulders and splaying out one hand, as though to say, 'What's all the fuss about?'

And that is how the bullet caught him. We heard the shot, so close that my body convulsed with the sudden ear-splitting explosion. At the same time Manning seemed to be transfixed in that gesture. It can only have been a second, but it seemed an age that his body hung there, like a moving figure stilled in a snapshot. Then the revolver fell out of his hand and the cigarette out of his mouth. He seemed to move slowly backwards, his legs folded beneath him, and he toppled. The car lurched as the Sikh let out the clutch and pressed the accelerator. We began to career madly in reverse, swaying over the road; and simultaneously there was the deadly hammer of a machine-gun. The windscreen was shattered, and the steering-wheel spun in the Sikh's hands. Then the back of the car tilted downwards over the road's edge, and I thought we were all going over into the ravine; I hoped so, the smash would be over in a few moments.

But the front wheels clung to the road. The engine kicked and stopped, and we were at a standstill. There was an immediate onrush of little khaki figures with rifles and fixed bayonets. My own revolver had fallen to the floor. I searched for it blindly with one hand, but I knew it was too late. The Major fired one shot, wildly.

Then we saw half a dozen bright steel blades menacing through the windows, and as many blurred faces.

I expected to feel the steel, but when I got out on the slope it was the butt end of a rifle that hit me across the forehead, a kind of salutary warning, I suppose, and only hard enough to stun me momentarily. When I recovered and was clear-headed enough to take stock I saw that the Japs were pushing the car right across the road.

One of them, a private, was covering me closely with a bayonet. I moved a hand, and he shook the bayonet threateningly. His eyes were bright and zealous, and his teeth half bared. He looked rough and stocky, like the peasant types I had seen in the Fort at Cawnpore; but he was on the right side of the bayonet, and in his expression there was none of the rather pathetic and smiling philosophy. He was full of grim conscientiousness, ready to jab with the steel as a duty.

There was one officer amongst them. When he had finished directing the blockage of the road with the car, he gave orders to two of the soldiers to escort us away. The three of us were pushed together, and the bayonets flicked to indicate the direction in which we were to turn. We started to walk up the steep bank into the jungle. There was a path through the undergrowth, and we followed it in single file, the Major leading with a slow depressed pace. His head was hanging from sheer exhaustion and shock. He occasionally looked round at me over his shoulder, and I noticed that his face was infinitely more haggard than it had been twenty minutes ago. He looked like a condemned man slouching to the scaffold. I said to him in a low voice:

"It's not the end yet."

He looked back wearily and grunted, and one of the escorts shouted, full of officiousness, to shut us up. But I could hear the two of them, some yards behind us, talking between themselves, though I caught only snatches of their conversation; and although they were pretending with their tone to be tough soldiery, I knew they were full of excitement. One of them said:

"They are probably important officers travelling in a car like that."

"We shall get praised if they are."

"Who was it who shot the first one?"

"Kusano."

"Do you wish it was you?"

"It might be a good thing to fire such a fine shot, but . . ."

"We may have to shoot these if they try to escape."

"They would rather have them alive."

"I would like to have something off them as a souvenir."

"I would like to have the Indian's hat."

A few minutes later they became more daring, and one of them prodded the Sikh with his bayonet, ostensibly to make him hurry, but I believe it was only to see what would happen, and because they felt they ought to show some aggressiveness. Instead of increasing his pace the Sikh stopped in the middle of the path and swung round to face them, letting out a vituperation in Hindustani. The soldier behind him jumped back and held his bayonet levelled, glowering from behind it. He began to shout in Japanese, "Go on, get a move on," but the Sikh stood proudly and unintimidated. I was afraid that there was going to be trouble, and I said to the soldiers:

"It was unnecessary to touch him."

My use of Japanese seemed to take the wind out of their sails. They stared at me in surprise.

"You speak Japanese?"

"A little."

"Do the other two speak it?"

"No."

"Tell the Indian to continue walking."

I told him, and we set off again, but this time I went immediately in front of the Japanese, because I wanted to talk to them.

"It was very clever, catching us like that on the road," I said.

"No more transport will get through."

"What are your people hoping to do?"

"The Japanese are going to take Imphal."

"How do you know?"

"That is what we are told."

"And what are you going to do with us?"

"We are going to take you to the unit headquarters, and then we don't know what will happen to you."

We had walked about a mile from the road, uphill and through jungle all the way. Suddenly we heard a heavy gun fire close by us, and immediately afterwards two more went off, each farther away. Then the first fired again, and a moment later we saw it ahead of us, buried in the trees on a little promontory. The escort volunteered the information:

"They are shelling the road. You are lucky to have got out of it in time."

It was quite clear what had happened. They had sneaked in with their mountain artillery and got the range on to the road, and then blocked it and waited for a good catch. We had only been small fry; but now the lorries would be right under the shells. They were pouring them down for all they were worth from the three guns. As we came nearer, we could see the gun-crew working feverishly, reloading the moment the barrel had recoiled and was still. It was an awful thing, to watch this and be helpless; I wondered if the young fellows in the tanks were getting it too, the fellows who had talked about the Odeon Café and the flashlight girls.

Two or three minutes later there was some answering fire, and then the artillery dropped out and there was only rifle and machine-gun fire to be heard down on the road. It sounded as if a terrific battle was in progress. It went on for a quarter of an hour without a pause, and as we got farther away the sound of the shots became hollower and the machine-gun fire was like a sudden, rapid hammering. Once there was a resounding explosion, a mighty boom with half a dozen smaller ones in its wake; that must have been an ammunition car going up. Then there was a deep silence. We could hear the cries of birds and the ever-lasting rasp of the crickets. But the shooting had stopped, and it seemed like silence; and we could imagine the silence down below —the smoking chaos on the road.

"Perhaps you're also lucky to be out of it," I said to the escort.

"Saa . . . there will be plenty more of that."

"Do you like fighting?"

"Like it or not like it . . . it's a thing that can't be helped."

We must have walked three miles before we reached the encampment, and it took as many hours. There were a dozen little huts of the kind that are thrown up in a few hours in the jungle, of bamboo with straw roofs. Some distance away there were trenches and sentries on duty, and a platoon or so of soldiers squatting on the ground eating rice. They all watched us curiously, and one shouted: 'Banzai!' and the others laughed. Then they went on eating, and we stood together in a group whilst one of the escort disappeared into a hut. I could hear them talking about us:

"Do you think they'll cut off the black one's beard?"

"Will they send them back to Japan?"

"They ought to make them clear up the bomb damage in Mandalay or Rangoon."

"It's a pity we don't take women prisoners and then we should know what to do with them."

"They don't look very frightful."

"They are probably ashamed of being taken prisoner."

After a time we were taken to one of the huts and put inside, with a guard at the entrance. There was no furniture, and we sat down on the ground, leaning against the bamboo sides. I looked at my watch and saw that it was half past five. It seemed impossible to realise that the same morning we had got up at Dimapur and motored through Kohima with our own troops all round us, and that six hours ago we had been drinking tea at the rest-camp; and that then Manning had been alive, not cherishing life and yet somehow immensely alive. Now he was dead, but cleanly dead, thank God, and dead as I think he would have wished, extinguished in the midst of that gesture: 'What's all the fuss about? What does it matter, anyway?' I rather liked to think that he made the gesture, not at us at all, but at the sniper who he knew was going to kill him. Not that I think honestly, deep in his heart, he wanted to die—I believe he was no less afraid than the rest of us. But that elevated him in my mind; and though I had only come with him in the train and up the Brahmaputra, I thought that I had lost a friend. He was a good person. He had sold water-softeners from door to door, and made no success of his Rangoon cinema; and he thought his own life was a failure. But he was good; and he was dead.

And I had hardly a scratch, only a dull bruise on my forehead where the rifle butt had hit me. My watch was still going from yesterday's winding in Dimapur, and my clothes were untorn, the clothes I had bought with Sabby in the Army and Navy Stores in Bombay when the war had seemed infinitely remote—something I had already been through, not something I was going to go through again. I still had the tin of cigarettes in my pocket that my parents had sent out from England, and my wallet.

I remembered suddenly—in my wallet there was a photograph of Sabby. I had always intended to destroy it if I went near the front line; but I had thought I was safe enough in taking it to Imphal, and I had forgotten it until now in the excitement of events. It was a stroke of good luck that so far we had been searched for nothing but weapons.

I took out my wallet and found the picture. It was taken in the Himalayas, and there was Jennifer's hand in it, too, and half Margaret's face. And Sabby was full of the wonderful air, and you could see her eyes brimming with happiness. I would like to have kissed it, a thing I have never done before, kiss a photograph; but I was afraid of the guard glancing down from the doorway, and I kept it hidden beneath my knees, holding it for a moment before I tore it into tiny pieces. I felt treacherous, as though tearing up the happiness. But to have kept it would have been more treacherous, and in any case the happiness was gone. I pushed the pieces into the ground between the bamboos.

11

The Major was a broken man. He was almost twice my age, and he had been through the last war and been brave in it; his medal ribbons ran into two rows over his pocket. Before this war, the World War II, he had been in the railway offices in Leeds and on the point of retiring. He had joined up again as a Transport Officer, and made his way via the railway stations in Cairo, Bombay and Delhi to Dimapur. He had been two years in India, and in another two years he would have gone home; and he wanted to go home because he hated India. He hated everywhere but Yorkshire, and in this hut in the jungle, cramped on the floor and guarded by a Japanese First Class Private, he looked as though he was finished.

He took all the responsibility upon himself and despite my reassurances was filled with remorse. He insisted that had he not suggested we came in his car, we should have been in the convoy that must still be near Kohima. Furthermore, Manning would still have been alive. It was wrong of him, above all, to have let Manning get out to remove the tree.

He expected to be shot. They would spare me, he said, because I spoke Japanese and would be of use to them; but his own hours were numbered. They wouldn't bother to take him right back to the rear, and waste their food supplies on him in the jungle. He showed me a photograph of his wife and two children, a dreadful posed study by a Boar Lane photographer, and made me promise to visit them after the war. I was to tell them that he had no fear of death and that his only concern had been for them. And—whatever I thought of him for his behaviour in the car—I was to say to his son: 'Your father was a fine man.' His son believed in him and must never be disillusioned. I told him there was no need for me to promise to do these things; we would both live through this, and perhaps even escape. But he insisted. I promised, and he began to weep. The Sikh hung his head respectfully.

Some rice was brought us. It was only a small quantity, but it was given graciously by a private who was delighted with this duty. He bowed in the doorway with the bowl in his hands, and when I thanked him he said:

"It is scarcely sufficient, but . . ."

"Please don't mention it," I said.

He wanted to stay and talk. He asked one or two questions quickly. Were we very miserable? Surely as I spoke Japanese I knew Kyushu where he lived? Did our badges mean we were very high-ranking officers? Then because he was afraid this conversation would receive official disapproval, he bowed several more times and said, "Indeed, thank you, thank you," and left.

We were still chewing the rice when an NCO appeared in the hut doorway. He said savagely in bad English:

"You prisoners. Move outside quickly."

We trooped out, leaving some rice in the bowl. There was another escort waiting at attention with rifles and bayonets. We fell in with them and marched a hundred yards to a point in front of the huts, beneath the jungle trees. The NCO was shouting at us, presumably telling us to march smartly, but whether his orders were in English or Japanese I could not tell. When we halted the escort turned about and we did likewise. We remained at attention, waiting. The NCO went into one of the huts, and ten minutes later he came out behind an officer.

I could see by the badges on his collar that this officer was a Lieutenant. He was a small man, not more than four foot six, but brisk and swaggering. His face was hard and bony, and his eyes were like bright black beads. At his side there was a sword. It was too big for him, almost trailing on the ground, so that it made him look like a child strutting about with a grown-up's weapon.

He strode up to us and glared at each of us in turn. His eyes were burning. He held his hands behind his back, and kept his shoulders erect to lose nothing of his height. Then he said, using the tersest form of the verb:

"Which of you speaks Japanese?"

"I have a slight knowledge of it," I said.

"You have been to Japan?"

"No."

"Where did you learn it?"

"From friends."

"You can understand me?"

"If you don't speak too fast."

"Very well. I wish you to listen to my words, and afterwards to convey their meaning to the other two men."

He began to swagger up and down in front of us. In any other circumstances it would have been tremendously comic to have seen this: his chest thrown out and his sword dangling behind, and his speech as pompous as his walk. I did not understand it all, but I got the gist of it, and it was to the effect that we were now the captives of Dai-Nippon, whose present Emperor, the Son of Heaven, was the direct descendant of the Ancestral Divinity Amaterasu Omikami; and then there was a lot more history like a newspaper article on Japan, and it was all to tell us that to be a captive of a Power with such a heritage was a better fate for ourselves than to be free men of an inferior nation. It also seemed that by the Emperor's will we were to receive clemency, though we were not to interpret this as meaning that we were to be precluded from getting our deserts. Henceforward our allegiance was only to the Emperor, in the direction of whose Palace—and this he indicated with a rigid finger—we would sometimes be called upon to bow. Furthermore, when in a short time we were asked a few simple questions it devolved upon us to answer them, any recalcitrance on our part being an insult to the said Emperor, and therefore punishable by any number of ingenious means. "Do you understand that?" he said.

"I understand your words," I said.

"Very well. You will all bow in the direction of the Imperial Palace."

I said to the other two in English:

"You had better bow at that tree; it will save a lot of trouble."

We inclined our bodies. People have before now been put to death for refusing to do no more than that, and I admire them for having the courage of their unwavering principles. But I knew I was not that kind, and I made myself think of this hypocrisy as a joke, and I thought what a laugh Peter would get out of this bizarre scene of a Major, a Sikh and myself lined up somewhere in the jungle bowing to the Emperor Hirohito beyond a continent and a sea.

After that the Lieutenant strode up to me and glowered at me. He looked at the shoulder-straps on my bush shirt.

"What are those?"

"They are my badges of rank."

"You have no rank now," he said.

He reached up and tore off my Air Force rings savagely, dropping them to the ground. When he was close to me I could see how tightly the skin of his face was stretched over his cheekbones. His cheeks were hollow, so that his jaws projected, and his nostrils were wide and black. Only his eyes had a hard, steely life.

He glanced at the Sikh's rank badges and passed by; it was to try to humiliate us, I suppose, leaving the Indian with his rank. He went on to the Major, staring intently for a moment at the woven crowns on his shoulders.

"What rank is this man?" he said.

"*Shosa.*"

He smiled, and ripped off one of the shoulder-straps. The Major raised one hand and placed it firmly over the other. The Lieutenant's smile disappeared and he glared angrily.

"Tell him to take his hand away," he said to the NCO.

"Remove hand."

"I retain my rank although I am a prisoner," the Major said.

"Remove hand."

The Major kept his hand in place. I saw that the other hand by his side was quivering; but there was a new defiance in his face.

"May I have permission to strike him?" the NCO said.

"No. The Indian will strike him. Tell them both to take a step forward."

They stepped forward, and the Major still had his hand on his shoulder. The other shoulder of his shirt was torn where the strap had been stripped off.

"Face together," the NCO said.

They turned inwards.

"You, Indian, strike the Englishman on the face."

The Sikh remained perfectly still.

"You understand English?" the NCO said.

"I understand."

"Then I order you to strike the Englishman."

"I will not strike my superior officer."

The NCO interpreted this to the Lieutenant. The Lieutenant went up to the Sikh and stood nearly in front of him. He was like a little swollen-chested dwarf beside the other grandiloquent figure. The Sikh was looking into the sky over his head and his strong black beard was motionless. From the side I could see the white of his eyes and the noble curve of his nose. I could also see from the set of his face that nothing was going to make him carry out this order.

Infuriated, the Lieutenant swung his clenched fist and hit the Sikh's jaw. The Sikh was stone-still like a statue.

"Tell him to hit the man like that," the Lieutenant said.

"You are ordered to strike your officer like that," the NCO said.

"For God's sake do it, man," the Major said in a low voice. "It doesn't matter."

We waited, but the Sikh did not move. His arms were frozen at his sides.

"I'm sorry, sir," he said. And then he made a dash. He pushed between the Major and the NCO too quickly to be grabbed, and before the guard could raise his rifle he had leapt a trench twenty yards away and started through the trees. But there was no chance for him. He must have known there was no chance. A rifle went off by my side, and he went on running for a few seconds; but only loosely from the momentum, and gradually folding up. Then he sprawled forward on the ground and writhed over on to his back. He went on writhing, on to his face again as though trying to rise. The Lieutenant began to walk over to him. He walked slowly, concentrating on the powerful anguished body with deadly intent. He came to the trench, and it was two and a half feet broad, so he walked slowly round the end. I said to the guard: "Shoot again!" but he kept his bayonet turned towards me to prevent my getting away, and the other guard was looking after the Major. A dozen other soldiers had come running out of the hut and were making for the spot where the Sikh was still twisting in agony. They fell behind the Lieutenant, and watched him in fascination as he slowly drew his sword. They stood quite still as he raised it with both hands above his head; and at that moment the Sikh was also quite still. The sword came down, and I did not see what happened, but there was no more movement at the spot, and the Lieutenant turned round, the soldiers falling back to make way for him. He came back to where we were standing, the

214

hilt of the sword in one hand, and the point resting on the fore-finger of the other. He held it for us to see. The bright steel was smeared with fresh blood like a butcher's knife. Then he handed it to the NCO and, pausing before the Major, he tore off the second shoulder-strap.

CHAPTER IV

I

WE were interrogated separately in the Lieutenant's hut. I was dreading an interrogation, knowing the difficulties of keeping steadfast silence in the face of threats. But I knew nothing, anyway, of the military set-up; and the Lieutenant's method was transparent, and it seemed easy to lie.

Ten minutes ago he had shown me the bloody sword; now he received me with a grin that bared his two rows of prognathous teeth. He slapped me on the back. It was obvious that he had never slapped anybody on the back before, but he had heard that Englishmen slapped each other on the back, and he meant it to be a winning gesture. He sat me on the floor of the hut and gave me a cigarette.

"It was a great shame," he said, "that we had to kill the Indian. But I am glad it was the Indian and not one of you."

"Oh yes," I said.

"As I have said, we wish to treat you with clemency."

He went on pretending to be jovial. He talked for a long time in a grim, casual way to camouflage the questions that followed, but when the questions arrived they stood out in ludicrous relief. I pretended in turn that I did not recognise his traps, and allowed myself to fall headlong into each, but with harmless replies. I could see him purring with success, and the cold smile of stretched yellow parchment over bone became genuinely warmer. But when he began to drop the camouflage and demand information directly, and I became more manifestly evasive, all the softer light died immediately and he was hard and glittering again. His eyes were black and glassy, and the line of his cheekbones was ruthless. He started to recall the bloody sword, and to hint at other dark things, and I had to adopt new tactics, pretending to try to hold out on him, and finally give way under threat, but still feeding false stuff. It was childishly simple this, because he could not bear to think he was being fooled and losing face. It was so simple that I began to wonder if he knew what game I was up to and would suddenly order me out to be shot. But he looked pleased when he sent me back to the hut. Afterwards the Major went in, the NCO interpreting. He was away two hours, and when he returned he looked so ill and haggard that I asked at once if he had been physically ill-treated. He shook his head.

"They wanted to know all kinds of things that I had no idea about."

"What did you do?"

"I said I didn't know."

"That's fatal," I said. "Tell them anything. Any answer satisfies them."

"I didn't know the answers," he said as though he were dying. "I wouldn't have told them if I had known."

"Of course you wouldn't."

"They're swine," he said. "Did you see him cut off the Sikh's head?"

"Yes, I saw."

"My God, with a sword."

"It's death whichever way you do it," I said. "It doesn't matter whether it's with a sword or a bullet."

"It does matter. It's in cold blood when you do it with a sword."

"The Sikh was too far gone to see it."

"I saw it, though. You saw it. He just cut off the head with his sword. That little pompous swine . . . cut off the Sikh's head. He was a fine man, my driver!"

"Yes," I said. "I'd like to have seen those two matched in a fair fight."

"I'd like to fight that Jap. But I'm too old. I'm done for now. I'm finished."

"You'll be all right," I said. "We'll get out of this soon. You don't think we're going to let them sit on the main Imphal Road, do you? When they start to retreat, we'll get out of it somehow."

I told that to myself, to cheer myself as well as to cheer the Major, but I was only nursing a tiny seed of genuine hope. I knew that if they had to retreat in a hurry, the Emperor's clemency would be bitterly interpreted; and if they advanced we should get sent back to the rear once their lines of communication were working properly. Meanwhile they were taking no chances. When it was dark, besides leaving a guard on our hut they clapped us in handcuffs and joined us together by a chain. They gave us a little more rice and some brackish water. I drank the water because my throat was parched and rough and the rice was like sawdust. After that we lay down on the ground without covering, facing each other, and tried to sleep. I awoke once in the night to hear my own terror-stricken voice, and find myself tugging violently at the chain, almost tearing away the Major's arm. I could see the guard's silhouette in the doorway as he rushed in to silence me. He was about to strike me with the butt of his rifle when I stopped shrieking in time: we were too near the 'enemy' for sound or lights to be welcome. For the rest of the night I was feverish, conceiving fantastic plans of escape that in the morning were unthinkable.

The next day from sunrise there was the noise of two brisk battles in progress—one down towards Imphal and the other in the direction of Kohima, and both presumably on the road. At midday some more prisoners were brought in. A barbed-wire compound had been constructed, and we saw a dozen battle-worn British soldiers and a few Indians brought in and confined. We were not allowed to communicate with them, until I was called in and told to interpret for the Lieutenant, whilst the NCO interrogated on his own. The first man was a little fellow from Exeter, or somewhere like that. He was dazed and stupid. The Lieutenant asked some questions about tanks and numbers of men and positions, and I passed them on vaguely and had vague replies, misinterpreting them wholesale. I thought this would either bring my life to a quick end if I was discovered, or else earn me the privileges of a collaborator, giving me a chance to escape. At any rate, the risk was worth while. After the intimidated private a rough, bland-faced sergeant was brought in. He strolled between the guards and looked around the hut and at us as though he was a contemptuous sight-seer in a foreign town.

"Tell anything but the truth," I said.

"I'd like to tell that bloke the truth," he said. "The truth about that ugly mug of his."

I kept the insolence out of the replies, but his face was superbly derisive. The Lieutenant slapped him, and he sat stolidly with an unchanging expression, muttering to me. He went out between the rattling bayonets, having lost none of his Cockney aplomb.

In the afternoon, chained to the Major, I was allowed to take

217

exercise. We walked round the huts in the jungle, in front of an escort. I had delayed the time purposely until five o'clock because from the huts I had seen a wireless in the open under the trees. It was a transmitting and receiving set, with an operator sitting before it on a camp-stool. When we passed by I said:

"What is the news?"

The operator looked amiable. He was young, with a flat nose and wide mouth.

"This isn't for listening to the news," he said.

"But you could do so."

"It won't get Japan."

"It would get India."

"I suppose it would, but . . ."

"I would like to hear the news," I said.

"You had better continue walking," said the guard.

"The Lieutenant wouldn't mind us listening to the news. It's good news for you. I hear you're going to take Imphal."

"Do the English say we are going to take Imphal?" the operator said.

"You will find out if you tune in."

I told him the wavelength and he moved the dial hesitatingly. He pulled the earphones down over his ears, whilst I waited breathlessly. He listened in silence for a long time, and the guard kept his bayonet ready in case we were up to some monkey-business. He was doubtful that we should be doing this at all, but I had made good friends with him when he was guarding the hut by letting him tell me about his family, and he didn't want to push us on. He thought we were high officers, and treated us with some respect, using the politest language.

"This is English propaganda news," the operator said, taking off the earphones.

"Please let me listen."

"I can't do that," he said.

"I'm not going to touch your set."

"It is an impossible thing."

"Just for a moment," I said.

"I will get into trouble."

"There is nobody to see."

He scratched the top of his head with one hand, looking ridiculously apish in this characteristic gesture of uncertainty.

"*Saa* . . . I don't know what I ought to do."

"It is all right," I said. "There couldn't be any harm in it."

He handed me the earphones tentatively. I tried not to snatch them with too much eagerness. Without waiting to put them on I pushed one ear-piece against my ear, and there was Sabby's voice, just as I had heard it before, her rather sing-song wireless voice.

I was drunk with joy. The single night as a captive had seemed to carry me beyond a great ravine—a ravine of distance and time —that had made Sabby in some way less real to me, more of a marvellous dream. Now suddenly her voice brought her right to my jungle prison. For though it was no more than her voice and she was only reading news-script, I could see her wrinkle her nose at me and feel the gentle caress of her hand, as when a familiar melody awakens old memories that once accompanied it. And since yesterday it seemed as though a year had gone by—an age in which anything might have happened to Sabby. It was like hearing good news after months of anxiety, and it reminded me that for Sabby it was only a normal twenty-four hours that had passed.

She was talking now about Burma. 'British and Indian forces are attacking the two road blocks which have been established on the Imphal-Kohima Road. . . .' Could she guess, I wondered, that I had been caught by this unexpected inrush of the Japanese, and in what circumstances I was listening to her? Was she afraid for me? If only I could have called back to her through the wireless: 'I'm listening to you—I'm alive!' But there could be no calling to her, no writing to her; for months, for more than a year perhaps, I should not be able to send her word. The days would go by, one by one, and no letter would come from me. She would not even be told that I was missing. The telegram would go to Tewkesbury. 'We regret to inform you—your son—missing.' My parents would not tell Sabby, because I had never written to them that I loved Sabby, knowing with what consternation they would have read, 'a Japanese'. Probably Peter would tell her eventually.

"That is enough. Give them back."

The operator was all of a sudden afraid of what he had done. He could not account for my sudden show of happiness because however the news was worded it was bad for the British. He was suspicious and annoyed with me or himself. I handed him back his earphones.

"Thank you," I said. "That is interesting. Your army seems to be sticking to the road."

"Of course. It is the invasion of India. We have been told so by our officers."

II

The second night in the hut was worse than the first. To begin with, I had accepted the chains with resignation, and had thought the chance would present itself to escape. Now a deep depression came over me, and I had to close my eyes and try to imagine there were no handcuffs round my wrist, because a sudden panicky hatred of them kept shooting down my spine. I was afraid that if I lost control of this I would become hysterical and try to tear them away madly.

My body was sore already with lying on the hard ground, and there were new pains in my belly that felt like dysentery again, a likely thing after the foul water we were given to drink.

I asked the guard for a cigarette. He gave me one and the smoke calmed me, but it did not assuage the dull pain of depression. To get away from the thoughts of Sabby and of home, I began to discuss ways of escape with the Major. He was full of despair, but he played the game for the sake of playing it, and we agreed, knowing that it would come to nothing, to try something on the following night. I went to sleep at last, going over our scheme again and again in my mind. In the morning we had only to look round the camp once to see that it was impossible. Even if we throttled our own guard with the chain that linked us without attracting attention, we had to get past the bunker positions and the sentries. It was suicide. At night suicide seemed preferable to years in a prison camp. But in the daylight life seemed better.

Then the Major was taken away. They came in and took him without any explanation, and I saw the other prisoners being led from their barbed-wire compound. They were all handcuffed. They formed up near my hut and the Major looked back at me sorrowfully. He was the most tragic of them all. I saw their backs as they went off down the jungle tracks, with an escort as numerous as themselves, and it was the last I saw of them, the last I saw of the Major.

Down below on the road the battle burst out sporadically. A single shot fired seemed to bring all the guns in the neighbourhood into action, and for twenty minutes or so there would be the uninterrupted sound of shelling. But in both directions the sound was retreating, which meant the Japs were widening their block and pushing our troops back towards Kohima and Imphal. It also meant that if ever I made a break, I should have farther to go. There were a great number of British aircraft over the battle area, and I could hear them all day long. Once one flew right overhead. It was a Hurricane, and I could see the four cannons sticking out of the wings. One of the Jap soldiers watching out for aircraft from the top of a tree beat a shell-case for all he was worth, and at the sound everyone dashed into trenches, scurrying between the trees. I was taken out by my guard, but the Hurricane had disappeared long before we had reached the trench. I hoped that all the movement might have attracted its attention, and that it would come back and strafe us. Those cannons could have put the place in confusion, just what I was waiting for. But the noise of its engine died away, and we all climbed out of our holes and trooped back.

In the afternoon I engineered my walk at the same time, and we went past the wireless-set.

"May I listen again?" I said.

"No, it is not allowed."

"I shall ask the Lieutenant," I said.

"I advise you not to do that," the operator said.

"I shall certainly do so."

"Then I request you not to mention that you have already listened."

"I won't mention it," I said, "if you will let me listen again."

"I am not going to do that. I will listen myself and tell you the news."

He twirled the dial, and for a while he was absorbed in what he heard, but the earphones were close against his ear and I could hear nothing at all.

"Go away and come back," he said.

We strolled about for ten minutes, the guard carrying the bayonet pointed at the small of my back all the time. When we came back I said:

"What did you hear?"

"The Japanese have got four road blocks between Imphal and Kohima, and they are also on the road north of Kohima."

"And the British?"

"He said they were not afraid of Imphal being captured, but it cannot be true."

"He?"

"The man who read the news."

"It was a man?" I said.

"Yes, today it was a man."

"A woman didn't speak at all?"

"No," he said. "Yesterday there was a woman."

The next day I was not allowed out of the hut at all. I asked the guard why I was not to have exercise, and he said he did not know but that Lieutenant Nakamura had given orders. I saw nobody but the guards who came and stood in front of the hut, but I came to know all of these well, because they were mostly simple peasant folk, none of whom had been in the army more than a year. It was not difficult to scratch through the façade that the army had given them, and once that was done they spoke sentimentally of their longing for the day to go home. But they did not really think they would ever go home; they all had a fatalistic belief that death was waiting for them in the jungle. I said:

"When you move forward, why don't you hand yourselves over to the British? You will be well treated and get good food."

I thought if I could encourage one to do this, I might get him to help me escape, too; but it was a futile attempt. They were less afraid of bullets than they were of the shame which they believed such an act would bring upon them, and, only a prisoner myself in their charge, I could not break down that belief.

As I was unable to talk to the wireless operator again I persuaded one of them to do this for me, asking him to inquire about the news, and only incidentally about who read it. On the following day it was a man's voice once more. I began to grow desperate, and during the night my imagination found the worst explanations for Sabby's absence. All my first reactions to Margaret and Jennifer's letter reared up again, but in these more unfortunate circumstances they came with more force. That dark, numb core inside me began to burn. My heart was burning, too, a sensation I had never had before, and the worst sensation I had ever known, because it was both physical and mental; a slow, fearful torture, impossible to resist. It began to stifle me, and in my frustration I swore that if in two more days I did not hear that Sabby was speaking again, I should try to get away in the night, however hopeless success seemed. To remain here and to believe that Sabby was suffering and perhaps dying was a continuous death for myself.

The next day it was the same: the news was read by a man. I

wanted to break my way out then, rush out of the encampment in daylight like the Sikh. A kind of madness was upon me, and if I had given myself up to this madness, that is what I should have done, and in five seconds I should have been no more alive than the Sikh. But I held on to myself, and it was like keeping myself from vomiting or from giving way to drunkenness, knowing that it was touch and go. All the mad urge was tingling through my body. I sat down on the earth floor of the hut and gripped the bamboos behind my shoulders, looking out of the doorway instead of at the walls, which added claustrophobia to my frenzy.

Then on the following morning shortly after dawn another Hurricane came over. It dropped two light bombs, one either side of the bashas, and not until the explosions had died was the shell-case beaten from the tree-top. Again there was a wild scattering and there was nothing to be seen but running figures. The aircraft circled and came back with all its cannons opened up, and looking back over my shoulder as I ran to a trench, I could see it swerving from one side to the other, raking the whole encampment. I dropped down in the shallow hole. All round there were little explosions and earth spurting up. Then there was only the sound of the Hurricane's engines fading, and everyone waited, raising only their heads above ground level to see a dozen of their comrades sprawling dead or dying. Some seconds later it came in to attack again, only a few feet above the tree-tops, this time setting two of the bamboo huts on fire, but not my own amongst them. After that it made off on a straight course and at speed, its job done.

There was excitement but no loophole for myself. The Lieutenant came across at once to the trench where the guard had taken me. He threw out his hands towards the scattered corpses.

"The death of these Japanese warriors," he said, "will be paid for by a hundred times their weight in British blood. I am only sparing you because you will be of use to us."

He slapped my face with all the angry force he could muster. He was a foot smaller than I, and he had to reach up to do this, but he was powerful and the shock was stunning. His eyes were full of the hard light of hatred.

"Handcuff him to the tree," he ordered the guard.

It was a large tree, and my arms would not go all the way round. When the handcuffs were linked to my wrists, the metal cut into the skin and I was held tightly against the trunk. I could not slip my arms up or down, and I was standing almost on tip-toe. At first I pushed up on my toes to take the weight from my arms, but my feet soon grew tired and I let myself hang. It seemed as though my arms were going to tear away at the sockets or that the steel would cut through my wrists. For half an hour the pain was intense. I bit a piece of jutting bark with my teeth and played little games with myself to distract some of my attention. I pretended the bark was Sabby's nose, and I shook it. Then I carried on an imaginary conversation with her.

"Darling," I said, "it's not really true that you're going to die, is it?"

"Now I have been so happy, it doesn't matter to die."

"Why didn't you tell me what was wrong?"

"Then you would have been kind because you were sorry for me, and I only wanted you to be kind because you loved me a little bit. You did love me a little bit, didn't you, darling?"

"I loved you with all my heart."

"When I said that, you told me it was a criché and I couldn't mean it."

"Cliché, darling," I said.

"Please don't scold, I shall never learn to speak proper English."

"Say cliché, then."

"Darling, you said it was a criché, and I didn't really love with heart. So perhaps also it is just a criché for you and you don't love with heart."

"It's my heart that's burning."

"Not counting heart, you are in such bad pain."

"When you were in pain, you didn't show it," I said.

"Darling, I am so ashamed and miserable because the Japanese are making your pain. Don't you hate me when you think I am Japanese?"

"I don't think of you as Japanese."

"How do you think of Sabby?"

"I think of her as a woman."

"Sabby is Japanese woman."

"She is any woman," I said.

"What does it mean, darling—any woman?"

"It just means woman."

"I am not Indian woman. I have not got fine carriage like Indian woman."

"You have got a fine heart," I said.

"It is selfish heart, because it thinks of nothing but Michael."

"Please let it go on thinking," I said. "I'm not going to let this kill me. This pain is nothing and soon it'll be over. I'm going to get back to you somehow. Whatever you do don't die before I get back. When I'm with you I shall make you want to live, and all our happiness has only been the beginning. You're going to marry me and come back to Tewkesbury. When my parents have seen you they can't help loving you, and we are going to have a beautiful life full of gentleness. Soon there will be no more of this pain. This is a test, darling. It's a test for both of us, and it's not going to beat us. I'm going to come back. I promise you I'm coming back."

I was left embracing the tree until late in the afternoon. During my life I have seldom had to suffer pain, and I did not endure this heroically; but I learnt the lesson of heroics—that the determination not to be defeated by pain lessens the agony like a drug.

When I was released from the tree the handcuffs were at once put round my wrists again, and another short chain was attached with which to lead me through the jungle. All afternoon I had seen the troops moving off from this position with their equipment, and now I was taken by the rearguard. I don't know whether they had intended to make this move, anyway, or whether the Hurricane had frightened them away, but at any rate we left behind us all the empty huts and trenches, and we crossed the spot where Lieutenant Nakamura had with great courage used his Samurai sword to cut off the Sikh's head. We went in single file down the jungle tracks, and a guard in front of me held my chain and the guard behind me held a rifle, so that even when an aircraft came over and we buried ourselves in the under-growth, it was hopeless to attempt to get away. Besides, I was exhausted, stumbling along anyhow to keep up and prevent the handcuffs dragging on my bleeding wrists. Since I had become a prisoner the only food I had been given was rice in small, inadequate quantities, and though I had not cared greatly about this yet, I could feel the effect now in the weakness of my body. I experienced sudden spells of dizziness; but I reeled on through them until my head cleared again.

Fortunately we only marched a couple of miles, though at times the track led steeply upwards. The new position for the head-quarters was on the crown of a hill, with encircling trenches and bunker positions with narrow entrances down steps of earth. I was led down into one of these deep bunkers that they called the 'Guard Room', and found myself in the company of a sergeant and two or three privates.

"Am I going to live with you?" I said.

"You will spend the night here."

"I'd like you to remove my handcuffs," I said.

"It is not allowed," the sergeant said. "As far as I am concerned, it is all right for you not to have handcuffs, but I must obey orders and it can't be helped."

"Then please will you let me sit down?"

"Please make yourself comfortable without ceremony."

I sat down on the earth floor with my back against the side of the bunker. It was beginning to get dark, and there was only a tiny flickering paraffin lamp that turned the faces of the soldiers a deeper yellow and painted them with shadows. They all had a thick stubble above their mouth and round their chins. I remembered that I had a stubble, too, which had been growing since my last shave in Dimapur. I ran my hand all over my face, wondering how I looked. One of the soldiers saw me and grinned. He pulled a metal mirror out of his pocket and held it up in front of me.

"Is it interesting?"

"I've changed since I've been with you," I said.

"You are making more of a soldier's face than when you came."

"I feel more like a soldier," I said.

Partly because of the light, I looked so ridiculously macabre that a little ripple of laughter went through me. But it did not come into my expression. My eyes looked very black and wild, and my hair was matted and dusty. My cheeks seemed to have receded, giving a new prominence to my cheekbones. My mouth also stood out with big, dry lips. I studied this for quite a time, trying to bring myself to realise that I was really seeing myself. But I could not reconcile this savage reflection with my feelings, for although I was aching and weary and could feel with every bone this severing from a past life, and in this respect was changed, the real core of me was there as it had always been. All my loves and sentiments and friendships, and all the impressions of my past life, all the things that had built me, were there in the core, hard and real. I knew that, in seeing them like this, I was learning more about myself than I had ever learnt before. But

226

what I saw in the little dented mirror, held by the hand of a Japanese soldier who was quivering with amusement, was only one moment of myself, myself as a prisoner-of-war, miserable and uncouth.

Later on I was given a small handful of rice and a can of water. The guards were friendly and full of curiosity; I was still a museum-piece to them, and they were half-awed because I could speak Japanese. They had seen Englishmen before in Japan, but I was the first they had ever met, although for years they had been learning to hate the English. They asked endless questions about my home, and how I felt about becoming a prisoner and how my family would feel. Would they be able to lift up their heads? And after the war, would I be able to go back to England?

'I may go back before that,' I thought. But I said: "I have dysentery. Will you kindly escort me outside."

The sergeant detailed a man, and we began to climb the steps at the end of the bunker. I turned back:

"I can't manage with these handcuffs," I said.

"Very well," the sergeant said. "You may have them off to go to the lavatory." And he added to the escort: "Be careful."

We went up the steps again, the escort with a pistol in his hand. There was no moon now, but the stars were brilliant and I could distinguish the outline of the trees, and after a moment the trunks took shape in the darkness. There was a heavy jungle smell. There was no sound from the other trenches, but in the open slit-trenches that marked the perimeter I could distinguish the heads of sentries at intervals of a dozen yards. From beyond came an occasional cry of a bird or animal and the interminable sound of crickets; but down on the road there was silence.

Under a tree a hole had been dug as a temporary convenience. There was no privacy, except that provided by the night. The guard stood facing me a few yards away, and all the time the revolver was in his hand, and I had seen him click the chamber into position. In the trench he had talked amicably, even with respect; but he was not taking any chances.

I had really got dysentery again, badly. The pains kept grinding my stomach. I stayed for a long time under the tree, and then ten minutes after we had returned to the bunker I had to go out again. The soldiers laughed. They knew what dysentery was from experience. When I came back they made jokes, and one said: "It is hardly worth putting him back in handcuffs." But I

227

was chained into them again, all the same, so that I couldn't grab one of their rifles and start trouble.

I went out six or seven times and the guard began to get careless. He came with me, but when I sat down at the tree he paced backwards and forwards, so that half the time his back was turned to me. I pretended to be more ill than I was. In the dugout I laid my head back against the wall and closed my eyes and tried to look even more ghastly than I had appeared to myself in the mirror. When I went out it was with sluggish, painful footsteps.

It was after midnight. The sergeant's good humour suddenly turned to impatience.

"This can't go on," he said. "Do you want to be chained to a tree again outside?"

"No," I said. "I would hate that."

"Then you must control yourself."

"Let me go once more," I said.

He took off the metal links and I dragged my way up the steps. The night seemed to be getting lighter, but at the base of the tree it was almost totally dark. I took my place there and waited, whilst the escort strolled off for a dozen yards and returned. It was impossible to make a direct dash, because before I reached the perimeter trench, thirty yards away, he would have heard my movement and turned and shot me, or called to the sentry. I had worked out another plan during my visits here, not infallible, but the best I could do. I sat there in the awful stillness and knew that the next ten minutes would settle everything; whether I should ever see Sabby again, whether I should see anybody again. It was going to be life and freedom or death—if not with the first bullet, then with Lieutenant Nakamura's once-christened sword.

It took all my strength of mind to bring myself to make the first movement. I was in a kind of suspense wondering if it could be that I should lack this strength; but in the midst of this doubt I found myself moving. I stood up. I could see the silhouette of the guard's head as he paced away from me. I put my hands above my head and grasped the branch I knew to be there, forgetting all my pains and my weariness. I bent my elbows and pulled my legs slowly upwards. My head followed in the backward somersault— the same movement I had learnt on the bars in the gymnasium at school, but then only with the fear of being laughed at for failure, and now with a fear that was too great to realise completely in that moment. Then I was resting on the branch with my stomach.

228

I remained like that while the guard returned. From my position I might almost have dropped down on to him and throttled him before he could utter a cry. I would have done that, I suppose, had there been no alternative; but I had got to know him in the dugout, a little fellow with a timid blink—he had been an assistant in a porcelain shop a year before, and I could imagine him selling some piece of crockery with pride. He was too human and simple to kill alone and at close range. I knew he would put a bullet into my back if I ran away, but only because he had been caught up in the war and given a gun, and for that I felt no bitterness towards him.

After a few moments I stood up on the branch, clinging on to the trunk, and felt my way to the next branch, ten feet above the ground. It was thick and steady, and I worked my way along it until I was close to the foliage, and sitting ready to jump. Then I waited.

The guard was patient. It was ten minutes before he tentatively peered at the tree base. I could just make out his form in the shadows as he moved hesitantly. Then I heard him say:

"Have you finished?"

There was a silence. He was quite still, and I could imagine the horror dawning slowly upon him. He said again, with a quaver in his voice:

"You . . . have you finished?"

He stood for another second, and then he went up to the hole and felt about with his arms. He touched nothing but the tree trunk, and panic came into his movements. He walked round the tree looking into the undergrowth, and I heard him say softly, so that the sentry should not hear and learn of his negligence:

"Come out of there or I shall shoot. I shall shoot."

He had no torch, because lights were forbidden, and in the darkness he became suddenly terrified. He knew now I had got away and there was no concealing it. He scurried like a rabbit back along the track to the dugout.

I jumped. I hit the ground clumsily, recovered my balance, and began to run. I ran at right angles to the track to the dugout, towards the nearest perimeter trench. It seemed an interminable distance. I saw the trench getting nearer, and then I saw the sentry, and it was only the back of his head. He was guarding the encampment from outside attack and was not listening for unusual sounds within. I could make out the trench clearly. I leapt it a few yards from the sentry. As I flashed by I saw from the corner of my eye that his rifle was at his side, and not already in position, as I had feared. He began to turn his head, but the rifle had not moved as he disappeared from my sight. That gave me a few seconds' grace. I kept my head down and bolted straight forward, aiming at the space between the trees that I had previously noticed. It was forty-five yards to the nearest cover, but downhill, and against the dark background I knew that I would make a difficult target. All the same, I felt terribly exposed. I was in the firing line of at least three of the sentries, and I ran with half my mind concentrating on the small of my back, expecting a bullet there; I was three-quarters of the way and nothing had happened; I could hear nothing from behind. I thought that something must happen now. A sudden new terror exploded inside me, and electrified my legs, which went out of my control. I was afraid of falling, because I was going too fast down the hill. But I drew level with the trees that would cut me off from immediate danger. Then I tripped over something and sprawled forward headlong.

At the same time there was a frightful metallic clattering a few yards away. I lay on my face, and it seemed an age before it came to me what had happened, but it may not have been more than a few seconds. I had fallen over the trip-wire that the Japs had strung up to warn them of anyone approaching in the dark, and the clattering was only tin cans. I got up. I had to make myself move now the initial impetus was over. I went forward, stooping. There were only a few yards and I would be behind the trees, and at night no one would follow. I moved a hand to part the undergrowth, and at the same time, just above the elbow, I felt myself struck. The sound of the rifle came simultaneously. My arm was knocked forward, and there was a pain that spread at once to my shoulder. It was not severe. I went into the undergrowth and knew that no more bullets could reach me. There was another shot, and a whizzing through the air, but I had solid tree trunks behind me now. I pushed on, feeling my way with my left hand and letting my right hang at my side, crooked at the elbow. I could only go slowly, because there was no light here at all, only the black tree-tops showing against the profusely starred sky. I did not know where I was going, and I didn't care so long as it was away from the camp. Fortunately the undergrowth was not thick, and I kept finding places where there was only grass, through which I could pass quickly. I scarcely noticed the sharp blades cutting my hands and face. Once I stopped and listened in the direction from which I had come. There was no sound, only insects and the occasional dash of an animal. I didn't care about the animals or the snakes either, because their danger was nothing after the danger I had escaped. They could not rattle bayonets at me or shut me up behind barbed wire for years.

After a while I stopped again and leant against a tree to rest. I was exhausted with the hard work of going through the jungle blindly, and I wondered if I was losing much blood. There was a long, dull pain in my arm, and I couldn't move my elbow. I ran my hand down the sleeve and found it sodden, so I unbuttoned the front of my bush shirt and began to pull it off. When I tried to raise my right arm I found it stiff and heavy as though it was weighted with lead, so I used my left hand to slide the shirt off it. I stood naked from the waist, and the air was cool, drying my perspiration. I looked at the wounded arm, but it was too dark to see anything except the blood which seemed quite black on the paler skin. I touched the flesh with my fingers and found where the surface was broken. As far as I could tell, the bone was all right, and I thought the bullet had passed through. It was nothing: I would have paid more dearly than that for this night in the jungle alone.

I put my foot over the shoulder of my bush shirt on the ground, and with my left hand tore off the sleeve. It was tough material, but I tore down the seam, and I wound the whole sleeve round my arm as a bandage. Then I put the bush shirt on again, and lay down on the ground on my side, with the injured arm on top.

During the night of broken sleep I dreamt that Lieutenant Nakamura was emptying a machine-gun into me at point-blank range. I woke up and could still hear the machine-gun crackling, only it was a long way away on the road into Imphal.

CHAPTER V

I

In the morning I started to unwind the sleeve from my arm, intending to look at the wound in the daylight, and turn a cleaner patch against the skin. But the material was glued to the flesh, and it was painful when I tried to pull it off. I thought the pain was a good thing, since it showed there was still life in the arm although I was unable to bend it or raise it from the shoulder. But I had no water with which to wash it, and I was afraid that if I tore away the bandage the bleeding would commence again; so I wound up the ends and tucked them in without uncovering the wound.

In whichever direction I went the going was equally difficult. I could find no tracks and I had to break my way through the intertwined vegetation without a knife and only one arm to help me. It was impossible to avoid the steep hillsides; there was nothing but hills here, chain after chain of pointed hills a thousand feet high, riven with narrow valleys. Descending, I kept slipping, crashing downwards until the undergrowth caught me up and I could stand again. My hand was bleeding with clutching at thorns and knife-like grasses. When I tried to climb, I slipped back often, and each time I lay a little longer to recover my spirits to go on. The only guide to direction was the noise of battle on the road. At least I supposed it to be on the road still, though in both ways the sound was receding as though we were being pushed steadily back. It was no use my making back towards Kohima; in the camp I had heard that the Japs had formed a road block a short distance from this side of the village, and beyond it too, and were certain of its fall. They were also certain of Imphal, for that matter, but they had got farther to go to reach it, and, anyway, I was closer to our lines in that direction. I reckoned the shelling was ten miles away, and that if I went parallel to the road for ten miles, and then curved in to meet it, I should be well on the right side. I tried to keep along the valleys, but they twisted perpetually and led me from the right direction, so that I could not avoid climbing altogether. Now and again I saw a Naga village perched on a hill-top, but I was afraid of going near it because, although I had heard the Nagas were friendly, the Japs were likely to be there, commandeering the rice and trying to conscript labour.

More hampering to my progress than my injured arm was my dysentery. There was little food in my stomach for it to play on, which gave it all the more scope with the walls of my bowels. It seemed to be tearing them to bits. This disease had never been really painful for me before, only inconvenient; and now the pain itself did not matter, for the circumstances made it easy to bear, but it drew on my strength which had already been diminished by loss of blood. It drew its own toll of blood, also. At first I stopped for it, but that became too tedious and took too much time, so I just went on, thinking I was already so ragged and filthy it made little difference. One sleeve of my shirt had gone, of course, and the buttons had been ripped away. The bottoms of my trousers were shredded, and everything was covered with bloodstains and grime from sleeping nightly on the ground since I was captured. But all this meant no more than the equally dishevelled face I had seen in the mirror, because it did not seem to be myself, despite the bodily discomforts that went with it. Or, at any rate, it was only a part of myself, the part that was living this moment, the particular section of film that was passing through the machine. My real self, the accumulation of all the film that had passed already, I was carrying intact out of the jungle; and still, whatever happened, whatever was done to me, nothing could destroy that. Once, when Sabby had said to me 'No one can ever take away all our happiness, darling', I had thought, without saying it, that time could take it away. But I knew differently now, because I knew that the happiness was with me in the jungle as all the sadness was also; and that was why I could not think of myself only in terms of rags and dried blood and a ten days' growth of beard.

I went until midday without feeling a strong need for water, then it came upon me as though my body had suddenly realised it was being neglected. I had not seen any water all morning, not even in the valleys, and I began to worry over this, knowing that lack of a few cupfuls could drive me back to the Japanese.

I pushed on for an hour, reckoning by the sun that it was one or two o'clock, and then I came across a track and turned along it. I was more likely to find water that way, though I was more likely to find Japanese, too; so I proceeded circumspectly. I had only gone a few hundred yards when I saw some movement ahead, and I dived into the undergrowth. I lay on my belly where a section of the path was visible through the tangled vegetation. It was a whole company of Japanese, marching in single file. They were carrying full packs and water-bottles and rifles, and were moving forward to the road. They went in silence, and their faces looked expressionless and dead. If I had held a machine-gun I could have mowed them down without compunction, because at this distance they seemed less like humans than like some formidable species of jungle-born animal. And yet I knew that this was not so —that their appearance, like my own, spoke only of the moment,

233

and that somewhere buried within all their equipment and khaki and set soldiers' faces were stores of sentiments and memories, and that each one of them who trudged past me was in some way different from the rest.

I let them go by, and then set off along the track in the opposite direction. In a few minutes there was more sound ahead, so I got down again. A string of mules came by, sturdy, big-eared animals carrying enormous loads. Some had machine-guns strapped to them and heavy boxes of ammunition. A dozen soldiers escorted the train, behind which another platoon followed in single file. They passed slowly, and I had to remain perfectly motionless, because I was only a few yards from their legs.

When they had disappeared I cut off into the jungle again, thinking it too dangerous to continue along the track. The dryness of my throat and mouth was making it difficult to salivate. I had read so many tales of men who had suffered from thirst on a raft or in the desert, and of how the torture had turned them into gibbering idiots, that the fear of this happening to myself produced a nervous reaction that made the effect worse. I had also been perspiring freely, and I knew all the water had to be replaced.

I thought that in some of the valleys there must be water, so I worked my way downwards again. I had been walking and floundering through the undergrowth all day, but I hadn't covered more than two or three miles. Now I had to go on regardless of direction, only to find water. Food didn't matter yet—and even if I found some it would be useless with nothing to drink.

I reached the bottom of the hill, and it flattened out and rose again without any water course. There was nothing for it but to go on. I pulled my way up the next hillside thinking now of nothing but my thirst. It was not unbearable, but great enough to give me an unpleasant premonition of what was in store.

I found a promontory from which I could look over the tree-tops and survey the country. I could still see nothing but lines of hills, with a few clearings in the jungle and no water at all. I chose the deepest valley between two hills, almost a ravine, with a mountain rising behind that looked like a watershed. It took an hour to reach it, and the sun was dropping low on my left, over Cawnpore and Delhi, and Peter and Sabby. I got down into the ravine where there was a deep gloom. The whole of the bottom was buried in undergrowth. I stepped into all the tangled vegetation and parted it with one hand and foot. There were the smooth stones of a stream-bed, but I could neither see nor hear water, so I dropped on my knees and felt between the stones. It was all bone dry. I pulled at the stones and felt beneath them, but there was not even dampness. It had been dry since the last monsoon and was waiting for the next. The next was not for a month at least, and by that time I should have gone mad and died, or gone mad and gone back to the Japanese.

I got up from the stream-bed and climbed the side of the ravine again. I knew what I was going to do now—go on with all the determination I had, straight towards our lines, without wasting any more time searching for water that wasn't there. With this decision I felt less thirsty, and able to move more strongly against the entangling growth. I shook my feet free angrily. I wasn't going back to the Japanese to have my head cut off by the arrogant little ape Nakamura; and I wasn't going to die either, because I had to see Sabby, and anyway our people weren't more than a few miles away. Men had survived journeys a hundred times worse than this, and they didn't have to see Sabby. I would go on all night and get through tomorrow. If I got through tomorrow water didn't matter. It didn't matter if it took until the following day: you could go most of a week without drinking. In any case, the sun wasn't burning on my skin because of the trees, and that was different from the desert or an open raft. I was going to get through all right, and with this wound I would be sent to the rear at once, and I should be with Sabby in a week. The thirst was nothing when I knew I should be with her as soon as that.

It became dark quickly. The vast wildness of the jungle faded and there was only the blackness and the faint outlines that made my immediate world. Everywhere the crickets rasped and hissed and screamed, and all kinds of other new noises began. There may have been the same noises in the daytime, but at night they sounded new, as any noise sounds new in a cathedral when you have heard it only in the street. It was rather like a cathedral in the jungle at night because of the stillness that sounds only emphasised, and because the stillness was awe-inspiring, and there was some power in it the nature of which it was impossible to comprehend. I tried to struggle on, groping my way from tree to tree, one arm dead at my side. I went on purposely until I was too tired to care where I lay, and I dropped down suddenly and remained where I had dropped, biting a stick that fell across my face, for that kept my parched lips apart and the tongue from the roof of the mouth. The temperature fell quickly and the cold ate at my exposed limbs, and went through me. It was a long night, the longest I have ever spent. It dragged itself out until I could no longer believe that this was one night only; but I thought I must somehow have slept through the day and woken up only to suffer another. I counted what I thought were minutes; and over each I seemed to labour as though it was a full stage on a steep hill, with the top far away out of sight. I thought it must be three or four in the morning, and in order to give myself the surprise of seeing the light before I expected it, I pretended that it was only midnight. But there was no pleasant surprise, for had it been only dusk I would have expected the light sooner. Finally, I gave up waiting for the dawn, believing this night was really endless; and then it came when I had almost ceased to care. I got up at once, thinking in the cool morning I could make good headway, particularly as my thirst seemed to have diminished. When the sun began to shine through the upper branches of the trees instead of between the trunks, I reckoned I had put a mile behind me. I began to feel light-hearted, believing that when the noise of battle began I should find myself level with it. Then all of a sudden I saw the ravine in which I had searched for water on the previous evening, and despair banished all the hope in me. I had somehow confused my directions despite the position of the sun to show me I was wrong—and now the day was advancing and the high sun was heating the air, and the air was burning in my rough throat.

There was no firing to be heard. I wondered if it was Sunday and the armies were observing a day of rest. I tried to work out the day of the week, going over the days from the Thursday on which I was captured. I marked each in my mind by an incident, but each time I reached three or four I lost count, and the time became confused. Anyway, it didn't matter what day it was, there was no battle to guide me, that was the point.

I used the sun, and went south, still parallel to the Imphal Road. Later on I came upon an encampment of Japs. Luckily I heard them first and got down out of sight, but it took me a long time to skirt the area, cautiously crawling most of the way—and with one arm useless it was a terrible business that exhausted me. When at last I tried to stand up I collapsed and had to lie resting for a time. I was weaker than ever, with a pain spreading through my body like a poison from the shoulder of my wounded arm. I had left the bandage on still, and dare not remove it, partly because I knew I could do nothing and partly because I was afraid the sight would revolt me. All over the arm a dirty blue-green colour was spreading, and in places the flesh had been scratched and torn by thorny growths. The dysentery was nothing now. I had dried up with no food or water in my stomach, and there were only pains that didn't matter. But there was a burning pain round my head like a red-hot steel band. It was this that made me cry. I could have kept myself from crying, but this would have taken energy that I needed, and I let myself weep. It did not matter weeping in the jungle when there was nobody to see. Once I had started, enormous convulsions began in my breast, but there were only tiny tears on the end of them, squeezed out as though my body had not enough water to spare for this. I put my face on the ground and bit the earth until the waves that shook me had subsided. Then I got up and went on, but stumbling half blindly. I felt utterly broken and hopeless.

Yet something kept holding me up, some strength that no longer seemed my own. It was as though I had passed from reality into a dream; and the dream brought with it the blessing of timelessness. I ceased to count or care about the hours. But I know that when I came at last upon the river course, the sun was low amongst the trees.

I could not see any water in the river at first, only the white stones that were evidence of a torrent in the rainy season. I was too dazed to rush upon them in excitement. I went on stumbling up to them, and I fell down there before I knew whether or not there was water. Then I heard a faint trickle. It came into my ears slowly, growing louder, like a sound that wakes one from sleep. I listened to it for quite a long time before I turned over and pulled away a stone and saw the dancing reflection of the light. I tried to push my head down, but there was not enough room between the stones, so I shifted one or two more for the length of my body, and as I touched the water with my lips I felt it like tender fingers caressing my limbs. I turned my head sideways and the water ran into my mouth. It was a moment or two before I could contract my throat muscle to swallow. When I succeeded I could feel the liquid pass down the channel to my stomach. My throat was still hard and the first gulp made no difference. I swallowed six or seven times more, and each time it was a great effort, and I felt enormously wearied and could not bring myself to swallow again. It vaguely occurred to me I had found this water too late. It did not matter very much. All I wanted to do was sleep. I closed my eyes and the water splashed into my mouth and over my face, and I was too tired to think of anything but the dark sleep that was creeping over me and the very gradual extinction of pain.

II

I woke up and it was night. A very soft, starry night with a feathery wind blowing. I could not think where I was. I had been dreaming of Bombay and the house on the hill, and I woke believing myself to be on a soft mattress, with a white pillow under my head and Sabby snuggling up to me, stroking away with her long fingers the dull pain in my forehead. Very gradually the fingers became water and the pillow a round stone, and there was no Sabby at all, only the feeling of space around me and the slow realisation that this was jungle. I remembered that my body had been sick. I could not feel my body now. There was no pain in it, and below my throat there might have been nothing. I wondered if it were all dead and only my mind was living, and to test it I made up my mind to move my leg. I managed to shift it a few inches. Then I moved my arm, enclosing a stone in my fingers, but I could not grip it tight enough to lift it. It was only a small stone.

I tried to get up. I began to count five, intending on the five to concentrate all my energy into the effort. I counted slowly, because there was a reluctance in me to do this. When I reached five there was a short spasm in my body that expended itself before I had raised myself at all. There seemed to be a force holding me to the ground, my own dead weight. I thought I would try getting up the other way, so I shifted my top leg over slowly until I was lying face downwards instead of on my side, and I pushed upwards on the one sound elbow. I raised myself an inch or two and then dropped back exhausted. I lay with my face pushed into the stones, thinking that I was dying.

I did not really know why I was dying, whether it was weakness from the days I had lived on a few handfuls of rice and these last two days on nothing, or whether it was the poison from the wound. Whichever it was, I ought to have been stronger. If I had been a soldier, I could have come easily through this. But I had been sitting too long behind a school desk and cooped up in the

238

fort at Cawnpore; and I had been eating well and growing soft, not lifting a box myself because there was always a bearer. I was not dying a tough fighting death, but falling effete by the wayside. I was deeply ashamed of my defeat, and I knew that in my weakness I had betrayed Sabby. And I had betrayed Lord Durweston, whom I had promised that I would look after Sabby; and I had betrayed myself.

I did not care how long this night lasted. It was not like the last, one aching minute after another, but a timeless suffering in the heart. And after a time there began to come back to me certain scenes from my life, and with them a curious sense of detachment, as though they were from the life of a stranger. And I fell to wondering how it was that my own life had been built up of these scenes, and not of others; how it had come about that with all the world to be born in I had been given life in a place called Tewkesbury in the Midlands of England. And what power was there beyond my own will that had thereafter shaped my destiny? Had it been preordained that I should escape from Burma, to find waiting for me in India a year of intense happiness? And that I should be abandoned at last on the stones of a river-bed in Manipur? How strange a place in which to die! I had somehow never thought of myself coming finally to grief in so remote a spot. . . . But it was always in the last reel that you got the biggest surprises.

Yet now it seemed to be at hand, I saw nothing to fear in death. It was leaving life that I dreaded—leaving Sabby, perhaps in pain and deeply unhappy. I wanted more than anything else to be with her, to hold her frail body tightly and kiss away her enormous tears; and I wanted to show her love in the warmth of which she must grow well. And I wanted to be alive to see Sabby grow old, for with age there would come to her a new beauty of gentleness and serenity. I loved her for what she would become no less than for that part of her that I knew; and if I regretted dying, it was more than anything because I should never see her like this and could not help her to live through the misery of the present.

"Darling Sabby," I said. . . . "Sweet, darling Sabby" . . . and I could hear my own voice amongst the stones, and I thought somehow that she might hear it too, and remember as I was remembering the loveliest moments of our happiness—when she had held the towel between us in her first bedroom in Bombay, and we had kissed with lips only faintly touching; and the night I came back to her from Rosie, and those times when we had lain under a pine-

239

tree overlooking Jali Tal; and the night we had first gone to the new house together and dined together on the balcony with the lights of Bombay like a jewelled carpet below; and at Agra in the moonlight, the exquisite confusion of happiness and sadness . . . all this, and underneath it the fusion of our love. I had been taught to love and to know the meaning of gentleness and generosity . . . but these were only seeds planted in me, and were only beginning to grow into a real knowledge that would bring a serenity into my life. I was dying with all my old selfishness and ignorance . . . and it was too soon. I hadn't begun to live.

"But, darling, you were always living person." I could hear Sabby's voice so clearly.

"You have to die once," I said to her in my thoughts, "to know how rich life can be."

"Darling, can you love life and Sabby at the same time?"

"It is really the same thing."

"Then won't you please come back to me?"

"I don't think I shall be able to."

"But you are not going to die. You are too young to die, darling, and I am not going to let you be killed by a bullet sent by Japanese man. I shall make you better."

"If anyone could make me better, it would be you."

"Really, you're not going to die."

"Let's have a pact then," I said. "Neither of us will die."

"You keep pact. It doesn't matter about me."

"Don't say that. You must promise."

"All right, I promise, darling. Please will you promise too?"

"I promise that I'll do my best," I said.

"That is cheating."

"I know it is. But I'm terribly tired and I've got to go to sleep now. Please will you kiss me once more?"

Dawn was breaking behind the hills, and a pale light suffused the sky to the east over Burma. A few miles to the west a heavy gun began its morning work. A machine-gun coughed in reply. Over my face the stream water splashed gently, cool from the mountains. But it was the soft pressure of Sabby's lips that I felt as I passed dreaming into sleep.

III

When I opened my eyes again I was puzzled to see blue sky and the branches of trees moving overhead. I thought for a moment:

am I dead? Then at once I knew I was not, and I was about to try to sit up when I saw a face over me with long, dark eyes and a flat nose. I shut my eyes again.

I was lying prone on a crude bamboo stretcher. I could feel it being borne sturdily and hear heavy boots on the earth. When I looked through my lashes, without fully opening my eyes again, I could see the backs of the two men in front. They were small-statured, with broad shoulders, and the hair was black on their necks.

I kept my eyes closed because I wanted time to think. I was sick with despair. There was a good deal of other pain in my body, but this utter black dead weight of despair held me like a girder fallen across my chest. In my mind were the confused pictures of a second captivity, infinitely worse than the first because this time I should be secured beyond hope of escape; and I should be mercilessly punished for this blundering attempt to get away, which had gained me only a wound and something like death. I felt as though I had died once, been through the awful process of dying, only to find myself back where I had started. It had been a swindle.

I did not think I was going to die now, unless they wished to let me do so. But in that case they would have left me to become a carcass where I lay, and not waste the strength of four good soldiers in carrying me back. I wondered why they were bothering to do this.

Looking up again, I said in Japanese:

"Please will you give me water?"

The face I could see had wide cheekbones and dark eyes. The man returned my gaze with a flicker of humour, and he glanced at his companion who held the other rear handle of the stretcher.

He said at last, in laboured accents:

"You do not speak English?"

"Of course," I said. "I am English."

"You are now better?"

"I would like some water."

"At the top of this hill, I will give you my bottle."

"Where are you taking me?" I said.

"To the field hospital."

"Take me back to the British!" I began to plead with desperation. "If you take me back, I'll see you're well treated. Please take me back!"

He looked puzzled and then he smiled again, and I thought he was smiling at the naïveté of my suggestion.

"Of course we are taking you back to the British," he said.

I pondered over his tone for a few moments, wondering why it had seemed to lack sarcasm. Was he only saying this for kindness. . . .? My mind was not functioning properly, and I couldn't make it out. 'Of course we are taking you back. . . .' He spoke English, this man; and he had not understood my Japanese. Yet he looked like a Japanese. . . .

"We are Gurkhas," the man said, as if reading my thoughts.

My face did not seem to be laughing, but my joy came in gasps, and my eyes must have lost all their dead, despairing look and begun to live and sparkle.

"Gurkhas?" I said after a long time.

"Yes. What did you think?"

"Of course you are Gurkhas," I said. "Your hats. . . ."

I ought to have noticed their hats, but all I had looked at was their features, and with Mongolian eyes and swarthy skin they were not unlike the Japanese.

"What time is it?" I said.

"Three o'clock."

"And what day?"

"Wednesday."

"It's April, isn't it?"

"The fifth of April."

"I shall always remember the fifth of April," I said. "Talking to friends again."

At the top of the hill I had a long draught from a water-bottle, and death was a long way behind.

"I will try to walk," I said, and started to push myself up from the stretcher which they had laid on the ground; but then I found the recovery was in my mind and my body was still sick. I caught sight of my arm. I had almost forgotten it, and it was a shock to see this dead thing at my side, and at the same time become aware of the offensive odour of the bandage. They would have to cut off the arm. A pretty beastly business. . . .

"You are all right?" said the Gurkha who spoke English.

"Yes," I said. "I've been talking too much, that's all."

"We will continue. In an hour we shall reach the hospital."

I felt very ill all the rest of the way back. I wanted to be sick, and my stomach went into convulsions, but nothing came except a mouthful of water. My head was dizzy. I opened my eyes sometimes and saw troops passing along the track, and there was a good deal of fighting going on somewhere. It seemed to break out afresh every quarter of an hour or so, with a frenzied din of machine-guns and rifles and metal whizzing through the air. When I heard it I felt ashamed of the self-pity in which I had been indulging. That stuff out there was worse than anything I had experienced, worse than a fortuitous rifle shot and pseudo-death in a river-bed. All the same, I wished I was right out of it. They could have my arm if only they'd take it quickly and send me back to Sabby. Whatever happened, I must get back to Sabby. My body was tired and starved and poisoned, but it had not forgotten how to yearn . . . all of it was yearning for her, yearning through its fears.

It was half past four when we reached the hospital. I was put in a bamboo hut, and a medical orderly brought a bottle of soup. A little later another patient was carried in, with a bayonet wound underneath his right breast. The orderly said the doctor would be along in a minute. I tried to think of something to say, but there were no words in my head. It seemed ridiculous to lie side by side in silence, when you might come from the same town, and here you were wounded in the Indian jungle. In the end I worked up a sentence, and said:

"It's funny having soup for tea."

He said nothing at all, and afterwards the doctor came in and looked at him, and signalled at once to the orderlies to take him out. Then he came over to me, and began to cut off the bandage from my arm.

CHAPTER VI

I

I was taken off by ambulance that night. I had still got my arm, and the doctor said there was hope of keeping it: they would have to decide down in Imphal when they would tell the effect of the first-aid. My luck seemed to be in all round. Touch wood, I thought, and I felt the side of the stretcher with my left hand, because I needed quite a bit more luck yet.

It was dark in the back of the ambulance. For a time we crawled at a few miles an hour over a rough track, and then I felt the smoother surface of a good road under our wheels. This was the Imphal Road, someone said; and I calculated that we must be about fifteen miles nearer Imphal than the spot where a fortnight before we had run into the road block. Only two weeks ago! It seemed more like two years since we had stopped at the rest-camp near Kohima, and sipped tea and said we would be in Imphal in a couple of hours. Since then Manning had been shot and the Sikh slaughtered, and the Major's spirit broken. Yet even those things had passed into the back of my memory; and it surprised me to find that I had to grope there for a clear picture of Manning's appearance. But in time I should remember him easily again. Time would set the events of the last fortnight in perspective, and perhaps enable me to understand those things which so puzzled me. Why, I wanted to know, had we been allowed to sit blithely in the rest-camp when all this had been round the next corner of our lives? And why was I alone allowed to escape? What pattern was working itself out, what scheme was there behind events? Or was there no pattern and no scheme, only chaos and endless unguided change? Perhaps to know the answer you must know God. Even the belief that I was dying had brought me no nearer to Him. Would Time do that, also?

I let myself relax. All the time I had been with the Japanese I had not relaxed, and now it was a luxury to give myself up freely to the motions of the ambulance, and know that friendly hands were at the wheel. I lay watching three red cigarette-tips moving in the darkness; and each time one was placed between lips and glowed brighter, lighting a friendly soldier's face, a new warmth of gratitude glowed in my heart.

Running swiftly on the level road of the plain it seemed only a short while before we came to our destination. At once our stretchers were carried from the ambulance and up steps; and then there was a hospital ward, and a bed with white sheets and a pillow, and there was a nurse—and it all came back to me how I had come out of the jungle before and been through this, and it came back with a queer sensation that it was a repetition of something from another life, and that I was remembering ghosts.

I wanted to sleep. But the nurse came and washed me and put me into pyjamas, and her hands had a friendly efficiency. Then a doctor came, and he did something to my shoulder, but I was drifting away into a delicious unconsciousness, and I did not know until the morning that I was going to keep my arm.

244

I was overjoyed; but the most thrilling event of the morning was sending a letter to Sabby. I raised my knees so that I could write it against them without lifting my body, and I used my left hand. The writing was like a child's, but I thought it would amuse Sabby if she didn't worry too much about my right hand. I told her I had cut it; and since I could say nothing of what had actually happened, I filled a few pages with all the things we were fond of saying to one another, and sealed the letter and gave it to the nurse. I wondered how long I should have to wait for a reply. And I wondered, too, whether I should get sent back to India. Here in Imphal they had got the wind-up—and no wonder, for the Japanese were coming in from the mountains on every side. The Corps had gone into a 'box', and even the hospital staff had their battle positions. There was no road left open for retreat. But the airfield was in use, and already the worst casualties were being flown out to Assam. I began to pray that I, too, might be thought sick enough for evacuation.

In my room there was a wireless, and that afternoon I had it tuned in to the Delhi wavelength. The suspense of waiting was unbearable. I knew that if Sabby spoke, all my fears would be wiped out in an instant and the colour of my life changed; but that if she didn't, there could be no relief for my anguish. She didn't speak. It was a man's voice, but for me only a blankness.

I had to tell the whole story of my capture and escape to a Captain, who sat by my bedside scribbling like a reporter. He kept saying: "A wonderful experience, since you came out alive." But it did not seem to me wonderful, and anybody could have had that experience in exchange for a straight run through from Kohima to Imphal. Then the next day Peter came.

For a time my happiness at seeing him left me speechless. He strode into the small ward wreathed in smiles, and his moustache seemed to be grinning on its own, and he seized my loose hand, which I shook madly in his. He had been sent to Imphal to take my place after I had been reported 'missing'. He had come in by air; and only now, after three days, had he heard of my presence in hospital.

"I've wasted an awful lot of sympathy on you," he said. "You're an old fraud! I thought you were dead, and I've played the part of a grieved friend with a histrionic talent that amounts almost to genius. And here you are looking the picture of health. Why couldn't you at least have brought a few Japanese prisoners back with you, to have something to show for your escapade?"

"I would have done," I said. "But I didn't know you'd be here to interrogate them."

"Of course I'm here—and feeling very important. There's nobody here who can test my Japanese, so that it's all right feeling important. I'm a key person. And it's most desperately exciting being in a box, entirely surrounded by the enemy. It'll provide stories to dine out on for years. Though, of course, when we demonstrate the box on the table, with the help of the cutlery and the cruet, we won't say that we could have escaped perfectly easily by air."

"That's what I want to do," I said.

"You don't want to get out?"

"Yes, I do."

"You don't really think that one bullet is enough to get you retired off on a pension?"

"It's enough to get me retired out of Imphal," I said.

"What a bitter disappointment you really are! We all expected you to do something heroic, and then come back and say it was nothing at all and anybody would have done it. Instead you get yourself into this bungalow, when everybody else is living in bashas or tents or nothing at all, and start shooting the hell of a line about it."

"I'm going to get out of Imphal, all the same," I said.

"I suspect the real reason is that you're pining for Sabby."

"Yes," I said. "I think that's the real reason."

I told him that I thought Sabby was ill and that nobody would be looking after her, and just for a moment the tender part of Peter glowed through the shell.

"In that case," he said, "we'll have to get your evacuation fixed up at once. It would have been nice to have you here—but if you want to know the truth, I think being in a box is a mug's game. The Duke of Wellington, or whoever invented boxes, must have been out of his senses. Boxes are too damned difficult to get out of whether you've aeroplanes or not; and I'd much rather dine out on stories of how I spent the war at Simla drinking *burra pegs* at the Cecil."

"You're an impossible person to understand," I said. "You're my best friend, and I still don't know whether you'd prefer to be in Imphal or Simla."

"I don't know myself. But if I have to be in Imphal, I'm sorry you won't be here to talk to. You're the only person who doesn't understand me, and that's very refreshing. Anyhow, you'll have a great story for your free dinners in country houses: how you flew out of the box in the last aircraft to leave before the sides caved in and your remarkable friend Peter died at his post."

"Doing what?"

"Oh, doing something really incongruous. Discussing Frank Harris and Oscar Wilde would be rather good. Or do you think it's better for me to have a rifle which I fire to the Last Round?"

"That would be much more incongruous."

"Very well, I'll have a rifle. And please don't forget to tell everybody how I died on the battlefield. Tell your adopted daughter."

"I'll tell her," I said.

II

I had no difficulty in getting sent off by aircraft, because they wanted to make room for the steady flow of casualties that was coming in. It was ten days later when the drugs had got a grip on my dysentery again, and my only real trouble was the plaster cast that encased my arm. I was allowed on my feet to save space for another stretcher in the aircraft; but nothing I could say would make the authorities send me straight to Delhi. They told me I should be bundled off to bed again as soon as we reached the hospital in Calcutta, and I could reckon on another month there at least. And I thought to myself: so this is where I shape my own destiny for a change. . . .

Peter came to the airfield to say goodbye.

"I've got a feeling that I'll come through this war all right," he said. "And so will you."

"You don't happen to have a feeling about Sabby?" I said.

"I leave that to you. Maybe Sabby will be all right, too."

"Maybe?"

"Oh, she'll be all right."

"You never really told me what you thought of Sabby," I said.

"She's the sweetest creature I've ever known."

"That sounds like my own thoughts."

"It's what you wanted to hear, isn't it?"

"Of course it is."

"That's why I said it."

"All the same, you sounded as though you meant it."

247

"I say all the right things in the right way. And I mean quite a lot of them, as a matter of fact. I mean it when I say I'll miss you. And if you ever want a shoulder to cry on, here it is."

"I'd say that works the other way round, too, only you don't cry."

"I don't have to—I'm not in love. I've never been in love, so you said."

"I was wrong. Of course you've been in love. It's in every line of your book."

"I got stung a bit in France. But not enough to cry."

"I'm almost crying now," I said. "Let's say goodbye."

"All right. Goodbye."

"I'm coming back. I'll get myself sent out again when my sick leave's over."

"I'll have finished all the dangerous jobs for you then. You'll come back just in time for a rest in the monsoon."

"You won't know when I'm crying in the monsoon," I said.

It was seven o'clock in the morning. We took off from the airfield and made a circuit over Imphal, and then headed off westward. The whole of the Manipur plain lay below us, flat as a lake and encircled by hills. We looked down and knew that the Japanese were below us now, not a dozen miles from Imphal. What colossal impudence they had, butting their way into India like this! We'd broken all their bridges in Burma, and shot up their stores and their men and their aircraft, and we'd even put a couple of landing-strips for ourselves right down in their midst; and yet still they'd pushed their way through these impossible hills and surrounded our base, and there was no hope of getting them out altogether before the rains begun. We'd do it eventually, of course; no one had any doubts about that. We would extricate them from these mountain ranges and ravines, and drive them out of Burma. But how long was it going to take? Already we'd been four and a half years at war; could we suppose it would take less than the same time again? There was a time when I used to think of the war as something to get out of the way so that we could go on with life—as though the war would take a period out of life without being life itself. Instead these war years had brought the profoundest experience of all, and had moulded me more than my years at school. Now it had become difficult to imagine the world at peace—newspapers that were not full of front-line communiqués and friends who were not soldiers. It was difficult to think

248

of oneself as a civilian; as someone who caught buses and tubes, and wore flannels, and went boating on the Avon, and had a bed with an eiderdown and a set of favourite books on the polished oak table. . . . Yet if ever I went back to this life again, wouldn't it be equally difficult to think of myself as I was now, and to recapture the atmosphere of a scene like this? And as though to impress it upon my own mind and make it easier to recall in the future, I looked round at the wounded men on the stretchers, and out of the window to the jungle-covered hills moving away below; and I thought of the heavy plaster cast on my arm and of the apprehension within myself that was heavier still. And I knew that however dim this became in the future there was no escape from it now; that life had to be taken moment by moment, and you could neither hold up time to preserve your happiness nor hasten it to take away your sorrow. Peter had said, 'If you want to cry . . .' If I had to cry I would do so, and that would be part of my life.

At ten o'clock we landed at Calcutta. Two ambulances from the hospital came alongside the aircraft on the tarmac, and orderlies carried out the stretchers.

An orderly said to me:

"Can you manage yourself, sir?"

"Yes," I said. "Which ambulance?"

"There'll be room in the first."

I went over to the leading ambulance, and stood around for a few minutes whilst they filled it up with the stretchers.

"This ambulance?" I said.

"Yes, sir."

I waited until the orderly had gone back into the aircraft, and then I began to walk away. I walked over to the control tower without looking round. I went in, and there was a Squadron-Leader sitting behind a desk.

"Have you got an aircraft going to Delhi?" I said.

He looked at my arm all done up in plaster and supported by a sling.

"Rather," he said. "There's always something going."

"I'd like to get a lift."

"You haven't booked a passage?"

"No," I said. "I've just come from Imphal."

"Well, we'll fix you up all right," he said. "You don't want to travel by train with a groggy arm like that. Hang on."

I looked out of the window and saw the first ambulance starting off. It came over the tarmac and passed behind the control-room, and a minute later the second followed it away. Nobody seemed to have noticed I was missing. My medical papers had been taken with the others, but it would be some time before they found out what had happened. By that time I should be in Delhi with Sabby. I didn't mind what happened so long as I found Sabby.

"There's a kite going in an hour," the Squadron-Leader said.

"I can get on it?"

"We'll squeeze you in."

I found a canteen and bought myself a lemonade and a packet of cigarettes. The air in Calcutta was terribly sultry. Inside the plaster my arm felt swollen with the heat, and my hand was burning where it stuck out at the end. I poured some cold water over it, but when it had dried it seemed hotter still. I sat down under a fan. Soon I became restive, and I went outside again, my battledress jacket soaking up perspiration. It was a badly fitting jacket that I had been given in the hospital at Imphal, and my olive-green trousers were very large and baggy.

When I went back to the control-room the Squadron-Leader said the aircraft had been delayed half an hour.

"What time will it get to Delhi?" I asked.

"Six o'clock."

"It won't be later?"

"It might be seven. You're in a hurry?"

"No," I said. "I just wondered."

I had to wait another three-quarters of an hour, and then I was taken over to an aircraft. I stood back whilst some senior officers got in, until a Brigadier took my left arm and said, "After you, old chap." I was still nervous that there was not going to be enough room, but when everybody had sat down there was still an empty seat. We got away before midday, and the relief of escaping into the air again was tremendous. It was the last lap, with Sabby at the end of it. We flew over Bengal and Bihar, and then along the River Jumna, and after we had been going some hours somebody shouted in my ear, "If you look out now you'll see the Taj Mahal." I peered down and there was the old town of Agra, a cluster of roofs in the dry, broken country. Outside it, on the brown river, the Taj stood like an ivory miniature, only whiter than ivory gleaming as though it had just been washed. It came as something of a surprise to see it like this—in the sunlight, and from so great a distance. I had thought of it only in the moonlight, and with Sabby and me on the grass at its foot; but now I realised that this way in which I had remembered it was only a moment in its own life, a moment that was gone and forgotten by all but ourselves.

This miniature beneath us had nothing to do with our memories. It was the famous monument of Shah Jehan, to be pointed out by one traveller to another as they swept over it at two hundred miles an hour. And as such I did not care for it; so I sat down again, and waited for the last hour to drag itself to a conclusion.

CHAPTER VII

I

WE reached the Willingdon airport soon after six. I went straight out on to the road and found a tonga, and gave the driver the name of Sabby's hotel. It was a long way, first through the avenues of the new town and then the bazaars of the old. The hot air streamed on to my face, drying my lips and my throat. There were heavy smells in the bazaars, and the flies were swarming thickly everywhere. The bells of the horse jingled all the time. I was jolted about, perspiring and dirty, and longing to get to the hotel. The journey seemed to go on for ever. Pedestrians and cyclists got in the way of the horse so that we were constantly brought to a standstill. We went slowly. My arm was paining me badly and was chafing against the plaster. I would have torn the plaster off, only I had nothing to do it with. I began to pray: 'Please may I find Sabby at the hotel. I will give anything for that. Please, please let Sabby be there.'

When we arrived at last, I remembered I had no money to pay the tonga man. Peter had given me a rupee in Imphal, all he had on him, but I had spent that on cigarettes in Calcutta. I told the man to wait and went into the hotel. I went straight up to Sabby's room. I knocked and listened: my heart was banging inside me after the speed I had taken the stairs, and it was the only sound. I stood breathing through my dry throat. After a while I tried the handle. It turned, but the door was locked.

I went downstairs again and walked through the dining-room and the lounge. Everybody looked at me with curiosity; I suppose it was because of the lump of dirty plaster and my dishevelled appearance. I looked at them, and through them, because Sabby was not there. She was not outside on the terrace. I went to the clerk at the reception-desk.

"Miss Wei?" I said.

"Yes, sir," he said, obsequiously tilting his head on one side.

"Well," I said, "is she here?"

"Yes, sir."

"Where?"

"Kindly wait, sir. I will see for you." He began to search in a register.

"I know her room number," I said. "Do you know where she is?"

"Yes, sir. I will tell you." He went on pushing his finger down the page. "Miss Wei is in Room No. 37."

"I know that—but where is she now?"

"You may try the room on the first floor. It is No. 37."

"Yes, yes," I said. "But she isn't there now. Did you see her go out?"

"Yes, sir."

"What time?"

"I don't quite follow you, sir."

"Miss Wei," I said. "Did you see her go out today?"

"No, sir."

"Do you know who she is?"

"She has Room No 37."

"For heaven's sake get the manageress," I shouted at him.

He climbed off his stool and came out of the office into the hall. He spoke to a bearer as though he were describing a murder that had taken place, with fussy speed. The bearer also began to rattle away, and they stood there holding a long conversation. I interrupted.

"The manageress," I said. "Memsahib. Fetch her, will you?"

"*Atcha*, Sahib," the bearer said and disappeared.

I waited in the colonnaded porch. It was dusk, and the air was terribly heavy and oppressive. I never liked Delhi. I always thought it was soulless, and I always came to it with a kind of dread. It was in the middle of the dry, ugly plains, and it was hardly more hospitable than the plains themselves. Now a deep hate for it began to rise in me. I wanted to find Sabby and take her away to some place where the sky gave sun and rain generously, where there were trees and flowers in profusion. Whatever happened, I must take her away. Sabby was a sweet blossom that in Delhi could only shrivel and die.

The bearer came back, and began to gabble to the clerk.

"Well?" I said.

"The manageress is out," the clerk said.

"Where's the telephone?"

"Here, sir. You may use this phone."

I looked through the directory and found the number for the broadcasting station in New Delhi. I dialled the number. A ringing tone sounded for a long time, and then an apathetic voice said: "Hullo."

"Is that the broadcasting station?" I said.

"Is that what?"

"The broadcasting station. The wireless station."

"No, it isn't."

I rang off and dialled again, and got the same voice, a little more piqued. I slammed the receiver down without answering and went back into the lounge. There was a Colonel there whom I had seen when I had visited Sabby before. He was reading an old copy of the *Illustrated London News*.

"Excuse me," I said. "Do you know where I can find a friend of mine who lives here—Miss Wei?"

He looked at me over the top of his spectacles.

"Who are you?" he said.

I thought. 'What the hell's that got to do with it?' but I said politely:

"My name's Quinn. I've just got back from a forward area."

"I can see that."

"I'm looking for this friend of mine—a Chinese."

"I've seen a Chinese girl here, but I don't know her."

"Have you seen her today?"

"I can't remember when I've seen her. You'd better ask Mrs. Betterton. I believe she's an acquaintance." He indicated an elderly lady across the room, and looked down into his magazine again.

I went over to the lady and began to question her.

"Please can you tell me," I said, "have you seen Miss Wei lately?"

"Miss Wei? Why, yes, of course . . . she's been in hospital, you know."

"In hospital?"

"She's been there for some time."

"What's the matter with her? Do you know anything, please . . .?"

"I understand it was an operation—on her head, I'm afraid. I've heard nothing else."

"What hospital is it?" I said.

"The King George Hospital. I'm afraid you're very worried. If I may do anything at all . . ."

"No, thank you," I said. "I'll go to the hospital at once."

I got into the tonga outside. The driver was resting with his legs up over the side. He clambered down painfully and fiddled about, trying to light his oil lamps. It seemed minutes before we started, and I was quivering with impatience. I said "Quickly!" and he whipped the horse into life. I didn't care about the horse then, so long as we went quickly. We had to go through the old city again. The bazaars were brightly lit, and there was a lot of shouting and a metallic voice coming from a street loudspeaker. We passed a tonga with two officers and a girl, looking very gay and a little drunk. One of them shouted out to me some passing remark. I couldn't bring myself to reply or smile, but I went on staring at them. They thought that was funnier still and produced another taunt. Then they forgot about me and their tonga fell behind. We passed out of the gates of the old city into the open avenues of the new, back towards the airport. At last we turned into the drive of the hospital.

I jumped off the tonga and ran in. It was a beautiful new building, cool and clean inside after the dusty heat of the outside air. The corridors were like the polished marble of the Taj. An Indian at the desk in the entrance hall stood up.

"You wish treatment?" he said.

"No, I'd like to see Miss Wei."

"Miss Wei," he said. "Very good. Will you please wait in this room."

"Please take me to her straight away," I said.

"I am sorry, you will have to wait. It is always necessary to wait."

I stood in the bare room. There was a table, and plain chairs, but the room looked empty, with its high, bare walls and stone floor. A fan purred on the ceiling. I stood underneath it, and my forehead was cold as the perspiration dried away. I took out a cigarette, and went to a corner of the room out of the draught to light it. The smoke was rough on my dry tongue and throat, so I dropped it on the floor, a long, white cigarette, and trod on the end. I sat down and looked at it on the wide expanse of clean floor. I knew I ought not to have put it there. It was a dirty thing to do, to stamp out a cigarette on the floor of a spotlessly clean hospital. I ought to remove it. If anyone saw it they would think I had no respect for their beautiful polished floor. In hospitals it was necessary to have floors like that, and it was hard enough to keep them clean without people dropping their cigarette ends everywhere. I would really have to remove it—if only I could make myself get up from the chair. But this dead-weight inside me would take some shifting . . .

"You wish to see Miss Wei?"

There was a Sister in the doorway in white starched uniform.

"Yes," I said. "Miss Wei." I got up with sudden energy.

"You're an old friend?" she said, right in the doorway.

"A close friend," I said.

"I shall have to tell her. I can't let you go straight in."

"Why not?"

"It might be too much of an excitement. I'll go and tell her, and after a little while . . ."

"She's all right, isn't she?" I said.

"She's had a bad time. It was a dangerous operation."

"But now?"

"Now we're waiting to see. We've been waiting ten days."

"Please go and tell her," I said. "Tell her it's Michael."

"Oh yes, Michael Quinn," the Sister said. "She's spoken about you."

"Please tell her. I might be able to help her. I'm sure it would help if I could see her."

She went away, closing the door softly. I looked at the door, and then I looked down and caught sight of the cigarette again and it already seemed hours since I had dropped it there. I picked it up and looked around for somewhere to put it. There was no ash-tray in the room, and there was no window. I was about to push it through the grid of a ventilator, and then I thought better of it and stood in the centre of the room, with the thing in my fingers, trying to make up my mind what to do. I could feel the wind of the fan playing loosely with my hair. I felt in my pocket to see if there was a matchbox in which I could stuff the cigarette;

but whilst I was going so I suddenly realised I didn't care a damn what happened to the polished floor, and I threw the end down and screwed my foot round on top of it as though I was grinding it into the earth. It served the floor right for looking so infuriatingly immaculate and smug. I hated the whole room, which was as unfriendly and disheartening as any room could be. I was just on the point of going out and waiting in the corridor when the Sister came in again.

"It's all right," she said. "You can go in now."

"What did she say?"

"She didn't say anything, except with her eyes."

"And her eyes?"

"I think she wanted you to come," the Sister said.

We began to walk down long corridors. The Sister went in front, with soft shoes, her white skirts rustling. Then I saw a figure squatting outside a door. It was Bahadur. He rose with his back against the wall, with a slow smile lighting up his face. There was a lot of sadness in his eyes.

"Bahadur," I said.

"Michael Sahib."

"I thought you'd be here."

"She is waiting for you," he said.

I lifted up the bamboo screen over the doorway and went in. Sabby was lying on her back with only a sheet over her. All the top of her head was in bandages. Her face looked very small and pale on the pillow.

I went over and sat on the side of the bed. I could not say anything at all, because there was a lump blocking my throat. I watched her and saw enormous tears coming into her eyes. They swam all over her large, brown eyes and ran down the side of her face. Her throat was quivering. Her lips were smiling, and her eyes were smiling too beneath their mist. Then she began to sob. She sobbed gently, still smiling, and the tears covered her face. I dropped down and buried my face in hers, and I did not know whose the tears were any more. I ran my lips over her wet face, and I could feel her hands clutching my back. After a while I began to bite her tiny ears, and her nose, and she sobbed again, and when I sat up I saw more happiness in her face than I had ever seen before, glistening in the tears themselves.

"Darling, I can't see you," she said.

I felt for a handkerchief and had not got one, and so I wiped her face with the sheet, dabbing the water out of her eyes, and then I did the same thing to my own.

"Darling Sabby," I said. "My poor sweet Sabby, what have they done to you? You've got a turban like an Indian."

"And something has happened to you," she said. "Something has gone wrong with arm."

"It's only a little wound," I said. "It's all right now."

"You've been hurt, darling."

"The only thing that hurt was worrying about you. And you knew this was going to happen. You knew, didn't you—all along?"

"Yes, darling, I knew."

"You ought to have told me."

"I didn't want anything to spoil happiness. It was just selfishness, you see, wanting all the time to keep happiness. I didn't want to think of end. I ought to have told you about end."

"There isn't an end," I said.

"Yes, there has to be end. Please don't mind, darling, because it has been beautiful, and I loved you so much."

"Why didn't you get Margaret and Jennifer?" I said. "They'd have looked after you. They promised me that they would."

"Darling, I didn't want to give nice young people sadness. I didn't want to give you sadness, either; but now you are here, I am terribly glad. Everything is all right now, so long as there is no hurt in arm."

"There's no hurt," I said.

"Could you please lean to kiss, then."

"I'm awfully dirty."

"I like you when you are dirty and have funny clothes. Why do you wear funny clothes, darling?"

"My others got torn in the jungle."

"Poor darling, you have been in jungle again. Did it give you nasty sores?"

"No more sores," I said. "And I'm not in the jungle any more. I'm with Sabby, and I'm going to kiss her and make her well."

I put my left arm underneath her shoulders, and felt her small body against me. Her face was warm and soft under my lips. She closed her eyes and I kissed the white lids, and then I lay sideways on the plaster cast of my arm and put my face against the side of hers.

"You're just the same, darling," I said. "You have the same

soft, womanly smell. In the jungle I used to think about how you smelt."

"I am different Sabby," she said. "There is no hair under turban. Do you hate Sabby without hair?'

"I don't mind. I wouldn't have liked it if they'd taken off your nose. But your hair will grow again, and the second time it's always more beautiful."

"Darling, wouldn't it be a good thing to lose nose?"

"It would be a catastrophe."

"You always said it was comic nose."

"It's the only one that would suit you."

"Then Sabby has comic face to match?"

"Not really. It's rather a nice face."

"You didn't love me just for face? Once I heard you say that is why somebody loved, just for face."

"I love you for your hands, too."

"Is that all, just hands and face?"

"No darling, for everything else too. You're the only person I've ever loved for everything about them."

"Won't you love somebody again for everything?"

"No—no one but you."

"Please will you love somebody else and be happy? I won't mind."

"Darling, when we're married . . ."

"No, please don't say that," she said. "You promised you would not talk about that. We're not going to get married."

"Didn't you want to marry me?"

"Yes," she said. "Yes, darling, that is what I wanted with all my heart."

II

After half an hour the doctor made me leave, and all Sabby's protests were of no avail. But he said that I could come back in an hour if I wanted to say another good-night.

Outside in the corridor I spoke to him.

"She's all right, isn't she?" I said. "She's got plenty of strength to pull through?"

"You thought so?" he said.

"She can't be dying. There's too much life in her."

"It was a brain operation," the doctor said. "It's not always successful."

258

"But it was ten days ago already."

"You never can tell," he said. "You've got to be brave and wait. She's a very brave woman, and you'll do well to emulate her."

"I know," I said. "She's much braver than I am."

"She's not been expecting to live. It was a slow growth that took two years."

"Why didn't she have an operation earlier?"

"She might not have had those two years. She'd have regretted that."

"And she's been in pain?"

"In the last year she must have had a great deal of pain."

"And I didn't know!" I said. "I was just being happy, and all the time she was suffering and dying . . ."

"There was nothing you could have done."

"There'd have been some way I could have helped her."

"You can help her now by being strong," the doctor said.

"All right, when I'm with her I'll be strong."

"That's no use, she'll know at once if it's only when you're with her. You've got to be strong always."

"Yes, of course, you're right," I said. "I'll try to be strong always, like her."

I couldn't bear to pass the time in the waiting-room, so I walked out of the hospital. There was a moon coming up—yellow with the dust that had blown off the plain. It was the first moon of this size that had risen since our night at the Taj. That was only a month ago, then. Not quite a month—twenty-five days. But it was impossible to count a time like that by the calendar. Time is a personal matter. Once Peter had quoted to me from Wilde: 'Suffering is one very long moment. We cannot divide it by seasons. . . .' That was it—one very long moment. . . . Had it been like that for Sabby, an endless moment?

I went down the drive and on to the road. My tonga was still waiting by the gate. As I walked past it the driver called out after me.

"I don't want it yet," I said.

He thought I was trying to get away without paying and brought the tonga after me.

"Four rupees," he said.

"Presently."

"No more waiting. Four rupees."

"I'm coming back," I said.

"Pay now."

"I haven't got it now."

I walked on down the pavement, and he kept the tonga alongside, the horse's bell tinkling. He was calling at me all the time, demanding his money. I ignored him consciously, and soon I forgot about him altogether, thinking of Sabby. I went on for about a quarter of an hour, and then I turned round, and he was still on the road near me, muttering in Hindustani. He turned the tonga round, too, but I didn't get into it because I wanted to pass the hour walking, although the air was insufferably hot and my arm angrily painful with so much jolting during the day.

At ten o'clock I returned to Sabby's room. She was lying still, with the table-lamp by her bedside casting a soft light on to her face. She smiled at me with a slow smile, but most of the smile was in her eyes. Her eyes looked more than ever beautiful in this light, deep and brown and generous and terribly loving. When I saw her eyes my own love for her welled up, and if I had not resolved to be strong I could have cried again with the intense joy of loving and the sadness within it all. I sat down on the edge of her bed, and found her hand under the sheet and took it in mine and pressed it against my body.

"Was I horrid just now?" she said in a small, soft voice.

"Why should you have been horrid, darling?"

"Saying not to talk about marriage."

"Of course you weren't. We won't talk about it now. We'll talk about it some other time."

"Darling, please talk now."

"What shall we say about it?"

"After war, what is our house like, darling?"

"It all depends whether we live in London or the country."

"Let's live in country. Sometimes we can make spree to London."

"Then it will be a very old house in Gloucestershire. It will probably only be a cottage, because we shan't have any money, but it'll have fine old beams and a good smell, and in winter we'll sit in front of a huge log fire."

"What will happen in summer?"

"In summer the garden will be full of gorgeous flowers, and you'll spend all your time walking amongst them and arranging them in bowls in the house."

"How will Michael spend time?"

"I shall spend my time being an old bore telling people about India and the war, and a strange night we once spent in a hospital in Delhi."

"Won't you work a little bit?"

"That is why we shall live in a cottage, so that I don't have to do much work. Perhaps I'll run a little stall on the roadside, and sell plums and apples and very lurid-coloured drinks."

"Can I help, too, please?"

"You can give teas in the garden, darling. Everybody will always stop at our cottage, just to see you."

"Because I am curiosity?"

"No, because you're beautiful like the flowers. And you'll have a flower in your hair like you did when we were in the Himalayas."

"Can we have little ponies, too, like Himalayas?"

"We'll try to afford ponies. We'll grow red currants, which make a lot of money, so that we can keep ponies."

"Do you think Bahadur will also come?"

"Bahadur's got a family in India, and I don't think he'll want to come to England."

"Let's pretend that Bahadur is there."

"All right," I said. "We can pretend."

"Shall we go away for holidays?"

"If you get tired of the cottage we can go away."

"No, darling, I shall not ever be tired of cottage, but it is fun to go away."

"Very well, we'll go to Wales and I'll make you climb mountains."

"You will have to pull Sabby up, darling."

"I shan't do anything of the kind."

"That will be very mean."

"Darling, you're crying. Is that because I'm mean and am going to make you walk up by yourself?"

"No, it's only a little escaped tear."

"There is no need for tears any more now."

"It is a happy tear. It is because I am very happy."

"Honestly?"

"Yes, darling, honestly."

"You said it right this time—you said 'honestly'. You're getting very clever."

"Once you said you would rather I said honestry."

"I don't mind which you say, so long as you're really happy."

"Don't I look happy, darling?"

"Yes, you look happy."

"I would like you to lie close, and then I should be more happy still."

I lay down on my left side and put my head next to hers on the pillow. She moved her body closer to mine, and I could feel it trembling through the sheet. I pressed myself against her, and gradually the trembling stopped and she lay quite still and peaceful.

"I shall get into trouble for lying on your sheets with dirty clothes," I said.

"Please don't go, darling. I don't mind dirty clothes."

"The nurse will make me go soon."

"Don't let's think of future," she said. "Let's think what has happened in past. I would like to think about mosquito-net."

"We'll have to have a mosquito-net in England to remind us."

"Darling, you looked so nice under mosquito-net. I am sure nobody has ever looked half so nice."

"*O-seiji*," I said. "Do you remember where you first said that to me?"

"In ghari when you took me to bazaar. You said complimentary things to me."

"O course," I said.

"You didn't mean them?"

"Yes, I did, darling."

"It's your turn to remember something now."

"I remember you when you were a schoolmistress, hanging up the duster by the side of the blackboard where there wasn't a hook, and then wondering why it had fallen on to the floor."

"You are nasty tease."

"And I can remember you saying, 'When it's at home, what's a Bombay duck?' because you had heard the expression, and you wanted to show me you could speak good idiomatic English."

"It was good, wasn't it?"

"Yes, darling, only it sounded so quaint I didn't know what you meant."

"I think you are horrid to me."

"I loved you for those things as much as for your eyes. But I said much funnier things in Japanese."

"I loved you for that, too."

"Do you think it's been a good thing to be in love?"

"Darling, I hope it has been a good thing for you?"

"It's been the most beautiful and heavenly thing that ever happened," I said. "But what about you?"

"Darling, it has been like going gently to sleep and having lovely dreams. It has not been like living at all."

"I think it's been like living," I said. "And everything else is like being dead."

III

When the nurse came in she said:

"If only you could see what you look like! One of you with your head bandaged and the other with an arm in plaster. You might have been throwing each other down the stairs."

She looked at her watch and then sternly at me, and I knew I would have to go, because Sabby was tired and drowsy. I remembered I had nowhere to sleep, and no pyjamas or washing things. I forgot all about Sabby's room at her hotel until she suggested it herself, and then I thought I would like more than anywhere else to be there. Bahadur had the key and I could take him back with me in the tonga.

But that meant not seeing Sabby again all night. She was ill and I wanted to be with her all night; I wanted to sleep at her side. Being in her bed would not be like sleeping at her side, and if she woke with her head paining her I would not be there to try to draw away the pain with soft kisses.

"I'd like to stay," I said to the Sister.

"I'm sorry, that would be impossible."

"But I'll sleep in the chair," I said. "I won't disturb her."

"The doctor has said she must be left alone."

"Then let me come back once more. I'll go away for an hour, and then come back just for five minutes to say good night."

"It won't have to be more than five minutes next time."

"All right," I said. "I promise it won't be longer than that."

Bahadur was still waiting outside. He had been waiting outside all evening, like a watchdog. He had slept two nights by Sabby's door, and he was going to sleep there again. But I told him that in an hour I would take him back to the hotel, and we would return together in the morning. He still had the sad, troubled look in his eyes, and he nodded with a kind of dumb comprehension.

263

"Don't worry," I said. "Everything's going to be all right. She's going to get well now."

A smile came into his face but his eyes were the same, and their hopelessness frightened me, so I turned and went down the corridors and out of the building again, and there was the tonga-man waiting for me on the steps.

"Go now?" he said.

"I'm sorry," I said. "You will have to wait longer."

"Pay money."

"I'm coming back," I said.

He came after me angrily, a huge, untidy turban balanced on his brown forehead. I felt sorry for him; he was afraid he was being swindled. But I had no money. I would have given him my watch, but the Japs had that and there was nothing else on me of value. I would get some money for him; I would get it from Sabby, or borrow it from the nurse, or get the hotel to pay him.

"Wait in the drive," I said.

"Six rupees," he said. "Pay six rupees."

"I'll pay you afterwards."

He went on trotting at my side on his bare brown feet. He was skinny and old and very angry, and his moustache was like a brush that had seen better days. I let him come on a hundred yards, and then because his presence became suddenly irritating, I turned on him ferociously.

"Go back and wait!" I said.

He stopped and stared at me uncertainly, and with selfconscious defiance he repeated: "Six rupees." I went on and left him standing.

I walked along the avenue, where the street lamps lit the dry dusty leaves of the trees with a yellow light. The moon had risen high now and was very bright, and the sky was pale all around it. In the air was the dry dust, and my feet were dusty on the pavements.

But I was thinking only of the clean, fan-cooled hospital bedroom and Sabby's face on the pillow. I thought of Sabby's lips, warm and soft and passionate against my own, and her living hands. I did not believe that she was going to die. I did not believe that her body could be dead, nor that the deep well of affection and gentleness in her eyes could dry up. Sabby was warm and living, and I loved her and she could not die. And knowing this, a new joy grew in me, grew out of all the heavy dread in my belly

264

like a profusion of blossoms growing suddenly out of the heavy, dark trunk of a cactus. I felt buoyant, loving everything, the dust and the dirty figures huddled on the pavement, and the angry tonga-man. And I loved Sabby exultantly; the love kept rising in me afresh, rising like the swell of a tide, and was in me everywhere, in my back and my shoulders, and like a soothing ointment in my encased arm.

It was half past eleven, and I turned back, walking swiftly. When I arrived at the hospital gates it was ten minutes too soon. I might have gone in; but I thought if I went in then I should have to leave ten minutes earlier. I wanted to go on looking forward to going into her room and saying good night. So I waited outside.

When I went in it was very still in the hospital, and my footsteps echoed in the corridors. There seemed to be nobody about. The corridors were dim because only a few lights had been left burning. I was thinking as I went: it will be terrible, just saying good night and then leaving her. It will be like going away for months. I would like to sleep outside the door like Bahadur, and then I could look in at her often and sometimes kiss her in her sleep.

I went down the last passage. I heard a door opening, and the Sister came out. It was Sabby's door. The Sister came slowly along the polished floor towards me. She walked as though she was very tired. And then she stopped and I went on towards her, but I did not pass her because she had stopped in the middle of the corridor and she was looking at me with her tired eyes.

"I will really only be five minutes," I said.

"The doctor is in there now," she said.

"Do you want me to wait?"

She said nothing; her headdress was beautifully white but her eyes were very tired and grey.

"Well?" I said.

"You did know this would happen, didn't you?"

"What would happen?" I said.

"Half an hour ago—she died suddenly."

"Died?" I said. "Sabby?"

She nodded, and all I could see was her face nodding and nodding in the pale electric light, and her grieved eyes watching me framed in their white linen.

"Yes," she said, and I heard her voice through clouds as though it came from another world. "We knew it would happen suddenly. And without any pain. There was no pain at all. She was very happy when she died. She told me after you left that she knew she was going to die. She didn't want it to be long for your sake, and it was just as she wanted it. She wanted you to know she was happy." I felt her hand on my left arm. "You would like to see her?" she said.

"No," I said. "I don't want to see her. I couldn't bear to see her not living."

"You would like to rest here, then?"

"No, I don't want to rest."

"There is nothing we can do for you?"

"No, there's nothing," I said.

CHAPTER VIII

I

I WENT back between the blurred walls. I caught a last glimpse of the Sister as I turned the corner, motionless in the corridor staring after me. Then I saw all the doors go by, and the Indian clerk at the desk in the entrance hunched over his book. I went out and down the steps.

A figure stood in front of me—a yellow turban and brown face —talking to me. I could only hear his voice faintly. I tried to remember who he was; and then I saw the horse and tonga, and it came back to me, like something out of time long past. It came into my consciousness, and then it sank again like a piece of wreckage on the surface of the sea, and I simply stood there waiting to grasp it again. At last I heard myself saying:

"I'll get your fare for you. . . ."

I turned and went back up the steps and along the corridors, and somewhere I ran into Bahadur. We stared at each other for a long time. He tried to say something, but only his throat moved.

"I've got no money," I said.

His hand went slowly to his shirt pocket. He pulled out all the notes there and held them out to me without looking at them. I went through them and found a ten-rupee note and handed the rest back. He shook his head, so I put them in his pocket for him.

"I have to pay a tonga," I said.

He managed to say:

"We will go back to the hotel now?"

"No," I said, "I'm not going back."

"You have no place to sleep."

"I'll find somewhere," I said. "I'm not going back to the room."

"You will need Bahadur."

"I'm going by myself."

"Tonight you must have Bahadur to take care of you."

"No," I said. "You stay here, and I'll come in the morning."

I went out again, and the tonga-man came out of the shadows and stretched out his hand. I put the note into it, and he examined it carefully, then he touched his turban and grunted and went back to his tonga, and I heard the tinkle of the horse's bell as he went off down the drive.

I began to walk along the pavements under the dry trees. The night air was still hot and the moon was high and vivid. White-clad figures passed me like ghosts. I walked on anywhere, without effort, without thinking. I saw a few shop signs, and then the entrance to a cinema with the last-house crowds coming out in a waft of cool air. Then the window of Davico's. I remembered it had been at Davico's that I had met Peter after my convalescence in Simla, and it was there that I had first heard of going to Bombay. This came with a burst of pain; but the pain soon died. Inside I felt utterly dead. I somehow did not think of Sabby.

I came to the circle of grass. A few beggars and couples and drunks were lying about, and here and there was a bed of flowers. The moon drained out the colour from the flowers, but some were night-scented and the air was heavy with their perfume. I moved out of their aura, loathing it. I did not want to look at or smell the flowers. I wandered away and lay down. The ground was hard like a board. I dropped my head back, and there was nothing but the sky, livid with the moon. I tried to think about the moon, but my brain had stopped functioning. I could only feel deadness, immensely heavy deadness, weighing me down to the dry, hard earth.

It seemed longer than all the rest of my lifetime that I lay there. But when I got up the hands of a clock in the circus only pointed to one o'clock, a single hour since the Sister had stood in the corridor with tired grey eyes. I started to walk again. A new weariness had come over me and I had to drag my feet. I made myself walk, because I wanted to tire myself out and drop down and die; only I was afraid I would not die, but would wake up from a weary sleep to something that was worse than death.

I saw the brightly lit entrance of an hotel, and I turned into the drive. It was a huge modern building, white and floodlit. I went up the steps. At the reception-desk in the hall there was an Indian in evening dress."

"I want a room," I said.

"I am sorry," he said, smiling apologetically. "That is impossible. We are booked up until June."

"Put me anywhere—it's only for tonight."

He looked all over me, at my dirty green clothes and my arm in plaster. He felt sorry for me because of my plaster.

"I will try," he said. "Wait, please. I will inquire." He picked up the telephone.

I waited, but I did not care much what happened. I had to wait a long time, walking up and down the big hall. I was still waiting when I saw a man and a woman come in together through the doorway. They were very smartly dressed and handsome, and their arms were linked. The woman had soft hair brushed in a sweep over her shoulders. They came the length of the hallway, and then they saw me, and hesitated and stopped, and it was Mario and Dorcas.

"Michael!" Mario said. Only there was a questioning note in his voice because he was not certain that it was me.

"Mario."

"My God," he said. "I thought you were . . . Oh, my God," he said. "What have you been doing to yourself?"

"I'm all right," I said.

"When did you leave Imphal?"

I could not think at first. The truth seemed impossible. Then I worked it out.

"This morning," I said.

"But what are you doing here?"

"I'm trying to book a room. What are you doing?"

"We were married yesterday," Mario said. "This is our honeymoon. We are going to the hills tomorrow."

"That's marvellous," I said. "It's wonderful. When I'm clean I'd like to kiss the bride."

"How is Sabby?" Dorcas said.

"Sabby?"

268

"Have you seen her lately?"

"Yes," I said.

"She's all right?"

"Oh, rather, yes."

The receptionist came up and grinned at us.

"There is a small store-room," he said. "In which we may put a bed."

"You must come into our room," Dorcas said. "You're in an awful state—you can't look after yourself with that arm."

"I shall be all right," I said. "I'll go into the store-room."

"He'll come with us," she said to the Indian.

"You're on honeymoon. I'd rather sleep in the store-room."

"You won't do anything of the kind," Mario said. "We've got a camp-bed, and one of us can sleep in the bathroom."

I went upstairs with them and into their room, because I could not argue any more. It was a wide, airy room, and cool under the fan. I sat in the arm-chair while Dorcas went into the bathroom and changed her evening dress for a silk dressing-gown. Mario began to fix the bed. They were both very capable, and good to look at, and terribly in love. I could see they were in love by the glances they gave each other and the way their hands lingered in contact.

They tried to make me sleep in their own big bed, with its soft mattress and huge white mosquito-net. I had to protest a great deal before they let me have the camp-bed in the bathroom. But I did not want to upset them; and also I wanted to sleep in the bathroom, because I somehow dreaded to go by myself into the voluminous folds of the net, and lie in the wide bed, as I had dreaded the scent of flowers that brought with it pain. It was better to go on being dead inside. I still felt dead and heavy, and I wanted them to hurry up and leave me alone on the bathroom camp-bed.

I did not tell them about Sabby. To tell them I would have to put it into words, and I was afraid of the words. Besides, I didn't want them to be sad. I wanted them to go on smiling and loving and having their honeymoon. I wanted to have the sadness to myself, and everything else to go on. I was rather jealous of the sadness.

When they had made up the bed I went into the bathroom, and Mario helped me off with my clothes and put on me a pair of his own pyjamas. They were beautiful pyjamas of black silk, expensive and tasteful like all Mario's things. Then I lay on the bed, and Dorcas came in and sponged my face and washed the filthy hand that was protruding from the plaster. She washed my fingers carefully and in between them, and dried them as carefully with a towel. Mario sat on the edge of the bath and talked cheerfully.

"You look better now," he said. "When I first caught sight of you I thought you were one of the war-dead risen from the grave."

"We're going to see you back into hospital in the morning," Dorcas said.

She put a sheet over me and tucked it in at the sides, and then Mario brought a small table from the other room and put it at the bedside, with a glass of water on it, and cigarettes and his lighter, because I was unable to strike matches. They stood together in the doorway, closely shoulder to shoulder, Mario dark and suave, and Dorcas with a sunburnt skin, rich against the cascade of fair hair, and her frank, competent English eyes.

"Where did you say you were going tomorrow?" I said.

"We shall see you're all right first. Then we're going to Kashmir."

"It's lovely in Kashmir in April."

"We're looking forward to the mountains."

"You wait until I've made you climb them all," Mario said.

"You can carry me up if you like. Otherwise I shall sit at the bottom and sip cool drinks. Don't you think that's only fair?"

"Oh yes," I said. "You mustn't let him bully you."

When they went they turned off the light and closed the door gently. I heard their soft voices from the next room. There were two dull bumps that were probably Mario's shoes falling to the floor. Then I thought I could hear the sound of Dorcas brushing her hair. She brushed for a long time, and afterwards she put some things down on the glass surface of the dressing-table. A little later there was the click of a switch, and the only light under the door was the faint orange light of the bedside lamp. Then that was extinguished too. They went on talking for a time, but only occasionally and in voices that were only a murmur through the intervening door.

The bathroom was dark except for the pale bars of moonlight

270

that marked the screened window. I stared up into the blackness. And then out of the deadness within me, gradually, very gradually, a swelling began to emerge, pushing its way upward. Softly at first, and afterwards hugging the pillow to stifle the sound, I began to sob.

THESE ARE PAN BOOKS

John Steinbeck
SWEET THURSDAY

Boisterous, light-hearted story of Cannery Row, derelict Californian seaside town, by one of America's most famous writers. Some disreputable but lovable characters plan a marriage for their unhappy friend, Doc the scientist. (2/6)

Lew Wallace
BEN-HUR

The magnificent tale of a prince of Jerusalem who was thrown into slavery by his boyhood friend, yet lived to become as rich as Caesar. One of the most famous books ever written, it glitters with the splendour of the old Roman Empire, resounds with the clamour of an ancient land in ferment. Now filmed again by MGM. *Illustrated*. (3/6)

PICK OF THE PAPERBACKS

THE WIND CANNOT READ

"An excellent piece of writing . . . very good indeed . . . the author proves himself to be a novelist of the right kind, able to sketch rapidly and vividly a scene, a character, a setting, and to keep his narrative moving at a good pace."—J. B. PRIESTLEY (*Bookman*).

"He writes economically and vividly, is not afraid of emotion."—ANTHONY POWELL (*Daily Telegraph*).

"Extraordinarily poignant." — HOWARD SPRING (*Country Life*).

"The freshness, charm and unashamed romanticism hold one in subjection."—MICHAEL SADLEIR (*Sunday Times*).

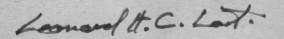

THE FILM

The film version of *The Wind Cannot Read* was shot in Eastman Colour at Pinewood Studios and on locations in India, starring

Dirk Bogarde and Yoko Tani

with John Fraser and Ronald Lewis

Directed by Ralph Thomas
Produced by Betty Box

for

THE RANK ORGANISATION